Also by William Heffernan

BEULAH HILL
THE DINOSAUR CLUB
CORSICAN HONOR
TARNISHED BLUE
RED ANGEL
SCARRED
BLOOD ROSE
RITUAL
THE CORSICAN
WINTER'S GOLD
ACTS OF CONTRITION
CAGING THE RAVEN
BRODERICK

CITYSIDE

by William Heffernan

AKASHIC BOOKS
New York

©1999, 2003 by Daisychain Productions, Inc.
Published by Akashic Books
Originally published in hardcover by William Morrow & Company
All rights reserved
First paperback printing

Design by Melissa Farris, Sohrab Habibion, and John Yee
Cover photograph ©Ernst Haas/Getty Images
ISBN: 1-888451-47-5
Library of Congress Control Number: 2003106946

Printed in Canada

Akashic Books
PO Box 1456
New York, NY 10009
Akashic7@aol.com
www.akashicbooks.com

This book is for Brishen and Tess,
who arrived too late for the last one.
And, as always, for Stacie.

Author's Note

Parts of this novel are based on real events, but it is completely a work of fiction. The characters are fictitious, a blending of men and women I knew during my years as a newspaper reporter into single individuals. None is intended to be any one person, although most could have existed.

ACKNOWLEDGMENTS

I would like to thank the many people who helped in the research and writing of this novel. They include Dr. Michael Baden, an extraordinary pathologist and an extraordinary man, who shared some of the secrets of New York's medical community; Drs. Joseph Haddock and Richard Grunert, who lent their medical expertise; James Wade and Zachary Schisgal, for their excellent editorial advice and support; and, finally, all the men and women with whom I shared so many exciting, funny, wonderful years, in slightly insane newsrooms.

(1)

New York City
A Monday in May 1975
The woman's hands fluttered in her lap like the wings of a frightened bird. She glanced at the clock, then lowered her eyes and stared at the hands dancing along the fabric of her dress, almost as if seeing them for the first time, perhaps even wondering if they might belong to someone else. She clenched her fists, ending their flight.

Her eyes again went to the clock on the wall, and she sighed. There were five other people in the waiting room, and she wondered what illnesses had brought them here. They were all reading magazines and seemed content to wait. Perhaps they didn't want to know, she thought. She understood that. Understood it too well.

She had left her Brooklyn apartment at five-thirty so she

could have some time with Roberto at the hospital. She had been forced to leave him sooner than she wanted, just to be on time for this appointment. Then she had sat here, waiting for forty-five minutes now, realizing after the first half hour that she would also be late for work. She told herself that her boss would yell. He always yelled. But he wouldn't fire her. Not this time. He would dock her pay instead. Just as he always did. He looked for chances to do that. She began to calculate what it would mean to her already stretched budget. But it wasn't important. She would find a way to stretch it again, just as she always did. Only her son mattered. Now only her little Roberto was important.

Jennifer Wells knocked lightly, then opened the door and stepped into a well-appointed office in the faculty-practice section of the hospital. There was a smile on her young, pretty face, fixed there as it always seemed to be whenever she came near her employer.

Dr. James Bradford was seated behind his desk perusing a real-estate prospectus for a Florida shopping mall. He pulled his eyes away from the figures and peered over the half-glasses perched on the end of his nose. The corners of his mouth turned up slightly at the sight of the young nurse. Jennifer had worked for him nearly six months now, but unlike most of her predecessors, she had failed to become part of the wallpaper. He understood why, as he studied her perfectly fitted uniform. Today she was wearing her one-piece whites. He felt mildly disappointed. Although he appreciated the perfect shape of her legs, he much preferred the uniform slacks ensemble. The woman had one of the most magnificent asses he had ever seen.

Bradford raised his eyes to her face. Pretty and pert, he thought, with bright blue eyes that seemed to jump out from beneath tousled blond hair that, in his imagination, always made her look as though she had just climbed out of bed. He chided himself for the thought. As the hospital's chief of service for cardiac surgery, and the top-ranking member of its university-affiliated faculty, he was expected to be beyond such libidinous predilections. But this woman, he told himself, made all such restraint impossible.

Bradford allowed a small smile to form. "Yes, Jennifer?"

Jennifer's own smile widened. "Mrs. Avalon's still waiting," she said. "You had her scheduled for eight."

Bradford glanced at his watch. Eight forty-five. "Give me ten minutes, then show her in." He looked at the corner of his desk. "And bring me a fresh box of tissues," he added.

He saw Jennifer's smile vanish. She's seen the boy's file, he thought. And she's acknowledging your compassion.

"Oh, I almost forgot," she said. "Maggie asked me to tell you Dr. Gruenwalt called to confirm your golf date on Wednesday."

Bradford snorted. "Yeah, I guess I'll have to let him win. He's referred five cases this month."

Jennifer let out a small, happy laugh. "Oh, and Maggie said your wife called. She wants you to get tickets to that new Broadway show, *The Wiz*. She said you should call her back right away."

"Then you better give me fifteen minutes," Bradford said, the irritation in his voice palpable.

Jennifer smiled again. In complicity? he wondered—a signal that she understood his dissatisfaction? She was twenty-five, twenty years his junior. Not much at all—perfect really, he told himself. His wife intruded on the notion. She, too, had once filled his mind with similar thoughts. Now she simply drained his bank account to *overfill* her very expensive clothing.

Jennifer spun around and started out the door, and Bradford again wished she had worn her slacks. He wondered if he should say something. Perhaps he should. They had known each other for six months now, and it would be interesting to see what her response would be.

Maria Avalon sat in the visitor's chair, staring anxiously at the doctor, waiting for him to raise his eyes from the chart on his desk. He seemed so self-assured, so successful, so different from the doctor at the clinic who had referred her here. This man wasn't as pleasant, she decided—he was much more distant— but he looked more like a doctor. His hair was gray at the temples, and he wore those half-glasses, just like the doctors she had seen on television. He even dressed like those doctors. His blue shirt was starched and crisp and clean, and she could tell the striped silk necktie he wore was expensive. Even his long white hospital coat was starched and had his name embroidered on the breast pocket. Maria only wished he would look up and speak to her, but she was too frightened to say anything. Bradford let out a weary sigh, then closed the chart he had been reading. He glanced up and was genuinely surprised by the beauty of the woman seated across from him. He had been concentrating on the medical file when she had entered his office, and he hadn't really looked at her. Now he took in her very-light-coffee complexion, the large almond-shaped brown eyes and full lips, which together made her seem both alluring and vulnerable. He removed his glasses and smiled. Her dark brown, nearly black hair, hung to just above her shoulders, and it gave off hints of red in the harsh fluorescent light. She was quite appealing, he thought, as he discreetly took in her demurely crossed legs. A bit older than his nurse, Jennifer. Late twenties, he guessed. But every bit as lovely.

Then he changed his mind. No, not that lovely. Not on second glance. It was the woman's hands that had forced him to reappraise—rough and work-worn and bearing the marks of small, partially healed cuts. And then there was her clothing—a simple flower-patterned dress that was really quite cheap, probably homemade, and her plain, plucked-from-a-bin tennis shoes. Definitely discount-store variety.

"I'm afraid the news isn't very good," he began. He watched her hands close into fists, the knuckles turn white. There was a tightening at the corners of her mouth, and he suddenly feared she would begin to cry. "Let me try to make this as simple to understand as possible." And as quick, he added to himself. "At your physician's request, I examined your son and confirmed the initial diagnosis. What . . ." Bradford hesitated and glanced at the chart again to check the name. "What Roberto has is a congenital defect of the heart. Basically, he was born with a small hole—only a pinprick, probably—in the chamber of the heart that pumps blood back into the body. It's grown over time, which is why he's shown a gradually increasing weakness and loss of energy." He drew a deep breath, preparing the worst news. "The child is dying, Mrs. Avalon. It's only a question of time. And surgery is the only way to reverse that process."

He watched the woman's lips begin to tremble and glanced at the corner of his desk to make sure the fresh box of tissues was in place. He hated crying in his office. It was disruptive, and he was never certain how to deal with it. He struggled to look as reassuring as possible, then hurried on. "Now, this is far from hopeless. It's 1975, and open-heart surgery is quite advanced and quite effective. The heart is no longer the mystery it once was. We've even been doing transplant surgery for the past eight years, and that's far more complicated than the procedure your son would need."

"But he's only five," Maria whispered. Her jaw trembled, and her eyes were suddenly awash with tears. She seemed to struggle with it, then fight back the emotion.

Bradford twisted in his chair, discomfited by the threat of further tears. "Children handle this surgery far better than older patients. I've performed dozens of these procedures, some on patients even younger than your son. They all survived, and every one is doing quite well." He paused as if weighing his next words. "But it is important not to wait any longer than necessary. Your son's condition is deteriorating, so it would be best to move ahead quickly."

Maria bit her lip, uncertain about how she should respond.

Bradford glanced at the chart again, his eyes narrowing with disapproval. "I don't see anything here about insurance," he said. "And I must point out that this is a rather expensive procedure, both from the standpoint of the surgical team *and* the hospital. Even before surgery, a great many tests are required, and"—he glanced at the chart again—"Roberto would have to remain hospitalized throughout that period. Then there's the postsurgical care—fairly long in itself—and some rather expensive medication." He shrugged, watched her chew on her lower lip. "Do you have *any* insurance?" he asked.

Maria shook her head. She hesitated, as if struggling for the correct words. "But I have a job, and I can get another one, too. I can pay you. I can give you money every week until everything is paid. The hospital, too."

Bradford stared at his desk and blew out a long stream of air. Then he looked at the woman and smiled. "Mrs. Avalon, let me try to explain. This is a private teaching hospital. That means it's supported by the university and the medical school with which it's affiliated. Unfortunately, neither the university nor the hospital is designed to take on patients who present this kind of financial risk. And neither looks very favorably on surgeons who impose that type of risk on them." He raised his hands and let them fall back to the desk in a gesture of helplessness. "There are public institutions, of course, places like Bellevue and Harlem Hospital. Their function is to treat uninsured or charity patients." He let his hands rise and fall again. "Regrettably, public hospitals do not have the facilities for this type of advanced cardiac surgery. They can treat your son to some degree—provide medication, monitor his condition, and so forth. But I won't mislead you. Surgery will be needed eventually. There is no other hope. And for that a teaching hospital is really the only choice. It's why the doctor at your clinic sent you here. But . . ." He paused, extending his hands out to his sides. "A teaching hospital cannot function as a public hospital. We do some charity work, of course. But we simply cannot afford to assume the costs of these types of very expensive procedures." He sighed. "So . . . simply put, the money would have to be guaranteed in some way before we could even schedule the surgery."

Maria stuttered momentarily. "H . . . H . . . How much money?" There was a look of fear in her eyes, and her fists were held even more tightly in her lap.

"We're talking eighty or ninety thousand dollars," Bradford said. "Probably closer to ninety." He watched the woman's face fall, seemingly crushed beneath the weight of his words. "And I'm afraid at least eighty percent of that would have to be guaranteed in some way before we could begin." He paused a beat, then went on to ask what he knew was a useless question. "Do you have any relatives or friends who could help?"

Maria Avalon shook her head. "No. But I will find the money," she said. "I promise you I will find it."

Bradford smiled. It was the kind of smile one gives a small child who has said he can fly. He nodded. "When you do, please contact me immediately, and I'll get things rolling. In the meantime I'll authorize your son's release from the hospital. You can take him home tonight. Just try to keep him as inactive as possible."

When Jennifer entered Bradford's office a half hour later, he handed her Roberto Avalon's chart. "The mother has zip for insurance," he said. "I doubt we'll be hearing from her again, but file this as an ongoing case anyway."

"Should we be expecting the results of any tests?" Jennifer asked.

"No, no tests. I didn't order any." He noted the surprise on her face. "I've given her a free consultation. I can't give her free tests, too." Bradford gave a regretful shrug. "In fact, the child is being sent home today. The hospital's already absorbed the cost of a bed for three days. And that's about as far as they're willing to go. So just file it and we'll see what happens. Who knows, maybe the mother will come up with the money." He sat back, allowed the look of regret to fade. Jennifer tucked the chart under her arm and turned to leave. Bradford's voice stopped her.

"Before you go, there's just one other thing." He smiled as she turned back to face him. "I wanted to talk to you about your uniform," he said.

"My . . . my uniform?"

"Oh, it's nothing to worry about," Bradford said. "Just something I thought we might agree on."

Tuesday, 3 A.M.

Frankie Fabio, affectionately known to friends as Don Cheech, waddled up the wide marble steps of Brooklyn's 78th Precinct. He was short, perhaps five-seven—and plump, about a hundred and eighty pounds—but he walked with a swaggering arrogance that few short, fat men ever achieved. To do this he held his head tilted slightly back, which allowed him to look along his nose at whomever he encountered. The pose was augmented by a permanent smirk that complemented the arrogance reflected in his eyes. It told all he met that he knew they were full of shit.

Frankie swaggered toward the high desk that dominated the dingy, dimly lit waiting area. He was dressed in a tan sports jacket over sharply creased brown trousers, with a wildly patterned sport shirt open at the neck. A gold cross was visible against his hairy chest. As he moved forward, he took in the name tag of the sergeant who occupied the desk, trying to recall if he knew this gray-haired, balding old hairbag. Frankie had spent twelve years of his newspaper career as police bureau chief for the *New York Globe*. Now, as an assistant city editor, he liked to intimidate young reporters by claiming that during that time he had spoken to every cop above the rank of sergeant. But this hump—this Kowalski—didn't ring any bells at all. He pursed his lips with displeasure. Tonight of all nights you gotta run into the one fucking Polack you missed, he told himself.

Fabio removed his press card from his wallet and held it up. "Frank Fabio, assistant city editor for the *Globe*," he said. "I understand you got one of my troops upstairs."

The sergeant looked up, glanced casually at the press card, then looked down again. "That's right," he said.

"So, I wanna see him," Fabio said.

"Good luck," Kowalski said. "Take a seat."

Fabio's cheeks flushed. "Take a seat? A seat? I don't think you understand me. I wanna see him . . . like now!"

The sergeant looked up and sneered. He was fat and unnaturally pale, and his cheeks were filled with the thin red lines of burst capillaries. "Fuck you. You'll sit and wait like everybody else."

Fabio's jaw dropped in disbelief. "Listen, you hump, maybe somebody didn't explain something to you." Fabio began jabbing a finger to emphasize certain words. "Right now, *you* have got one of *my* people in custody. Right now, *I've* got the deputy commissioner on his way down here to sort this bullshit out. *You* play this fucking game with me, when he gets here I'm gonna have him sort *you* out."

Kowalski glared at him. "Hey, big shot, you want my ass, you got it. Next week I got my thirty years in. You can come down here and watch me throw in my papers. Then you can plant a big guinea kiss on both cheeks." His lips curled into a snarl, and he spoke through his teeth. "Until then, it's like I said: *Fuck you.*"

Fabio's face turned scarlet. "You son of a bitch! You don't think I can find a way to rain on your fucking parade? You just watch me, you piece of shit."

"Frankie, Frankie, take it easy." Fabio turned and saw Mike Murphy hurrying toward him. Murphy was deputy police commissioner for public affairs, and an hour earlier Fabio had awakened him and told him that he had better get down to the Seven-eight. Murphy was in his late thirties, a big and once beefy Irishman, with a red face and now doughy body, each the result of an ongoing love affair with Jack Daniel's. Before accepting an appointment as one of the city's pseudo cops, he had been a political reporter for the *Globe*, and, as such, he had little doubt about what Fabio could and would do if provoked.

Murphy stared at the desk sergeant in disbelief. "What the fuck is the problem here?" he snapped.

"This guy's telling me he wants to go upstairs," Kowalski said.

"So let him upstairs," Murphy snapped again. "What the hell's the matter with you? We're not goddamn enemies here."

"Policy says no unauthorized personnel beyond this area, unless escorted on official business," Kowalski said. The sergeant's tone had become calm, cool, and indisputably unctuous. Fabio could feel the smirk hiding behind the deadpan exterior.

"So I'm escorting him," Murphy growled. "You have a problem with that?"

"Whatever the commissioner wants," Kowalski said. He glanced at Fabio, allowing the smirk to enter his eyes.

Fabio turned to Murphy as he pointed a finger toward the desk. "You know, it's bad enough one of your clowns rousts one of my people. Now I've got this hairbag giving *me* shit. But, hey, why not? I'm only an editor for the biggest fucking tabloid in this country." He glared at Murphy. "I thought we could work something out here, Mike. But this whole damned thing is taking a very ugly turn."

Murphy raised his hands, as if trying to fend off Fabio's anger. "Frankie, calm down. We're going to work everything out if it's at all possible. Let's just go upstairs and see what the story is." He drew a breath, as if dreading his next words. "And we've got two reporters up there, not one."

"What?"

"Whitney Morgan was with Burke when he got busted. They busted her, too." He drew a breath. "Apparently she didn't want to notify the paper. I guess she figured Burke was already doing that. She used her call to get hold of her old man's lawyer. He's supposed to be on his way in from Long Island."

"Jesus fucking Christ." Fabio stared at the ceiling, rolling his eyes. "And what did your resident geniuses charge *her* with?"

Murphy studied his shoes. "Same as Burke. Disorderly conduct, resisting arrest, and assaulting a police officer."

Fabio looked to one side and started to chuckle. "Little Miss North Shore Wasp? Little Miss Vassar graduate? A broad whose rich little ass has never passed so much as a fucking fart? She assaulted one of your cops?" The chuckle turned into a full-throated laugh. "Jesus Christ. When your humps decide to fuck something up, they don't go halfway, do they?" Fabio shook his head in disbelief. "Maybe I should just call it in to rewrite now. Tell the desk to save some space on page three."

Murphy took Fabio's arm. "Come on, Frankie. Let's just find out what happened before we do anything. Okay?"

"Of course." He laughed again. "I can't wait to see what else these assholes did." Fabio's eyes snapped back to the desk sergeant. "And don't think I'm forgetting you, you prick."

Kowalski fought to keep the deadpan in place. "I'm here till next Wednesday, sir. I'll be happy to help you in any way I can."

Fabio sneered at him. "You'll be fucking amazed at what I can do in eight days," he said.

Murphy and Fabio entered a windowless interrogation room, further crowding the space already taken up by a uniformed sergeant and four patrolmen. Billy Burke sat in a straight-backed wooden chair, his hands cuffed behind his back. There was an abrasion on his left cheek, but he was otherwise unmarked. He also appeared to be sober, something Frankie Fabio was relieved to see. Whitney Morgan occupied another chair a few feet away, her hands cuffed in front. Her very lovely face glowed with mortified rage.

"What is this shit with the handcuffs?" Fabio demanded. He turned on Murphy, feigning outrage.

Fabio knew very well why handcuffs were in place—at least on Burke. Burke was six-two, an easy two hundred ten pounds, and even at thirty-eight very little of it was fat. Years ago he had been a starting safety in the Big Ten, and had been known as a ferocious hitter. Fabio had seen that ferocity only once. But it had been enough. An Aussie correspondent had gone after Burke in Costello's, a major newspaper watering hole. The Aussie, a hulking asshole who turned bullyboy whenever he was drunk, had tried to take Burke's head off with a roundhouse right. It had proved a serious mistake. Burke had left him on the barroom floor, unmoving for almost five minutes. Fabio had been certain the man was dead.

"Take the handcuffs off," Murphy growled. He glared at the uniformed sergeant.

Fabio walked over to Whitney as the cuffs were removed. She had short, dark hair, cut to accent high cheekbones, vivid green eyes, and a small, straight, very patrician nose. She was beautiful in a very definite Waspy way, with a trim, slender body, about which Frankie had enjoyed untold fantasies. Office rumor claimed that she had been sharing that body with Burke for the past six months.

"Are you okay, Whitney?" Frankie asked.

"I just want to get *out* of here," she said through clenched teeth.

Frankie noticed that the tailored, dark blue suit she wore showed barely a wrinkle, even after hours in this hellhole precinct. He touched her shoulder reassuringly. "It won't be long."

Turning, he went over to Burke. "Billy, my lad." He raised his chin, indicating the abrasion on Burke's cheek. "They do that to you?"

Burke gave him a small, bitter smile. "The arresting hump. *After* I was cuffed."

"That's a fucking lie." The words came from a heavyset cop, about Burke's size. He had thinning hair that was turning gray—about forty, Fabio guessed—and there was heavy swelling on the right side of his jaw. From a very good left hook, Fabio decided.

Frankie turned to Whitney. "You see this clown hit Billy?" he asked.

Whitney nodded. "Yes, I did."

"Was Billy cuffed when he hit him?"

"Yes."

Frankie turned and walked over to the cop. His name tag

identified him as Grady. Fabio's head was tilted back, giving Grady the full value of his "you're full of shit" look. "So it's a fucking lie, huh?"

Grady glowered at him. "That's right. It's a fucking lie."

Fabio took a step back as though he had been struck. Then he started to laugh. "Hey, Commissioner. Come over here and get a whiff of this hairbag. He smells like he's been sucking on a bar rag."

Murphy closed his eyes and shuddered. Then he turned to the uniformed sergeant. "Did you test Burke and Miss Morgan for alcohol?" he asked.

"No, sir," the sergeant said.

"You've had them here for—what—three hours now? So why didn't you test them?"

The sergeant's jaw tightened. "There didn't seem to be a reason to, Commissioner."

Fabio had gone back over to Burke. He turned toward the sergeant, then inclined his head toward the arresting cop. "Did you test Grady?"

The sergeant stared at him, his eyes blank. "No."

Fabio turned to Murphy. "Who was riding shotgun?"

Murphy turned back to the sergeant for an answer.

"Officer Muldoon," the sergeant said.

A young, slender officer took a step forward. Fabio looked him up and down. No more than a year out of the academy, probably less, he decided. He also noticed Muldoon was wearing a different precinct insignia, indicating he had been "flown in" for the night, either because Grady's regular partner had been off or—as sometimes happened with trouble-prone cops—because nobody else in the precinct would ride with Grady.

Fabio put on his glasses and looked at the insignia more closely. "You work out of Coney Island?" he asked Muldoon.

"Yes, sir." To Fabio, the young cop looked as though he wanted to be there now.

"You get flown in here regularly?"

"Just this week, sir."

Fabio turned toward the sergeant. "If the *Globe's* lawyers check the patrol sheets, you think they're gonna find that somebody gets flown in every time Grady's on patrol?"

The sergeant's jaw tightened, but he maintained the blank stare. "I wouldn't know, sir."

Fabio laughed. "Yeah, I bet you wouldn't." He turned back to Muldoon, noticed that the young cop was standing as far away from Grady as he could get. "You see what happened tonight?" he asked. Fabio had removed a reporter's notebook and a pen from his pocket. Had he pulled a pistol, the effect on Muldoon could not have been greater.

"No, sir," Muldoon said. "I was in the patrol car, trying to raise the precinct on the radio."

From behind Frankie, Billy Burke let out a low laugh. "Jesus, I thought I remembered you standing right next to that clown. I even thought I remembered you grabbing him when he went for his gun after I knocked him on his ass."

"No, sir," Muldoon said. "I was in the patrol car. I didn't see anything."

Burke let out another laugh, and Frankie turned toward him. He raised one finger to his lips. "Not another word, my troop," he said.

"Yes, my Cheech," Burke said. He grinned at the floor and shook his head.

Frankie turned to Murphy. "You wanna dance this fucking dance some more, or should we just leave now and maybe—just maybe—forget it ever happened?"

Before Murphy could answer, a tall, gray-haired man was led into the room. He went immediately to Whitney. Frankie watched them confer in whispers, then turned to Murphy, keeping his own voice as low as possible. "Of course, it may be too late." He watched Murphy's facial muscles dance against his cheek. "But if you want, I'll see what I can do?"

Murphy turned away from the roomful of cops, took Frankie by the arm, and led him out into the hall. "What's it going to cost me?"

Frankie inclined his head toward the interrogation room. "A minor contract on Officer Friendly in there," he whispered. "And another small one on that hump desk sergeant."

Murphy drew a deep breath. "See what you can do."

Outside on the sidewalk Billy Burke placed a hand against the small of his back, arched his shoulders, and stretched. He was dressed in jeans and a houndstooth jacket that looked as though he had slept in it. Three buttons had been torn from his blue checked dress shirt. "Sorry you got dragged out of bed, Cheech." Burke glanced at Whitney. The look on her face forced him to turn away.

Whitney's lawyer had gone to retrieve his car so he could drive her home, but Frankie glanced around just to be sure. "It's not a problem, but Murphy may decide to bend some ears at the paper, just to cover his ass. So you better tell me everything that happened."

Billy shook his head. "It was stupid, Cheech. This cop, Grady, was half in the bag. I think he spotted the press plates on my car and decided he was going to break my chops. Anyway, he pulled me over and told me I'd run a red light. Then he started mouthing off—said he was sick of newspaper and television assholes who thought they could do whatever they wanted. Before I could say anything, he started ranting about that cop in Brownsville, the one who shot that black honor student last month. He said the kid was a scumbag junkie and that we ruined the cop's life by playing him up as some trigger-happy kid killer." Billy rubbed his eyes. "Hell, I should of just kept my mouth shut and taken care of it the next day. I knew then he was half loaded. His damn breath almost knocked me over. Instead, I told him where to get off; told him I was going to let his captain know he had a drunk working for him." He gave Fabio a regretful look. "That's when he really lost it. He grabbed me by the throat and pulled me out of the car, spun me around, and started patting me down." Burke let out a low laugh. "All this time his partner—this young kid he's riding with—is begging him to cool it. I think he could see his brand-new cop career headed straight for the toilet." He shook his head again. "That's when Whitney got out of the car to find out what was happening. She came up behind Grady and asked what was going on, and he turned around and belted her. One shot, right to the chest. Just like they teach at the academy. Knocked her ass over teacups." He let out a long sigh. "And that's when I lost it and decked him."

"If you'd kept quiet in the first place, you wouldn't have had to play Sir Galahad." Whitney was staring into the street as she snapped out the words.

Billy let out another breath and looked to the heavens. Frankie ignored her, thinking, And if you'd kept your cute little ass in the car, I'd still be in bed. He glanced at Billy. And you probably would be, too. With her.

Frankie stared at Burke, wondering how long it would take him to mend fences with the lady. He was a good-looking guy— wavy black hair with a few flecks of gray starting to show through, soft green eyes contrasted against rugged features that seemed a bit world-weary. Frankie had known Burke for seven years, and not only liked the man but respected him. Early on he had made Burke his protégé considering him the best reporter he had ever encountered. Until a few years ago there had been no question in Frankie's mind that Burke would be the paper's next city editor. But when his chance came, Burke's life had been falling apart, and any hope he had of running the city desk fell apart with it. And his life was still falling apart. You could see it in his face. It was a deep, personal pain that seemed to sit behind his eyes. Frankie understood that pain, knew what had caused it, and he silently prayed it was something he would never experience himself.

He forced the thought away. Right now there was a more pressing problem. He took Billy's arm and led him a few steps down the sidewalk.

"I need you to listen up a minute," he began. "You know and I know that a certain city editor is gonna ask some very pointed questions about this tomorrow. And he's gonna be hoping for answers that will put you in a pile of shit." Frankie raised his hands as though speaking a regrettable truth he wished he could change, but a truth nonetheless. "Look, if this had happened to one of his fucking pets, he wouldn't give it a second thought. But it happened to you. So if he doesn't get the right answers, he's gonna jump all over your ass, and he's gonna love every fucking minute of it. Now, you got two choices. You can tell him to fuck off and end up working in Queens for the next three months, or you help me put together a story he's gonna buy."

Billy stared out at the traffic moving down Flatbush Avenue. "What do you need to know?"

"First, tell me what the hell brought you two out to Brooklyn."

"Fate," Billy said. He gave Frankie a lopsided grin. "Actually, we came out for a late dinner at Monte's. Whitney heard it was a wiseguy hangout and wanted to see it." He grinned again. "She said it would be *interesting* to eat with a bunch of hoodlums." He let out a short laugh. "Those were her exact words."

"Jesus Christ."

"Hey, she works for the *Sunday Magazine*." He laughed again. "I think she expected to see the Godfather scarfing down a plate of scungilli. Anyway, we were heading back to Manhattan when that clown pulled us over."

Frankie turned and beckoned for Whitney to join them.

"Billy says you came out here for dinner," Frankie said when she reached them.

"That's right. Coming to Brooklyn was my second mistake of the night." She gave Billy an icy look, making it clear what her first mistake was.

Frankie ignored her and pushed on. "The copy of the report Murphy gave me says this happened a little after eleven. Why'd you both wait so long to call the city desk?"

Whitney's face turned a deep red, and she looked away.

"That's the way Grady played it," Billy said. "He took us to the central booking station, had us strip-searched, booked, then put in holding cells for a while before they brought us here to the Seven-eight. We weren't allowed any calls until we got here. I think his sergeant was pissed when he found out that happened—I could hear him snarling at Grady out in the hall—but by then there was nothing he could do."

Frankie glanced at Whitney. Her back was rigidly straight, and she was still staring into the street. The revelation of the strip search had deepened the color in her face. He tried to visualize her being told to bend over and grab her ankles. He couldn't quite manage it. And the female holding cell, given the area, had probably been loaded with the evening's collection of skags and hookers. He fought off a grin and decided it might be quite a while before Billy again climbed between those lovely legs.

"Okay, let's go home and forget about it. Leave the damage control to me. This moron, Grady, did enough things wrong I should be able to bury him with our fearless leaders."

"What's going to happen with us?" Whitney asked. "Will we have to go to court?"

Frankie shrugged. "Grady says he won't drop the charges, and even his bosses can't make him if he wants to play hard-ass. But I'll call the Brooklyn DA. He's a politician. He knows better than to play games with us. Don't worry about it. The worst that's gonna happen is he'll ask the judge to adjourn the case in contemplation of dismissal. That means you'll appear in court, you'll go home, and six months later the charges will be expunged from the record. I'll take care of any questions at the paper. But if anybody there asks you about this, you make sure you don't tell them any more than you told me. The cop was a drunk who had a hard-on for the media, and you two were just innocent bystanders. That's it. End of story. You got that?"

"I'm not sure I want to let it drop," Billy said. "I think Whitney and I should file a complaint with the Civilian Review Board."

Frankie stared at him, blinked, then let out a barking laugh. "Bullshit." He tapped one finger against Burke's chest. "You listen to your Cheech, my boy, and just let it die. The powers that be are *not* gonna be happy about this. Just keep our beloved city editor in mind. You are *not* one of Lenny Twist's favorite people. And your star isn't exactly in the ascension with the other editors either. So drop it and let me handle it."

Billy drew a deep breath. "Cheech, if that drunken asshole stays on the street, sooner or later he'll kill some poor bastard. Christ, if he did this to a newspaper reporter, what the hell do you think he'll do to some black or Hispanic kid who happens to piss him off? We'll have another Brownsville all over again."

Again Frankie tapped Burke's chest, emphasizing each word. "That . . . is . . . not . . . your . . . problem. You let *me* take care of Grady."

"What are you going to do?" Whitney asked.

Frankie stared at her, as if she, too, were about to propose something stupid.

"I'm not disagreeing with you," she said quickly. "In fact, I agree with you completely. I just want this whole thing over with, and I certainly don't want any trouble at the paper." She paused a beat. "But . . . well . . . I *am* curious."

Frankie nodded. "Okay. But this is for our ears only." His lips formed a self-satisfied smirk. "Let's just say that later this morning, our good friend the deputy commissioner just might run a little check with personnel to find out where Patrolman Grady lives. Then, later, he just might have a little talk with the chief of patrol and express his concern about the horrendous understaffing at whatever New York City precinct is the farthest one away from Grady's house." The smirk disappeared, and he let out a sigh and shook his head in mock sadness. "It wouldn't surprise me at all if that Irish asshole ends up working as the broom in that precinct." Fabio's smirk returned, decidedly evil now. "A few days after that happens, I think Patrolman Grady also just might get a little phone call. And when he gets that call, somebody just might ask that Irish prick how he likes sweeping floors and cleaning locker rooms and if he ever thinks about us when he drives his fat Irish ass all that way to work each day." Frankie's smirk grew. "There's also a certain bigmouth desk sergeant who's supposed to retire next week. Except I think his paperwork just might get lost. Maybe for a couple of months. In the meantime he might be doing a little foot patrol with all the skells in Times Square."

Billy studied Frankie and found himself enjoying the man's outrageous bravado. Fabio looked quite pleased with himself. His dark hair was slicked back, accenting a sharp widow's peak, and his head was tilted so he could look at them along the length of his nose. His pudgy body seemed puffed up like a victorious rooster, Billy thought, one who fully expected to have his way. He glanced at Whitney and knew his own plan for Grady didn't have a prayer. There would be no chance with the Civilian Review Board without her corroborating statement. The look on her face told him not even to ask.

He shook his head. "Okay, Cheech. We'll play it your way."

Frankie glanced at Whitney to confirm what he already knew—that there would be no opposition in that corner either. Satisfied, he turned back to Billy. "That's a good troop," he said. "Where's your car?"

"They left it on the street where they busted me."

"When Whitney's lawyer gets back, I'll take you over there." He grinned. "With a little luck, some of it might still be there."

(2)

Billy Burke was still half asleep when he got off the elevator on the seventh floor. He turned left and groped his way toward the editorial reception area, where he pulled a time card from a wall rack and punched himself in for the day.

When he turned around, he noticed the people waiting for the first time. There was an extremely tall, cadaverously thin man dressed in a stovepipe hat, black frock coat, and trousers. He sported a dark beard, minus a mustache, and there was a counterfeit mole pasted on his cheek—a perfect facsimile of Abraham Lincoln. A few seats away sat a woman in Gypsy garb, large hoop earrings adorning each lobe. There was a wire cage on her lap that held a sleeping chicken. Next to her, looking decidedly uncomfortable, were two business types, then a man dressed in a New York Yankees baseball shirt and cap. The ballplayer let out a gurgling gasp, and his head jerked so violently to one side Burke was surprised he hadn't dislocated his neck. Four seconds later the gasping spasm was repeated.

Burke blew out a stream of air and turned to the small desk that occupied one corner of the waiting area. He stepped closer, bent toward the aging receptionist's ear, and whispered, "Good morning, Thelma. Full moon?"

Thelma rolled her eyes. "Is it ever."

Burke grinned at her. Thelma was well past sixty. Her husband had been a foreign correspondent for the *Globe*, killed twenty-one years ago while covering the Korean War. His meager pension had left her almost penniless, until pressure from the Newspaper Guild had placed her behind the reception desk. She had taken to it immediately, and had ruled that post with an iron hand ever since. No one passed into the newsroom without her approval. And few were found deserving.

Thelma beckoned Burke to come even closer. "One of the loonies is yours," she whispered.

Burke glanced back over his shoulder, finally settling on the Gypsy with the chicken. He turned back to Thelma. "The Prophetess?" he asked.

"In the flesh." Thelma gave him an all-knowing smile.

Burke let out a long sigh. He had never met the Prophetess in person. She had been telephoning him weekly for six months now, promising to put him in direct contact with God, assuring him he would become privy to the news *before* it happened. There would be a small fee, of course, which she insisted the paper would be happy to pay.

Burke had been amused. That first call had caught him on a slow day, and foolishly he had played along, telling her the paper would require some proof of her powers. The Prophetess had promptly predicted a plane crash—no time, no place, just a crash. God would provide the details only if He knew she was being paid. Burke had promised to take her offer directly to the publisher. Five days later a military transport went down in North Carolina, and the Prophetess was back on the phone. Had the paper given her a hundred dollars, photographers could have been at the scene, she had insisted. Burke had hung up on her. This time it had not been a slow day. Still, she continued to call.

Burke leaned in closer to Thelma. "Tell her I'm out of town," he whispered. He hesitated. "Better still, tell her I've been transferred to a different office and that Pete Stavos has taken over all my Manhattan sources."

Thelma looked at him in mock horror. "Pete's crazier than she is. If you think I'm going to deal with that . . ."

"Hey, maybe they'll hit it off." Burke glanced over his shoulder and judged the Prophetess to be about forty-five. He turned back to Thelma. "They might even fall in love," he offered. "Pete loves chickens."

Thelma stared at him. "Good God," she said. "Imagine if they had children."

Burke entered the newsroom and headed for the far corner where his desk was located. The room was enormous, with more than two hundred desks pushed together in groups of four. The desks were equipped with typewriters, telephones, and imitation leather chairs, the last of which produced endless and senseless turf battles. For some, a particular chair became their kingdom, and many of the more proprietary reporters and editors had personally claimed a favorite, even going so far as having their names stenciled on the back so it could be quickly found if moved by those who worked the night or lobster shifts. Some, Burke believed, would gladly surrender their wife's virtue before they gave up their chair, and being found seated in someone else's could provoke anything from ill-humored umbrage to snarling hostility.

Burke flopped into his own unmarked chair and picked up a copy of the paper's final edition. The lead story told of riots in Boston over the court-ordered busing of twenty-one thousand schoolchildren. It was more than he cared to deal with. He put the paper down and looked across at Eddie Hartman, one of the three other reporters who shared that particular group of desks, dubbed the "Eagles' Nest" by its occupants.

"It's Tuesday, Eddie. Did you remember to hide Stavos's chair?" he asked.

Hartman fluttered bushy eyebrows and grinned through his thick mustache. "It's in the photo lab. That Greek fruitcake will be screaming all day about the chemical stink on it. Probably threaten to sue the paper for maintaining a hazardous-waste site, then leave work early to have his fucking lungs X-rayed."

"And send the bill to the publisher," Burke added. He smiled at the scenario. It probably wouldn't be far off the mark. Stavos was certifiable. A year ago, when the paper had declared editorially that "the so-called Watergate scandal" was nothing but a house of cards, Stavos had become so enraged he had thrown his typewriter through a nearby window. The typewriter had fallen seven floors and had left a small crater in the sidewalk on Forty-third Street. It had also narrowly missed a visiting parochial-school group, which had just completed a tour of the paper. The following day Hartman, a devout atheist, announced his plan to "make the world safe for Catholic-school children." He would drive Pete Stavos into an insane asylum—something their fellow deskmate, a transplanted Brit named Tony Rice, had characterized as "carrying coals to Newcastle." The disappearance of the chair—now a regular Tuesday and Thursday happening—had become an integral part of Hartman's campaign.

Burke noticed that Hartman was now grinning at him. He was a small man, no more than five-six or -seven, in his mid-forties, with longish, graying hair and a flowing mustache. When he smiled, his teeth seemed to peek through the mustache like a rabbit peering out of a bush.

"What?" Burke asked.

"I hear you were a naughty boy last night." Hartman was a longtime police reporter—referred to as the Chief, sometimes the Little Chief, by his peers—and his "untold sources" within the NYPD were said to be second only to Frankie Fabio's.

Burke remained silent, and Hartman's grin widened.

"The Six-Pack will not be amused," Hartman added. He was referring to a hated clique of editors and assistant editors, led by city editor Lenny Twist and metropolitan editor Mitch Coffee. Hartman himself had dubbed them the Six-Pack, due to their after-work propensity for guzzling beer. But their drinking habits hadn't impaired the control they exerted over the newsroom. Collectively or individually they could undermine a reporter's career. They did this by means of an office shit list, which saw talented senior reporters dumped onto the night or lobster shifts for a month or more, or temporarily reassigned to obscure bureau offices in Long Island or New Jersey. Burke, Hartman, and their fellow deskmates Tony Rice and Fred Costa had each endured several of those punishment tours, each earning the dubious rank of shit-list regular.

"Yeah, I'm sure I'll hear about it. But I've got my Cheech on the case," Burke said.

"Hey, good luck, pally. But remember, even a rabbi as talented as Frankie can only do so much." Hartman's eyes twinkled. "I'm afraid that beating on one of New York's Finest just might produce some retaliation from the Patrolmen's Benevolent Association. They might even reduce the Six-Pack's Christmas booze donation by a case or two. And that's something they would *never* forgive."

"Has our aging hero committed yet another unspeakable act?"

Burke glanced up and found Tony Rice hovering beside him, displaying a double row of capped teeth. The Brit was dressed in a tan suit, starched blue shirt, and a solid yellow necktie.

"Heavens, don't we look smashing today," Burke said.

Rice beamed at the sarcasm, stretched out his hands as if preparing to take a bow, and said, "Nothing very special, my dear chap. Only my normal sartorial splendor."

Burke turned back to the Chief and found him staring at the ceiling. He and Rice—whom the Chief had renamed Lord Haw Haw—had an ongoing and very one-sided fashion battle. The Chief's penchant for flamboyant leisure suits and open-necked polyester sport shirts—he had an unquenchable need to dress like an off-duty cop, Burke believed—made the contest a joke.

"He looks like a fag," the Chief said. He stared at Burke. "Am I right? Does he look like a fag?"

Burke ignored the question. Rice slid into his chair, still beaming. He turned to Burke.

"So tell me, you naughty boy, what have you done?"

"He was out last evening with the lovely Lady Whitney," the Chief offered in his best British accent. "And for her ladyship's amusement he knocked the stuffing out of one of our lads in blue. Unfortunately, the copper was *not* amused and proceeded to lock up both their asses."

Rice squirmed in his chair, his smile turning into a broad grin. "I love it. Now, give me all the details. Don't leave out a thing. Did all that violence throw her into fits of passion? Did she tear off all your clothes, my dear chap, and fuck your tiny brains out? Tell me everything."

Burke repressed a smile. "When I last saw her, she wasn't speaking to me."

Rice's grin widened. "Unquestionably a ruse. She undoubtedly went home and masturbated into the wee hours."

"Don't talk like that," the Chief begged. "I don't want her to do those things unless I can watch."

Rice leaned in close. "Tell me, dear boy, were you both strip-searched?"

Burke nodded. "Indeed."

"Oh, God," the Chief moaned. "I think I'm gonna come."

"Not here, you won't. It pisses off the cleaning woman."

They turned and found Frankie Fabio giving them all his "you're full of shit" stare.

"My Cheech," Burke said.

"My troop," Frankie replied. He gave Burke a pitying look. "Our beloved city editor would like words with you," he added.

"Great," Burke said. "Now if I find out I have cancer of the throat, my morning will be complete."

"Exactly. But if you keep your mouth shut, you just might not end up working in Queens." Frankie tapped the side of his nose. "I recommended you for a story he's hot for, so just take his shit for a change, and you'll probably walk out of there still working cityside."

Burke let out a half groan, half growl. "Yes, my Cheech," he said.

Lenny Twist's office was a glass-fronted square, furnished with an oversize metal desk, cushioned visitor's chairs, and a leather sofa. The wall behind the desk was covered with the various awards Twist had won as a reporter. There was a conspicuous blank space in the middle of the wall, symbolically left empty for the Pulitzer Prize Twist endlessly claimed he had been "fucked out of."

Twist sat behind the desk, half glasses perched on the end of his nose, his attention given to the page proofs of an ongoing series that detailed the city's deepening financial crisis. He was a short, skinny man, with a hairline that was disappearing faster than his thirty-six years warranted, and closely set—piggish, Burke thought—blue eyes that held all the warmth of an Alaskan lake. To Burke he was a ruthless, self-serving little shit who would stop at nothing to get what he wanted. Grudgingly, he also had to acknowledge that Twist was the best working city editor he had ever met.

"Frankie said you wanted to see me," Burke began.

Twist continued to stare at the proof sheets. "How long have you been in this business?" he asked without looking up.

Burke groaned inwardly. "Seventeen years," he said.

"And how long have you worked at this paper?" Still he refused to look up.

Burke fumed, but held himself in check. He and Twist had started at the *Globe* within months of each other. Both had been correspondents in Vietnam—Burke for UPI and Twist for AP. They had been rivals during those early years, each taking the other's measure at varying times. That rivalry had continued at the *Globe*, where each man soon had come to be considered among the paper's top reporters. Later each had been a candidate for the city editor's job. But Burke's marriage had been falling apart at the time, and Twist had used that "instability" to outmaneuver him for the post. When offered a lesser promotion—assistant chief of the paper's Washington bureau—Burke had been forced to decline for personal reasons. From that moment on, Twist saw to it that no other offers came his way.

"I've been here seven years," Burke said.

Twist looked up now. "And what was your last little fiasco? No, wait. Let me tell you." He glared over the top of his glasses. "You went to that party when they closed the old police headquarters, and you got loaded and tried to piss on the mayor's shoes."

"That wasn't me," Burke said. "That was the Indian." The Indian was Alex McDermot, a hulking reporter who, whenever he was in his cups—which was often—had an irrepressible urge to urinate on people. When not, he was a lovable and talented writer who vied with Tony Rice for the paper's best features.

"Oh, excuse me," Twist said. "Then it must have been that fucking cadaver you stole from the funeral home."

Burke stared at the floor and said nothing. The stolen-body story was true enough. It had happened three years ago, when his marriage was collapsing and he was drinking heavily. It had involved the corpse of a fellow reporter who had worked for the *New York Post*. The reporter had been stricken with terminal cancer, and he had promised his mistress that she could hold a wake and funeral for him when he died. He had then implored his closest colleagues—Burke among them—to see that his wishes were carried out. Following the wake and funeral arranged by the reporter's less-than-loving wife—and after the family had left Brooklyn's Greenwood Cemetery—the casket holding the body had been tossed into the back of Burke's Jeep Wagoneer for transport to Westchester County. Unfortunately, the funeral director had raised a large stink with the medical examiner's office over the illegal transport of a corpse, and the *Globe*, the *Post*, and the *News* had been forced to call in numerous chips to keep their participating reporters from being prosecuted.

"This was different, Lenny. This was a drunken cop with a hard-on for the press. It wasn't something I planned." He was looking at the top of Twist's desk, not the man. Admitting a negative truth to Twist was painfully hard. Burke forced his eyes up. "But it was stupid, and I should have handled it a lot better than I did."

Twist sat back and nodded. "A moment of truth. I'm stunned."

Burke ignored the sarcasm and kept his mouth shut as Fabio had advised.

Twist shook his head, showing his disgust. "The *Globe* will provide a lawyer when the time comes, but Frankie tells me he thinks it can be squared away before then." He stared hard at Burke. "He also tells me *you're* not pressing any charges. Is that right?"

Burke nodded. "Yeah, that's right."

"I'm glad to see you're showing sense about something. We don't need to go to war with the cops over petty shit like this."

Again Burke kept his mouth shut.

"All right. Let's put this crap aside." He gave Burke another

hard look. "But I don't want any more of it. Understood?"
"Understood."

Twist nodded, more to himself than Burke. Submissiveness
pleased him. He brought his hands together in a soft clap. "All
right. Let's get back to newspaper business. I've got a story for
you. A damned good one." He paused, gave Burke his serious
editor look. It was a practiced gesture—one designed to let you
know he was uncertain whether *you* were good enough for the
story. He blew out a breath, as if coming to a reluctant decision,
then continued.

"We got a call from this little nurse the other day. Seems she
works for this very successful, high-profile heart surgeon. Manhattan practice. Big bucks. The guy's chief of cardiac surgery at
University Hospital and heads up the surgical teaching faculty
at the medical school. Big man in the medical community. The
whole enchilada." A glimmer of pleasure came to his eyes. "Anyway, this very successful doctor has a patient. A five-year-old kid
named Roberto Avalon. Lives on Fifth Avenue in Brooklyn.
Probably Puerto Rican. Single mother named Maria Avalon.
The usual story." Twist's eyes narrowed like a man ready for a
fight. "Except this little kid has a hole in his heart." He raised
one finger. "A hole that, sooner or later, is going to kill him . . ."
He paused for effect. "Unless he has open-heart surgery—which
happens to be our doctor's specialty."

Burke felt a knot in his stomach. This was the big story. The
one that was supposed to bail him out of trouble. Keep him
working in Manhattan, at least for now. Jesus. And it had to be
about a sick kid, an innocent five-year-old dropped into an un-
caring medical maze. He felt the idea hit at him like a hammer. It
was the last thing he wanted to confront at this point in his life.
But how did he say no without putting himself on a fast track
back to the shit list? He watched Twist lean back in his chair, looking, Burke thought, a bit like the cat who'd been asked to investigate the disappearance of the canary. He decided to remain silent,
allow Twist to play out the whole scenario to his full satisfaction.

"But there's one little problem," Twist continued. "Little
Roberto's mom doesn't have any insurance, and the doc and the
hospital want eighty percent of the fees in hand before they'll
agree to do the surgery."

"How much does the operation cost?" Burke asked.

Twist gave him a cold, heartless stare. "Ninety large. Which, if my second-grade math is correct, means that Roberto's mom has to come up with at least seventy-two thousand bucks before our doctor picks up his knife or our hospital agrees to dust off a bedpan."

Burke felt the knot in his stomach tighten. "So what do you have in mind?" he asked.

Twist tilted his head to the side and continued to stare at Burke. "You don't seem surprised; you don't seem outraged by this."

Burke gave him a look of regret and formulated a quick lie. "It's what we just talked about, Lenny. I've been in this business for seventeen years. Nothing surprises me anymore. And I ran out of outrage about ten years back."

Twist let out a short, barking laugh. "Good. My one worry about you was that you'd become a fucking bleeding heart over this one." He raised an eyebrow, making sure it was understood that he was talking about Burke's personal life and an unmentioned problem that was very much a part of it. "This story is too big. It doesn't need a reporter who gets emotionally involved."

"Not a chance," Burke said.

"Good, because there's more to the whole thing than I've told you." Twist leaned back in his chair and linked his fingers, resting them on a minuscule paunch. "You remember how back in the sixties the city set up the Super Hospital Administration."

Burke nodded. "Vaguely. I don't remember all the details."

Twist sat up and pushed a folder of library clips across his desk. "It's all in here. Read it." He sat back and linked his fingers again. "Right now I'll give you a quick history. Back then the city was having trouble finding people to staff its public hospitals, which is not surprising, considering what fucking zoos they were, and still are. Anyway, part of the Super Hospital concept was that the large private teaching hospitals would assume some of the staffing responsibilities for the public hospitals. Their medical schools and the hospitals themselves would provide residents, interns, and attending physicians, along with certain specialists where needed. In return the city would pay the medical schools some pretty heavy bucks to cover those salaries and the cost of administering the program, with enough left over to make it worthwhile for the university."

Twist leaned forward again. "According to our little nurse, certain private hospitals have figured out a way to scam the city. And just guess who's into this little scam right up to his rosy, red rectum."

"Our big-time heart surgeon."

"Indeed." Twist clapped his hands again and rubbed them together, a man at the dinner table ready for a feast.

"How much are they clipping the city for?" Burke asked.

"The nurse claims it's been going on for a while, so it's gotta add up to big bucks. She says University Hospital seems to have found a way to get almost all their attendings and specialists on the city tit, as well as a slew of residents and interns." Twist grinned. "We're talking a couple of hundred docs who've been sucking up money for at least five years, so we could be talking well over seven figures here." He tapped the side of his nose with one finger, indicating a secret. "Of course, the attendings and specialists never actually work at the public hospitals, except a few who show up every month or so to consult on cases. Hell, most of them probably don't even know they're on the city payroll, since the money goes straight to University Hospital and then gets divvied up with the medical school and the university itself. But the nurse claims that payroll records will show that all these docs are at the public hospitals every week—sometimes two, sometimes three, sometimes four days. The residents and interns actually do show up, so the public hospitals are happy. Hell, they'd be happy to get Jack the Ripper in there to relieve some of the bedlam. And, of course, the people running the public hospitals have no way of knowing who University Hospital is putting on the public tit, or what those phantom physicians are supposedly doing at their hospitals. In the meantime, the university gets some of its own hospital nut covered, some of its medical-school costs covered, and the attendings and specialists who are actually running the scam—guys like our big-time heart surgeon—probably get to pocket some extra cash without disrupting their lucrative private practices."

"So how do you want to fit all this together? The kid, the hospital, and the scam being run on the city?"

Twist hunched over his desk like a bear over a freshly caught salmon. "I want even more than that. Here's how I see it: The kid's our starting point." He raised a finger. "But only our starting point. You meet with our little nurse and get all the medical details. You also get everything you can about this prick doctor. How much money he makes, what country clubs he belongs to, where he likes to go to lunch, if he and the missus go to the opera, museum openings, whatever." Twist leaned farther forward and stared up at Burke. "When we get ready to slam this guy, I want to be able to paint him as Dr. Big Bucks, complete with all the trappings."

"When we get ready?"

Twist nodded. "That's right. When we get *ready*. Because this story is going to be orchestrated to perfection. I want you to play this story the same way Muhammad Ali boxes. I want you to float like a butterfly and sting like a bee." He rubbed his hands together rapidly, almost as if trying to produce sparks for a fire. "You're gonna start with the kid as if that's our only concern. But while you're doing it, you are going to investigate this doctor and the administrator of the hospital until you know what time they shit in the morning. Our little nurse can help you with these things, but even that's just going to be your starting point. Where you're really going to need her is to find a way to get you into the hospital's payroll and personnel records—the surgical records as well. Getting that stuff for the public hospitals won't be a problem. If the city's paying University Hospital, the medical school, whomever, for having certain docs working at Bellevue or Harlem Hospital or anywhere else, there will be public records in the city comptroller's office detailing who worked where and when. But to prove it's all bullshit, you're going to have to get into University Hospital's records, and probably the medical school's as well. Then we'll be able to show that when the city paid Doctors X, Y, and Z for work at a public hospital, they were actually working at University, or teaching a class at the medical school, or slicing up some private patient in the operating room." Twist's face filled with anticipated pleasure. "Wouldn't it be lovely if our big-time heart surgeon—the same guy who won't help little Roberto Avalon until he gets eighty percent of his dough up front—was actually carving up some Park Avenue matron while the city was paying him for consulting on the case of some homeless bag lady at Bellevue?"

"What about the kid and the mother? When we start, how big do you want to play them?" Burke tried to keep any reluctance out of his voice.

"Big, big. After you meet with the nurse, you go out and meet with *mamacita*." He raised a finger. "First we want a feature story about little Roberto. Maybe we'll want half a dozen stories. If the public catches on to this thing—and they will, if you do the job right—we can run Roberto stories for a month, maybe more." He waved a hand. "You know what to do—a good, gut-wrenching feature. Little boy can't play baseball anymore because of his heart. Shit, find out who his favorite player is on the Mets or the Yankees, and we'll blackjack the son of a bitch to come visit the kid." He raised both hands, the index finger of each pointing up. "But here's the kicker. The *Globe* is going to start a fund for Roberto. A fund that Joe Citizen can contribute to for little Roberto's operation. Got it?" He seemed to puff up with pleasure. "Hell, we'll inflate the cost of the whole damned thing. With all the aftercare he'll need, it shouldn't be hard. Special hospital bed for his room, twenty-four-hour home nursing. Christ, it'll be a piece of cake. Anyway, we'll raise enough so his mother can go back to Puerto Rico and live like a fucking queen."

"How soon before we start going after the doc and the hospital?"

"That depends on how quickly you can nail it down. But it's got to be solid. No loopholes, no escape hatches for the hospital, the doctors, the medical school, the university itself. We take no prisoners on this, got it?" Twist waited for Burke to nod agreement.

When he had, Twist let out a sneering laugh. "You remember a few years back, that big-shot doctor the IRS nailed for deducting hookers on his tax return? Claimed they were physical therapists?"

"I remember," Burke said. "The paper had a lot of fun with that one."

"You bet your ass we did." Twist leaned forward, the bear hovering over the salmon again. "Well, it just so happens that our hooker-friendly doctor worked at this very same hospital. And that's exactly the way I want to paint *these* bastards. So we investigate them inside out. Look for any juicy personal stuff we can find. And all the while we're nailing down this scam they're running. Then, as soon as I'm sure we have enough, we go after the bastards, the doctor, the hospital administration, all of them; paint them as members of The Rich Boys Club who are willing to let little Roberto die. We talk about their big incomes, their fucking country clubs, and we use every goddamn thing we can dig up on them. Then, as soon as they start to cry foul— which they will—we slam them with the scam they've been running on the city. Hell, maybe we'll even bring up the doc who tried to write off blow jobs on his tax returns." He leaned back and stretched out his arms. "Hell, we'll be able to say anything we want. Their asses will belong to us. *We* will be the court of public opinion on this. We can even demand that the city hold hearings, maybe appoint a commission to find out how many private hospitals have been playing this little game. And we can start digging to find out how many other little kids have been denied medical care while these bastards were lining their pockets. I don't think it will be hard. I think once we publish, people will start coming out of the woodwork with one story after another."

Twist sat forward and raised both index fingers again. "But until then we don't know anything; we're not looking into anything. It's just this one poor kid we're trying to help. We don't know anything about any greedy surgeon or heartless hospital who won't save this kid's life until they get their money. All we know about is poor little Roberto. And let's change the little fuck's name to Bobby, by the way. There's no point in telling the world that he's some fucking bongo player who'll probably be burglarizing their homes in ten years." He brought his hands together and shook them to emphasize the point. "We don't want anything to taint this story, because we're not going to nail just this one doc and this one hospital. We're going to nail the whole stinking health-care system that lets the little Robertos of this world happen while doctors and hospitals get fat." He gave Burke a long, hard stare. "There could be a Pulitzer in this. The big one. The Meritorious Service Award for the paper. You understand that?"

The knot in Burke's stomach had become the size of a boulder. He had never seen Twist so hot for a story. "I understand."

"Good. Then see Frankie. He's got the nurse's phone number. Get together with her tonight and get this thing rolling. And get out to Brooklyn and see *mamacita* and the kid, too. You're still going to have to pull regular assignments, but I want you working on this thing every spare minute. Got it?"

Burke nodded. There was no way out. "Got it," he said.

Twist gave Burke a long, steady stare. "You can do yourself a lot of good with this. You can mend some fences that need mending." He held Burke's eyes. "You understand that?"

"I understand."

"Good." He eyed Burke again. "One other thing. When you get this thing rolling, if you need some uninterrupted time, come and see me. We'll work something out to free you up."

"I'll let you know."

"Do that. And keep me posted on what's happening. I want to hear from you at least once a week." Twist jerked his thumb toward his office door. "Now, get the hell out of here and go win this paper a Pulitzer Prize."

(3)

Jennifer Wells was tall, slender, twenty-five, and beautiful—the kind of woman who could take your breath away, Burke thought. Until she started to talk. Then it all disappeared, and a very intense bitterness seemed to ooze from every pore. And nothing—not the deep-blue eyes, the tousled blond hair, or the very sensual lips—could hide it.

Burke thought about that as they sat across from each other in the small Columbus Avenue bar that Jennifer had chosen for their meeting. She had insisted on the place, claiming it was close to her apartment and far enough away from University Hospital to ensure no one she worked with would see them. She had sounded nervous, perhaps even a bit frightened on the telephone, but when they were seated across from each other, the bitterness had overcome everything else. Yet, to Burke, it didn't seem to be directed at any one person or thing. Not even her boss. It was just there—not quite hidden by that very beautiful smile.

The bitterness didn't concern Burke all that much. It was not uncommon in a news source. Very few people brought information to a newspaper because of some "great moral purpose." Inevitably there was an ax that needed grinding. The ax was something that always had to be treated cautiously.

He wanted to know what this woman's particular ax was, but he knew better than to push the issue. He would find out in time. Just as he always did. People who brought information to a newspaper never realized that a good reporter investigated his source first. Just to make sure he wasn't being sandbagged.

Burke smiled across the table. There was a cup of coffee in front of him, a glass of wine before her. In the background Harry Chapin's hit song "Cat's in the Cradle" could just be heard on the restaurant's muted stereo system.

Jennifer was dressed casually. She had obviously gone home to change before meeting him, dumping the nurse's uniform he was sure she wore at work, now dressed in very tight bellbottom jeans that were meticulously adorned with designer-inspired patches and an I LOVE NY T-shirt, sans bra. There were sunglasses stylishly perched on top of her hair—placed there, it seemed, more to accent her high cheekbones than for convenience.

Burke let Jennifer tell him about the boy, the five-year-old who was scheduled to die from complications of a birth defect—especially the complication that he had been born poor. Burke put aside his personal discomfort, his reluctance to deal with it. It was a sad story, but not exactly man bites dog, Burke thought. And there was some hope after all. This time this one child might escape his birthright because Lenny Twist wanted a Pulitzer Prize for his office wall.

When Jennifer had finished telling him about the boy, Burke shook his head in apparent disbelief, playing into the woman's outrage. "Tell me about your boss," he began. "I want to understand this guy."

Jennifer let out a little snort that didn't match all the other beautiful parts of her—except maybe it did, Burke thought. "He's a big guy, you know what I mean?"

"You tell me."

She seemed to notice the hint of skepticism he had put in his voice, and she gave him a beautiful smile, one intended to melt any resistance. *The woman knows just how good she looks,* Burke thought. *In that way she's a lot like Whitney. She turns it on when she wants to or thinks she needs it.* But with this woman there was also a very real anger behind it. He wondered if he responded to the beauty, would he meet the anger as well? He had known women like that—women who for some inexplicable reason pushed their beauty or sensuality at you, then became angry when you responded to it, who seemed to take a positive physical response as a rejection of everything else.

"He's a rich, successful, middle-aged white man. Do I need to say more?"

Burke stared at her and nodded. He paused a beat. "I know some rich, successful, middle-aged white men who wouldn't turn their backs on a dying kid." He paused again. "Not many. But some."

"Yeah, well, Dr. James Bradford isn't one of them. He thinks the world and everybody in it should worship the ground he walks on." She gave Burke a hard, cold stare. "This little boy is dying. That's not even a question. He has a year, tops. Maybe only six months. Maybe only one month. It depends on how many more episodes he has and how serious they are."

Burke watched as she brought a big carryall-type purse up from the floor and placed it on her lap. She reached in, pulled out a stack of photocopies, and dropped them on the table. Burke stared at the small pile of papers, trying to fight off a smile. They were photocopies of the doctor's federal-income-tax returns. *He wondered if Lenny Twist had called her after they spoke and had asked her to bring them.*

"Where'd you get these?" he asked.

"The office files."

Burke nodded. *Nothing illegal for him or the paper,* he thought. *For Jennifer Wells? It only matters if she gets caught. And it'll be your job to make sure she doesn't.* But that, he knew, would be the easy part. It wouldn't be the first time he had claimed that documents he was not legally supposed to have had arrived anonymously in plain brown envelopes. The public liked to think reporters readily went to jail rather than reveal a source. It was a myth, something that happened rarely and only when convenient, unprovable lies couldn't be used to safeguard that anonymity.

As far as this woman's theft of private documents was concerned, Burke decided he could live with that and use the woman to get even more. But first he needed some answers.

"How long have you worked for Bradford?" he asked.

"Just about six months."

Burke couldn't hide his surprise, and Jennifer seemed to bristle under it, take it as a rebuke. She reached out and tapped a finger against the photocopied tax forms.

"You see how much money the good doctor made last year?"

Burke looked at the line indicating Bradford's taxable income. It was a mid-six-figure monster.

"He makes more than ten thousand bucks a week. You think he couldn't afford to help this one little kid, gratis?" She sensed Burke about to object and hurried on before he could.

"You know this ninety thousand we're talking about for this operation isn't all his. He's not being asked to give up that much money. He only gets a part of that. Oh, sure, it's the biggest chunk of all the docs involved, since he's the primary surgeon, but the hospital's chunk is bigger, and all the other docs on the surgical team, combined, are bigger. And you know what? If *he* agreed to give up *his* chunk, the other docs would go along, and so would the hospital."

Burke held her eyes for a long minute. "Why?" he asked.

"Because it's the way the game is played. All the other surgeons on the team are picked by Bradford. They owe their piece of the action to him. So if he says, 'Hey, guys, just this one time, I think we should do one for free,' it's ninety-nine percent certain they'd go along. They might not like it, but they'd do it. They sure as hell wouldn't tell him to kiss off and risk losing future fees." She shook her head. "It's all part of the game— believe me. And it's the exact same thing Bradford would do if some big cardiologist who referred a lot of cases came to him and said, 'Hey, Jim, I have a special situation here, and I need your help on it.'" She had been speaking quickly and now took time to draw a deep breath. "Look, Bradford isn't the first surgeon I've worked for, and believe me, they all play it the same way."

"What about the hospital?" Burke asked.

"If Bradford pushed it, the hospital would go along, too."

"Why?"

"For the same reason, and because he has weight there. All the surgeons do. They're the *big guys* in any hospital. They bring in the big bucks. And even more important, this isn't something that happens every day. An individual surgeon gets something like this thrown at him maybe once every two or three years, tops. So the hospitals can afford to indulge a particular surgeon once in a while. They don't like it, and they definitely have to be pushed a bit, but they'll do it."

"So why won't Bradford?"

She sneered at him. "Because he's a god, and gods are supposed to be paid for the miracles they perform." She paused, staring him down. "There's also the little matter of the scam they're all running on the city. Didn't your editor tell you about that?"

"He told me," Burke said. "And we're more than a little interested."

"But you're going to do something about the kid, right?" Her beautiful eyes were filled with doubt and distrust now.

"Of course." Burke put as much assurance in his voice as he could muster. "It all fits together, as far as we're concerned. There's no story without the boy." He leaned forward, hoping it would emphasize his sincerity. "But we are concerned about documenting that final part of the story. To do that we'll need to get into the hospital's records, the medical school's, too, if possible. We'd like to show where these doctors were actually working when the city thought they were at Bellevue or Harlem Hospital or wherever. That means payroll records, surgical schedules, duty rosters—the whole ball of wax. And I can't just walk in and ask for those things." He gave her his best smile. "I could, but they'd just laugh in my face." He raised a finger, as if in warning. "And it would also tip them off about what we're looking for and give them a chance to cover it up." He shrugged. "So I need you to help me find a way to get to those records without anybody knowing about it. You see my point?"

Jennifer paused, thinking it through. "I'll get you in," she said at length. "It won't be easy, but it can be done. You'll just have to guarantee me that my name won't come up if you get caught. I don't want to lose my entire nursing career over this thing." "They can tie me to the rack and put hot pokers to my feet. Your name will never come up." Burke's eyes became serious. "Hell, the paper would fire me if I gave you up." He paused a beat. "Seriously, we'll meet maybe one more time to set things up. After that we'll never be in the same room together, and if I'm ever asked, I'll deny even knowing you. You, on the other hand, can telephone me at the paper if you have any questions or problems—in fact, I'll need you to do that from time to time. I won't risk calling you. I'll just return your calls at whatever number you leave. Other than that you won't exist after I start working on this." He studied her face, trying to gauge her reaction, and decided that she seemed satisfied. "So that leaves only one question," he added. "Are you sure you can get me access to these records?"

"I can get you in where you have to be, but I won't get the records myself."

"I understand. But are you sure you can get *me* in?"

Jennifer let out an unladylike snort. "I told you that I worked for Bradford for six months. But I've been at the hospital for four years. I know how the place works. And I know its weaknesses." She lowered her eyes and shook her head. "Do I ever. If the public only knew how many weaknesses there were, nobody would go near that place."

Burke smiled at the sarcasm, nodded. "If we pursue this— and I can't foresee any reason why we wouldn't—there are also a few other things I'm going to need from you."

Jennifer stared at him. "Like what?" The suspicion in her eyes now carried to her voice.

"First I'm going to want to keep tabs on him. It's what I meant when I said I'd need you to call me from time to time."

"I don't understand."

"Like where he eats lunch—especially any fancy joints that he goes to. Dinner reservations, too. Like something special he might have for himself and his wife at the Russian Tea Room or someplace like that." He raised his hands, then let them fall

back to the table. "Or a night out at the opera, a museum opening, that sort of thing."

He watched Jennifer's face, the small hint of pleasure that
had come to her eyes. She was getting the picture, and she
seemed to like it quite a bit. He made a circular gesture with his
hand. "Eventually I'm going to want to contrast how little
Roberto lives with how Dr. Bradford lives. And I'd like to have
some photographs of him doing his thing. It will just be a lot
easier if I know when he's going to the country club or the
opera or to Lutèce for lunch, rather than follow him around
every day for a month. You think you can find those things out
and tip me off?"

Jennifer smiled. "His secretary makes all his appointments
and reservations. She even does it for his wife. Our desks are
right next to each other in the office."

They were both smiling now. Burke toyed with his coffee. He
was ready to push the woman a bit, discover exactly what kind
of ax she was grinding.

"Tell me a little bit about Bradford. Something on a personal
level, if you can." He tried to make his words sound innocent,
nonthreatening. "Just so I know what kind of person I'm dealing with," he added.

Jennifer stared at him for several seconds. "He's a pig," she finally said.

Burke laughed. "Okay, that's a start. But give me an example."

Jennifer drew a breath, then told him about Bradford's request
that she wear slacks to work each day. Her features twisted with
each word, permeated with all the bitterness she obviously felt.

"Does that give you some idea?" she asked.

Burke noted that the restaurant's stereo system had appro-
priately switched to Linda Ronstadt's "You're No Good."

He fought off a smile. "Yeah, it sure does," he said.

A woman came toward their table, dressed in a one-piece
jumpsuit and tottering on a pair of platform shoes that were the
latest fashion craze. Burke watched her approach, mesmerized
by the unstable footwear. The shoes boggled his mind. That so
many young women would subject themselves to wearing them
amazed him even more. The woman stopped beside him, bent
and kissed Jennifer on the cheek, then slid into the chair next to

her and immediately began to stare Burke down, almost as though she had read his thoughts. She, too, was tall, slender, and attractive, despite a heavy dose of powder-blue eye shadow and Barbie-pink lips. She also had a very hard edge. Someone not to be messed with, Burke decided.

"This is my roommate, Adele," Jennifer said. She turned to Adele. "This is the reporter I told you about."

Adele gave Burke a "don't tread on me (or mine)" look that Burke immediately picked up on.

"Nice to meet you," Burke said. He used his best, nonthreatening smile. He had a strong feeling that Jennifer might back away from the entire project if Adele decided not to like him. He enhanced the smile with an offer of a drink.

Adele accepted and returned the smile, temporarily putting his mind at ease. He quickly ordered her a glass of white wine, knowing he would excuse himself and exit soon after the wine arrived. It was a cardinal rule professionally. Don't screw around with a winning hand.

Burke smiled again, but to himself this time. He was thinking about Dr. James Bradford, by Jennifer's account a very talented, very successful, and very self-satisfied man. The inner smile grew. He wondered how pleased the good doctor would be with himself if he ever discovered just how much his admiration of Jennifer Wells's buns had cost him.

Tuesday, 7:30 P.M.

Fat Vinnie Fagen sat behind the desk doing his imitation of a giant Buddha—a Buddha with a telephone pressed to each ear. Fagen was an enormous man, a six-foot-one, four-hundred-pound behemoth, whose girth seemed to swallow up his regulation-size gray-metal desk, turning it into some child's toy that had been plunked down in the middle of the newsroom. A thatch of reddish-blond hair sat atop Fat Vinnie's head, the hair on the sides cut so close the skin showed through. It made his very round head look like some mammoth vegetable, Burke thought, as he stopped before the desk and listened to Fat Vinnie growl, first into one phone, then the other.

"This racket is for the New York Press Club. You got that? All

of a sudden I'm not sure I'm making myself clear about that."
This into one phone. "Fuck you. We want the boat for the whole
night. We'll tell you when to head back to the dock. If the har-
bormaster bitches, we'll deal with it." This into the second
phone.

"No, no booze." To the first phone again. "The Patrolmen's
Benevolent Association is taking care of the booze, and the fire-
fighters' union is handling the beer. From you I just need hors
d'oeuvres. But I want hot and cold—the good stuff—and
enough for three hundred people. I end up with trays of cheese
cubes and rolled-up pieces of salami, neither one of us is gonna
be happy."

Burke fought to keep a smirk from his lips as he listened to
Fat Vinnie negotiate "donations" for the press club's annual
boat ride around the island of Manhattan.

Fat Vinnie had created the extravaganza five years ago, so it
was extremely close to his heart. It involved commandeering
one of the tour boats that circled Manhattan five times each
day—at no cost to the press club, of course. The boat was "donated" for the entire evening, as were the food, the booze, and
the cost of the five-piece band who provided the entertainment.
The event was a guaranteed success. Every politico from the
mayor on down attended—at fifty bucks a ticket—along with a
smattering of legitimate celebrities, who were ingratiating
themselves to the critics who had "invited" them, and a very
heavy handful of professional wannabes, who had been invited
by no one and who had literally begged for the privilege of buying a ticket. All of it, of course, delighted Fat Vinnie, who touted
his watery gala as second in importance only to the annual
black-tie dinner hosted by The Inner Circle.

That event charged the attendees one hundred dollars, fed
them a barely passable meal, then forced them to watch the
city's political reporters put on a musical revue that poked fun
at the very politicians whose annual "donations" kept their organization financially afloat.

Finally Fat Vinnie growled good-byes into each phone and
looked up at Burke.

"Well, well. The villain of the hour." He shook a scolding,
sausagelike finger. "First, let me say that the PBA is not amused.

In fact, you've become their prick of the month. One of their board members even asked if you were going on the boat ride." Vinnie let out a heh-heh-heh sort of chuckle. "Like if you were, you might not be coming back."

"They have no sense of humor," Burke said. "I'm surprised they didn't threaten to make the press club buy its own booze."

"They wouldn't fucking dare." Vinnie offered up a large shrug. "But you gotta appreciate their viewpoint. They're not supposed to have a sense of humor about these things. Not when it comes to one of their own getting an ass-kicking. That's just plain embarrassing." He let out another laugh; this time it was more of a snort. "The cops are supposed to be the ass-kickers. Remember?"

"They were. After I was cuffed."

Fat Vinnie raised his eyebrows. "Are you shitting me?"

Burke tapped the abrasion on his left cheek. "I was lucky. The young kid who was flown in to ride shotgun for the drunk I hit pulled the bastard off before he had a chance to really get started."

"Then fuck him and the PBA together. I hear any more I'll tell them they're lucky you didn't file charges." He raised his eyebrows again. "You're not, are you?" A note of concern had entered his voice.

He nodded approval as Burke shook his head. "It's better that way. For everybody."

"Don Cheech is taking care of the drunk," Burke said. He wanted Fat Vinnie to know he hadn't caved in completely.

The fat man let out another heh-heh-heh laugh. He was wearing a polyester shirt, the top three buttons undone, revealing a hairless, fleshy chest and a gold horn hanging from a chain. He reached inside the shirt and began scratching himself absentmindedly. "Believe me, whatever Don Cheech dreams up will be better—and longer-lasting—than anything the Civilian Review Board woulda done. And it won't have every cop in the city looking to break your balls."

Vinnie rubbed his hands together as though dismissing the subject. "Now, what can I do you for?"

Burke pulled a parking ticket from his inside pocket and dropped it on Vinnie's desk. "When I went back to pick up my car, this was on the windshield."

One of Vinnie's "unofficial" jobs for the press club was fixing parking tickets. As the club's liaison with the city's Parking Violations Bureau, he handled every ticket given out to the editors and reporters of each of the city's newspapers, television and radio stations, and other newsgathering organizations. The arrangement made sure that no press-club member ever paid a parking ticket. The theory behind it all was that it helped provide easier access to the news and was a public service granted only to reporters working on breaking stories. In reality tickets were fixed for every press-club member, whether he received them while working or while paying a visit to his favorite squeeze. It was a privilege that was also extended to members whose jobs never took them out of the newsroom at all.

Vinnie picked up Burke's ticket and placed it in a thick folder. "Consider that part taken care of," he said. "You got time for a beer or two?"

"Not tonight. I've got to head out to Brooklyn for an interview that Twist set up."

Vinnie raised his eyebrows again. "All messages from the mountaintop must be obeyed."

"Indeed," Burke said. "Especially by those of us struggling to lower our position on the shit list."

Vinnie gave him a big-cheeked smile. "Hey, be a good boy and you could drop down to number two. You never know."

(4)

Burke stared up at the building, one of the last remaining tenements in this very upwardly mobile Brooklyn neighborhood known as Park Slope. Indeed, gentrification had hit big time here. It had begun three long blocks away at Prospect Park, the city's one true rival to Manhattan's Central Park; then it had freight-trained down the sloping hill that gave the area its name, moving through the blocks of row houses that first crossed Seventh Avenue, then Sixth, until finally coming to an abrupt halt at Fifth. Up the block, the reason for the sudden stop was clear. The rows of brownstones, so valued as renovation prizes by the young stockbrokers and lawyers and MBAs who were fleeing the high-priced, cramped apartments of Manhattan, ended at this corner. Below Fifth Avenue run-down apartment buildings intermingled with warehouses and commercial buildings, all of it untouched and unwanted by the newly arrived gentry. This remaining part had been left to the poor, who lived in the small railroad apartments and who now joined their new neighbors each day for the subway ride to equally dissimilar jobs.

Before its discovery and newfound affluence the neighborhood had been quite different. It had been dominated by first- and second-generation Italians who worked the city's docks. And, as it did in all the city's old-line Italian neighborhoods, the Mafia had maintained a strong foothold as well. Even now a few of the old Italians remained, resisting the temptation to sell out to well-heeled newcomers and leave the homes where they had raised their children. And the mob still occupied a clubhouse only two short blocks from where Burke now stood—this one the dominion of Carmine "The Snake" Persico, an aptly named and currently incarcerated capo of the Colombo crime family. Now the lingering old families and the hoodlums who once protected and preyed on them were little more than oddities, misplaced persons among the youthful joggers who pounded the pavement each day in their overpriced running shoes and designer togs.

Burke crossed the street to the building where Maria Avalon lived. It was a squat rectangle, four stories high, that took up all of Fifth Avenue between First and Second streets. The upper floors were devoted to tenement apartments, a fact made clear by the occasional bit of furniture or drying wash that had been placed out on fire-escape landings. The ground level was a mix of fast-fading commercial establishments lined up like mourners at a wake—a dry cleaner, a minuscule bodega, a plumber, a down-at-the-heels clothing store replete with racks of cheap merchandise decorating the sidewalk and GOING OUT OF BUSINESS signs pasted to the windows.

The entryway to the upstairs apartments was jammed between the plumber and the bodega. The outside door opened into a small foyer with a wall of mailboxes, most of which were hopelessly vandalized—a regular pastime for junkies hoping to steal newly arrived welfare checks.

A second door led to a dark, narrow staircase. Burke glanced over his shoulder to make sure he wasn't being followed by any entrepreneurial thugs, then climbed the stairs to the second floor, his nostrils filling with a mélange of cooking odors that seemed to permeate the walls. He had often wondered why the buildings of the poor always gave up those small secrets. He had lived in such a building as a child—after his father was killed in an industrial accident—and he had always hated it, felt shamed when friends visited, understanding in his child's mind that the smells somehow marked his own poverty.

When he reached the second floor, he found the building bisected by a central hallway. Maria Avalon's apartment, 2C, faced the rear. Burke knocked lightly and waited. The door was opened by a slender, well-worn woman with graying hair. She had a soft, gentle face that did nothing to hide her fifty-something years, and she stared at him with open curiosity.

"Are jouse the newspaper?" Her voice had a heavy Spanish accent.

Burke tried to hide his surprise. The woman seemed much too old to have a five-year-old son.

"Yes, I'm from the *Globe*. I telephoned earlier this evening."

"I am . . ." She tapped her chest. "Consuelo Torres. Maria's mother. Roberto's *abuela*. His, um, granma, yes?" She added a vigorous nod, asking if he understood.

Burke immediately felt foolish. "Is Roberto's mother . . . um, your daughter here?" The feeling of foolishness grew.

"She is pooting Roberto in his bed. He wants to stay up when he hears someone is coming. But . . ." She smiled, then placed prayerlike hands against the side of her face, indicating the child had fallen asleep. She laughed, took Burke's elbow, and pulled him into the apartment. "Jou come in. Come in."

Burke found himself in a small living room and was immediately struck by both its obvious poverty and its cleanliness. The floor was covered in ancient linoleum, yet it gleamed under a heavy coat of wax, and a nylon area rug had been placed on top of it, adding color and warmth.

The furniture was old—items probably gathered from the secondhand shops of Goodwill or the Salvation Army—and each piece showed signs of careful repair. There was a large convertible sofa, two mismatched easy chairs, and a pair of heavy pine end tables, each holding massive porcelain lamps from the 1950s. The walls were decorated with inexpensive lithographs and a collection of photos, each showing a small boy with various adults. Burke let his eyes continue around the room. An old black-and-white television sat in one corner, its rabbit-ears antenna spread in a wide V. Burke stared at it. It was tuned to *All in the Family*, and Burke could hear Archie Bunker screaming at his son-in-law, the Meathead, as some malfunction in the vertical hold made the screen flip maddeningly. He ground his teeth. There had been a similar set in his own boyhood apartment. It, too, had never worked properly, but like this one's, its rabbit ears had always been incongruously spread in the same false sign of victory. He drew a breath and dismissed the derogation, against both his childhood and this woman he had yet to meet. Perhaps, in a place like this, just surviving with *this* much was victory in itself.

The grandmother excused herself and hurried off to get her daughter. Burke walked to a window that overlooked the rear of the building. Rising up the hill were the abutting rear gardens of the brownstones that lined First and Second streets.

What must it be like, he wondered, to look out each day at other people's gardens? To look at their flowers, at the safe, private place where their small children play, and to know nothing like that exists for you or your child and probably never will?

The thought was broken by the sound of a door opening. Burke turned and saw Maria Avalon for the first time. She was dressed in jeans and a plain, pale-blue T-shirt that accented her brown, almond-shaped eyes and light-coffee complexion.

She's beautiful, he thought, and immediately wondered why that surprised him.

She was about five-foot-five and appealingly slender, perfectly proportioned, although neither clothing nor demeanor made any attempt to emphasize the fact. She smiled and stepped toward him, haltingly extending her hand. The word "demure" came to his mind.

"I'm Maria Avalon, and you must be the Mr. Burke who called." There was only the faintest hint of an accent.

He took her hand and immediately felt the slightly rough, work-worn texture. It, too, surprised him, and again he realized it should not.

"Please call me Billy."

She smiled, her eyes giving off a bit of mischief. "Like the gruff goat?" She laughed. "I just read that story to Roberto tonight. He loved it."

Burke smiled back. "I was hoping to meet him."

Maria's eyes became distant, as though she had been forced to remember something. She let out a breath. "He gets so tired. It's his . . . illness." She spoke the final word as though she didn't want to.

"Can you tell me about it? What the doctor said? And the hospital?"

Maria's mother came out of the bedroom before she could answer. "Meester Burke. Jou want some coffee?"

"Yes, thank you."

"Not for me, Mama." Maria lowered her voice. "Her coffee is too strong. If I drink it at night, I can't sleep." Her mother grumbled something in Spanish from the kitchen, and Maria grimaced. "She heard me. She says I don't know good coffee when I have it." She gestured toward the sofa and chairs. "Come sit down. I'll try to explain what the doctor at the hospital said."

Burke listened for the next fifteen minutes, the coffee Maria's mother had brought growing cold on the table before him. The story was essentially the same one Jennifer Wells had told, although Maria Avalon's version lacked the nurse's hostility about James Bradford's insistence that he and the hospital be paid up front. It's because she's used to that treatment, Burke thought, used to it the way anyone who's poor gets used to it.

"What do you do? Your job, I mean."

"I work in the garment district. In the cutting room of a women's clothing company." She hesitated, as if trying to decide whether to tell him something. "Until last year I was going to Brooklyn College part-time. It was my first year, and I could only go part-time, but I thought if I could finish, someday I could get a better job." She paused again. "But then Roberto got sick, and I couldn't be away from him so much . . ." Her words trailed off.

"So you quit?"

She nodded. "Yes. I had to. Between school and the extra hours I have to work sometimes, I just couldn't be with Roberto enough. And we need the money, so I couldn't give up the extra hours."

Burke tried to estimate how much money the woman could earn each week in a garment-district cutting room. It was obviously not a full-time job or, if it was, it was one paid off the books. Otherwise she'd be in the garment-workers' union and would have some type of insurance. He decided to leave that question for later, rather than force her to admit that her employer wasn't paying taxes on her salary. It really didn't matter. Not for his purposes. Part-time or off the books, what she could earn would not be much.

"We're talking about a lot of money for Roberto," he finally said. "Do you have some money, or the ability to get some?"

Maria leaned forward, urgency entering her voice. "I can get a second job. I can pay them everything I make. Every week. If they'll only let me pay that way."

"Even if it means being away from your son?"

She stared at him as though he had suddenly revealed himself as a fool. "If he doesn't have this operation, there will be no time . . ." Her words died again, and tears began to form in her eyes. She brushed at them, then willed them away.

Ninety thousand bucks, Burke thought, and paying it off with a second job. It wasn't a big surprise that neither Bradford nor the hospital was willing to put much faith in that kind of offer.

Burke let out a breath. "I'm hoping we can help you. The paper, I mean."

Maria leaned forward, eager anticipation visible in her eyes. "But how? It is so much money."

"We'd like to run a story about Roberto—several stories, really—about his illness. We're hoping people will be willing to help."

She reached out and took his hand, gripping it tightly. "Do you think so? Do you think they might?"

Burke felt an electricity in her touch. The woman was attractive in so many ways. He pushed the thought away. It was something he couldn't afford to feel. "Yes, I think they will. If the story is written the right way, I think it will touch people and make them want to help."

There was a noise behind them, and they both turned. A

small boy stood in the doorway of the bedroom. He was thin to the point of being frail, and his face was dominated by two large brown eyes. He was a beautiful child, and he looked at them timidly, then hid his face behind the teddy bear he was carrying.

"Roberto. Why are you out of bed?" Maria jumped to her feet and hurried to the child. She scooped him up as if he weighed nothing at all and hugged him to her. The child whispered something in her ear, and she turned to Burke and smiled.

"He said he heard voices and wanted to meet the man he heard talking. He thinks you are very big." She looked at the child again and laughed. "But he's just nosy." She drew out the final word, kissed his nose for emphasis, then carried him back to the battered sofa.

The boy sat on her lap, his face buried against her shoulder, his head turning ever so slightly so one eye could take in the large man seated next to him.

The sudden appearance of the child made Burke feel surprisingly uneasy. He tried to ignore it, to do what he had to do— draw the child out. "How old are you?" The child didn't respond. "I bet you're four."

The child thrust out a hand, showing five splayed fingers.

"You're *five?* I don't believe it. I was just kidding about you being four. I thought you were at least *nine.*"

Roberto started to giggle against his mother's shoulder, then stole another look at Burke. "Five," he said, then buried his face again.

Burke noticed Maria's hands moving gently over the boy's body, stroking, comforting. She leaned down and whispered something, then turned the child on her lap so he was facing Burke. The boy smiled shyly but didn't avert his eyes.

The child's face startled Burke. From across the room he had seemed slender, perhaps even frail, like someone recovering from a bad case of flu. Now, up close, Burke could see the hollowness around his eyes, deep, bruiselike smudges, so heavy they looked like Halloween makeup. He let his gaze drop, scanning the child's body. Beneath the pajamas he could see how painfully thin the boy's arms and legs were. The child was dying. The thought hit with unnatural clarity, and he suddenly felt like an intruder, like someone who had stumbled into a wake where he didn't belong. He had come to the boy's home knowing that the child was dying, but not truly understanding, not allowing himself to accept the fact.

He pushed it all away, forcing himself to concentrate on the job he was there to do. He leaned forward, keeping his voice soft. "I work for a newspaper, Roberto. And I want to write a story about you. Will you tell me the things I need to know to make it a good story?"

The boy's face became serious, and he nodded.

Burke extended his hand. "Let's shake on it."

Roberto took two of Burke's fingers in his small hand and gave them three vigorous shakes. He started to giggle again. There was a mischievous glint hidden in those brown eyes, Burke realized. Then the boy spun around and again buried his face against his mother.

She stroked his head, then kissed it. "And now it's time for *somebody* to go back to bed."

The boy didn't protest, and Burke could see his eyes were already drooping. He watched Maria carry her son across the small living room and through the bedroom door, and found himself fighting off an unbidden thought: Would she be performing that simple, maternal act a year from now. Six months from now?

When Maria returned, Burke had his reporter's notebook and pen in hand. "I promised your boy a story." He smiled across at her, trying to put her at ease. His questions would get very personal, very explicit, and he wanted her to feel comfortable with him, confident that neither he nor the paper would do anything to harm them. He couldn't help wondering if that confidence would be warranted.

Maria's lips tightened momentarily, then she let out a breath. "I will tell you anything if it will help Roberto."

Three hours later

Burke sat in the soft leather reading chair, his feet propped on a matching hassock, as he reread the notes he had taken. The chair was the one luxury he had allowed himself in his otherwise sparsely furnished apartment. The cost of an apartment on the Upper East Side of Manhattan had seen to that—even for the modest three rooms he now called home. The remaining furniture, given his other expenses on a rent-impoverished budget, had been bought on the cheap. But since he was seldom home and rarely brought anyone there, it had never seemed to matter. Besides, the high-rise building had an elevator and a respectable southerly view of the Manhattan skyline. It was clean and orderly and well run, and unlike the apartment of his childhood, there were no cooking odors in the halls.

He had arrived back at his apartment and had immediately begun reviewing his notes. He had interviewed Maria Avalon for two hours, and her words filled almost half the notebook's pages.

Roberto was born in New York, two years after Maria and her husband had arrived from the colonial city of Ponce on the southern coast of Puerto Rico. Burke had vacationed there once years ago, and he recalled the small, elegant hotel where he had stayed, the horse-drawn carriages lined up in front to carry tourists along the narrow, flower-laden streets of the city's center, the long empty beaches and gentle sea that stretched along that Caribbean side of the island. He had also seen the other part of that city, the impoverished houses that were little more than shacks dotting the hardscrabble roads on the outskirts; the men, women, and children along those roads, some holding strings of crabs they had plucked from the sea, some squatting behind rows of conch shells or next to braziers of cooking food, all of which they hoped to sell to those traveling past.

Maria had come from that poverty, had fled to New York with her young husband in search of something more. But the new life they sought had overwhelmed her husband, the barriers of language and race, the very city itself proving too much for him. After the first year he had begun staying out at night, hanging out with his friends on the mean streets of their neighborhood. Soon he had become involved in drugs, first marijuana, then heroin. When she had discovered his addiction, she had begged him to get treatment, then, learning that she was pregnant, had threatened to leave him if he did not. Finally he had agreed, had enrolled in a methadone-maintenance program, and their lives had returned to some degree of normalcy. Then Roberto had arrived, a child who was constantly ill, forcing them to spend every available cent on doctors and medicines, and these new pressures had only added to her husband's uncertainties and despair. Suddenly he began staying away for days at a time, and she realized he had returned to the needle as a way of salving his growing fears. So she had told him to leave, told him she would not have drugs in the home where her son lived. She had believed the threat would bring him to his senses, force him to again give up the drugs. But he had left without the slightest protest. He had abandoned them and fled back to the island, or to somewhere else. She had never been certain which, and discovered she did not care. She filed for divorce and moved to a new apartment, hoping he would never find them again.

Maria's mother, Consuelo, had come after Maria's husband had fled, and they struggled to make a new life. They worked together at first, cleaning other people's homes. Maria studied evenings to improve her English, got a better job as a waitress, and finally enrolled in an adult-education program at Brooklyn College.

Then the bottom fell out of her life again when Roberto's health began to worsen. Suddenly he seemed to grow weaker almost daily. By then Maria had a steady job in the garment district, and she was forced to leave school so she could spend more time with her son. At first various doctors failed to diagnose his illness. Then an internist at a neighborhood clinic had discovered a congenital heart disorder—a small hole, apparently there from birth, that had begun to enlarge, and which would in time claim his frail body.

Burke laid the notebook in his lap and reached for the glass of bourbon that sat on a side table next to his chair. It was not a family history that would please Lenny Twist. It lacked the clean innocence he would prefer—a poor but loving family suddenly faced with overwhelming burdens. But Twist would move his mind around that obstacle if the rest of the story—the important part of the story—held up. He would tell Burke to ignore the *unpleasant* facts, to lose the part about the drugs, to simply state that the father had been unable to handle the pressures of a sick child and had abandoned him. Burke could play up the mother's heroic struggle, Twist would say—Burke could almost hear him using those very words. A young mother, alone, with no one to help her but her own aging mother, who worked each day cleaning other people's houses. It was a natural tearjerker, something that would make every reader wonder what new horrors lay ahead for the two women and the small, sick boy. Burke could see the entire scenario Twist would lay out, and there was no question it would work—for the paper.

His hand trembled as he sipped the amber liquid. He didn't want this story, didn't want to be within a hundred miles of it. Most of all, he did not want to get too close to this dying child.

He stared across the room at the floor-to-ceiling bookcase that covered the wall opposite his chair. Mixed among the books were photographs of a woman and a child, pictures he looked at every day to remind himself of what his life had once been. Julia and Annie, his wife and his daughter.

One of the pictures—his favorite—showed them sitting on the lawn before a small, two-story house. Julia and he had bought that house when she had become pregnant. It had been a typical middle-class move. They had decided to escape the confines of their cramped Manhattan apartment and give their coming child the space to run and play with other children. He studied his wife's face in the photograph. Her dark hair hung to her shoulders, and her smile was wide and happy, reflecting the joy that filled her soft brown eyes as she sat there next to their two-year-old daughter.

He had watched that joy begin to weaken, then fade away shortly after the photograph was taken. At age two and a half their daughter, Annie, suddenly began to lose the verbal skills she had just acquired. Then, over the next six months, she gradually lost interest in speaking altogether. Strange, repetitive body movements followed, comic at first, then growing more and more disturbing. Their pediatrician had simply smiled away their concerns, and they had struggled on for another year, watching their daughter become increasingly distant and withdrawn, never seeming to need comfort in times of distress, preferring her toys and stuffed animals to any contact with either his wife or him.

Annie was five when the doctors finally diagnosed her as severely autistic, six when they concluded that her condition would never improve. Institutionalization was the only option offered, and he and Julia had resisted it at first, had struggled to care for Annie at home.

The last photograph he had of them together was taken two weeks before Annie had entered the institution where she now lived. In that photo his daughter sat on a white cast-iron garden settee next to her mother. Behind them the flowers Julia had planted were in full bloom, contrasting sharply with the distant, vacant look in the child's eyes. In that final photo his wife seemed battered and beaten. The broad smile of the earlier picture had become little more than a fixed grimace, and the light that had filled her eyes was replaced by something almost as vacant and uncomprehending as the eyes of their child.

Julia had left him six months later. They had not divorced, only separated, but it was clear that being together, then or in the future, was something too painful for her to endure. Early on they had tried to see each other from time to time, but the guilt she was so desperately struggling to escape only intensified when they did. And so they stopped meeting. Now they saw each other only occasionally, when their paths accidentally crossed during visits to the institution where their daughter lived. They spoke on the phone, of course, but only at times when decisions about their daughter's care required discussion.

Julia had returned to her career as a magazine writer, and in the three years since their separation had risen to the rank of senior editor. To his knowledge she had never seriously dated in those three years, and he doubted she would ever remarry. He knew with an inner certainty that if she did, she would never agree to have another child. Nor would he.

Burke's thoughts returned to Maria Avalon and to her mother and to little Roberto—"Little Bobby," as Twist would have him called. Without Twist he never would have heard of these people. Maria and her young child simply would have remained part of a faceless, suffering mass, except for Lenny Twist's hunger for a Pulitzer Prize. He thought about that prize—achievable now in Twist's mind by publicly pillorying the doctors and hospitals who turned their collective backs on children like Roberto. Deserved? Undoubtedly, to some degree. But also a multifaceted question—the contraposition of which he would never touch. That wasn't the job Twist had set out for him. He was out to catch villains and to win a prize. And what about Roberto if there were no prize to be won or villains to be caught? Would the *Globes* and the Billy Burkes of this world still be there? The answer was obvious. And what did that say about the paper and about himself? He let the thought die, not wanting to deal with it. It was all moot anyway. He drew a deep breath and sipped his bourbon. There was no escaping this story. That was the one, indisputable certainty. If he rejected it, for whatever reason, Twist would use it as proof that he no longer had what was needed to be considered for major assignments. He would have him reassigned to some far-flung outpost— Queens or New Jersey or Long Island—where Burke would live out his remaining career covering community news. He could leave the paper, or course. His credentials would get him a job on most of the major newspapers in the country. But not in New York. Lenny Twist would see to that. He would use his position to make sure those doors remained closed. And Twist knew Burke could not afford to let that happen, that he could not leave the area where his daughter was institutionalized. So, like it or not, the story was his. Burke would do as he was told. It was a fact of life he preferred not to think about. Soon Maria and little Roberto would be in the paper's hands. And in his. Those thoughts, for now, were unnerving enough.

He looked back at the photographs on the bookcase and wondered if he would soon be failing another child, another mother. What was it Bradford's nurse, Jennifer Wells, had said? The boy had a year at best. Maybe only six months. Maybe just a month if serious medical episodes occurred. He pushed the thought away, hardened himself to the reality. He took a long drink of bourbon. He would be visiting his own child in two days. He had already arranged time off from the paper. It was Annie's birthday, and he suddenly realized he had yet to buy her a gift. He wondered what one bought a nine-year-old girl who lived in a world he could not even imagine. But there would be a gift. He would find something. And if he remained there throughout the visiting hours, he might see Julia as well.

(5)

Burke hit the newsroom at 9:45 A.M. and was immediately assigned to rewrite. Harry Mulligan, the early-rewrite man had called in sick, and the city desk already had reporters chasing down three homicides.

Burke had planned to dive into the Roberto story, had actually convinced himself that he wanted to. It was something he could easily have started from home. Now that was out the window, and he cursed himself for coming into the newsroom fifteen minutes early. He knew better. Anybody who had been in the business for more than six months knew better. When editors needed a body, they looked around the newsroom and found their strongest horse, and reporters who wanted to avoid the first "shit assignment" of the day simply kept out of sight. Now he was stuck and could only sit and wait for the reporters to call the city desk and see if the various killings were judged "good murders"or "bad murders."

It was an editorial decision made five times each day, given the city's murder rate, and one that always rankled Burke. "Bad murders" were those that involved blacks or Hispanics, which in New York newspaper parlance would be termed "banjos" or "bongos" and then summarily dismissed. The only way the killing of a black or Hispanic would be considered newsworthy would be: one, if the victim was a celebrity or public official; two, if it involved an honor student wrongly gunned down by a cop; or three, if it provided a natural tearjerker—an innocent mother or child accidentally killed in a disaster or a drug war.

A "good murder," conversely, would involve the wrongful death of almost anyone who was white, ideally a young, white female found in her Upper East Side apartment strangled with her own brassiere. It was madness, but Burke had long ago given up on this blatant racism that permeated the New York media. He had simply surrendered to it, and to the rationalization used by those who perpetuated it at every newspaper and radio and television station. The reasoning, he had found, was unassailable, because no one with the power to change it would listen to an argument against it. It went simply: Whites bought newspapers and listened to radio and television news, and whites weren't interested in ghetto murders. Blacks and Hispanics did not buy newspapers or follow radio or television news reports, ergo stories of interest to blacks and Hispanics were not newsworthy. Although he doubted the validity of the argument, Burke recognized that it was ingrained in the collective media mind-set like some false historical premise. Even so, he had once had the temerity to suggest that blacks and Hispanics might actually gain an interest in the news if those daily offerings had any bearing on their lives. The idea, which he put forth at a *Globe* editorial meeting, had been met with raised eyebrows. When he had persisted, pointing out that the existence of publications like *Ebony* magazine proved his point, the eyebrows only went higher. It was clear to all present that Billy Burke was out of the mainstream of media wisdom.

At eleven-thirty Burke was released from the rewrite desk. The three murders had turned out to be one banjo, one bongo, and one Times Square derelict, who, though white, fell into one of the few categories of white men who did not rate any ink. The reporter covering the murder, however, was told to follow up later in the day just in case the investigating detectives discovered that the deceased derelict had been a respectable citizen before his fall to the gutter. Even a white derelict had an outside shot at becoming newsworthy.

Before being relieved from rewrite, Burke handled two stories—one about a fire in Brooklyn that involved the rescue of three children and another about an elderly woman run down by a drunken cabdriver—then returned to his desk in the Eagles' Nest and found Eddie Hartman and Tony Rice working their own potential stories on the phones. Fred Costa, the fourth member of their group, had his feet up on his desk, the wide bellbottoms of his trousers hanging about his ankles. He was carefully cleaning his fingernails. A bottle of champagne sat at his elbow.

"I see there's been another transportation disaster," Burke said.

"Bus crash in Idaho. Tour group of senior citizens. Four dead. Dozens maimed." Costa's face became a mask of wicked pleasure. "One of the great tragedies of our time," he said.

Burke shook his head in mock severity. "Obviously a two-day assignment."

Costa's eyebrows fluttered. "At least." He tugged at the wide collar of his synthetic white shirt, then readjusted the Windsor knot on his oversize paisley necktie. "I'm sure the city desk will want in-depth interviews with the relatives of the victims," he said.

Costa was the paper's transportation reporter, and in addition to covering news from various regulatory agencies he was usually the lead reporter on any plane crashes, train wrecks, or other transportation mayhem. He was also an incorrigible libertine with a stable of steady girlfriends, many of whom worked as secretaries at the agencies he covered. To feed this avocation, Costa regularly scanned the wire services for any accident that might warrant a few lines in the paper. Finding one, he would immediately write a short item for the city desk, then call his wife in Long Island and tell her he was being sent to cover the "disaster," thereby clearing the way for an evening or two with one of his squeezes. This chicanery was made foolproof by the newsroom's internal switchboard, which allowed calls to be transferred to reporters anywhere in the world. The switchboard, manned by eminently bribable copyboys, maintained a list of reporters' locations and phone numbers—real and imaginary. For a ten-dollar gratuity they would happily add a reporter and his imaginary destination to that list and tell any in-calling spouse that she was being reconnected to that phony location. The call would then be transferred to a real phone number left by the reporter. Once the system (and the bribes) were in place, Costa would be free and clear. Should his wife telephone that evening, searching out her hardworking husband, the call would be passed on to the squeeze's apartment. Burke could visualize the scene, as the young lovely of the evening answered her phone with the words "Idaho Hilton," before passing the receiver to Costa.

Burke left Costa to his sexual plottings, picked up his phone, and called the Avalon apartment in Brooklyn. The previous day he had arranged a one-on-one interview with Roberto. When the grandmother answered, he explained he had been delayed and asked to come out later in the afternoon.

That set, he dialed Whitney Morgan's internal number at the paper. It was time to mend some personal fences.

"I'd like to see you," he said when Whitney answered.

There was a long pause before she said, "I'm not sure I want to talk to you." Her voice was soft, not angry, and Burke picked up on the "I'm not sure" part of her message. It was a signal that said "Coax me."

Whitney worked for the *Sunday Magazine,* and he pictured her sitting in her individual cubicle, one of the perks provided to the five writers who worked that section of the paper. It was a cushy job, with each writer getting two or three weeks to turn out a single piece. Whitney's specialty was long, in-depth articles on prominent, high-profile people. She was known for leaving her subjects shredded by the article's end, but she did it with such delicacy and apparent innocence that they seldom complained—or perhaps even noticed. Her last piece was about a magazine editor who had ridden an overbearing ego to personal celebrity. Whitney used his own self-serving proclamations to slice, dice, and hang him out to dry. When the editor read the article, he promptly offered her a job.

"I really feel bad about the other night, and I thought we might talk things over," Burke said. "I have to be out in Brooklyn by two-thirty or three. I thought we might be able to have lunch together. You pick the place?"

There was another long hesitation. Another good sign.

"I don't want to talk in a restaurant," she said finally. "Why don't you pick up some Chinese—nothing too spicy—and meet me at my apartment in half an hour."

Burke leaned back in his chair and stared up at the ceiling. Lunch in Whitney's apartment would end in only one place—where it always did—her bed. Life was good. "I'll be there in thirty minutes," he said. "Chinese food in hand."

When Burke hung up the phone, he found Tony Rice grinning at him.

"Don't smirk at me, you limey fop," he said.

"Do I detect love blooming yet again, my dear chap?" Rice's smirk grew.

"You're going to detect my large colonial fist at the end of your palmy British nose, dear boy," Burke said.

"Hit the limey fag," Fred Costa said.

Rice sucked in breath through pursed lips. "God, I love it when you Americans are violent. But say no more, dear boy." The smirk returned. "You will, of course, give me all the sordid details when you return, won't you?"

Burke's reply was interrupted by the crash of a chair against a desk. He turned and saw the chair spinning in the aisle behind him, obviously propelled off the foot of Pete Stavos, who now rumbled after it, shoulders hunched like an angry Cro-Magnon. He kicked the chair again, sending it another ten feet down the aisle.

"Peter, my dear boy, what *is* the matter?" Tony Rice fought off the giggle that was rising to his lips.

Stavos was a short fireplug of a man, no more than five-seven, with a square, stocky body that seemed to match his blocklike head. He looked, in fact, like a *set* of children's building blocks dressed in a suit, his only distinguishable features being a slightly hooked nose that bent to the right and a shock of salt-

and-pepper hair that made him appear dignified until he opened his mouth.

"Dear boy, tell us what's wrong," Rice repeated.

"Fucking gorillas," Stavos snarled.

Fred Costa, his feet still imperturbably propped on his desk, twisted his head around and grinned at Stavos. "Is it Pattycake's birthday again?"

"Of course it's her birthday," Stavos snarled. "That fucking gorilla has a fucking birthday every three months." He turned back toward the city desk and raised his voice to an ear-splitting shout. "And I've covered every one of that fucking ape's birthdays. Every fucking one. Because the fucking assholes who run this newspaper claim they haven't got anybody else who can cover a fucking story about a fucking ape with a fucking birthday cake."

Stavos's face was scarlet with self-induced rage. He was pushing fifty hard, and Burke, who always envisioned him blowing the tops off blood-pressure gauges, fully expected one day to watch him fall over dead in the middle of the newsroom.

"And how old is our beloved Pattycake this year?" Tony Rice asked.

Pattycake was the pride of the Bronx Zoo, the first and only of its gorillas to be born in captivity. She was also a favorite of the city's children, owing largely to the flamboyant birthday stories the *Globe* had run every year since the gorilla's birth— stories invariably written by Pete Stavos. The event had become an annual newsroom joke to everyone but Stavos.

Now he turned on Rice, glaring through narrowed eyes, not quite certain if he was being mocked.

"She's seven," he snarled. "And if you're so fucking interested, why don't you write the fucking story, you fucking limey hump?"

"But, Peter, dear boy, I wouldn't dream of taking this story away from you." Rice batted his eyes innocently. "Besides, I could never hope to match the warmth, the drama, the empathy you've brought to the story all these many years."

Stavos began to laugh in spite of himself. "You son of a bitch. You sound like those humps on the city desk." The laughter turned into another snarl. "I told them we should do the real story. Tell the fucking public how every goddamn year those monkey-loving assholes at the Bronx Zoo throw a party for some banana-sucking ape, instead of having one for all the fucking kids in the South Bronx who've never *had* a fucking birthday party."

"And what did they say?" Burke asked. He thought it was the first rational thought he had heard Stavos utter in the past year.

"They said Pattycake sells newspapers, and the bongos in the South Bronx only read *El Diario* anyway. The fucking racist scumbags."

"It's an outrage," Eddie Hartman said. He wiggled his bushy eyebrows, twitched his mustache. "We ought to put a contract out on this knuckle-walker. Talk to some of the wiseguys down on Mulberry Street. TV news would go apeshit for this story—pardon the expression." Hartman framed a headline in the air. "I can see it now. 'Pattycake Slain in Gangland Hit. Gorilla Found with Banana Shoved Up Its Ass. Film at Eleven.'"

"I love it," Stavos said. He raised his chin toward the city desk. "I'd pay those humps to let me cover that fucking gorilla's funeral."

"So why don't you whack her out yourself?" Costa suggested. He swung his feet off the desk and turned to face Stavos. "When nobody's looking, we'll get somebody to open her cage. You can be waiting around the corner in a fucking truck, and when she steps out in the road—bam, No more birthdays for Pattycake." Costa widened his eyes and gave a confirming nod. "Hell, that even makes it a transportation story. I can travel to zoos all around the country to get their reaction."

Tony Rice rounded on Costa. "I am astonished that you would turn the demise of this noble beast into yet another opportunity to get laid."

"Nah, nah, nah, nah," Hartman said, ignoring the others. "Forget that. No trucks. It's too complicated. You could have a flat tire, a dead battery, and blow the whole deal. Just stop at some hardware store on your way to the zoo and buy a box of rat poison. Then, when nobody's looking, sprinkle that shit on her birthday cake. One bite and Pattycake's off to that great big banana tree in the sky. And if they catch you, we plead temporary insanity. We claim the city desk drove you to it."

"What's temporary about Pete's insanity?" Burke asked.

"Ignore him," Hartman said. "The hardware store. Rat poison. And don't worry about a thing. I can get us a judge who hates fucking monkeys."

Frank Fabio's voice bellowed across the newsroom, telling Stavos to get moving or he'd miss the birthday party.

Stavos glared back across the room. "I'm goin', I'm goin'." He lowered his voice to a stage whisper. "But first I'm stopping at a fucking hardware store."

Burke watched Stavos storm off, then turned to Hartman. "That's great, Eddie. What are you gonna do if that fruitcake actually poisons the gorilla? I figure that makes you an accessory before the fact."

"No question about it," Costa said. "It's a clear case of conspiracy to commit gorillacide. You'll do ten years at Attica, and your asshole will be the size of the Holland Tunnel by the time you graduate."

"I'm afraid I may have to testify against you, dear boy," Tony Rice said. "Much as it will displease me to do so."

"I hope he tries," Hartman said. He let loose a simultaneous wiggle of eyebrows and mustache. "And I hope the gorilla catches him and rips his loony head right off his shoulders."

Whitney Morgan's apartment was only five minutes from the *Globe*, a second-floor walk-up in a stately brownstone that sat incongruously between two massive high-rise buildings just off Lexington Avenue.

They lay beside each other in Whitney's queen-size bed, their bodies glistening with sweat, the Chinese food Burke had brought growing cold in its containers in an adjoining room.

Burke had barely begun his apology for the fiasco with the Brooklyn cop when Whitney had started unbuttoning his shirt. Now their clothing lay scattered across two rooms, and as he lay there looking at the haphazard trail, he found himself thinking about Hansel and Gretel and the bread crumbs they had strewn behind them so they could find their way home.

Burke leaned up on one elbow and ran a finger along the fine line of Whitney's jaw. The bones of her face were delicately etched, classically beautiful, her eyes under long lashes a deep emerald green. She had small, perfectly formed breasts, a narrow waist, and long, slender legs, the body of a well-toned dancer, and the first time he saw her crossing the newsroom he stopped what he was doing and simply stared.

"Do you want to talk about the other night?" Burke asked. "I still feel guilty about you being dragged into it."

Whitney raised her head from the pillow, eyed him with skeptical amusement, then lay back and smiled at the ceiling. "I don't think so. I know it wasn't your fault—not entirely—but I still think it could have been avoided." A small smile played on her lips. "God, I keep thinking about that holding cell they put me in. There were two prostitutes in there with me, and they were not to be believed."

"How so?"

She giggled. "You should have seen them. They were both wearing these outlandishly low-cut hip-huggers and tank-tops, and one of them had one of those ridiculous yellow smiley faces painted on her stomach just below her navel, with an arrow beneath it that pointed down toward her crotch." Whitney giggled again. "Anyway, they wanted to know if I was turning tricks, too. Apparently there was some kind of sweep going on, and the cops were rounding up all the streetwalkers they could get their hands on. When I told them I wasn't a working girl, one of them said I was lucky, because all the johns she had serviced that night had been *enormous*."

"Enormous?"

"As in hung."

"I see. What a pity."

"Apparently it was for her. I gathered she had already serviced quite a few, and she claimed she hurt so much she couldn't sit down." Whitney bit her lower lip mischievously. "She told me the last guy she had, had a dick that was twelve inches long—*soft!*" Whitney widened her eyes. "Have *you* ever seen anybody that big? I sure haven't."

Burke laughed at the question. "I don't think so, but I never looked that closely—with an eye toward measurement, I mean. I took showers with some pretty big guys when I played football, but I don't think I ever saw anyone with that kind of equipment. But you have to understand, staring those

conditions was considered bad form. It made people nervous."
He glanced down at himself, then back at Whitney. "I'm glad I
don't present that difficulty."

"Liar, liar," she said. "All men want women to think they're
hung like horses."

"Only until they're eighteen. Then they realize the charade is
useless. Revelation outs the truth in the end." Burke leaned
down and kissed the tip of her nose. "But if you're interested in
conducting a survey, I've heard rumors about Fred Costa."

"Really?"

"I met one of his squeezes at Costello's a few weeks back, and
she kept referring to him as 'old donkey dick.'"

Whitney wrinkled her nose. "Not a very alluring allusion."

"He seemed quite pleased with it, actually."

"He would. The man is such a blatant libertine. I hope his
wife catches him and he wakes up some morning and finds out
she's given him a dickectomy."

Burke feigned a shudder. "Is that what you'd do?"

Whitney let out an evil laugh and jabbed a finger into his
chest. "That would be the pleasant part."

Burke pulled the sheet over his loins. "I don't think I even
want to hear the rest," he said.

She eyed him slyly. "I think you're reasonably safe. You see, I
know you're still in love with your wife." She reached out and
toyed with the hair on his chest. "And that's okay. I just want
you for your body anyway." She stretched like a cat. "You see, I
have a very detailed plan for my life, and home and hearth isn't
part of the picture right now." She reached out for his chest hair
again and urged him toward her. "But that doesn't mean I
couldn't get jealous if you decided to have more than one girlfriend."

Burke winced as she pulled his hair, then bent down and
kissed her forehead. "Message received," he said. "So, since my
wife doesn't want me back, I guess I'm stuck with just one girlfriend."

Whitney gave him a coquettish look. "You are until I get tired
of *you*," she said.

Burke gave her a pained look. "Touché," he said, as he sat up
and retrieved his watch from the bedside table.

"You have to leave?" Whitney asked. There was an audible pout in her tone, but it was not sincere, rather a practiced "little girl" response she had cultivated.

"Soon," he said. He bent down and kissed her forehead again, playing the game.

"Tell me about your interview."

He told her, starting with the small, sick child and ending with Twist's plan to nail the doctor. He alluded to financial hanky-panky at the hospital but withheld the details. Spreading it around at this point would be foolish. Newspaper reporters were notorious for their big mouths.

"That's a terrific story," Whitney said. "It's exactly the kind of piece that can put you right back on top."

Burke was jolted by the words. Had he fallen from the top? And if he had, had it been that noticeable, even to someone who worked in the isolation of the *Sunday Magazine?*

"There's a lot to do before I have it nailed down," he said. "A lot of digging. The part about the boy is pretty straightforward, and it sounds like the paper is willing to get behind it and get the kid the operation he needs."

"He won't live without it, right?"

"That's what I'm told."

"What a terrific tearjerker. You'll have old ladies sending in their bingo money. And when you nail that surgeon"—she let out a cold laugh—"he won't be able to walk down the street without people hissing at him."

Burke thought about that, about the glee it seemed to give Whitney. It wasn't just her, of course. Since Watergate the mindset of the media had changed dramatically. No longer was it enough to expose a wrong or reveal a problem that adversely affected people's lives. Now a specific villain had to be pilloried. Public punishment was required even if the identified villain was only part of a system gone awry. He recalled a story he had written years before. He had been a young reporter working for UPI, assigned to their Newark bureau. A police commissioner in a suburban New Jersey town had been accused of taking bribes to overlook a mob bookmaking operation. The evidence had surfaced during a widely publicized wiretap the FBI had run against a Mafia don, and the commissioner was an ancillary catch. But the media had descended with knives drawn, delighted with the tale of a corrupt cop. Later, after the commissioner's trial and conviction, Burke had happened by his home and noticed a handicap ramp leading to the front door. He made some inquiries with neighbors and learned that the commissioner's wife suffered from a severely advanced case of multiple sclerosis. It had been a prolonged battle, the neighbors revealed, and treatments had eaten up the commissioner's insurance coverage and nearly bankrupted the man. Burke was stunned by what he, and everyone else, had missed. It did not excuse the corruption, but it did help explain it. It was an internal story, even better than the one that surrounded it. It was the human element that no one had looked for, so no one had found. Today, Burke thought, it would be ignored even if it were found. It was a reality about the news business that disturbed him, but it was something he could not change. It was simply the way things were. Now—with Watergate fresh under their belt—there seemed to be no limit to the media's callousness.

"When do you think you'll have it all together?" Whitney asked.

"The kid's story can go almost immediately. Actually, they want several pieces on him while I try and dig up the rest of it. As far as that part goes?" He shrugged. "A week, two weeks. It really depends on how easily I can get to the information."

"God, I'd love to work a story like this," Whitney said. "Nail some smug bastard who's willing to let a kid die. Jesus, he reminds me of my relatives."

{ 6 }

Roberto sat on the couch, occasionally glancing toward the kitchen, where his grandmother busied herself preparing dinner. It was almost five o'clock, and the sounds of chopping and slicing had turned into aromatic simmering smells and begun their intrusion into the living room. Burke found it distracting, and surprisingly disturbing. Initially it made him realize how hungry he was, to think of the food left uneaten at Whitney's apartment. Then, as the sounds and smells intensified, Burke recognized the almost subliminal comfort he felt just being there; how long it had been since he'd witnessed the preparation of a simple evening meal. He'd been talking to the child for the better part of two hours. They'd covered school, the few short weeks Roberto had been able to spend in kindergarten before illness had forced his withdrawal, his favorite television show—*Happy Days*, with the Fonz—and finally his favorite baseball team—the Yankees.

"So, who's your favorite player?" Burke asked.

The boy thought about it, then his face erupted into the type of broad, enthusiastic grin only children can achieve. "Roberto Ramirez," he said. "He's the best guy on the Yankees. He hits home runs all the time."

Burke smiled at his choice. The Yankee outfielder had become as well known for his nighttime carousing and brushes with city cops as he had for his booming home runs. "I think maybe you like him because his name is Roberto," Burke said.

The boy's grin turned sheepish. "He's cool," he said. "I think he's from Puerto Rico."

"Does being from Puerto Rico make him cool?" Burke asked.

The boy's eyes danced with mischief. "That makes him the coolest," he said.

Burke laughed, and Roberto began to giggle. Ramirez was actually a Cuban, born and raised in Miami, but Burke saw no reason to disabuse the boy of his mischievous fantasy. He thought he remembered something from the paper he had brought with him and flipped it open to the sports page. There it was, a photo of Ramirez swinging from the ankles, the ball already in the catcher's mitt. The headline above the photo intoned, RAMIREZ SLUMP CONTINUES.

Unable to read, Roberto satisfied himself with the photo. He climbed down from the sofa and began swinging an imaginary bat. "Another home run," he squealed.

Before Burke could stop him, he began to run imaginary bases in the living room. When he swung back toward "home plate," he suddenly stopped and began gasping for breath. Burke went to the child and sat him on the floor. Through his shirt, he could feel the child's heart pounding. His own heart, he realized, was also hammering with fear.

"Are you okay?" He watched as the child nodded. He was still trying to catch his breath, and Burke scooped him up and placed him back on the sofa.

"Do you want some water?" he asked, not knowing what else to suggest.

The boy shook his head. Gradually his breathing began to ease.

"Are you sure?" Burke said. "Your mom will skin me if she comes home and finds out I had to take you to the hospital."

The boy giggled. "I'm okay now. I'm not even tired." He tried to squirm free, but Burke held him in place.

"Wait a minute. Wait a minute. You want to see a story I wrote in the paper?" he asked, trying to distract him. The boy's breathing had returned to normal, and now his eyes widened. "You wrote one in there?" he asked, pointing at the paper that sat on the small coffee table. Burke could see his child's mind working up a question.

"Did you write about baseball?" the boy finally asked. "About Roberto Ramirez?"

Burke shook his head. "I'm afraid not. Nothing that exciting." He had brought the paper to help break through any initial tensions and now found himself using it to force the boy to rest. He showed him a story he had written for that day's edition. It involved a bungling bank robber, who had passed a note to a teller, then grabbed an offered bag of money that was loaded with exploding dye. The robber ran from the bank and hailed a cab to make his getaway. As the taxi pulled up, he ripped open the bag of stolen loot to "make sure he had enough to pay the driver" (as he later explained to police), only to have the bag explode in his face and cover him in purple dye just as a patrol car was driving past. When the cops reached the bank robber, they found the cabbie choking him, incensed that his hack had been splattered with the unseemly color. Burke loved the story and had given it every comic twist he could. But the story didn't seem to impress the child at all, and Burke hastened to explain that it would be in all the papers that were sold in the city that day. That idea seemed to fascinate the boy, and he stared at the paper now as if trying to connect the printed words to the man who sat beside him.

"You know, the story I want to write about you will be in all those newspapers, too. It will be in every newspaper that's sold that day."

Roberto stared at him for a minute, his five-year-old mind surrounding that idea. "When you write the story will you have to write it in every one of the newspapers?" he asked.

Burke fought back another laugh. It was a stunning idea, and he had a sudden image of himself sitting in the press room furiously typing his story as sheets of newsprint flashed by. The question was so naïve, yet so perfectly logical, he didn't know how to reply.

He was saved by the reappearance of Roberto's grandmother. The woman had given him coffee when he arrived and refilled his cup whenever it was empty, each time moving on tiptoe as if entering a sickroom or the sanctuary of a church. He'd told her she was welcome to remain while he talked to her grandson, but she had insistently refused, as if her presence might somehow harm his work. As she came again now, coffeepot in hand, she made shushing sounds as a way of apology for having interrupted him even that much.

His question about newspapers forgotten, the child spoke to her in Spanish, and Burke's rudimentary understanding of the language made him suspect he was asking about his dinner. Her reply—*"Arroz con pollo"*—confirmed the suspicion.

The door to the apartment opened, and Maria Avalon came through, instantly filling the room with one of the most beautiful smiles Burke had ever seen. The child slid from the couch with effort and started toward his mother, and Burke suddenly realized how much more slowly he was moving. He felt an instant wave of guilt.

Maria picked him up and began kissing his cheeks, making him giggle.

As Burke moved toward her, he began to apologize. "I'm sorry. I think I really tired him out. He had a little trouble breathing just a minute ago."

A sadness crept into Maria's eyes. She shook her head, dismissing the apology. "It is something we all do. He seems so strong one minute. Then the next it is gone."

She took Roberto back to the couch and sat him on her lap. She sniffed the air. "Mmmm, something smells good. I think my mother is trying to impress you. I also think that she wants you to stay for dinner."

Burke was stunned by the suggestion. "I . . . I don't want to intrude on your family."

Maria's smile engulfed him. "Please," she said. "We have so little way to thank you for what you are doing. And Roberto would like it, I can tell." She tilted her head and looked at the child. "Wouldn't you, Roberto?"

Roberto leaned into his mother's ear and whispered. Maria fought back a laugh.

"He says he wants you to stay." She paused. "He also says you don't write about baseball for your newspaper." She arched an eyebrow. "Is that true?"

Burke reached out and stroked Roberto's cheek. "Yes, I'm afraid that's true."

"Well, do you at least know someone who writes about baseball?"

"Oh, yes," Burke said. "I know the person who writes about the Yankees, in fact."

Maria leaned back and looked at Roberto wide-eyed. The child's eyes widened as well. "I think you can stay, then," she said. "Don't you, Roberto?"

"Can the man who writes about the Yankees come and visit me?" he asked.

Burke started to laugh. "Playing hardball, huh? I'll see what I can arrange. Okay?"

"Okay, okay." The child was jumping in his mother's arms.

Consuelo Torres oversaw the dinner like a symphony conductor, spooning out large portions of *arroz con pollo* garnished with slices of papaya and mango. The food was sweet and aromatic, laced with spices Burke could only guess at, and it turned a simple meal of chicken and rice into a feast that teased eyes, nose, and palate.

"Mrs. Torres, this is delicious," Burke said. "I eat so much restaurant food, I forget how much I miss home cooking."

Consuelo cocked her head, a slight glint in her eyes. "Jou are no married? Jou don' have a wife to cook?"

Out of the corner of his eye Burke saw Maria twist in her chair, then Consuelo jolt slightly in hers. He realized that the younger woman had kicked her mother under the table. He fought off a smile.

"I am married," he said. "But my wife and I separated three years ago."

Consuelo moved her chair so she'd be safe from Maria's kicks. "Jou no divorced?" she asked.

Burke shook his head. "It just never became an issue—for

either one of us, I guess. So we never bothered."

"Jou have children?"

"Mama," Maria snapped. "You're being so nosy."

Consuelo waved her hand, dismissing her daughter's objection. "We have a daughter," Burke said. "She's nine. In fact, her birthday is tomorrow." He hoped the next question wouldn't come. He always hated it when it happened.

"Jou daughter, she live with jou wife?"

Burke lowered his eyes, shook his head again. "She's sick, Mrs. Torres. She lives in a hospital." He looked up at the woman's stricken face and softened his own features to let her know it was all right. "She's autistic. It's a disease that makes her act strangely, and she has to live in a special hospital so they can care for her."

The woman's eyes seemed to mist with regret, even sadness, Burke thought, and he felt washed in the warmth of her compassion. She reached across the table and squeezed his hand. "Jou have a picture?" she asked.

Burke took a photo from his wallet. It was the same picture he kept on the bookcase in his apartment, Julia and Annie next to each other on the garden settee.

Consuelo held the picture delicately as though it were a treasure she was afraid of harming. She passed it to Maria. "Jou daughter is beautiful," she said. "*Muy, muy hermosa.*"

The telephone interrupted their conversation, cutting off any need to reply. The women's pity had been palpable, and Burke felt overwhelming relief as he watched Maria move away from the table. Moments later she extended the telephone receiver toward him. "It's your office," she said.

Burke took the phone and immediately became the target of a barely coherent assault. It took a moment to realize he was listening to the *Globe's* night city editor, Sam Soule, who without preamble had launched into an excited babble about a murder at a Catholic church "just around the corner from where you are."

Soule barely paused for breath. "Look, you're the closest reporter I've got to the scene, and I need you to get there quick. We just picked it up on the police radio. The victim is supposed to be a nun, and the cops already collared some asshole at the scene, so everybody and their brother will be headed out from Manhattan. I've already got a photographer on the way. But you should be able to get there ahead of everybody. Listen, if it is a nun, pull out all the stops. You hear me? I want everything on this. Unless we go to war, it'll be the lead story tomorrow. And try to talk to the perp. Offer the detectives anything they want for an interview. You got all that?"

Burke stared at the floor and shook his head. Soule was an idiot who panicked every time a major story broke on his shift. He had been hired from a New Jersey paper four years earlier and still had no idea where anything was located in Manhattan. Brooklyn and Queens were like foreign countries to him. "I've got everything but an address, Sam," Burke said. "It would help if I had an address."

"Oh, yeah." Burke could hear Soule cursing under his breath as he fumbled around on his desk. Finally he found the address. The church that was supposedly "just around the corner" turned out to be in the Bay Ridge section of Brooklyn, a good fifteen minutes away by cab. Burke jotted the address in his notebook.

He replaced the receiver and turned back to the two women and the child. Roberto's grandmother was still holding the photo of his wife and daughter. "Bad news," he said. "I'm afraid I have to leave." He felt a sudden sense of escape just saying it.

Patrol cars were scattered like fallen dominoes, bubble lights left flashing, doors left ajar, the time-honored way of announcing the great urgency with which the police had arrived. The front entrance of Mary Immaculate Church was cordoned off with yellow crime-scene tape, and as Burke climbed the stone stairs, he could see two detectives just inside the barrier. He knew one of them. Mike Hanrahan was a burly, red-faced, cigar-chomping detective sergeant with whom Burke had downed many an off-duty beer during a three-month punishment reassignment to Brooklyn the previous year.

Hanrahan turned as he came up the stairs, removed the cigar from his mouth, and pointed it at Burke's nose. "I heard about you, hump. You out here to cover this story or to try and kick some poor cop's ass?"

"Cover the story," Burke said. He extended his hand over the yellow ribbon of tape. "Besides, I'm not sure if I could take you or not."

Hanrahan took Burke's hand, squeezed it harder than necessary, and grinned. "It's good you don't wanna try. It's been a long fucking day, and I'd hate to have to kick your ink-stained butt all the way back to Manhattan just to prove a point." He shoved the cigar back into his mouth and talked around it. "So what are you doin' in Brooklyn? That little fracas at the Seven-eight get you back on the shit list?"

"Close, but not this time." He returned the grin. "I just happened to be in the neighborhood, so the city desk dropped your little caper in my lap. Whatayagot?"

Hanrahan's face hardened. "Somethin' nobody should have to look at on a full stomach. Or an empty one." He motioned back toward the closed church doors. "A sixty-eight-year-old nun, for chrissake. Looks like she caught this junkie scumbag trying to jimmy the fucking poor box. For her trouble she gets raped, then gets her throat slit for good measure."

"You caught the perp?"

Hanrahan raised his chin toward the street. "He's in the back of that patrol car. Two uniforms were driving by when our hero comes running down the front steps covered in the nun's blood. Says now the cops beat his ass and how he's the victim of police brutality. It was me who caught him, he'd be bitching from inside a fucking body bag."

"I'd like to see the body and talk to the perp," Burke said. He glanced around. "Before the rest of the ghouls get here."

Hanrahan let out a snorting laugh. "Hey, I'd like you to suck my cock, but I figured there was no point in asking."

"C'mon, Mike."

Hanrahan eyed him up and down. "All right. I figure we owe you one for what went down at the Seven-eight. I know that asshole Grady. He's a fucking souse shoulda been thrown off the job years ago." He removed his cigar and pointed it at Burke's nose again. "But you didn't get nothin' from me. Agreed?"

"You got it, Mike. I never even talked to you."

"You never even fuckin' saw me," Hanrahan said.

* * *

The nun's body lay in a pool of blood just inside the front doors of the church. Burke's initial view of it came in a blaze of light as a police photographer documented the crime scene, preparing a portfolio of pictures that twelve unlucky jurors might one day be forced to carry forever in their memories.

The first thing to strike Burke was the woman's horrible nakedness. Her black habit had been pulled up and her white cotton underwear ripped away, exposing the frail, wrinkled legs of an old woman and a semen-stained thatch of gray pubic hair. He felt instant shame and quickly raised his eyes to the woman's face, only to find himself looking down into a glassy-eyed mask of horror, the mouth stretched wide in a now-silent scream, the starched white wimple below her chin turned crimson where the knife had opened her throat from ear to ear.

He averted his eyes again and found himself staring at the woman's hands. They were clutching the large rosary beads she wore around her waist, the fingers of one hand pressed against the figure of Christ on the cross. He turned his back on the scene.

"Jesus."

"Yeah, it's a beauty, ain't it?" Hanrahan said. "And the perp is bitching that the uniforms roughed him up." He let out a grunt. "You wanna bet some ACLU hump ain't holding his fucking hand by tomorrow morning?"

Burke glanced to his right, into the interior of the church. Candlelight bathed everything in a soft glow and cast shadows on the somber statues of various saints. He took a deep breath and immediately regretted it. The heavy copper smell of drying blood overwhelmed his senses. He gagged and stepped quickly to the front doors. "I gotta get outta here."

"That's a good boy," Hanrahan said. He pushed Burke forward. "Puking on a crime scene is a definite no-no."

Outside, Burke sucked in a heavy dose of filthy New York air. "Jesus," he said again. He looked to his left. A large brick parochial school stood next to the church, looking like every parochial school he had ever seen. "This nun teach at the school?" he asked.

"Yeah, she used to teach there. For about twenty years, according to the head nun. You go to Catholic school as a kid?" Hanrahan asked.

Burke nodded. "Eight years."

"The nuns ever take a ruler to your knuckles?"

Burke nodded again. "About once a week."

"Shit, you musta been one of the good kids. Anyways, this nun retired from teaching about three years ago. Since then she kinda took care of the church—changing the flowers, the candles, making sure the cruets for the wine were filled, shit like that. It's why she was here tonight."

Burke took another deep breath, then pulled his notebook from his pocket. "You got names on the nun and the perp?"

Hanrahan gave them to him, along with the approximate time of the attack, the time the two uniforms had first seen the perp, and a detailed—if perhaps fictional—account of the perp's attempt to flee the scene and his subsequent attack on the arresting offcers.

"We got his ass cold. We got the murder weapon. We got the nun's blood all over his fucking clothes. We're missing only one fucking essential here," Hanrahan said.

"What's that?" Burke asked.

"The fucking electric chair," Hanrahan said. He pulled the cigar from his mouth and spit a piece of tobacco toward the street. "You still wanna talk to this asshole?"

"Yeah, I would."

Hanrahan jabbed his cigar toward a patrol car with officers standing beside each rear door. "You sit in the front passenger seat and talk to him through the wire cage. Then you get your ass out of here before the rest of the fucking vampires show up." He called out to the two uniforms guarding the patrol car, pointed at Burke, and gave an approving nod.

Burke reached out and squeezed Hanrahan's shoulder. "Thanks, Mike. I owe you."

"You bet your sweet Irish ass you owe me," Hanrahan said. "And I intend to collect."

"You a fucking cop?" the perp asked.

Burke stared through the wire cage that separated the front and rear of the patrol car. He removed his press card and held it up for the man to see. The perp's name was William Racine. His street name, according to Hanrahan, was Willie Rancid. He

was a small, skinny, hollow-faced junkie, with skin the color
and texture of thirty-year-old paper.
    "You wanna tell me what happened, Willie?" Burke asked.
"Just so we get your side of it."
    Willie's body twitched. Lank, filthy hair hung down across his
forehead. His mouth was swollen and twisted into a sneer.
"What do you think, I'm fucking stupid?" he snapped.
    Burke looked back toward the sidewalk. If he hadn't felt so
sick to his stomach, he would have laughed at the question. Do
I think you're stupid? You go into a church to pull a major caper
like robbing the goddamn poor box. You get caught by a sixty-
eight-year-old nun, and the best response you can come up with
is to rape and murder her. Then, to make your getaway, you run
out the front door covered in her blood and right into the arms
of two cops, who were probably on their way to a goddamn
doughnut shop. No, Willie, I don't think you're stupid. He looked
back at the man. "Hey, Willie. You just want me to write up the
cops' side of the story, it's okay with me." Burke started to get out
of the patrol car when Willie's high-pitched voice stopped him.
    "These fucking cops, they beat me up," he said.
    Burke slid back into the seat. "Hey, these cops said you were
waving a knife at them."
    "That's bullshit," Willie snapped. "They already took the knife
outta my fuckin' pocket. They already had me cuffed and every-
thin'. It's all bullshit, man."
    "So why'd you kill the nun, Willie?"
    Willie started to jump up and down in his seat, still hopped
up on whatever drug he had taken. "Hey, man, I didn't kill nobody. The cops planted the knife on me. I didn't do nothin', not
a fuckin' thing."
    Burke shook his head. "Hey, Willie, you want me to help you,
you gotta help me here. Look, you already told me the knife was
in your pocket. You're covered in the nun's blood. You're running out of the church. You've got the poor-box money in your
pocket."
    "Hey, I never even got in that poor box," Willie shouted.
"That fuckin' nun, she was all over me before I even got the
thing opened."
    Burke stared at him, letting what he had just blurted out set-

tle in his weak little drug-juiced mind. "So, Willie, I understand why you killed her. But I don't understand why you raped her. She was sixty-eight years old."

"Hey, that old bitch got what she deserved, man. She started whackin' the shit outta me. She had no right to do that, man. She didn't even give me a chance to get the fuck out of there. She just started smackin' me. All I did, I just paid her back, tha's all."

Hey, that old bitch got what she deserved, man. Burke slid out of the car. Willie's high-pitched protests followed him, but he ignored them. He had the quote he wanted. The paper would undoubtedly run it under Willie's mug shot. And Willie? Fuck him. Let him spend the next thirty years in an eight-by-six-foot cell with a series of mutant bikers drilling his ass for oil. Couldn't happen to a nicer skell.

Burke started to walk away. There was a teenage kid coming toward him on the sidewalk. He was a white kid, but his hair had been braided in cornrows, a style favored by many blacks. He was wearing a Fleetwood Mac T-shirt and a pair of bellbottom jeans that swallowed his shoes. There was a boom-box radio on his shoulder, and the kid was bobbing his head to the music, apparently oblivious to the mayhem that surrounded him. Burke recognized the song as Captain and Tennille's "Love Will Keep Us Together," the big hit single of the year. He hated the song almost as much as he hated boom boxes and the morons who carried them.

One of the patrol cops reached out and grabbed his arm as he was moving past. "So you gonna write up that shit about that pervert getting his ass kicked?" the cop snapped. He had pronounced the word as "prevert."

Burke looked at him. He was short and stocky and sallow-faced, maybe twenty-three, twenty-four years old, but there was already an angry cynicism permanently marking his face.

The kid with the boom box was next to them now. The music had changed to some blaring Pink Floyd tune, and Burke had to raise his voice to be heard. "I think Hanrahan was right."

"How's that?" the cop shouted back.

Burke began walking again and called back over his shoulder. "He said you should of shot the prick."

{ 7 }

The heavy, cloying scent of pine detergent failed to mask the underlying odor of urine. Walking down the long hallway, Burke realized it was a smell he had come to associate with his daughter. The pale, industrial-green walls were another association, as were the cracked, dull gray tiles of the floors and the occasional shrieks that came from individual rooms. Depression ruled here. This was a place forced upon those who lived behind the walls and those who visited, and merely crossing the threshold produced a sinking sensation that remained throughout each visit.

He hated coming here, had felt that way from the beginning. He thought the feeling would dissipate over time, but it had not. It remained, had become even more entrenched, as had the guilt he endured each time he acknowledged it.

A middle-aged nurse looked up and smiled as he approached.

She was a large black woman with soft, patient eyes. They had come to know each other over the years.

"Good morning, Ms. Collins," he said.

The woman glanced at the wrapped present Burke carried. Her smile broadened, flashing a bit of gold at the corner of her mouth, "We have a birthday today, don't we?" she said.

Burke felt his anger flare. He wanted to tell the woman that *we* didn't have anything today. That it was *Annie's* birthday, although she probably didn't have the slightest *fucking* idea that it was. Instead he smiled and asked, "How is she today?"

"It's a good day," the nurse said. "And your wife is here. She brought a cake."

Burke forced another smile. A good day, he thought. One without tantrums or hysterical outbursts. A day when Annie would play with her toys, unaware or not caring about the presence of anyone or anything, lost in a solitary world that he could neither enter nor understand. Yes, a good day. Another that would see a mother weep soft, bitter tears and a father wish he were somewhere else.

He opened the door to Annie's room and stopped short. Annie was sitting on Julia's lap, her long, lean, nine-year-old body curled in fetal comfort. It had been months since Annie had allowed herself to be held. Julia smiled at him, her face tender and content. Annie simply stared, curious at his arrival, perhaps even wondering who he was. The last thought ripped at his heart, so he quickly put it aside.

"Hi," he said, smiling at his wife.

"Hi. Are you here to see the birthday girl?" She kissed the top of Annie's head.

"I sure am." Burke went to them and knelt down in front of his daughter. He kissed her cheek, then extended a box wrapped in glossy blue paper with a large, gold stick-on bow. Bright, shiny colors fascinated the child, and she immediately reached for the gold bow and pulled it from the package, ignoring the box.

"Do you want to see what's inside?" he asked. "I think it might be something you'd really like."

"*I* want to see. Let me help. Please." Julia reached out and began unwrapping one end of the box. Annie ignored her, cocking

her head and curiously turning the gold bow in her hands.
Burke watched his wife slowly unwrap the package, struggling to bring as much drama to the event as possible. Annie remained uninterested, lost as she always was in her own
unfathomable moment in time. He continued to watch them,
struggling to recapture what he had felt years ago, the joy that
had surged through him just seeing them together.

Julia's soft, dark hair was shorter now than it was in the picture he kept on his bookcase. No longer shoulder-length, it was
cut just an inch or so below her ears, sculpted, really, in a slight
curve that set off the delicate, almost fragile lines of her face.
Her light-brown eyes seemed less pained now than they did in
that last photograph, but he knew that was a temporary condition, fully dependent on what the remainder of this day held.
She's still so beautiful, he thought. Even at thirty-four, when
most women begin to show the effects of time, she carries herself with that same soft, gentle grace that first attracted you.

He looked at his daughter. Beautiful, too. The same soft, dark
hair as her mother, hers now tied in twin ponytails, unbraided
and fixed with small white bows. The same lines in her face,
only less defined, still slightly plump and childlike, but clearly
destined to be striking one day. And her eyes—oh, God, her
eyes. Soft, light brown, beautiful, and . . . And oh, so vacant.
Burke stared at his daughter's eyes, silently praying for some
spark, some hint of animation. Annie's gaze was now fixed on
the far end of the room, seeing God-knew-what, empty of all
feeling and emotion and interest.

"Oh, look, honey. Look." Julia held up the doll. She glanced
up at Burke and raised her eyebrows. It was a Madame Alexan-
der, its lifelike face, its skin tones the epitome of the dollmaker's
art, this one dressed as a Scottish lass, complete with tam-o'-
shanter, white blouse, and a skirt in distinctive Highlander tar-
tan. And its eyes as blank as Annie's, Burke thought. Again he
pushed the thought away, hiding from the pain. He had paid
seventy-five dollars for the doll. Guilt money, without question,
and now his daughter studied her birthday prize with all the ex-
uberance she might hold for a bug found crawling across the
floor.

"Oh, Billy, this is so extravagant," Julia said. "This is the kind of doll you put on a shelf, the kind you collect." Her voice was soft, the words a gentle reprimand, her eyes telling him at the same time that she loved him for his foolish generosity.

Burke reached out and stroked his daughter's hair. "It's all right," he said. "Annie can play with it all she wants," then thought, There's enough of her life already on a shelf.

"Then let's have cake," Julia said. "And we'll let our new doll come to the party and have some, too." She placed the doll in her daughter's arms, then slid her gently off her lap and hurried off to a small table and began to remove a small white cake from a bakery box.

Burke sat in the chair Julia had vacated and again stroked his daughter's hair. She turned and looked at him, then hugged her new doll tightly and climbed onto his lap.

It sent a shock through him, and he felt a sudden intake of breath. He wrapped his arms around the child and held her tightly. When he released her, she turned and looked up at him, her eyes curious. Then she reached up with one finger and touched a solitary tear that was moving along his cheek. Holding it away from her, she studied it on the end of her finger as if it were some small, strange creature she had never before seen. This lovely little child who never cried, Burke thought— even when she was hurt—now studying a tear from her father's eye.

They had cake together, lighting nine candles, then blowing them out while Annie looked on. Julia's present was a beautiful dress trimmed in fine Irish lace, a party dress as impractical as his gift, dress-up clothing from a mother who wished her daughter could go to parties like other little girls.

Julia looked up at him and smiled, as if reading his thoughts. "I couldn't resist it," she said.

He could tell from the look in her eyes that she wanted Annie to change into the dress. He could also tell that she knew the angry resistance that might produce. He watched Julia fold the dress and place it back in the box, and he knelt next to his daughter.

"Annie, let's put on your new dress," he said. "Then you and your dolly can both have new dresses."

Annie stared off into space as though the words had floated

past her, unheard. Then she began to unbutton the simple red dress she was wearing.

They walked together on the grounds, across lush green early-summer lawns. Walking outside was one of Annie's favorite things, something they tried to do on each visit. Annie walked ahead now, still holding her new doll, the skirt of her new dress flouncing about her long, skinny legs.

Burke glanced down at Julia. Her eyes were fixed on the child—sad eyes that spoke of her lost maternity more clearly than any words. She was a small woman, no more than five-four, slender to the point of being delicate. He had often wondered how such a seemingly fragile creature had ever found the strength to give birth to a child—then wondered, unbidden, if he wished she never had, and hated himself for even the thought.

"I read your story in today's paper," she said. "Did that monster really say that poor old nun got what she deserved?"

It pleased him that she had read his story, although the story itself meant little to him. It was more that she was still interested in what he wrote and did. "He said it. And he meant it."

"That must have been horrible," Julia said. "Having to look at that poor woman's body, then talk to the cretin who killed her."

Burke thought about it, thought about the old nun, her brutally exposed body, the look of surprised horror on her face, her fingers pressed against the figure of Christ on the cross. He no longer regarded that part of his job as horrible. Over the years brutality had become so much a part of his life that he rarely analyzed his feelings about it. What did worry him from time to time was the absence of any feeling at all. That wasn't the case last night. He had been truly sickened by what he had seen, and he knew that when such things no longer had that effect, he would walk away from the job. At least he hoped he would.

"It was ugly. One of those stories you'd be happy to have someone else cover." He meant what he said yet also knew he felt a certain pride in the way he had handled it. He wondered if Julia could understand that, if anyone could. He decided not to risk talking about it and changed the subject. "I'm working on another story I'd rather not have."

Julia asked about it, and he told her about Roberto. He told her all of it, even the details about the suspected hospital scam. It marked the strong trust he felt in her.

"That poor little boy. But at least he has those two women. They sound incredibly strong." She hesitated, then looked up at him. "Why would you rather not have the story?" she asked. He could sense from her tone that she already knew the answer.

"It's personally painful. I don't want to get close to another child who needs help, and then find out again that I can't provide that help." He shook his head. "But that's not all of it. There's the other part of the story, too, and I just don't know how fair I can be. Or how fair I want to be."

"Is that because of Annie, too? Because of *her* doctors?"

He nodded, looking ahead at his daughter. "I'm still bitter about the doctors, about all the incompetence. All the years it took them to figure out what was wrong with her."

Julia looked down as they continued to walk. "It wouldn't have mattered. It wouldn't have changed the outcome for her," she said at length.

"It might have mattered to us," he said. He wanted to say more. He wanted to say that it might have changed the outcome for them, that they still might be together. But that was supposition on his part, and it was unfair to Julia.

She took his hand as they continued to walk, and he could feel the wedding ring she still wore on her finger. He accepted that for his answer, the one he wanted—be it true or not.

"Just put your anger aside and concentrate on helping that poor child," she said. "I know it's hard, but it's a chance to do something more than just cover murder and mayhem. In the long run it may be good for you." She paused a moment. "In a lot of ways."

She said it almost as though it might provide redemption, Burke thought, and he wondered if that were possible.

He squeezed her hand and smiled. "I could use you looking over my shoulder on this one," he said. "Sort of a rent-a-conscience."

Julia laughed at the idea. "You don't need any help with your conscience, Billy," she said. "You've already got one that's too big for the work you do." She squeezed his hand back. "But if you ever need to talk about it, I'm here."

"I may take you up on that," he said.

{ 8 }

Gerard LaFrancois looked at Burke with one eye suspiciously cocked. "So tell me, you big, gorgeous hunk of man, whose life are you about to make miserable today?"

Burke shook his head sadly. "Jerry, Jerry, Jerry. What a thing to say. Isn't it remotely possible that I came by just to see you?"

Jerry shook his shoulders as though a shiver had just coursed through his body. "Oooh, it's such a lie. But keep saying it. I love it when you lie to me."

Burke perched on the edge of the desk next to a copy of Saul Bellow's new novel, *Humboldt's Gift*. To Burke the book epitomized the contradictions Jerry presented to everyone. He was highly intelligent, yet everything he did was played out in high camp. He had once told Burke his life story, or at least that day's version of his life story. With Jerry one never knew.

Born Gerald Francis thirty-something years ago in Queens,

he had supposedly endured the religious fanaticism of a "very domineering, very Catholic mother" for eighteen years, then left home for college, promptly changed his name to Gerard LaFrancois, "and came flying out of the closet in a pink-sequined tutu." Burke had no idea what parts of the story were true. During another conversation Jerry had told him his mother had once been a contortionist in the circus, then winked slyly and claimed he had inherited "all of her talents" but put them to "much more intriguing uses."

Jerry drew a deep, weary breath, rose from his chair, and moved to a nearby filing cabinet with an intentionally mincing walk. He was a small, slender man—svelte was the description he preferred—with short, receding blond hair and a blond mustache that sat under his oversized nose like a well-barbered caterpillar. He turned back to Burke, threw out one hip, and sighed. "So what is it? I'm a busy little public official, you know."

Burke rolled his eyes at the flamboyant display. It was Jerry's way of ragging him. But as outrageous as he was, he was equally competent. He also happened to be the administrative assistant to the city comptroller, and as such held the keys to the kingdom as far as Burke was concerned. The city comptroller's office oversaw all the city's financial dealings and had the power to look into the finances of any public or private agency receiving city money. Burke had spent years cultivating Jerry as a source, and the effort had produced repeated dividends. He couldn't have cared less about the man's sexual orientation. He could sleep with goats as far as Burke was concerned.

"I need to take a look at some payroll records for city hospitals," Burke said. "Specifically, I need the payroll time records for the attending physicians, specialists, interns, and medical students from private hospitals who are providing services at city hospitals under the Super Hospital Plan."

Jerry gave him a quizzical look. "So you go to the city hospitals in question and ask them. It's all public record."

"Ah, there's the rub," Burke said. "You know how doctors cover up for each other. One visit from me and the telephones will be buzzing between hospitals. Then everybody will be pulling a Richard Nixon on me—one stonewall after another."

Jerry let out a long, exasperated breath. "So you want me to do the dirty work."

"It's just more practical, Jerry. If the city comptroller's office asks, it's just another compilation of statistics for some future budget report. If I ask . . ."

Jerry waved him into silence. "Let's cut to the nitty, you sweet thing. What's the quid pro quo for *this* office, and me in particular?"

Burke gave an exaggerated shrug. "Well-l-l . . ." He drew the word out. "Your boss could end up ordering a very politically charged investigation—and we both know how he wants to be mayor someday. And you could be the indispensable employee who hands it to him on a platter."

"Before you publish?"

"Could be arranged. Our beloved comptroller could be ready to pounce the day the story hits the street. And if you're especially helpful, we might even give him some credit in the piece itself."

Jerry pondered the idea, then grinned. "All right. All right. I get the point. But it's going to cost you something personal as well." The grin turned lascivious, then ended in a cackle at the horrified expression on Burke's face. "Don't worry. I'm not going to compromise your latent homosexual virginity—which we *all* have, you know." He gave Burke an exaggerated wink. "I'll settle for a sumptuous little lunch at someplace terribly expensive."

"You've got it," Burke said.

Jerry wiggled with delight, high camp again. "In that case I'll have the information in your office by Monday afternoon." He raised an eyebrow again. "Hospitals, eh? Did I ever tell you that I once thought about becoming a nurse?" He pursed his lips. "God, just the thought of all those virile young medical students wandering around with stethoscopes dangling from their necks. It's just *too* phallic for words."

Burke spent the afternoon writing the first of what Twist had dubbed the "Little Bobby" stories. Everything, it seemed, had become "little" to the man. Jennifer Wells had become "Little Nursie." Now Roberto was "Little Bobby." The boy's mother had become *"mamacita,"* the Spanish version of "little mother."

Burke wasn't sure if it came from Twist's own undersized physical stature or his oversized sense of importance, or simply the lack of stature and/or importance he ascribed to everyone else. Whatever the cause, it was beginning to annoy the living hell out of Burke, and he knew he was headed for trouble if he didn't keep that irritation under control.

Twist had scheduled the initial piece for Sunday's paper, had said he wanted "a real tearjerker," one "that'll get all the bozos reaching for their wallets before we ask them to." Burke took his time, crafting the piece. Twist would get his tearjerker, but it would be different from most. Burke was a believer in Robert Browning's dictum, Less is more, and he didn't want to abuse the *Globe's* readers with a blatant tale of woe. Instead he intended to state Roberto's illness, simply and clearly, then portray the boy for what he was, an exuberant five-year-old who loved baseball and who should be racing through a playground with the other neighborhood children—and who would be if his hardworking mother found the money to reverse his life-threatening condition. That was the key, of course, the subtle plea for help. Burke had been told to have a follow-up ready for midweek to keep that plea in the minds of the *Globe's* readers. He had decided to use Roberto's love of baseball for the next story. New Yorkers were suckers for the game, and even bigger suckers for stories about baseball heroes who went to visit sick children. It went all the way back to Babe Ruth and Lou Gehrig and the legendary tale of the home runs they once hit for a dying child. Burke intended to play the angle shamelessly. He had already gotten Stan Evans, the *Globe's* sports editor, to blackjack Yankee slugger Roberto Ramirez into paying the child a visit before today's game. It hadn't been all that difficult. Ramirez had recently been arrested following a brawl at an after-hours nightclub of dubious reputation, his normally impressive batting average was enduring a month-long slump, and his contract with the Yankees was up for renegotiation next season. In short, Ramirez needed some good ink, and Evans had played the Godfather, giving the slugger's agent an offer he couldn't refuse. "I told that hump that his boy could visit the kid and look like fucking Francis of Assisi, or he could turn us down and never see his name in the *Globe* again." The sports editor had spread his hands in self-congratulation. "Guess which one the hump picked?"

By three o'clock Burke had finished the initial story, shown it to Twist and received his imprimatur, then shepherded it through the final editing of the copy desk. At three-fifteen he entered the sports editor's office and found Roberto Ramirez slumped in a chair running a wide-toothed comb through a massive afro hairdo that made Burke wonder how he ever got a baseball cap on his head. A second man, dressed in a tan suit set off by an electric-blue shirt and yellow necktie, stood at his side. Stan Evans introduced him as Jack Freeman, Ramirez's agent.

Ramirez was not a big man. He was no more than five-ten, with an angular though well-muscled body and the cocky and slightly dissipated look of the perennial bad boy. He was dressed in skintight slacks, flared at the ankle, and a flowered shirt open to mid-torso, revealing a smooth, hairless chest and five pounds of gold chain. Burke felt an immediate dislike for the man.

Freeman introduced Ramirez, then took a deep breath when his client failed even to look up at Burke. The sports editor sat behind his desk studying the scene. Then he shook his head and busied himself with a phone call.

"How long this gonna take?" Ramirez finally asked in heavily accented English. He was studying his fingernails, ignoring Burke. "I gotta get myself some dinner before tonight's game."

Burke placed his hands on his knees and brought his face directly in front of the man. "I've got a *Globe* car and driver waiting downstairs," he said. "A photographer is going to meet us at the kid's apartment. It's going to take us about twenty minutes to get there." He paused for effect. "Then it's going to take as long as I say it's going to take." Another pause. "And when we leave, if that little boy isn't smiling, you are not going to like what you read in the newspaper. You got that, Roberto?"

Ramirez looked up for the first time. "Hey, man, you threatenin' me?"

Burke rose to his full height and grinned down at Ramirez. The smile never carried to his eyes. "You bet your ass I am."

Ramirez slowly pushed himself up from his chair. It was a

macho move, a veiled threat that quickly dissipated. Standing, he seemed to realize that Burke had him by four inches and about thirty pounds, and the look in Burke's eyes left little question about his willingness to use all of it.

The agent moved up to Ramirez and put an arm around his shoulder. "Hey, let's not get off on the wrong foot, okay?" He directed the comment to Burke, but it was clearly intended for his client.

"Just tell your boy to do the right thing," Burke snapped. "The car's in front of the building. He comes or he doesn't come. It's up to him." With that Burke walked out of the office and headed for the elevators.

Burke sat in front with the driver, leaving the backseat to Ramirez and his agent. Freeman kept up a steady prattle about Roberto's talents, the upcoming All-Star Game for which he was a certain pick, and the "bad rap" his client was getting in the press. Throughout it all Ramirez stared out the window, bored, pleased by none of it.

When they crossed the Brooklyn Bridge, Burke turned in his seat to prepare them for the scenario he wanted when they reached the child's apartment. He began by using the opening line that would appear in Sunday's first "Little Bobby" story.

"Bobby Avalon is a very sick child, sicker than any five-year-old boy should ever be." He glanced at Ramirez, who continued to stare out the window, still apparently bored, then at his agent, Jack Freeman, who was offering what he obviously considered a series of serious nods. So much for the impact of my lead sentence, Burke thought—at least with these guys. "He's seriously ill. That's the bottom line. He has a hole in his heart. It's a condition he was born with, but now it's getting worse by the day, and his life expectancy is running on the short side. Very short."

Ramirez was still staring out the window; Freeman was still nodding his head. Burke drew a breath, more in exasperation than anything else. "The boy's mother works her tail off in the garment district, but it's a low-paying, off-the-books job, and it doesn't carry any insurance. The father abandoned them when the child's illness became too much to handle. No one knows where he is, but he was into hard drugs when he left, so it's doubtful he could help the boy even if we found him. The boy's maternal grandmother lives with them and cares for the boy while the mother's at work."

"But the kid's a big Roberto Ramirez fan, right?" It was Jack Freeman, the agent still priming the ego pump for his client.

"Yes, he is. Mainly because Roberto plays for the Yankees—his favorite team—and because you both have the same first name."

The statement brought Ramirez out of his bored, catatonic stare. "This kid likes me 'cause we got the same name?" His tone was incredulous.

"He's five years old," Burke said. "He thinks it's very cool that a big baseball star has the same name as he does."

"Hey, tell this kid he's got the same name as *me*." Ramirez jabbed a finger into his chest to emphasize the point.

Burke glanced at the driver, whose name was Eddie. He was a big black kid, maybe twenty years old, who had quit school after the tenth grade to support his mother and younger brothers. The only difference between Eddie and Ramirez was that Eddie couldn't hit a baseball as far. Now Eddie was staring straight ahead, shaking his head. Burke groaned inwardly. "Whatever," he said.

"What will it take to make this kid well?" Freeman asked. "Moneywise, I mean."

"He needs open-heart surgery," Burke said. "It's his only chance. And between the doctors, the hospital, the postoperative care, and medication, it could go as high as ninety grand. The surgeon and the hospital want eighty percent up front before anybody picks up a knife. That's the bottom line."

Freeman made a whistling sound through his teeth. Ramirez said nothing.

"We're hoping to raise that money from the public," Burke said. "Of course, you gentlemen could probably write a check and take care of it yourselves," he added.

"Hey, why don't your newspaper just foot the bill?" Ramirez said. He was still staring out the window.

Burke turned and smiled at him. "Because the newspaper is run by businessmen, who think their job is selling newspapers. Small, dying children don't fit into that job description."

Ramirez grunted. "Hey, man, we're all businessmen. We all got expenses."

Freeman leaned forward in his seat. "Now, let's not quote Roberto on that," he said. "I'm sure somewhere down the road a reasonable donation isn't out of the question."

Ramirez's head snapped away from the window. "Hey, you talk for yourself, Jack. You get ten percent of everything I make. Every fuckin' dime. You wanna write a check, you go right ahead."

Freeman sputtered. "Look, we're all off the record here, right? I mean, we're not even at the kid's place yet."

Burke turned to the driver and smiled. "Hey, whatever you say. We're all businessmen, right, Eddie?"

"That's right," Eddie said. "I worry about my motherfuckin' portfolio all day long."

They pulled up behind a blue Plymouth with the *Globe* logo painted on the door. Jimmy Cogan, one of the *Globe's* better photographers, climbed out and walked back to their car. He was tall and thin, and his sharp features seemed pressed into a perpetual smirk. There were two Nikon cameras and three cased lenses hanging from his neck and shoulders.

Burke rolled down the window as he approached. Cogan glanced back at Ramirez. "Roberto doesn't look too thrilled to be here," he said.

"This the building we gotta go in?" Ramirez asked. He was ignoring Cogan, staring at the tenement and the ramshackle collection of stores that fronted it. "It's a goddamn shithole tenement. We all be lucky we don't get mugged. You shoulda brought some cops."

"Next time we'll get you a gig on Park Avenue," Burke said. He turned to Freeman, his eyes heavy with warning. "Have a talk," he said. "The way he treats this kid, that's what I write."

"Not to worry. Not to worry. Roberto loves kids. It's going to be great," Freeman said. He forced his features into a concerned, sympathetic pose. "What are the little kid's chances?" he asked.

Burke stared at him. "Not good," he said. "Not good at all."

Burke pushed the door open and climbed out. Freeman was now whispering frantically in the backseat.

Cogan seemed to be enjoying Burke's exasperation. "Hey, whadja expect? Albert Schweitzer? The guy couldn't hit a base-ball, he'd be working in a fucking car wash." He leaned back in the window. "Hey, Eddie, watch my car," he said to the driver. "After the garbanzos mug Ramirez, they may go after my cam-era equipment."

"Not a chance," Eddie said. "They'll be too weighed down with gold chains."

Roberto Avalon's eyes were like saucers when the door to the apartment opened. He was hiding behind his grandmother, peeking out from behind her skirt. Burke had called Maria Avalon that morning to tell her Roberto's favorite ballplayer would be stopping by that afternoon, and she had obviously told her son. He looked like a child getting his first glimpse of Santa Claus.

Burke and Cogan entered first, followed by a swaggering Ramirez and finally Freeman, who, briefcase in hand, had as-sumed the role of grand factotum following in the wake of his master. Burke couldn't help thinking about their respective roles five years down the road, when Ramirez, his career in eclipse, wouldn't be able to get Freeman to accept his phone calls.

Once inside the apartment, Ramirez's demeanor changed. He bent down, hands on his knees, his face only inches from the boy's. "Hey, my man," he said. "You know who I am?"

The boy's eyes practically glittered, his face the happiest Burke had seen it. "You're Roberto Ramirez. You play for the Yankees," the boy said. "You have the same name as me."

Ramirez threw a quick glance at Burke. "Tha's right, tha's right," he said. "An' I bet you gonna play for the Yankees some-day, too." He reached back with one hand, his eyes still fixed on the boy as if he were the only creature on earth, and Freeman, ready and waiting as though the scene had been choreo-graphed, filled the hand with an eight-by-ten glossy of Ramirez swinging a bat.

Ramirez whipped the photo around and handed it to the boy, and Burke could see it was already autographed: *To Roberto, from Roberto. Get well, the Yankees need you.*

Ramirez read the inscription, and the child's face brightened even further. Then the ballplayer scooped the boy up, carried him to the sofa, and placed him on his knee.

Burke was stunned. Charm and warmth oozed from the man, almost as though a switch had been thrown setting it loose. Even his features had changed. The sullen downturn of his lips was gone. The bored, self-centered stare had been replaced by an eager excitement over everything the child said. They began to jabber in Spanish like two old friends, and almost everything Ramirez said had the boy either giggling or jumping excitedly on his lap.

Cogan was busy taking photographs, so Burke turned to Freeman, who extended his hands at his sides as if to say, Go figure.

"He's a complex guy," Freeman offered. It was almost an apology.

Yeah, Burke thought. Either that or the guy's got a second career in Hollywood that'll make him even richer.

Maria Avalon came home a few minutes before five. She was breathless. She had gotten permission to leave work early and had run all the way from the subway, she explained. Ramirez was now surrounded on the small sofa, little Roberto still on his lap, Grandma seated next to him, Freeman standing at his shoulder, and Jimmy Cogan moving from side to side, still snapping away with his Nikons.

Ramirez stood as she approached, still holding her son in his arms, and his newfound charm immediately washed over her as well. The grandmother sat beaming up at them. Two hours ago she had loaded the table in front of Ramirez with plates of chorizos and slices of fresh bread, a cold rice-and-bean salad, cookies, and freshly brewed strong coffee, all of which she had replenished four times, mostly due to Jimmy Cogan's demonstration of a photographer's approach to free food. Now she gazed awestruck at her daughter and the famous Roberto Ramirez, and Burke couldn't help smiling at the wedding fantasy he imagined racing through her mind.

Maria thanked Ramirez and told him how much her son admired him and how he looked for his picture each day in the newspaper. The boy extended the autographed publicity photo toward his mother as though it were some religious relic. He had not let go of the picture since Ramirez had placed it in his hand.

Maria turned to Burke and reached out and took his hand. "Thank you so much, Billy," she said. Her eyes were glassy with tears, and her emotion surprised Burke, though he quickly realized it should not. Anything done for her child is a blessed gift, he thought. Anything done to make him happy, outside her family, was beyond any expectation.

"Mr. Ramirez wanted to come and meet Roberto," he said. "He thinks he's a very special boy."

He reached out to stroke the boy's hair, and the child suddenly threw himself from the ballplayer's grasp and encircled Burke's neck with his small, frail arms. Burke took the child to him and felt his hug tighten. Unexpected pleasure surged through him. Then he felt pain as his mind assaulted him with the memory of the last time he had been hugged by a child—his own child—the last time he had felt that unselfish surge of childlike love. It had been a very long time ago.

$$\{\ 9\ \}$$

The telephone jarred Burke awake at seven.

"You recognize my voice?" It was a male voice. Deep. A sense of amused urgency about it.

"What?"

A soft chuckle. "Wake up and tell me if you recognize my voice."

The cobwebs began to clear. Burke shook his head, driving the rest away. The voice. It was Dezi. Grant Desvernine. "Yeah, I recognize you."

"Okay. No names. I know how you reporters like to tape-record telephone conversations."

"I'm not taping this," Burke said.

"No names. Agreed?"

"Okay, you got it."

"All right. Last night we caught a kidnapping. A big one. One of Edwin Kaufman's kids. You know who he is, right?"

Burke sat up in bed as though hit with an electric shock. Edwin Kaufman was the founder and CEO of a family-owned chain of discount department stores that stretched across the United States. He was *the* bigwig in American Jewish circles, an intimate of the last two Israeli premiers and an unofficial adviser to the man who currently occupied the Oval Office. Every time a cabinet post or U.S. ambassadorship came up, his name was on the short list. It was said he always declined.

Burke grabbed a pad and pen he kept on his bedside table. "Which son?" he asked. "If I remember right, he has three."

"And a daughter," Dezi said. "They snatched Arthur. Twenty-two years old. He's a graduate student at NYU. Apparently he was just grabbed off the street somewhere. They're asking the old man for two million, cash."

"When did it happen?"

"Late last night. Your buddies in the media should be getting wind of it now. And all hell's gonna break loose." Dezi let out a soft laugh. "But this time you media vultures are in for a little surprise."

"What's that?"

"Seems our beloved leader has set up a little scam to keep you guys away from the action. He plans to have you all chasing your tails until he's ready to step up to the microphones and take the appropriate bows."

Now Burke understood the real reason behind Dezi's call. It was more than just a tip to give him a head start on a big story. Desvernine and Burke had been friends for years, going back to the days when Dezi headed the organized-crime section of the FBI's New York office. During his tenure in that job Dezi had often planted stories with Burke about New York's five Mafia families. The stories involved everything from supposed turf wars between families to internal struggles within individual groups. All had some basis in fact, since those occurrences were a constant within the mob. But they were also laden with heavy doses of bullshit, intended to wreak havoc at the lower levels of the various crime families. The stories were good copy for the paper, and served Desvernine's purposes as well. They stirred up trouble within the mob and on more than one occasion had helped make individual low-ranking mobsters believe their

livelihoods or even their lives might be in danger. Being the ve-
nal men they were, the stories had turned more than one into a
Bureau informant.

That all ended when Assistant Deputy Director John Patrick
Henry became the agent in charge of the FBI's New York office.
Henry, like his namesake, regarded himself as a patriot. The
Constitution of the United States was his bible, except for the
First and Fifth amendments, which he regarded as grave mistakes never intended by the Founding Fathers. He especially despised the media and upon taking control of the New York field
office had banned any contact he had not personally approved.
Dezi had ignored him and had paid the price. Henry had fallen
on Dezi like a building, and only Dezi's seniority and record of
success had kept him from being reassigned to Boise or some
other punishment post. But Henry had exacted another more
subtle revenge. He had removed Dezi from all fieldwork and reassigned him to a senior administrative post within the New
York office, turning him into a pencil pusher. Tips like the one
Burke was being offered today were Dezi's method of payback.

"So what's his scam?" Burke asked.

"Kaufman has three different apartments in the city, all of
them owned by his company. Two are used for various corpo-
rate purposes, and one is exclusively for his use—the one located
on Park Avenue and Seventy-eighth."

"So that's where he'll be?"

"Uh-uh. But that's the story our beloved leader has arranged
to have leaked from Kaufman's office. He knows it's gonna leak
anyway, like it always does, and he knows you clowns will be all
over it like flies on shit. So he's gonna play you guys with a little misdirection. Kaufman will really be at one of the other
apartments, a penthouse at Fifth Avenue and Seventy-fourth.
He'll be there with Henry and a handful of agents and technicians waiting for ransom instructions from the kidnappers, and
the phone company will transfer all calls to that location. Mean-
while, the Bureau will be putting on a big show at the Park Avenue address. A dozen agents going in and out of the building,
plenty of obvious Bureau cars parked out front. They intend to
lure all you guys in, set up barricades when you all show up.
Then, when the ransom delivery is set, they'll put on another big

show at the Park Avenue location and lead you guys on a wild-goose chase in the opposite direction of the real drop—New Jersey or Connecticut or where-the-hellever."

"And then the real ransom leaves from Fifth Avenue," Burke said.

"You got it."

"Who else is going to know about this?" Burke asked.

"Just you," Dezi said. "You owe me, buddy."

The words were followed by a dial tone in Burke's ear.

Burke telephoned the city desk and asked them to reach out for Twist.

"He's been here for half an hour," an assistant city editor said. "We've got a big kidnapping story. Half the staff is coming in. I've been trying to get you on the phone, but your line's been busy."

"Let me have Twist. I've got something on the kidnapping."

Twist got on the line with a growl. "What've you got?"

"I just had a call from my source at the Bureau," Burke began. He told Twist about Henry's plan. Twist grunted, then took time to think it through. He knew Burke had an unimpeachable source at the FBI's New York field office. He didn't know who, because Burke had always refused to tell him, but he understood from past stories that whatever the source said would be gold.

"All right, here's what I want. You get up to this Fifth Avenue address. I'll have a photographer meet you. First you confirm that Henry and Kaufman are there. Then I want you to send Henry a message. Tell him we want one exclusive photograph of Kaufman waiting by the phone for the ransom call. I want Henry in the picture, too, and any other FBI stiffs who are there. For our part, we promise to sit on the photo until the kid's released. You tell him we get what we want, we also keep our mouths shut and he can keep up his little charade on Park Avenue. But you also make sure he understands this: He plays hard-ass with us, we'll see to it he's got every reporter in this city climbing up the side of that fucking building."

The kidnap victim and his family rushed to mind, and Burke felt a sudden flush of guilt for the scenario that was about to unfold. At the same time he couldn't help admiring Twist's style. There was a touch of brilliance to it. He wasn't asking for an exclusive interview. Kaufman would have to be a fool to grant one, and he was far from that. And Henry, media hatred aside, could never allow it—not unless he wanted to kiss his FBI career good-bye. Twist also wasn't seeking an exclusive on any arrest, as some lesser editor might. He knew that too many factors could blow that promise, even if it were given—an all-too-typical leak from another agency, like the NYPD, for example—and that Henry, promise made or not, would fabricate one rather than risk the wrath of the media who had been left out in the cold.

Instead Twist had chosen something Henry could easily grant. Something he could later explain away as a necessary evil. He could even accuse the *Globe* of endangering the life of the kidnap victim by threatening to interfere with his rescue. He could make the *Globe* the lone bad guy—everywhere, that is, but in its own executive offices. There, that one photograph would be seen as a pot of money. The *Globe* would simply copyright it and sell it worldwide, and Lenny Twist would become the hero of the hour to the only people who mattered—those who would ultimately decide just how high his journalistic star would rise.

"We'll be putting a lot of pressure on the Kaufman family," Burke said. "It's a rough time for them." He threw the idea out more to soothe his conscience than in any hope it might change Twist's mind.

"Edgar Kaufman's a big boy," Twist snapped. "He'll handle it. And Henry's a prick who needs a lesson. You got a problem with that?"

"Not that part of it."

"Good. Then get going. And keep in touch. I want to know what's happening every step of the way."

Jimmy Cogan was waiting outside the Fifth Avenue building when Burke arrived. The cameras and lenses that would normally be hanging from his body were nowhere in sight. He had obviously been told to keep a low profile.

"Hey, this is becoming a regular rendezvous thing with us. People are gonna start to talk."

"Don't get your hopes up," Burke said. "Besides, you're too skinny for me. I like my boys on the plump side."

"Hey, it's like the guineas say: The closer to the bone, the sweeter the meat." He offered up a wolfish grin, then raised his chin toward the building. "So whadda we got here? They wouldn't tell me shit over the radio. Even told me to use landlines when I called back in. What's up?"

Burke filled him in.

"Hey, I can already tell you the feds are here," Cogan said. "I took a quick peek inside when I got here. You got two suits guarding the lobby like fucking tin soldiers."

"Are they wearing the shoes?"

"Oh, yeah."

Burke drew a long breath. Dezi had come through again, and he was about to make Lenny Twist a hero. Burke started toward the lobby. "Lets go talk to them. It's time to give John Patrick Henry a little Maalox attack."

Burke and Cogan entered the lobby and approached the two agents. FBI policy required all agents to avoid identifying themselves—even at crime scenes—unless doing so served their purposes. Instead they were expected to blend into their surroundings well enough to avoid identification. Burke looked over the pair as he approached. They were in their mid-thirties, clean-shaven and meticulously groomed, and each wore a suit and tie. Burke couldn't hold back a smile. Just two guys headed for early Sunday mass. Such a nifty disguise. Especially the bulge beneath their respective suit coats. Suits and shoes, he thought, always the fatal flaws in the feds' penchant for secrecy. Agents, like all cops, bought their suits off the rack, and even the finest tailor couldn't widen the chest areas enough to hide the telltale sign of a weapon. He looked down at the shoes the two agents were wearing. In the realm of failed disguises the Bureau went the cops one better. They had a deal with the Bostonian Shoe Company, something allegedly set up by old J. Edgar himself. Under that arrangement agents were allowed to buy two particular styles of that company's dress shoes at slightly above cost. It was a lovely deal— Hoover-approved and cheap. So all agents wore those two particular styles of shoes, and all reporters knew that they did.

J. Edgar could just as easily have hung signs around their necks.

"I need you guys to get a message up to Henry," Burke said when he reached the two agents.

Both men stiffened and exchanged a quick glance. One offered Burke a confused look. "Don't know what you're talking about, pal." The other agent remained silent.

Burke shrugged. "Okay, pal. My mistake. I guess we'll just head up to the penthouse." He glanced over his shoulder. "Better get your cameras, Jimmy."

When he turned back, the two agents had placed themselves squarely in front of him. They were both about Burke's size and looked capable of tossing him out into the street.

"I don't think so." It was the agent who talked. He did not look amused.

Burke offered his own confused look, imitating the agent, then took out his press card and held it up. "Hey, we can dance this dance, or you can pass a message on to Henry." He raised his eyebrows. "But if we dance, in about half an hour you're going to have a shitload of reporters and photographers camped in front of this building. And your beloved leader is not going to be happy when he finds out it could have been avoided." Burke shrugged. "Up to you, guys."

The two agents looked at each other again. "What's the message?" asked the one who talked.

Burke gave him Twist's offer.

"Wait here," he snapped, then turned and went to the elevator. The other agent remained planted in front of Burke, still silent as a stone.

It took fifteen minutes before the agent returned. He was wearing a self-satisfied grin as he exited the elevator—not a good sign. Burke decided to brazen it out and returned the smile.

The agent looked down at a notebook in his hand. "Mr. Henry would like to remind you about the criminal penalties for impeding a federal investigation." He looked up for Burke's reaction.

"Tell him I'm reminded." Burke held his own smile. "Is there more?"

"Yes, sir!" The satisfied grin returned to the agent's lips. "Mr.

Henry said that Mr. Burke should go fuck himself."

Burke threw back his head and laughed. "Tell Mr. Henry his message was received and that I'll pass it on to my editors." He turned to go, then looked back and winked. "Tell him he should also grab hold of his ass and hang on. It's show time."

Burke led Jimmy Cogan across Fifth Avenue and fifty yards into Central Park. He pointed up toward the building they had just left.

"That penthouse. Looks to me like it has a big terrace."

Cogan started to laugh. "You thinking what I think you're thinking?"

"Indeed. Let's get on a landline to Twist and get an okay."

"I love it," Cogan said.

The helicopter came in low over Central Park. Burke sat on the wall that separated the park from the sidewalk and stared up at Jimmy Cogan, strapped in a harness as he hung from the open hatch. The chopper was so low Burke could see him focusing his camera as the pilot pulled into a sharp bank above the street.

It took two more passes before the roar of the chopper produced results. On that final pass the chopper hovered, and Burke could see Cogan firing away. Then the chopper veered off and headed back to the East Side Heliport.

Burke continued to stare up at the terrace, and moments later John Patrick Henry appeared at the stone railing. He glared down into the street, eyes searching left and right. They finally settled on Burke, who was still sitting atop the wall. Burke raised his right hand and wiggled his fingers in a taunting wave.

When Henry disappeared from view, Burke took the portable radio Cogan had left him and raised the photographer on the *Globe's* frequency.

"Jimmy. You get what we wanted?"

Jimmy's voice came back, muffled by the noise of the chopper. "Perfecto, Billy. Perfecto. They all came out on the terrace. Henry, old man Kaufman, and a couple of other FBI stiffs. I had the motor on and shot the whole roll. Hell, there was even a telephone on a table out there, and they were standing right in front of it. How's that for fucking luck?"

"Beautiful, Jimmy. Beautiful. I'll see you back at the paper."

Burke let out a soft laugh, then pressed the "send" button again. "Either that or I'll call you for bail money."

Minutes later Burke watched Henry march across Fifth Avenue, two agents trailing in his wake. Henry was a moderately tall, moderately slender man with moderately handsome features. Mr. Moderately, Burke thought. The perfect incarnation of a bureaucratic executive—except now his face was a livid red and his blue-and-gold regimental necktie was uncharacteristically askew under his buttoned suit coat.

"Hi, Pat." Burke slipped his reporter's notebook from an inside pocket. "You have a statement on the Kaufman kidnapping?"

Henry stood in front of Burke, teeth clenched, facial muscles dancing along his jaw. "You just committed a federal crime, mister."

Burke looked around. "Sitting on a wall?" he asked. "That one must have slipped through Congress without me noticing."

Henry's mouth twisted with anger. "You sent that helicopter because I wouldn't give you what you wanted, and by doing so you impeded a federal investigation. That's a crime, mister."

Burke lowered his eyes and shook his head. "Hell, Pat, that chopper was a few hundred feet over my *head*. You were closer to it than I was."

"And that photographer you were with just happened to be in it. Right?"

Burke slid off the wall and stretched. "Could have been him, I suppose. But I never left here, so I really can't be sure." He returned the notebook to his pocket. "But if you want to arrest somebody from the *Globe*, I suggest you start with somebody who has the authority to put a photographer *in* a chopper. I'm afraid lowly reporters don't qualify." He shrugged. "Maybe the city editor. The managing editor. Or even the executive editor. What the hell, shoot the moon, Pat. Go for the publisher himself." He gave Henry as irritating a smile as he could manage. The words "Fuck you, you arrogant son of a bitch" rolled across his mind before he continued.

"But if you do, Pat, I think that old poof Hoover will be spinning in his grave. Because the Bureau will sure cover itself in shit."

The reference to J. Edgar Hoover and his alleged homosexuality made Henry stiffen from head to toe. He had been one of "Hoover's boys," one of a few select agents who had risen under the director's personal tutelage. And Henry had gone a long way under Hoover's ever-watchful eye—all the way to assistant director. It was rumored—from Burke's source Dezi and others—that he had overseen Hoover's black-bag operations of wiretaps, mail openings, and covert spying on any individuals or groups that the director had considered "un-American." But Henry's rise had ended with Hoover's death, and his subsequent transfer to head the New York field office had been considered a demotion, if not in rank then at least in power. Now, with the post-Watergate mood that permeated Washington, his past activities had allegedly cast a shadow and put his career on shaky ground.

Henry glared at him. "You think you're such a smart son of a bitch. But I'll tell you this, Burke: I'm going to get you. Maybe not this time, but if not, it won't be for the lack of trying. And sooner or later your ass will be mine." The glare turned into self-satisfied assurance. "And in the meantime, smart guy, if you think you'll *ever* get anything from the Bureau again, you're dreaming, mister."

Burke let out an easy laugh. "Hell, Pat, I haven't gotten anything from the Bureau since you took over the New York office. Neither has anybody else in the press." He winked at him. "At least not officially."

Henry stiffened. "Who told you we were here?" he snapped.

"A little bird. Whispered something about shoes." Burke stretched again. "Look, I've gotta go. I've got a photo caption to write." He pointed to the disarranged necktie under Henry's suit coat, then watched as the assistant director looked down and quickly straightened it. "I hope your tie isn't like that in the photo. Looks tacky. Very un-Bureaulike. Hell, Pat, that old queen Hoover would've sent you a memo, he saw that."

Back in the newsroom Lenny Twist was so jubilant over the photos that had come from Burke's tip that he assigned Burke to write the lead story, along with a sidebar about the FBI's failed attempt to snooker the press.

"Lay it on heavy," Twist said. "I want to zing the competition, too. But be subtle." An uncharacteristic grin crossed his lips. "Hell, fuck subtle." He waved his hand in the air, as though thinking with it. "Do something like 'While the New York press corps waited in vain outside Edwin Kaufman's posh Park Avenue penthouse . . .' Something like that."

Burke nodded, enjoying the moment. He could see the editors at the *Times*, the *News*, the *Post*, and all the radio and television networks grinding their teeth. "You got it," he said. "What about the chopper pilot? The feds going to bang him?"

Twist let out a grunt. "They're already trying. Henry's been onto the FAA. Told them he wants the pilot's license pulled for the max. That would be six months."

"We covering his ass?"

"We promised him we'd cover his salary for any period of suspension," Twist said. "Hell, I had to promise him that just to get him in the air." Twist gave Burke an all-knowing wink. "But we've got people on the phone to our friends in Washington as we speak."

The word "people," Burke knew, meant editors well above Twist's rank and influence, perhaps even the publisher himself. "You think we can squelch it?" he asked.

"The pilot won't get more than a slap on the wrist," Twist said. "Guaranteed. It'll cost us a few favors, maybe an endorsement down the road. But that'll be it."

Burke finished the sidebar and began assembling the main story. Information was coming in from reporters out covering every aspect of the kidnapping, and Burke was constantly on the phone taking down something new that had just developed. During lulls he sorted through stacks of library folders that covered every newsworthy detail of Edwin Kaufman's life and what little had been reported about his family and the one son who was now a kidnap victim. It was a frantic pace, a kind of ordered chaos that one old-timer had once described as a "juggling act performed by a maniac," and Burke found Twist and other editors regularly coming up behind him to add their own madness to the brew—to read over his shoulder, issue small grunts of satisfaction or displeasure, then to make pointed, sometimes useless, sometimes helpful suggestions.

Across from Burke, Eddie Hartman worked the phones, prying whatever information he could from his contacts at the New York Police Department. The kidnapping, like all such cases that involved ransom demands by mail or phone or the probable crossing of state lines, fell under the jurisdiction of the FBI. It was jealously guarded territory, but as much as Henry and his minions would have liked to exclude the NYPD completely, it was a logistical impossibility. Instead they tried to keep the New York cops assigned to help them as far out of the loop as possible. When that proved unworkable, they ordered the cops not to discuss the case with anyone but their FBI supervisors. That order, of course, was privately and promptly countermanded by the NYPD brass, who had no intention of flying blind on a high-profile, media-driven kidnapping. Therefore, the cops involved— sharing their bosses' intense dislike for the FBI and knowing whence their promotions came—passed on every iota of information as soon as it fell into their hot little hands. Those cops and their bosses were also more than willing to leak any derogatory information about their FBI counterparts to friends in the media.

It came as no surprise, therefore, that at six-fifteen that evening Eddie Hartman hung up his telephone and began to cackle wildly through his bushy mustache.

"You are *not* going to believe this," he said. "You are going to *love* it. But you are not going to believe it."

"What!" Burke demanded. His fingers were flying over the typewriter. They were fifteen minutes past the deadline for the paper's first edition—the bulldog—which would hit the streets at midnight, and he was already at work on an update for the city edition, which most *Globe* readers would buy in the morning on their way to work.

"They caught the kidnappers," Hartman offered with a flutter of bushy eyebrows.

"What?"

"That's right."

Burke spun in his chair and shouted to the city desk, "Lenny, over here, quick!" He spun back to Hartman. "Tell me!"

Hartman grinned. "They caught 'em. But that's practically a fucking sidebar. The FBI screwed up the ransom drop about four o'clock, and the kidnappers waltzed off with two million in cash."

"Details, details, damnit." Burke himself was laughing now. Hartman straightened in his chair, preening himself like a blue jay. "Well, it goes like this. The drop is in Prospect Park in Brooklyn, and old man Kaufman delivers the dough like he's been told—two million in cash, stuffed in two fucking garbage bags.

"Now, the feds are supposed to have the drop covered, but their surveillance team goes in the wrong entrance to the park— I mean, what the fuck does the FBI know about fucking Brooklyn?—and so they're fucking lost for about ten minutes . . ."

"And when they get there . . ." Burke prodded.

"You got it. They finally get their fucked-up asses to the spot, and all they got is a fucking tree with nothing under it, and the kidnappers and the loot are bam, shazam, fucking gone."

Burke was fighting down laughter even as he began to type a new lead to the story.

"Then, about a half hour later," Hartman continued, "these two NYPD narcotics dicks are cruising through Greenwich Village, and they see these two garbanzos going into a building on Christopher Street, and each one's got a garbage bag slung over his shoulder.

"Well, they don't know shit about the ransom, they just figure this is maybe one of the great hashish deliveries of all time." Hartman made a dunking gesture with one finger—like a basketball referee indicating that a shot counted after a foul. "So in they go. They probably figured they'd grab the stash and it would go directly into their own personal retirement accounts.

"Anyway, they follow these two clowns into the building, and when they start to open the door to their apartment, the two dicks push their way in behind. And, lo and behold, there's little Arthur Kaufman, sitting in a fucking Barcalounger, drinking a fucking beer."

"Alone?"

"You bet your ass, alone. No guard, no nothin'. He's watching fucking *Kojak* on the tube. Well, the kid just about shits when the two narcs realize what they got and flash their tin. These two garbanzos are fucking poofs, and it turns out little Arthur met them in a fucking S&M gay bar about a week ago."

"So it was a setup? The kid was ripping off his old man?"

"That's what the narcs figure. But little Arthur, he's quick on his feet. He's claiming these guys found out who he was at the bar and then set up a plan to snatch him off the street."

"How does he explain that he was there alone?"

"He says he thought one of the guys was in the hall. Said the guy told him he'd shoot him if he tried to leave."

"What floor was the apartment on?"

"First floor. With lots of windows the kid never tried to crawl out of. End of fucking story."

Twist was at Burke's side as Eddie finished, and Burke ripped a sheet of paper from the typewriter and handed it to him. "New lead," he snapped.

Twist read it aloud: "'Two alert New York City detectives rescued kidnap victim Arthur Kaufman late yesterday afternoon and arrested his two kidnappers after the FBI bungled a ransom delivery that nearly allowed the kidnappers to escape.'"

He looked down at Burke. "You sure of this?"

Burke was on the phone, dialing. He jabbed a finger at Hartman. "Eddie just got it."

"It's gold," Hartman said. "Seems that Billy-boy wasn't the only guy Henry told to go fuck himself today. He suggested the same thing to our beloved chief of detectives."

Twist turned and shouted toward the city desk: "Hold the bulldog for a new lead!" He turned back to Burke. "Get Henry for a comment."

"I'm calling now."

Twist turned to Hartman. "Tell me all of it."

Hartman began retelling the story, as Burke got through to the FBI agent in charge of press information.

"This is Billy Burke at the *Globe*. I need to talk to Pat Henry."

The request was met with undisguised disdain, typical of the Bureau press-information officer. The assistant director was tied up. There would be a press conference . . .

Burke cut him off. He reached out and snatched the new lead he had written from Twist's hand. "Listen up, shithead," he snapped. "This is the lead paragraph on our story. It's going to press in fifteen minutes, and Pat has got ten if he wants to comment on it. Otherwise we say the FBI declined comment, and we let it fly." Burke read him the lead.

The agent began sputtering on the other end of the line.

"Ten minutes," Burke snapped, and hung up.

"Okay," Twist said. "We include anything Henry says. And we go with everything Eddie came up with. We'll do a sidebar on the ransom being lost, and Eddie will share the byline. Now, I want you to cover our ass on the fag stuff. Old man Kaufman carries a lot of weight. Attribute everything to a high-ranking NYPD official and throw in 'allegedly' enough to give the copy desk indigestion. Go heavy on how the kid told the cops he met these assholes in a gay bar and how he was found alone in the apartment, drinking beer and watching television. We won't have to say much more for our readers to get the message. I'll get somebody to try and reach Kaufman, but that's going to be a waste of time. He's never going to go public on his kid fucking him over like this." He let out a low cackle. "I gotta get a new caption for the picture. Daddy and the feds waiting by the phone while junior watches *Kojak*. I think I'll use that *Kojak* line for a kicker—'Who loves ya, baby?'"

Pat Henry called back twelve minutes later. Burke was still typing frantically as he jammed the phone to his ear. Twist stood behind him, watching every word emerge from the typewriter.

"Hey, Pat, how's it hanging? You get a chance to read over our new lead?"

"You son of a bitch. This is bullshit. Absolute bullshit!" Henry was shouting into the phone. Burke stopped typing and held the receiver away from his ear.

"Is that your quote, Pat?"

"You listen to me, Burke. I have no comment whatsoever about this. But I'm telling you, you are way off base, and I'll bury your fucking ass if you print it."

"I like that quote even better, Pat." Burke tried to keep the laughter out of his voice. It was difficult.

"Where did you get this *crap?*" Henry demanded.

"Unimpeachable source, Pat. And that's exactly what the story will say."

"This is goddamn, unadulterated FBI-bashing. And if you're a party to it, I'll nail your hide to my goddamn wall. I'll tell your editors just what a two-bit, sleazy fucking excuse for a journalist you are, you son of a bitch. I'll—"

Burke cut him off. "Hang on, Pat. I've got an editor standing right here." He handed the phone to Twist. "The assistant director is not amused. He wants to tell you I'm a scumbag."

"I already know that," Twist said. He placed the phone to his ear. "Hello, Pat. This is Leonard Twist. Do we have a problem?"

The smirk on Twist's face grew steadily as he listened to Pat Henry's diatribe. Every so often he punctuated Henry's words with a judicious "Uh-huh" or a thoughtful "I see." When Henry finally ran out of steam, Twist quietly explained the *Globe's* position.

"Pat, this is the way it goes down. The story's solid. The source is solid, and I have complete faith in Billy Burke and the other reporters who've gathered the information."

He waited, listening, the smirk growing even wider on his face.

"Pat, I understand your unwillingness to comment. And I'm pleased to hear that you feel you've always had strong friendships here at the *Globe*." Twist paused a beat. "But earlier today, Pat, I sent a request to you through Billy Burke. One of your men brought back your response and gave it to Burke in the presence of one of our photographers. That reply was, 'Tell Mr. Burke to go fuck himself.' Now, Pat, I gotta say that wasn't very friendly. So, Pat, as far as the *Globe* is concerned—fuck you, too."

Twist returned the receiver to its cradle. "You're right," he said. "The man is not amused. Now, let's wrap this mother up."

It was nine o'clock before the story finally ended for the night. Pat Henry had held a press conference at One Police Plaza and salvaged what he could. He had stood with the police commissioner at his side, both men playing the role of conquering heroes—the chief of detectives had reportedly told Henry to shove it when he, too, had been invited to attend. True to form, Henry had tried to brazen it out. He had credited the two NYPD narcotics detectives with being "first on the scene" to make the arrest. The implication, of course, was that the FBI had been only moments away, but everyone let that pass. Henry did acknowledge that Arthur Kaufman had apparently known his kidnappers, but he judiciously left out the part about that acquaintanceship's having been made in an S&M gay bar and about Kaufman's having been left alone in the apartment while the kidnappers picked up the ransom. He also did not mention the ransom money's being lost.

The entire newsroom had listened to early television and radio reports about the kidnapping and Henry's subsequent news conference, and it was clear that the *Globe* was the only news agency with the titillating information that the assistant director had chosen to ignore. The *Globe* had it alone, just as the chief of detectives had promised Eddie Hartman they would. And that was a major coup, one of those rare instances for newsroom jubilation, and Twist had ordered in three cases of beer to celebrate.

Burke sat on the edge of the city desk rim next to Frank Fabio, sucking down his second beer and regaling Fabio with details of the "great helicopter caper," as it had now been dubbed.

Fabio was laughing. "So let me get this straight. Jimmy Cogan is hanging from the helicopter's open hatch, slamming away with his Nikon, and old man Kaufman, Pat Henry, and the other FBI assholes are all standing there with their dicks in their hands."

"That's about it," Burke said. "At least until Henry comes storming downstairs and threatens to do everything except have my ass drafted."

Fabio raised a cautioning finger. "He may still think of that, my troop. I always thought you'd look good in khaki."

"Yeah, but it would never work out. I almost flunked ROTC in college. Never could remember to clean my rifle. Actually set a school record for demerits."

Twist came out of his office and hurried toward Burke. "We got a problem," he began.

An immediate chill went through Burke. He envisioned a fatal error in the story he had just written, the one that was now spinning through the massive presses seven stories below. "What's wrong?"

"I just had a call from the kid's grandmother." He began snapping his fingers, struggling to remember the name.

"Roberto Avalon?" Burke asked.

"Yeah. Yeah. Anyway, she called, looking for you. When the phone at your desk didn't answer, they routed the call to me. The woman was almost hysterical. I could barely understand her. Anyway, it seems the kid was rushed to Caledonia Hospital in Brooklyn. I couldn't get her to tell me what exactly was wrong, but from the sound of her voice it isn't good. You better get your butt out there and see what's going on. Take a driver and a *Globe* car."

Burke felt his stomach sink all the way to his shoes. He didn't say a word. He just turned and headed for the elevator that led to the garage.

"And call the desk when you find out what's up," Twist shouted after him. "If the kid croaks, we need a story."

{ 10 }

Burke hurried down the wide hall of the cardiac-care unit, his eyes instinctively darting through the open doors of patient rooms. Sterile, antiseptic smells assaulted him, as did the quiet, squeaking sounds the nurses made as they moved along the tiled floors on heavily cushioned shoes. Just being there sent a chill through him, made him wonder if this might be the place where small, frail Roberto would die. He approached the nurses' station, and a small, plump woman looked up at him, her eyes both curious and challenging.

"I was told in Emergency that you had Roberto Avalon on this floor," Burke began.

"Visiting hours are over," the woman said, making it clear Burke was intruding on private terrain.

"I know. I just—"

"Are you a member of the family?"

"I'm a family friend. I just heard about it, and I wanted to see if I could help."

"It's all right, Nurse."

The voice came from behind the woman, and Burke glanced past her and saw a tall, painfully slender man of about forty. He was dressed in a white hospital coat, a stethoscope protruding from one pocket. He held a medical chart in his hand. A name tag identified him as Dr. Wilfredo Salazar. Burke recognized the name. He was the clinic physician who had referred Roberto to Dr. James Bradford.

Salazar came around the counter that stood like an impregnable barrier between the nurses and all who approached. He thought he detected annoyance in the plump woman's eyes, as though her authority had been unjustly usurped.

"I'm Billy Burke." Burke extended a hand.

Salazar took it, seemed to consider the name, then nodded. He had a narrow face that accented his receding hairline, a long, oversize nose, and unusually gentle brown eyes. Everything about the man exuded warmth, and Burke immediately felt comfortable with him.

"You're the newspaper reporter," Salazar said. "I read your story about Roberto in today's paper. I liked it very much."

Burke realized he hadn't even read the story himself. It was something he always did, just to be sure his work hadn't been savaged by last-minute cuts. Today he had been too overwhelmed by the kidnapping and had simply noted the teaser that had run on the front page. It had directed readers to the bottom of page three, the paper's primary news page. It had been excellent play, the best the paper had to offer.

"How's Roberto?" he asked.

"He's a sick boy. But you know that. We have him stabilized. And that's really all we can do." A hint of amusement came to his eyes. "Because of your story, all the nurses are treating him like a little celebrity. So he's getting very special care."

"Is he in danger?"

The doctor inclined his head. "Not immediately. Not right now. But we can only do this so many times. The child just gets weaker every day. And each episode reduces the amount of time he has left. Somewhere down the road his body simply won't be able to respond." He shrugged, almost in surrender, Burke thought. "It's a question of cumulative damage. If we're lucky, if we can limit the number and severity of these episodes, we may still be able to save his life six months from now. But the longer we wait, the greater the chance he'll never live a truly normal one. At some point, even if we correct the defect, serious damage will have been done."

"I was told initially he might have up to a year," Burke said.

"I'm afraid that's optimistic. Especially if these episodes continue."

The words grabbed at Burke. He had heard the same prognosis before, but now, here in this hospital, it seemed to hit with greater clarity. "Can I see him?" he asked.

Salazar nodded. "Yes, I think that would be good. The little guy seems to draw strength from the fact that people care about him. He's very frightened. So are his mother and grandmother. They're with him now."

They were moving down the hall, presumably toward Roberto's room. Burke took the doctor's arm, stopping him.

"Is there any way you can put pressure on this surgeon or the hospital?"

Salazar gave him a small, bitter smile. "I work with the poor, Mr. Burke. I am not what either the medical profession or the hospitals consider a prominent physician. I don't bring in the bucks. It's that simple."

"Perhaps if you—"

Salazar raised a hand, cutting him off. "Mr. Burke, I know what you'd like me to do. But I simply can't. I cannot get into a pissing contest with these people." He shook his head, a gesture of regret. "I'm a beggar, Mr. Burke. I'm the guy who's always asking them for something they don't want to give. And occasionally—not often, but occasionally—I get what I ask for. But if I attack them or their policies, I won't get anything at all. And that means some future patient will suffer. I just can't take that chance."

They started down the hall again. This time Salazar took Burke's arm.

"That doesn't mean I won't give you information," he said. "As long as my name isn't used, I'll give you everything I can to help this child."

* * *

Roberto saw Burke as soon as he entered the room. He smiled weakly from his bed, then raised one little hand and fluttered his fingers. The small, innocent gesture made Burke's emotions soar and sink almost simultaneously. Maria Avalon was seated next to the bed, and she turned with the child's gesture. Her beautiful face seemed battered. The lines around her mouth were deep with worry, and there were dark, sleepless bruises beneath her eyes. She gave Burke a plaintive look when their eyes met; then she came to him, closer than he had expected, and her head dropped against his chest.

"Thank you for coming." Her voice held an exhaustion that went beyond a lack of sleep. She raised her head and stared up into his face, then seemed to realize how close they were and stepped back. "My mother shouldn't have called you . . . bothered you at work. But she was afraid the hospital wouldn't let us in, and she didn't know who else to call."

She stood in front of him now, looking down at her feet. She was shaking her head as if she couldn't quite believe everything that had happened. Burke reached out and stroked her upper arm. He had a sudden urge to put his arms around her, to hold and comfort her. The idea frightened him, forced him to hold back. It was a closeness he couldn't afford.

He turned toward the boy, gave him a wink. Roberto tried to imitate the gesture. Again Burke fought to hold his emotions back, but it was useless. The boy's small, faint response had brought them out, allowed them to sneak up on him before he realized it.

The grandmother was seated next to the child and was stroking his head. She tried to speak but couldn't get the words out. Burke saw her lips tremble. The woman was clearly as frightened as her daughter.

He guided Maria back toward the bed. When he was next to the boy, he forced all concern from his face. "So what happened, my man? How come you're in bed?"

"Mama said I played too hard. An' I got sick." The boy gave him a weak, impish look.

Burke opened his mouth in mock shock. "Played too hard? Jeez, you *know* you're not supposed to do *that*." He sat on the edge of the bed. "You know you have to take it easy so we can do more stories for my newspaper. By the way, did you *see* your picture in the paper today?"

A grin spread across Roberto's face, momentarily masking all frailty. "Yeah. It was cool. I put it up in my room. My granma says you're a big shot. Are you?"

"Hey, you think they'd send some chump to do a story about you?"

"Does the story make me a big shot, too?" the boy asked, his voice so soft it was barely more than a whisper.

Burke laughed and shook his head. "You are a piece of work, kid."

Roberto looked at his mother. "I'm a piece of work," he said. Tears welled up in Maria's eyes. "Yes, you are," she said. She turned to Burke. "He made me go out and buy another newspaper, so he could have two," she said. "He said the story was so cool, he needed two of them."

Burke looked back at the boy and widened his eyes in surprise. "Hey, that's great. But if you think *that* was cool, you wait until *Wednesday*. That's three days from now. And *that's* the day there's going to be a picture of *you*"—he jabbed a finger at the boy—"with *Roberto Ramirez*! And when *that* happens, all your friends are going to know you're a piece of work, and they're also gonna think you are the coolest kid in town."

Roberto began twisting feebly in his bed, and his grandmother reached out and placed a hand against his chest to calm him. The boy ignored her efforts. "You think Roberto Ramirez will come see me again?" he asked.

Burke thought, Sure, he'll rush right over. He formulated a quick lie. "You know, he called me on the phone when he heard you were sick again. He said the Yankees had to go to another city to play another team. But he wanted me to tell you he hit a *home run* for you today, and he was sending you the baseball. *And* that he signed the baseball just for you."

Burke watched the child's eyes widen and his smile spread. He knew the Yankees sold individually autographed baseballs at Yankee Stadium, and he planned to go there tomorrow and buy one. Then he would simply forge a personal inscription.

"When will I get it? Tomorrow?" The boy was squirming

weakly in his bed again, and Burke suddenly feared he would push the boy into another attack.

"Whoa, whoa. Yes, you'll get it tomorrow. But Mr. Ramirez told me he'd only send it if you were quiet and did everything your mother and grandmother and the doctor told you to do. Okay?"

The boy settled back in his bed. "Okay. I'll be quiet. See?" His eyes were filled with five-year-old mischief.

Burke winked at him again. "You stay that way. And tomorrow you'll have your baseball."

"You promise?" Roberto's eyes were wide again.

"I promise."

"Yay."

In the hall outside Roberto's room, Maria took Burke's hand. "That was very sweet," she said. "Your baseball story made him very happy." She reached out and took his hand. "He thinks Roberto Ramirez is wonderful. But he thinks you're even more wonderful."

Burke studied the floor, his own not-so-wonderful life flashing through his mind. He looked up at her. "He's got a wonderful mother and a wonderful grandmother. That's what he should know about."

He stroked her arm again. "You look exhausted." He inclined his head toward Roberto's room. "What happened?"

Maria's face became washed in guilt. She shook her head. "He was just playing too hard. We took him to the playground and he was playing with other children. Then he just got weak, and he fainted." Tears filled her eyes. "It was my fault. Dr. Salazar warned me that he couldn't do that. His heart just doesn't work fast enough. But he was so happy . . ."

Tears started coursing down her cheeks, and before he realized what he was doing, Burke's arms were around her, his hand gently stroking her back.

"It's not your fault," he said. "It's not." He continued to repeat the words like a mantra.

｛ 11 ｝

They were in a small East Side restaurant close to Julia's office, seated next to a window that looked out into the lunchtime madness that thronged Madison Avenue. It was the type of place Burke normally avoided, an Indian restaurant that offered only meatless dishes. During the years they lived together, Burke had vigorously resisted Julia's penchant for vegetarian food, claiming his species had not fought its way to the top of the food chain so he could satisfy his hunger with roasted eggplants and tofu salads. But today was different. He had asked Julia to lunch because he needed her advice, perhaps even some degree of comfort, so he would eat what she fancied.

"Just think of it as giving some cow a one-day reprieve," she told him.

"I don't believe in reprieving cows," Burke countered. "They litter the landscape with undesirable fecal matter."

"Hmmm," she said. "Just like newspaper publishers."

Burke had telephoned Julia that morning after a long, contentious session with Leonard Twist. During that meeting he asked Twist to free him from all other assignments until he wrapped up the "Little Bobby" story. The child was too sick, he argued, and he wanted to move ahead before his condition worsened and any real chance to help him became moot. Twist dismissed his concern at first, then finally relented when Burke explained that information would be arriving later that day from the city comptroller's office that would allow him to start investigating the staffing scam University Hospital and its doctors were allegedly running on the city.

Then Twist had said something that had shaken Burke. He had finished explaining how he wanted the investigation conducted, and Burke was just leaving his office when Twist's words stopped him.

"I want you to nail these bastards," Twist had said. "Nail their asses to the wall. You do that and we've got a great story and a shot at a Pulitzer that nobody can take away from us. And we'll have it even if the kid dies."

Julia shook her head as Burke repeated Twist's parting line.

"That's so typical," she said.

He watched anger flood her eyes. Unlike most people, he thought, she looked even more beautiful when she was angry or annoyed.

"I mean, the story's the thing for all of them," she added. "They're just incapable of seeing beyond the headline."

He realized he had misunderstood her. He had thought she was talking about Twist, whom she had met many times when they were still together. But she had meant news people in general. Perhaps even himself.

"I read your story about the kidnapping," she said as she warmed to the subject. "All those hints the police laid out about the victim having met the kidnappers in some 'gay bar.'" She raised both hands and put imaginary quotes around the final words. "I can just see everyone running around today, trying to dig up anything they can about that poor man's sexuality."

"From what I heard this morning, the FBI has pretty much

quashed that notion." He was about to say more, then stopped himself. Julia did it for him.

"But your editors think that's because of his father's money and connections, right?"

He couldn't help smiling at her perceptiveness. "And they question whether the kid was part of it. Whether it was all a plan to rip the father off," Burke said.

"If it was, they'll arrest him. In fact, they probably would have already." She shook her head. "No, they just want a chance to titillate their readers. That's what drives them. That and catching someone doing something they're not 'supposed' to do." Again, she added the imaginary quotes.

"It's a good story if it's true," Burke said. He was feeling defensive about his own part in it, and it made him recognize again how much Julia's opinion of him still mattered. He thought about the helicopter and his role in sending it up. The victim had been the furthest thing from his mind then. All that had mattered was getting one up on Pat Henry—that and getting the paper what it wanted.

She seemed to recognize his discomfort. She reached across the table and laid a hand on top of his. "I'm not criticizing your story. You presented the facts as they were given out, and that's okay. What I'm talking about is the continuing process—all the effort that will be put forth to try and *make* something out of it. It's self-serving and it's gratuitous, and no one cares if it's true or not, or who it might hurt."

The words "gratuitous" and "self-serving" cut at him, as did the idea of not caring whom might be hurt. They hit too close to what he had done. Burke also knew she was right about the follow-up stories. He knew what assignments had been given out that morning, and the stories being pursued were very close to what she had described. But that was simply the way it was done. The media lived on controversy—it was their lifeblood— and he tried to tell himself she was being naïve to think it could ever be done differently. Especially after the enormous sense of power that Watergate had given everyone.

"I also think you have to keep all that in mind where this little boy is concerned," she continued. "You can't let him become a pawn in all of it, just to serve the paper's interest. If you end up proving everything you suspect about the hospital and the doctors, he could get lost in the feeding frenzy."

Burke nodded as he thought over what she had just said. "I think I can control it. Keep the focus on the kid. We're running a short piece tomorrow about him being hospitalized again. We would have run it today, but the paper was just too tight because of the kidnapping. Then Wednesday we'll run a bigger story about a baseball player who came to visit him. The idea is to get the public hooked on the kid. Then get a fund started that will raise enough money to pay the surgeon and the hospital bills."

He could see the doubt in Julia's eyes, and knew that somewhere—pushed far back in his mind—he felt it, too. He wondered if he was forcing a different brand of naïveté on himself.

"He sounds like a wonderful little boy. I hope you can pull it off." Her voice held all the doubt that showed in her eyes.

Burke fiddled with the glass of beer that sat in front of him. He looked across at his wife. She seemed more beautiful now than she had during the last years they had lived together, when the pain of their daughter's illness had left her looking haggard and beaten. She was wearing a sharply tailored blue suit that accented her light-brown eyes, and her medium-length brown hair gave off hints of gold and had been professionally styled to accent the delicate lines of her face. He still loved her. He knew that. And he wished they could live together. But their daughter's illness had put too many roadblocks in the way, created too many unspoken issues between them, and he knew all the pain would return if they tried. As much as he wished otherwise, there seemed little question that Julia was better off alone, even if he was not.

He pushed the beer aside and folded his hands. "The bottom line is, I still wish I didn't have the damn story at all. I don't want to fail another little kid who needs my help. Or another mother who's counting on me."

Julia's eyes snapped up, and her jaw tightened. "You never failed Annie. I know you feel you did, because I feel the same thing. But it's not true." She closed her eyes briefly. "And you certainly never failed me. It was just something we couldn't handle . . ." she paused a moment, then added, "together."

Her final words hurt, even though he had heard them before. They were more than he could deal with, so he pushed them away. "I do need your help. I think I'm just afraid because I've already gotten too close to the boy." He laughed at the way he had qualified the obvious, then shook his head. "God, have I gotten close to him."

"There was no way you could avoid getting close to the boy." She watched him nod. "What about the mother?" Her voice had become softer, slightly apprehensive. "Are you afraid you're getting too close to her, too?"

He hesitated. "To both of them, I guess."

She placed her hand on his again. "I hope you don't. Not the mother anyway. I don't think that will be good for anyone." Burke tried to ignore what she had said, but she pushed on. "What you're doing with this story is terrific." She let him absorb the compliment, knew he needed it. "I read your piece in Sunday's paper. It was beautiful, Billy. One of the best things you've ever done." Her jaw trembled slightly. "It made me cry."

Julia picked up her glass of wine, stared into it as if using it to compose herself. She put it down without drinking, then looked back at him. "So do the story. No one else will do it half as well, and I know you'll keep fighting for the child. And if you need a shoulder, I'll be here. I'll be here to help in any way I can."

Burke left the restaurant with a mild sense of relief. He had Julia's blessing, of sorts, and if not that, her support, and he knew he could push her concerns—as well as his own—far back in his mind. The story was his, and he'd make it work. Roberto would get his operation, and if Jennifer Wells knew what she was talking about, he'd even find a way to give Twist his pound of flesh.

Burke stepped off the curb and hailed a cab. His next stop would be Yankee Stadium. He had an autographed baseball to pick up, an inscription to forge, and a delivery to make to a small boy in Brooklyn.

He had called the hospital that morning and spoken to Maria. Roberto was scheduled to be released at eleven, with enough medication to keep him stable. He glanced at his watch. It was a little past two, and he was sure they would be just getting home. There would have been forms to fill out and a humiliating session with the business office over the family's inability to pay. He thought about Maria sitting through it all. It was just what the woman needed. A dying child wasn't quite enough. She also needed that feeling of inadequacy that bureaucrats and clerks regularly inflicted on the poor.

Burke's mind rang out a warning. Don't get too close. Just help the boy and walk away. You can't change their lives, and any false hope that you can will hurt everyone—even you.

Burke got back to the newsroom shortly before five. Roberto had been asleep when he arrived at the apartment, and Maria had left for work to make up some of the time she had missed that morning. He had left the baseball with Roberto's grandmother, and after deflecting her offers of coffee and cookies and sandwiches, had beaten a speedy retreat.

When he reached his desk, Burke found the packet of material Jerry Francis—AKA Gerard LaFrancois—had sent from the comptroller's office. It had arrived in the proverbial plain brown wrapper, sans note or any other identification, a method that would allow Burke to claim it had come from an anonymous source should the need arise.

He spent a half hour going through it. There were itemized time sheets for every doctor, intern, and medical student who had supposedly worked at Bellevue and Harlem hospitals, and records of the city's payments to University Hospital and its medical school for those services. The payments covered the past three years and totaled more than four million dollars.

Burke checked his watch. It was just after six, still too early to reach Jennifer Wells at her apartment, but he could do that later. He wanted to arrange their final meeting and set a plan in motion that would get him access to University Hospital records tomorrow morning. Jennifer had assured him she could get him in. Now it was time for Dr. James Bradford's nurse to deliver on that promise.

Burke gathered the papers and locked them in his desk. Reporters were naturally curious, which was a kind way of saying they were among the nosiest bastards on earth, and any papers left out were sure to be read. Information was a commodity—*the* commodity in the news business—and a good reporter would collect anything available, be it useful or not, then salt it away like a child stuffing pennies in a piggy bank. And like children, most would talk about anything they found. Costello's and other newspaper watering holes were always rife with information about who was working on what. Being in the know about "the big one that was about to break" added a certain cachet among one's peers.

Burke was just returning the keys to his pocket when Whitney Morgan slid her well-shaped bottom onto his desk, crossed her legs, and winked at him.

"Hi, sailor. It's been a while." She allowed her ankle to brush lightly against his thigh and smiled.

Burke gave her his best Bogart imitation. "Big stories. Breaking news. You know what it's like, sweetheart." He returned the smile.

"Oh, I know. You big-time news jockeys. Never a moment's rest." Whitney straightened her back and gave a little catlike stretch. It forced her breasts against the white silk blouse she was wearing and outlined the lacy bra that lay beneath. It drew Burke's eyes like a dog to a bone.

"But if you could find time to buy a girl a drink . . ." She paused for effect. "Who knows what might happen? She might even make you dinner."

Burke glanced past Whitney. Eddie Hartman was the only other reporter nearby. He was on the phone, but he was listening intently to Whitney's banter. His eyebrows fluttered wildly.

Burke stared up at Whitney and grinned. "That sounds like a terrific offer."

"I hope so." She gave him another coy smile. "When will you be ready to leave?"

"I just have to check with the city desk; then I'll make like a bird."

"Tweet, tweet." Whitney slid off the desk. "Call me when you're ready."

Burke watched her walk away. Behind him Eddie Hartman let out a low growl.

"Shut up, Eddie," he said. "Sit there and eat your heart out. But don't say a word."

Hartman growled again.

* * *

Burke stopped at the city desk, the horseshoe-shaped rim that operated as the paper's nerve center. The six-o'clock deadline for the bulldog edition had just ended, and the editors, having passed all the day's stories to the copy desk, were in a relaxed mode, talking over still-pending stories with their nightside counterparts who were just starting their shift.

Frank Fabio was leaning back in his chair, hands cupped behind his head, one foot propped against the edge of the rim. Ben Rostantino was standing over him, a sheaf of expense reports in one hand, an amused look on his face.

Rostantino was the comptroller for the news department, and as such was responsible for its vast budget and expenditures.

He dropped the bundle of expense reports on Fabio's desk. As assignment editor it was Fabio's job to approve all expenses submitted by reporters and photographers, something he usually did without either reading them or blinking an eye.

"You need to explain this to me, Frankie," Rostantino said. "Because as usual I am thoroughly mystified."

Fabio stared up at him, eyebrows arched. Rostantino was a short, plump man, with fast-thinning gray hair that matched his fifty-something years. He had a round, jolly sort of face and, comptroller or not, was one of the nicest men Burke had ever met. But he was also no one's fool, and he kept a tight reign on the news department's budget.

"Benny, my friend, demystifying things is my forte. Has one of my troops run afoul of your adding machine?"

Rostantino pointedly looked at the expense reports on Fabio's desk. "Seven of them," he said. "But I'm certain you can explain it all away."

Fabio's eyebrows rose again in mock amazement. "Only seven? And what did these miscreants do?"

Rostantino glanced toward the ceiling as if consulting the heavens. "It seems all seven of them managed to take the mayor out to lunch on the same day."

Fabio picked up the expense reports and began looking through them with feigned interest.

Burke, standing alongside, prepared himself for Fabio's response. It was a common ploy reporters used to hide the identity of a source—both from their editors and from any prosecutor or defense attorney who might one day prove smart enough to subpoena a reporter's expense records. To avoid that unwanted exposure, reporters simply substituted the name of the mayor, a city councilman, or some other public official, who would invariably back up their story if questioned. Over the years Burke had enjoyed hundreds of fictional lunches and dinners with everyone from the police commissioner to the governor.

Fabio placed the reports on his desk and made a point of smoothing out some imaginary wrinkles. He was well aware of the practice, which he had used many times himself. He was also aware that it rankled the business types who constantly groused about the news department's mammoth budget. He picked up a pen and began initialing each report.

"They all look fine to me," he said.

"Really?" Rostantino's voice held a hint of laughter in it now. He, too, knew how the game was played, although he would never admit it. Now he was simply going through the motions, keeping his own tail out of the wringer. He picked up the expense reports. "Just so I can explain it to my masters, would you mind telling me how seven of your reporters managed to have lunch with the mayor on the very same day?"

Fabio shook his head, as if dealing with a small child. "Benny, Benny, Benny. You know how the mayor is when he eats. It's just pick, pick, pick."

Rostantino let out a roar of laughter, waved the expense reports in the air, and started away. "That's beautiful, Frankie," he said over his shoulder. "I'd write a book about this place, but no one would believe it."

Fabio turned to Burke and winked. "Now that that's settled, what can I do for you, my troop?"

"I just wanted you to know I'll be out most of the day tomorrow."

"The University Hospital gig that our leader told me about?"

"Exactly."

"May God go with you, my son."

"Indeed."

Burke returned to his desk, picked up his phone, and dialed

Whitney's extension. "See you at the elevator in two?" he said when she picked up. He smiled at her answer, then replaced the receiver.

Eddie Hartman was staring at him. "I hate it when somebody's going to get laid and it isn't me," he said.

"I bet that happens a lot," Burke said.

"Fuck you," Hartman snapped back.

Burke grinned at him as he turned toward the reception room and the elevators beyond. "One can only hope," he said.

{ 12 }

Burke stopped at his desk the next morning to get some of the material Jerry Francis had sent from the comptroller's office. He had spoken to Jennifer Wells the previous evening, and she had agreed to meet at a coffee shop three blocks from University Hospital. The hospital's lunch and dinner hours and the evening shifts, she had claimed, would be the best times to search the surgical records that he wanted as his starting point, and she would have everything he needed to slip past its less-than-stringent security.

Burke went through the material quickly, compiling a list of surgeons and anesthesiologists, along with residents in various surgical fields, all of whom had supposedly worked at Bellevue and Harlem hospitals on certain dates. He had decided to start with the most recent year and work backward, under the assumption that those behind the scam would have gotten bolder with their phantom jobs as time passed. He still had nonsurgical physicians, residents, interns, and medical students to verify, but had decided to take the easiest route first—and the sexiest in terms of his story: namely, to determine if Doctor X was busy slicing up Patient Y at University Hospital when he was being paid for a day of surgical consultations at one of the city's very needy, but less prestigious, medical institutions.

Burke was just completing his list when Eddie Hartman sauntered in, suitcase in hand. He was dressed in his polyester best—pale-blue leisure suit, wide-collared shirt, and a napkin-size necktie.

"Are we off on a junket?" Burke asked.

Hartman wiggled his bushy eyebrows. "Chicago. That toddling town."

"Ah, the City of Big Shoulders. And what, pray tell, has happened there that forces you away from the Apple?"

Hartman dropped his suitcase next to his chair and put on a somber expression. "It seems last night that great American, and beloved Mafia don, Sam Giancana, was sent to the great cannoli factory in the sky." He made a diving gesture with his hand. "Down for the count. Seven bullets in the head and neck. Obviously a suicide."

"Probably depressed over his repeated failure to bump off Fidel Castro," Burke said.

"That wasn't Giancana's fault," Hartman said. "Castro hates Italian food, and everybody knows the wiseguys can't kill anybody unless they're eating dinner in an Italian restaurant."

Burke shook his head. "Imagine that. Castro saved by the old meatball-rejection syndrome. Who would of thought?"

"You heard it here first." Hartman slumped into his chair and turned serious. "Actually, you could do me a small favor before I leave."

"How's that?"

"You think your guy in the New York field office could set me up with someone in the FBI's Chicago Organized Crime Squad?"

"I can ask," Burke said. "Are you just covering the murder and Giancana's probable successors?"

"That and the funeral itself," Hartman said. "It should be a lovely affair."

"I hope you brought suitable clothing."

"Black shirt, white necktie."

"No spats?"

"Damn, I knew I forgot something."

Burke went to a more private phone and dialed Dezi's direct line. A few minutes later he handed Hartman a slip of paper with a phone number on it. "The guy who heads up the Chicago squad is Vincent Insulata. That's his home number. My friend will call him this morning and pave the way."

"You are a prince among princes," Hartman said.

Jennifer Wells was already seated in a booth at the rear of the coffee shop when Burke arrived. She looked anxious, and Burke noticed that she had worn a lightweight raincoat to hide her nurse's uniform, despite clear skies and warm temperatures. He also noticed that her uniform choice of the day included the white slacks favored by Dr. James Bradford.

"You're late," Jennifer said as he slid into the booth.

Burke glanced at his watch. It was eleven thirty-five, making him five minutes late. "I had trouble getting a cab," he said.

There was a paper bag next to Jennifer, and Burke raised his chin toward it. "That for me?" he asked.

She passed the bag across the table, and Burke glanced inside. It held a white lab coat, complete with a hospital ID and name tag for a Dr. John Rourke, a clipboard with hospital surgical forms attached, and a stethoscope.

"This is all I'll need?" Burke asked.

Jennifer flashed perfect white teeth, in what was more sneer than smile. She had a near-flawless beauty, Burke thought, but combined it with a deep-seated anger that made her decidedly unattractive.

"If you're a doctor and even vaguely seem to know what you're doing, no one will question you about *anything*." Her mouth twisted unpleasantly as she explained where the documents were kept in the hospital records room and the routine he should follow. "Just walk right in like you own the place, find what you want, then just hand it all to some clerk and tell her to copy it. The more arrogant you are about it, the more they'll believe you. If you were a medical student or intern—or God forbid, a lowly nurse—they'd tell you to piss off. But *no one* is going to say that to one of the resident gods. Not if they want to keep their jobs."

"What about the evening shifts?"

"It'll be the same, except there will just be a skeleton staff—one or two people. So you'll probably have to copy stuff yourself. But the copy machine's right there. You just have to sign the sheet with Dr. Rourke's name. Believe me, no one will question it."

"Who is this Dr. Rourke?" Burke asked.

Jennifer's eyes turned mischievous. "He works with Bradford. But he and his wife are on a month-long vacation in Europe. Except I bet you'll find Bradford has him scheduled to work at Bellevue the whole time he's away." She reached into her carryall purse. "Which reminds me. Here's a list of all the vacations both Bradford and Rourke have taken over the past four years, along with dates for conferences they've attended, and a list of all their surgical patients. I also have a list of the clubs Bradford belongs to—he plays golf at the country club listed there every Wednesday, by the way. There's also another list of social engagements he and his wife have over the next couple of weeks. There's even a museum opening at the Met that should let your photographer catch him in black tie."

Burke took the various lists and skimmed through them quickly. Among them was a *JAMA* article Bradford had written that included his photograph. He inclined his head in admiration of the woman's thoroughness. If he ever became seriously ill, he wanted her working his sickbed, he decided. But only if he was certain she liked him.

"Is there any danger that somebody in the records office will know this Dr. Rourke by sight?" he asked.

Jennifer gave him an incredulous look. "Bradford and Rourke don't deal with anyone at *that* level. The odd attending might go in there. But a surgeon? Especially one on the teaching faculty?" She shook her head. "Those clerks will be so flustered, they'll treat you like it was the Second Coming."

Burke sat back and thought it through. "First time out, you think it might be safer to go in at night?"

"Sure. It will always be safer at night. But it really isn't necessary."

"I'm just thinking about running into another doctor who might know Rourke."

"Just stay away from the surgical floors and that won't happen," she said. "And don't go anywhere near the doctors' lounge, the main cafeteria, and especially the physicians' cafeteria."

"The doctors have their own cafeteria?"

"You think they eat with mere mortals?" She reached out and patted Burke's hand. "You have a lot to learn about the medical profession."

Burke did not enter University Hospital until eight that evening. After meeting Jennifer he had decided to change his plan. Instead of going directly to the hospital, he returned to the paper and set up a photography schedule for Dr. James Bradford's upcoming social calendar, then took the rest of the afternoon off. Anticipating a late night, he went back to his apartment, grabbed some sleep to make up for the previous late and athletic evening in Whitney's bed, fed himself a tasteless TV dinner, then changed into his best shirt, tie, and dress slacks, all of it befitting a successful cardiac surgeon, he hoped.

Now dressed in the lab coat Jennifer had provided, the stethoscope protruding from a side pocket, Burke moved down a first-floor hospital corridor with all the authority he could muster. He also harbored the secret fear that some poor soul would collapse in front of him and immediately go into cardiac arrest. And what then, bucko, he asked himself—what do you do when you suddenly have a dozen nurses looking up at you, expecting you to save the guy? The answer came back immediately. You do the same thing you'll do if somebody tumbles to your phony ID—brazen it out, growl imperiously, then run like hell as soon as their backs are turned.

Burke's confidence perked up as he moved toward the records department and several passing nurses smiled and nodded. One even offered a "Good evening, Doctor," raising his hopes several notches.

The records department was a cavernous room with row upon row of eight-foot shelves, each filled with files in multicolored folders. Entrance was barred by a long counter, bisected by a four-foot-high gate, behind which sat ranks of desks, only two of which were now occupied.

The young man and young woman who manned those desks stared at Burke as he entered and pushed through the gate as though the room were his private fiefdom.

"Can I help you, Doctor?" the young man asked. He began to rise from his chair.

"No. I just want to check some old surgical schedules. I believe I know where they are." Burke snapped out the words with the same command he imagined Dr. Rourke would use. His tone seemed to freeze the young man to his seat.

The young man was plump, with a round, chubby face splattered with unpleasant blemishes. He wore glasses and a bad haircut, and there was a pocket protector stuffed with half a dozen pens protruding from his white shirt. The young woman, who looked to be in her early twenties, was the exact opposite— a pert, pretty, cheerleader type with blond hair sculpted into a winged Farrah Fawcett hairdo and enormous, though slightly vapid, blue eyes. She was dressed in a tight blue cotton pullover that accented large breasts, which as she leaned forward came to rest heavily on top of the desk.

Seeing the two clerks juxtaposed that way increased Burke's confidence. He felt certain that the young man would rather ogle the young woman than poke his nose into what Burke was doing. He also was reasonably sure the young man would not attempt to assert his authority to impress the young woman and thereby risk an embarrassing scene with a senior member of the medical staff.

Trouble came from a different direction, however.

The young woman approached Burke with a flirtatious smile. "If you need copies, I can help," she said. She spun around without waiting for a reply and turned on the copy machine that was only a few feet away.

Burke wanted to tell her to take her cute little buns back to her chair. He especially wanted to when he noticed the young man's glowering eyes as he watched his fellow worker strut her stuff.

"I'll let you know if I need help," Burke said. He kept his voice cool and superior, hoping it would drive the woman away.

Still, she lingered, so he decided to try another approach. He withdrew a five-dollar bill from his pocket. "Why don't you get all three of us some coffee?" he said. "I've been up since four, and I'm half asleep." He tried a smile this time, tried to make it as condescending as the suggestion he had just made.

The young woman took the five-dollar bill. "You should be in bed," she said. There was the hint of a smile on her lips, as though she were mentally adding, "With someone who's fun."

"I take mine black," Burke said. He turned back to the files.

He kept his eyes averted but could almost feel the young woman's hips swaying as she walked away. Within seconds of her departure the young man approached. It was as though he were securing the ground she had occupied—to keep her away when she returned, Burke decided.

"I'll make copies if you need them, Doctor," he said. "Wendy will just screw them up."

Burke decided camaraderie was needed. "One of those, eh? This hospital seems to be overrun with them."

"Yeah, but they're great to look at." The young man punctuated his remark with a yellow-toothed grin.

Burke had been looking through a file folder as he spoke. The name "Bradford" suddenly jumped out at him. Cardiac surgery, May 14, 1975. He flipped through the notes he had brought from his office and immediately smiled. Bradford had spent the morning carving someone's chest at University Hospital, while the City of New York had paid him for an entire day at Bellevue. The first glimmer of gold. He turned to the young man.

"Look, what I'm trying to put together here needs some concentration. When Wendy gets back, could you keep her busy with something else?"

The young man seemed to puff up. "Oh, sure, Doc. Sure. No problem."

Two hours later Burke had a manila envelope full of photocopies that covered the past six months of surgical procedures. Four more visits and that part of the story would be wrapped up. He started for the door. The young man was away from his desk as he prepared to leave. Wendy, still behind hers, smiled at him.

"Get everything you need?" she asked.

"Afraid not," Burke said. "Still a lot to do."

"Wish I could help." She pushed her lips into a slight pout.

"Are you here every night?" Burke asked. He was hoping she'd say no.

"Just three nights a week. My schedule at the medical school is too heavy for more than that."

Burke was stunned. He had assumed the young woman was nothing more than a dull-witted flirt.

"What year are you in?" he asked.

"Second," she said. "Next year I'll be working the floor here."

An idea began to form in Burke's mind. He perched on the edge of her desk. "Maybe you can help me," he said.

Wendy's entire face brightened. "I'd love to."

Burke smiled at her as he prepared the lie he had already worked out in case he was challenged. "What I'm trying to do is put together some proposed schedules for volunteer time at Bellevue and Harlem hospitals," he said. "The one part that's lagging behind is teaching schedules at the medical schools. I've called several times for them, but the clerks just can't seem to get them in the mail."

"Oh, I can get them," Wendy said. "I already have a copy of this year's teaching schedule. We get them at the beginning of the year so we can pick our classes and teachers."

Burke's hopes soared. "I'll need them for the past three years," he said. He hurried on. "I'm trying to develop a pattern of available time to ward off any arguments about people's schedules being too tight."

"I'm sure I can get all three years," she said. "I know I have the last two years myself. And I'm sure the third year will be on file someplace." She paused a moment, thinking. "You know, a lot of those schedules are kept right here, because a lot of the teaching is done right here. At least for the third-year students." She looked at him as though he were being silly. "But you know *that*."

Burke grinned as though acknowledging his foolishness.

"I'll show you where they are here, and then I'll get the others from school."

"If you could, it will be a great help. There's no rush on the schedules for the school," he added. "Sometime in the next few days will be fine." He paused to give importance to his next words. "I'd appreciate it if you could keep this between us," he said. "If word gets out about what I'm doing, resistance will start to build before I can get all my facts together. I'd like to avoid that if possible."

Wendy smiled up at him. "I'll be quiet as a mouse," she said. "Someone I dated once told me that real men hate noisy women."

Burke groaned inwardly, thinking, not for the first time, that the feminist revolution that had begun with Germaine Greer's recent book, *The Female Eunuch*, had a definite downside. He pushed the thought away. "I'm sure that would never be a problem for you," he said.

Wendy looked at him coyly. "Well, that might depend," she said.

Fred Costa was already banging away on his typewriter when Burke arrived in the newsroom the next morning.

"You must have the big one," Burke offered.

"Same old, same old," Costa said around the cigarette that hung from his mouth. "It's the annual transportation-beat blockbuster—our yearly attack on diplomatic parking. This year we've got a city councilman calling for the elimination of all DPL parking spaces."

Burke slumped into his chair, instantly pleased that he did not cover transportation. DPL parking was one of the paper's pet peeves and had become an annual crusade that delighted its readers. It was also laden with a level of duplicity that always amazed Burke. All diplomats were issued license plates marked with the abbreviation "DPL," which allowed them to park in special areas near the various UN consulates. Diplomats also regularly parked wherever they chose and were immune from parking tickets. The New York press also had special plates, marked "NYP," with an even greater number of special parking zones scattered throughout the city. They, too, parked wherever they wanted and had their tickets fixed by the New York Press Club. Several years ago, in an impish moment, Burke had included those facts in a story he wrote about the city's parking woes. The paragraph had been cut by the city desk.

It was a double standard that never ceased to amuse him—
only one of many—and Burke had often thought it might prove
enlightening to write a piece detailing the hypocrisy that surrounded the media. Another of the press' favorite stories involved travel junkets and other handouts furnished to
politicians by favor-seeking corporations. Yet reporters regularly boarded government-provided aircraft to follow the presi-
dent, the secretary of state, and other public officials around the
world. They also happily accepted free hotel rooms; the free theater tickets handed out daily by theatrical producers; free ad-
mission to major sporting events, or the circus, or the ice
shows, or any other extravaganza that passed through their
cities; free meals in restaurants; and most of all, free office
space in public buildings. His own newspaper utilized public office space in Washington, Albany, City Hall, each of the city's
five borough halls, the police department, and in all the federal,
state, and municipal courts. In each case the space, heat, lighting, and maintenance were paid for with public tax dollars—all
allegedly to promote the free flow of news.

Burke smiled at the blatant hypocrisy of it all. He also recognized that he was very much a part of that hypocrisy. He couldn't
count the number of free Broadway shows he had seen or the
number of times he had sat in Madison Square Garden to
watch the Knicks or the Rangers or a major boxing match. Only
last year he had invited a favorite uncle to New York. He'd taken
him to a game at Yankee Stadium, out to dinner at a well-
known steakhouse, then housed him in a suite at one of the
city's better hotels. His only out-of-pocket expense had been cab
fare. In each case his excuse had always been: It's there, so you
might as well take it.

A hand on his shoulder interrupted his self-deprecating reverie.
He looked up and found Lenny Twist staring down at him.

Twist inclined his head back toward his glass-enclosed office.
"I need a progress report," he said. "How about now?"

Burke nodded. "Be right with you."

He gathered his notes, then leaned over to Fred Costa. "I am
amazed this DPL story hasn't resulted in a bottle of champagne
sitting on your desk," Burke said. "I was sure it would produce
an evening of bliss with one of your many squeezes."

Costa glanced over his shoulder and sneered. "It's a New York story, pally. New York diplomats, New York DPL zones."

Burke patted his shoulder. "Ah, but there are also thousands of DPL parking zones in Washington. Certainly the city desk wants you to investigate how that illustrious city handles the problem."

Costa spun around and stared at Burke. "Damn," he said. "I never thought of that. Damn, damn, damn."

Arnie Goodman, one of the paper's political reporters, stood outside Twist's office as Burke approached. Twist was lambasting him about a story he had turned in, and Goodman's face was turning a deeper shade of red with each word.

"I asked you for a goddamn story about the city's fucked-up purchasing practices," Twist growled. "And all I get is a detailed account of how they've wasted money on office equipment over the past year."

"I thought that's what you wanted," Goodman mumbled. "I—"

Twist cut him off. "You thought that's what I wanted? Where the hell is your head, Arnie? This city is headed for the financial toilet. Everybody knows that. This is New York City, and it's in the worst goddamn financial crisis in its history. Think about that, Arnie. Fact one: The greatest goddamn city in the nation is about to go into default. Fact two: The politicians running the city have their heads so far up their asses, they've had to appoint a goddamn investment banker to head up the Municipal Assistance Corporation just to bail them out. So whose fault is it? Who's to blame? Those are the goddamn questions we want to answer." He waved Goodman's story in the air. "Now, look at what you give me. You give me a story that tells me city officials are wasting fucking tax dollars, which is about as newsworthy as telling me you saw a dog chasing a fucking cat." He closed his eyes and shook his head, as though he were dealing with a fool. Then he glared at Goodman again. "I want names, Arnie. I want city officials I can nail to the fucking wall." Twist held up the story Goodman had turned in. "What are you giving me *here*? Here I get a story about the city handing out contracts to replace office equipment that's only two years old. So what?

Governments have been wasting money for centuries. I asked for blood. I asked for bodies. And there are none here." He tossed the story back, and watched Goodman struggle to catch it in the air.

"I want to know which goddamn city official ordered these purchases, and what his goddamn connection is with the vendor. *That's* what I want."

"Maybe there isn't any connection," Goodman protested. "Maybe it's just typical—"

Twist cut him off again. "Don't give me that, Arnie. That's crap, and you know it. Your job is to find a connection. I don't care if it's just some political fundraiser that some politician and some vendor attended together. It's a connection, goddamn it, and I want it. And it's your job to find it." Twist tapped the side of his head. "Think, Arnie. And when you think, think Watergate. The days of just reporting government fuckups are gone. Now we don't just report fuckups. We report *who* fucked up and *why*. And we keep digging until we have a *why* that will give our readers answers. The right answers. Answers that will make them scream for some politician's head. And *that's* your job. Make no mistake about it. And if you can't do that job, I've got a dozen other guys who can. Do you get my meaning?"

Twist stared at Goodman until the reporter gave him a humiliated nod, then spun on his heels and entered his office. Burke hesitated, watched Goodman walk away. He felt humiliated himself, just for having witnessed the scene. Then he turned and followed Twist into his office.

Twist sat behind his desk, his hands steepled in front of his face, as if composing himself. The unctuous, prayerlike pose made Burke want to reach out and grab him by the throat.

"All right, you're next," Twist snapped. "What have you got so far?"

Burke reined in his resentment and filled Twist in, watching the city editor's eyes take on a glimmer of escalating pleasure with each example of payroll fraud he had uncovered the previous night.

"And this is only for the past six months?" Twist asked.

"That's right."

"How far back do you intend to go?"

"Three years. I want to show a long-term pattern of abuse."

"That's good, very good. The last thing we want is some hospital hotshot claiming our story is based on a handful of clerical errors. If we had a three-year record to point to, he'd be a laughingstock if he tried." Twist began tapping a pencil on his desk. "How long before you think you can wrap this up?"

"With luck, a week, two weeks tops."

Twist's eyes narrowed, and Burke could see him calculating the time. "We're not in a rush on this, especially if public interest takes off. And we want it to be solid above all else." He hesitated again. "I also don't know if I can keep you free of breaking news for two weeks straight." He held up a hand to ward off any objection. "I'll try, but I can't promise anything." He leaned back in his chair. "Right now I need more stuff on the kid. Money's started to come in, and we haven't even asked for any yet." He brought his chair forward. "The publisher's excited. He thinks we've got something that's potentially very big here. Needless to say, I don't want to disappoint him. He's already approved an advertising budget. We're going to start with some billboard advertising, some posters in the subway and some more on the sides of city buses. The ad boys will also start pushing our advertisers to see if they'll take some Jimmy Fund–type collection boxes for their stores, so we've got to goose our readers, get them even more interested in this kid."

Burke was surprised at how quickly things had begun to move. He also realized just how much Twist had riding on the story. And that spelled out only one thing. Movement—on Burke's end—would be critical. Long-term stories like this one always depended on the vagaries of fate and timing. In newspapers, today's stroke of genius easily became tomorrow's piece of shit. Sustained interest was a very unstable commodity. Once the smell of blood had left the water, editors and publishers moved on quickly to another part of the ocean. Even if there was still a story to be told.

"How about the struggle and sacrifice of the mother and the grandmother?" Burke suggested. "These are two very sympathetic and attractive women. And we've only touched on them."

He watched Twist's mouth wrinkle with displeasure as one eyebrow rose in doubt. Burke quickly added, "We'll tie it all around the boy, of course. Deal with the pressure his illness has put on them—and the threat that help may not come in time."

Twist's expression changed. The doubt was still there, but now he was nodding, acknowledging the possibilities.

"All right, we can try it. But I want the image of a small white coffin hanging in the background. Without saying it, I want you to paint a picture of little what's-his-name laid out in some run-down fucking funeral home." He gave Burke a sly wink. "And you can do that. I know you can. When it comes to jerking tears, you're a consummate pro."

Burke winced. "That's ugly, Lenny. Really ugly."

"Hey, you want this kid to get his operation, right? So get the bozos out there sniffling a little. Before you know it, they'll be reaching for their handkerchiefs and their wallets at the same time." Twist rubbed his hands together, then stood to signal Burke's dismissal. "That's the name of this story, mister. It's a fucking cash register. *Ka-ching, ka-ching.*"

{ 13 }

Maria Avalon glanced at the clock on the wall. It was four-forty. Only twenty minutes more and she would meet Billy Burke outside the building. He had telephoned and left a message with Rose; said he wanted to meet her and talk on her way home. Rose had smirked and teased her about having a new man in her life. She only wished, she thought now, only wished she could find someone to share her life with, find a decent man like Billy to be a father to her son.

All about her the frantic pace of the cutting room continued. She went through the motions of her job, her mind elsewhere. She unrolled the bolt of cloth on the table, stretched and smoothed it, then laid the pattern out on top, fitting it for the least amount of waste. The cutter was working at the next table and would move to her table soon. It was the final task of the day, this the last bolt of cloth she would handle. Until tomorrow.

She let her mind go back to Burke. Billy Burke. It was such a
little boy name for such a large man. She guessed he was in his
mid-thirties, maybe a few years older. He was a handsome man.
Not pretty the way her husband had been, but still handsome.
There was a rugged, worn look about him, and even though his
eyes were gentle when he spoke to her, there was something
weary in them, almost as though they had been forced to see
too much of life.

She readjusted the pattern, correcting it to avoid the loss of a
quarter inch of fabric. Her thoughts were still focused on her
own growing fantasy about the man. Then they struck back at
her, told her she was being a fool to even think about him that
way. She drew a long breath. What could someone like that see
in you—some Spanish girl who works in a garment-district cutting room, who goes home each night to take care of a sick little boy? Someone who isn't even educated, someone who
doesn't know anything about anything. Her hands fluttered
about the cloth. Stop being ridiculous. Billy talked to important
people every day, probably had lunches and dinners with them,
listening while they answered his questions about important
things. What if he invited you to one of those dinners. God,
everyone would laugh. You sitting there in one of your old
dresses, not knowing what to say to anyone, not understanding
anything *they* were saying to you. It was hopeless even to think
about it. She tried to force the thought away, but the image of
Billy returned. Her mind went back to the hospital, when he
had put his arms around her, comforted her. God, it had felt so
good to be held, to feel a strong man's arms around you. Not
like the neighborhood men you met the few nights you went out
to Spanish nightclubs hoping to find someone. All those men
with their macho bedroom eyes, the few you had danced with,
had allowed to put their arms around you, all moving their
hands to your ass and telling you how sexy you were. And, God,
sometimes it was even tempting, just for a minute or two. Your
body telling you how much you missed having someone to
make love with, how good it would feel to have someone want
you just that much.

Maria readjusted the pattern again. There was no point to it.
It was just something to do with her hands. Her husband,

Miguel, floated into her mind, and she realized she had not thought about him for a long time. They were such children when they'd come here, she told herself. And she had loved him so much. Now she couldn't even remember why, couldn't even remember what there was about him that made her love him. He'd killed all that with his drugs. Killed it and buried it so deep that she couldn't even remember how it was. Or why she had ever wanted him.

Billy would be different. He was a man, not a boy, even if he had a little boy's name.

The thought jolted her again. And he also had a wife and a child—a wife he never divorced. Never divorced because deep inside he must want her back. And a girlfriend, too. A man like him would have a girlfriend. Maybe even more than one. Beautiful, sophisticated women like his wife. You could tell that about his wife from the picture he showed you. A good mother, too. You could tell she was a good mother, you could see it in her face and her eyes and the way she held on to her child.

"Maria."

Maria looked up and saw Rose waddling toward her, her heavy body jiggling with each step—everything but her hair, which was bleached blond and stiff as a board from hair spray.

"Mr. Singer wants to see you," Rose said.

"Oh, God, what did I do now?"

Rose shrugged. "With him, who knows? He's been bitching at me all day." She waved her large, fleshy arm. "He spends his life making knockoffs, but to me he's supposed to be Bill Blass. What can I tell you, the man's a schmuck. But he's the schmuck who signs our paychecks. So go smile at him. Make nice. Make that little thing in his pants twitch, and then he'll be happy again. And if he's happy, we'll be happy. Or maybe almost happy. If I came home smiling someday, my husband would think I was *meshuggeneh*."

Maria followed Rose back into the office. It was a glass-enclosed box that allowed those within to look out into the various production areas, and within that box was another glass-enclosed box that was Bert Singer's private sanctum.

When she entered Singer's office, Maria noticed that the venetian blinds covering the windows had been drawn shut. It gave her some sense of comfort. When Singer fired someone, he did it with the blinds open and with much arm-waving and scowling. Longtime employees said it was always done that way. It was a message to everyone else, Singer's way of letting them know just how insecure their jobs could be if they displeased him.

Singer told her to close the door when she entered. He was seated behind a large, cluttered desk, and his white-on-white shirt and black-patterned silk necktie seemed almost iridescent under the fluorescent lighting that hung above his head. He was a short man, not much taller than Maria, about fifty-five years old, she guessed, but very trim, with stylishly cut hair and glossy, manicured nails. She had always considered him a reasonably handsome man—until you looked directly into his eyes. They were always cold and hard, even on those rare occasions when he tried to be friendly.

Singer put his hands behind his head and leaned back in his executive chair. "I've been reading about you in the paper," he said. "I want to know if you have a green card. Just in case Immigration comes around asking. They read the newspapers, too."

Maria watched his eyes drop to her legs. He seemed to roam their length from ankle to knee. "I'm from Puerto Rico," she said. "I don't need a green card."

"A lot of my workers claim they're from Puerto Rico," he said. "Then Immigration shows up, and I find out they're from Nicaragua or Costa Rica or God-knows-where. I don't need those kinds of problems." He had raised his eyes to her face. He pursed his lips as if he were considering her value, judging her.

"I have a birth certificate at home. I can bring it in tomorrow," Maria said.

Singer nodded. "Okay, you do that. Just in case somebody from Immigration shows up. Those bastards find one person who doesn't belong here and they check everybody. Then I've got all kinds of aggravation." He leaned forward in his chair and let his eyes drop again to her legs. "You know, you could do well here. You could even work in the office if you wanted. You're a good-looking woman, and I like to have good-looking women in the office. The buyers like that. They like to see beautiful

women when they're on buying trips." His eyes returned to
Maria's face. "But you'd have to be friendly, too. You understand?" He waited a beat. "I mean, somebody gives you a little
pat on the bottom, you can't get all bent out of shape. You see
what I mean?"

His eyes went to her breasts now, and Maria instinctively
folded her arms across her chest. "I like my job," she said. "I
like working with the women and the cutters."

Singer shrugged as if it didn't matter. "There's a little more
money, you know. Working in the office, I mean. Maybe even insurance. Who knows, it might help your son."

Maria lowered her eyes. Her jaw tightened. She struggled to
keep her voice even. "I've talked to insurance companies," she
said. "To see if I could afford to buy some. They said Roberto
wouldn't be covered for his illness because it happened before."

Singer's face turned into a scowl. He waved a hand. "Yeah,
yeah. It's preexisting. Still, it would be more money. But only if
you could be very friendly. Go out after work. Things like that."

Maria drew a calming breath. "I like my job, Mr. Singer. And
I have to go home to Roberto after work."

Singer leaned back in his chair and waved the back of his
hand at her. "Okay, okay. But think about it. You never know.
You might decide you'd like to try. And you bring in that birth
certificate tomorrow. Have Rose make a copy for our files."

{ 14 }

Burke was waiting when Maria came out of the battered old elevator. He angled his way through the crush of people rushing toward the front door, took her elbow, and joined the flow.

"Wow," he said. "You'd think the building was on fire the way everyone comes running out."

Maria smiled up at him. "They're just all trying to get to the subway first. It's like a race each day—everybody hoping to get a seat."

"Does anybody ever get one?"

She laughed. "Not during rush hour. But every day they still hope it will happen."

He guided her out of the flow, stepped off the sidewalk, and raised one arm. "Let's take a cab," he said. "Then you'll definitely get a seat."

"But it's so expensive," Maria protested.

"It's one of the joys of an expense account. We'll let the paper pay for it."

Wild, maniacal laughter interrupted Burke's words, and he and Maria both turned toward its source. A few feet away stood a tall, painfully thin man. He had tousled blond hair and a glazed look in his eyes. He was in his early twenties, and he was counting a wad of money.

The man laughed again, then reached down, pulled up one trouser leg, and stuffed the money into a loudly patterned sock that rose almost to his knee. Then he stood and smiled insanely.

"Boy, it's great to be out of the state hospital," he shouted. His head jerked erratically, first one way, then the other, as he took in the people rushing by. His movements reminded Burke of a bird. "Boy, it's great to be rich," he shouted again. "It's great to have money to spend on girls." Suddenly he spun around and began to march away in long, striding steps, his arms pumping up and down, his head still jerking from side to side.

After a half dozen steps he spun around again and marched back the way he had come. "Boy, it's great to be out of the state hospital," he shouted. "It's great to have money for girls."

Maria and Burke both started laughing.

"Who *is* he?" Maria said. "Is this *Candid Camera* or something?"

The marching man obviously heard her and stopped dead in his tracks. He turned to her, eyes even wilder. "I am the Sheriff of Nottingham," he said. "And it's *great* to be Sheriff."

He took a step toward them, and Burke held up a hand. "Okay, Sheriff, hold up there."

The man stopped and stared at him, eyes blinking.

"Look," Burke said, "I just saw Robin Hood headed down the block."

The man's eyes widened, and he jumped in place, spinning in the direction Burke had indicated. "Where?" he shouted.

"He just turned the next corner," Burke said. "You can still catch him."

The man raised a hand over his head. "And I will," he said. "It's great being the Sheriff of Nottingham," he added as he began marching away.

Burke and Maria watched him go, both of them laughing

again. Behind them a patrol car moved slowly through the heavy traffic, its siren blaring. Up ahead the marching man heard the sound and spun around. Spotting the patrol car, he raced to the curb, raised his arm, and began shouting: "Taxi! Taxi!"

Burke shook his head and laughed even louder. "I think the Sheriff may be headed back to the Nottingham funny farm," he said. He turned around and raised his own hand. "Taxi!" he shouted. He glanced back at Maria and winked. "It's great to have money to take girls on cab rides," he said.

Maria put both hands over her mouth. "You're as crazy as he is," she said. "You'll get us arrested, too."

"Like hell," Burke said. "The cops wouldn't dare. I'm a big shot. If you don't believe it, just ask Roberto."

A Checker cab pulled up next to them, and Burke quickly opened the door. A Checker was considered a prize catch by city cab riders, its roomy, limo-size rear seat and fold-down jumpseats large enough to accommodate five people or provide sprawling comfort for fewer passengers. Maria slipped into the rear and looked about in amazement as Burke gave the driver her address.

"This is wonderful," she said, the marching man now forgotten. "And some people go to work like this every day." The words were spoken with a sense of awe, as though it were impossible to imagine such a daily amenity.

Burke, who took a cab to work each morning, thought of a line Frank Fabio had dropped several months ago. They had been on their way to a night game at Yankee Stadium and were having trouble finding a cab. Burke had suggested they grab a subway. "I never travel with the unwashed," Fabio had said. Burke had been amused by the line. Now he looked at Maria and recognized the subtle cruelty behind those words.

"You don't use cabs very often, I guess."

Maria averted her eyes, and Burke noticed a slight blush in her cheeks. "I've never been in one before," she said.

Her hand rested on the seat between them, and Burke reached over and covered it with his own. She turned to him and smiled. He thought about his plans for the evening—a return to the records room at University Hospital, followed by a later visit to Whitney's apartment. He decided both could wait a day.

"Why don't we stop in and see Roberto and your mother, and then, if your mother doesn't mind baby-sitting, we'll go out to dinner, maybe take in a movie. There are two new ones out that are supposed to be pretty good. One's called *Jaws*. It's about a shark that eats up half a town. Then there's *One Flew Over the Cuckoo's Nest*. It's based on a very funny book—about a group of lunatics, just like our friend, the Sheriff of Nottingham."

Maria stared at him, her eyes blinking several times in surprise. Burke jumped in before she could speak, suddenly afraid he had overstepped his bounds. "Maybe only dinner, then," he said. "I just want to bring you up to date on the stories and tell you about some new ones we're considering."

"We could eat at home," she said. "You don't have to take me somewhere." She spoke the words shyly, and he realized she had just been overwhelmed by the offer.

"But I'd like to." He still had his hand on top of hers and now gave it a light squeeze. "We could take Roberto with us if you want. The movie might be too late for him, but he'd probably enjoy going out to dinner."

Her eyes brightened, and he could tell she was thinking how much she would like to take her son to a restaurant. He wondered if she ever had.

Then the light in her eyes faded, and he could hear regret in her voice. "I'm afraid it would make him too tired," she said.

"Then you and I should go," he said. "We'll spend time with Roberto. Then, when he goes to bed, we'll go out. I know a very good restaurant in Coney Island. They make the best lobster fra diavolo you'll ever have." He squeezed her hand again. "But we'll have to take another cab," he said.

Maria laughed at the idea. "Two cabs in one day. My mother will think we've lost our minds."

"Three cabs," Burke said. "We have to come home, too."

"Then she'll really think we're crazy."

Burke winked at her. "It's *great* to have money to spend on girls," he said.

Gargiulo's was just a block away from the boardwalk, a fifty-year-old Coney Island landmark, with high ceilings, starched white table linens, and gracious Italian waiters, none of whom were under fifty themselves. The restaurant defied the neighborhood, which had fallen victim to urban blight. Coney Island was no longer considered safe after dark, and the residents of the high-rise apartments that overlooked the water seldom ventured out to enjoy the cool evening breezes along the boardwalk and the beach beyond. Yet Gargiulo's still enjoyed a loyal clientele, made up primarily of native New Yorkers unwilling to give up a favorite eatery. They simply thumbed their proverbial noses at the street hoodlums and drove their cars into the restaurant's well-guarded parking lot.

Burke watched Maria study the menu. She had insisted on changing before they left and was now wearing a simple pale-blue summer dress with a lightweight white cardigan draped over her shoulders. She reminded Burke of a young girl out on a first date. No slave to fashion, Burke was dressed in what he considered his workday "uniform," a sports jacket over a cotton dress shirt minus necktie, jeans, and loafers. On days requiring more decorum he would forgo the jeans for a pair of khakis and don a tie. The five suits that hung in his closet were reserved for upscale dates, weddings, and funerals. It was a very personal sartorial statement, and one that would never get him a job at the *Times*. But he had never wanted to work there anyway. He had always found the irreverent writing style of a tabloid more to his taste.

Maria lowered the menu and gave him a slightly bewildered look. "There are no prices on the menu," she said.

Burke smiled at her. "There aren't supposed to be. The man gets the menu with the prices on it. The woman is not supposed to be concerned with such trivialities." He gave her a small shrug. "I admit it doesn't say much for the Supreme Court's new ruling about the equality of women, but it's considered very elegant."

"Then how is a woman supposed to know if she's spending too much money?"

"She has to watch for subtle hints."

"Like what?"

"Well, the woman orders first, okay? Now, when the man orders, if he suddenly tells her he's on a diet and only orders a salad and a glass of water, that's a good hint. Now, if he falls off his chair and faints, that's an even better one."

Maria was laughing. "Are there more hints?"

"Just one. That's when he excuses himself to go to the restroom—"

"And he never comes back," Maria finished for him.

"You got it."

"Do you have to go to the restroom?"

Burke gave her a sly look. "I'm not sure yet."

Maria was still laughing when the waiter returned to take their orders. What Burke hadn't told her was that he had never known a reporter or editor who had ever paid for a meal at Gargiulo's. They simply left an excessive tip for the waiter. Fearing that he might diminish his invitation to dinner, Burke had actually taken the owner aside when they arrived and explained that he *wanted* a bill for his meal. The owner had stared at him with open incredulity. Then, later—perhaps in appreciation for the miracle he had just witnessed—he sent a bottle of his best wine to the table.

When they had finished their dinners and were lingering over coffee, Burke told Maria about the money that had already started to come in for Roberto's operation. He then explained the advertising campaign the paper would be starting by the end of the week and his interest in doing an article about Maria and her mother.

The idea that a newspaper article might be written about her seemed to fly past Maria. All she had heard was that money was being donated for her son's operation, and she immediately began to question Burke about the amount received and how long it would be before Roberto's surgery could be scheduled.

"I really don't know what's come in so far," he explained. "It's being handled by another department. But I'll try to find out." He saw her chin tremble and realized she was close to tears. He reached out and took her hand. "I'm sure it will take a number of weeks. Maybe even a month or two. But we'll get what we need. I promise you."

A tear coursed down each cheek, and she quickly took her napkin and wiped them away.

"What's important right now is for me to get some more stories ready to run. Just in case I'm sent out of town. The paper would like to run two stories a week to keep the interest alive, so I'd like to have four or five set and ready to go."

Maria seemed to have difficulty forming a reply. She drew a long breath. "Anything," she finally managed. "I'll do anything you need me to do."

He smiled across the table. "You know, by the end of the week Roberto's picture will be on the sides of buses and in subway stations all over the city. He's going to be a very famous little boy." His smile widened mischievously. "He really will be a piece of work then. People will probably want his autograph. I hope he can write his name."

Maria choked back a sob, and tears filled her eyes again. "Yes," she said. "I taught him how to write his name last year."

Burke asked the cab to wait while he walked Maria to her door. Outside her apartment she turned to him, placed her hands on his shoulders, and softly kissed his cheek. "Thank you, Billy," she said. "Thank you for everything."

Burke's hands had gone instinctively to her waist. He stared into her very lovely face and realized how much he wanted to kiss her. "You're welcome," he said. He leaned forward and lightly kissed her forehead. "I'll come by tomorrow, and we can start working on the next few stories."

Maria nodded and stepped back. He detected a reluctance in her movement and again thought about reaching out for her. He knew it was the wrong message to send, but the desire remained.

He was about to turn and leave when she suddenly stepped toward him again and slid her arms around his neck. Her face rose to his, and she kissed him softly, tenderly, and he could feel her body against him and knew instantly just how much he wanted her.

Then she stepped back and opened her door. "Good night, Billy," she said. And before he knew it, she was gone.

Costello's was still a mob scene when Burke walked through the doors at ten-thirty. The East Forty-fourth Street restaurant was the preeminent newspaper watering hole, a raucous, noisy establishment five days a week, with an endless supply of New York reporters and editors and a varied assortment of foreign correspondents. Simply put, it was a boys' club considered a "must stop" for many, and it was steeped in a boozy tradition reflected in every item of its decor. It had a long mahogany bar that ran half the building's length, from the front door to a small scattering of booths and tables at the rear. Festooned behind the bar was an assortment of "historic memorabilia"—as the owner described it—including a walking stick that Ernest Hemingway had once broken over his own head to win a bet with John O'Hara. The walls were decorated with aging penciled cartoons that had been drawn by James Thurber to pay his often-outstanding bar bills, and regulars were invited to add appropriate items to the overall collection with the owner's approval. One *Daily News* reporter had added a stuffed hammerhead shark, allegedly stolen from a Florida hotel. It now hung above the backbar's mirror with a bottle of Harp Ale stuffed into its gaping jaws.

When Burke entered, a contingent of Brit and Aussie correspondents were holding court at the front of the bar, as they did every weekday evening. Tony Rice sat amid the jabbering throng. He let out a welcoming hoot that would have been appropriate had Burke just returned from a long journey. It was followed in kind by the Brits and Aussies.

Burke acknowledged the welcome by patting an arm here, grabbing a shoulder there, then found an empty stool near the bar's center. He ordered a Jack Daniel's and watched in admiration as John, the bartender, filled a rocks glass to the very brim without spilling a drop, then with a sleight-of-hand movement worthy of a well-practiced magician scooped up the twenty Burke had laid on the bar. Winking, he showed Burke the bill he had palmed and offered the warning, "Be alert, my lad. Be alert." It was a demonstration of the talent John reserved for unsuspecting tourists. Another of his tricks involved a serving tray. John would wet the bottom of the tray, then serve a round of drinks by laying the tray atop the target customer's change. When he removed the tray, several bills would be stuck to the bottom, thus beginning their route to John's very deep pockets.

It was said he earned thirty thousand a year in tips and another thirty as a very professional thief.

Burke raised his glass in salute, then took a heavy pull on the amber liquid. It would be a long evening and, he hoped, a mildly drunken one. He felt conflicted by what had happened at Maria's door. He had thought briefly about going to Whitney's apartment but had discarded the idea. Climbing into someone else's bed would not resolve the conflict. He glanced at his drink. And neither would pouring booze down his throat.

A hand slipped around his shoulder, and he turned his head and found Tony Rice grinning at him.

"You're being very unsociable, dear boy," Rice said. "We were hoping for some new blood to buy the next round of drinks. You know how stingy those Aussies can be."

"I thought it was the Brits who were tight with a pound," Burke said.

"Well, that's true, too. In any event, why don't you join us?"

"Not up to revelry, my dear chap," Burke said. "Deep thoughts, worrisome problems abound."

"Ah, let me play mother, then." Rice slid onto a stool next to Burke. "Buy me a scotch and I'll drown you in wisdom."

Burke ordered Rice a drink. He glanced around, looking for Tony's wife.

"Where's the lovely Theona tonight?" he asked.

"Working. Or so she says." Rice said the words with a bitter smile that failed to hide the pain in his eyes.

Theona worked for a high-couture magazine, and several years ago she had become involved in an affair with a fashion photographer. Tony had discovered the infidelity and confided in Burke. Later they had reconciled, but the pain whenever he spoke of her had remained in Tony's eyes. Burke had never told him that he thought the reconciliation had been a mistake. He often wished that he had.

"So, my dear boy, is it work or your love life that has driven you to this moment of despair?" Tony's eyes had softened, and Burke realized he truly wanted to help.

"Bit of both, I'm afraid." He took another sip of his drink, hoping the Tennessee sour mash would burn some clarity into his brain. "It's this story I'm working on. The sick kid. I'm just getting too close to it, too personally involved."

"Ah, that's bad business," Rice said. "Is it the lad you're getting too close to or the mother? I must say she sounds like a rather attractive woman in your stories."

Burke smiled at his perception. "Both," he said. "You know me, Tony. I never go halfway when I'm about to fuck up my life."

"Yes, isn't that true of us all?" Rice put a hand on his shoulder again. "I'm a bad sort to get romantic advice from, as you know. But if it was me, I think I'd do something rather simple."

"What's that?"

"I'd wait."

"Sound advice," Burke teased.

"Yes, I know. But it is good advice, I think." Rice took time to sample his drink, then continued. "The little lad is dying, isn't he?"

Burke felt the words hit, harder than he would have liked. "Yeah. That's the bottom line. Unless he gets that operation— and reasonably soon—he'll die."

Rice nodded. "Then the story has to be paramount. For the child, if for no other reason. And you know how cold and calculating you have to be on any story. You can't let your emotions get in the way if you're going to make it work." He shook his head, almost in wonder, Burke thought. "This is a rare one, Billy. A chance to actually do some good for a change, rather than just pillorying some poor bastard." He turned to Burke, a small smile playing across his lips. "I envy you. Imagine. An opportunity to do some small good, just this once."

Rice looked away and toyed with his glass. "As far as the mother is concerned, I suspect the lady's a bit vulnerable right now. No question about that, eh?" He picked up his drink and downed a fair amount. "I would imagine the child might be vulnerable as well. And you, old boy, are more than a bit vulnerable yourself—somewhat an easy mark for this type of situation." He turned back to Burke now. "You could end up being rather badly hurt if things go awry. And I would hate to see that. You've had enough pain where innocent children are concerned."

"I'll handle it, if I have to. I'm a big boy." Burke could hear the hollow bravado in his words.

"Ah, yes. Aren't we all." Rice pulled back his shoulders and put on a happy, somewhat silly face. It was a self-deprecating gesture, intended to include Burke as well. "Anyway, that's my wit and wisdom for the day. Wait, my dear boy. Get the job done for the lad with as little personal involvement as possible. Then wait another full month after the story is finished. Let everyone get back to their lives. All of you. Then, if you still feel as you do now, pick up the telephone."

Burke stood and finished off his drink, then placed a hand on Tony's arm. "Thanks. It *is* good advice. I hope I have the sense to follow it."

"I do, too." Rice put on the silly face again. "Are you off now?"

Burke nodded. "Home to bed."

"Pity, I thought we'd get thoroughly pissed together."

"Another night," Burke said. "I promise."

"Then I shall sit here and listen to the eminently interesting stories of my fellow countrymen—all of which I heard last night and the night before—while I await the arrival of my loving wife."

Burke ignored the self-mockery in Tony's voice. "Tell Theona I'm sorry I missed her."

"I shall, dear boy. Her disappointment will know no end." He raised a hand to his mouth and offered up a fake yawn. "Now, piss off, dear boy. Be a boring little shit and be off to bed."

{ 15 }

"Mama, I think you lost your mind." Maria tapped the sides of her head with the fingers of both hands. They were speaking in Spanish, as they always did when they were alone, and hand gestures were very much a part of their conversations.

Maria stared at her mother and shook her head. They were in the kitchen, cleaning up the dinner dishes. Maria picked up a plate, held it in front of her, and shook it. "It's crazy. We could end up in jail. Is that what you want?"

Consuelo rolled her eyes. "I told you, Spanish Louie says that won't happen. He says the police are part of it. The people he works for give them money."

"And you believe him? You know who he works for. He works for those gangsters down the block, those men who sit out in front of their social club all day scratching their bellies, waiting for people to bring them money. You want us to work for *them*?"

"Spanish Louie says with the two of us working we can make five hundred dollars a week. Sometimes even more. And we don't have to do nothing but collect people's money and then tell him what they want."

"Five hundred dollars?"

"That's right. And we can put it all toward Roberto's operation. In a month we could have two thousand dollars. Maybe we could go to the doctor then and give him the money, explain how we can give him that much every month and how the newspaper is collecting more, and then he'll say, Okay, I'll do the operation." She reached out and took her daughter's arm. "Then maybe we don't have to wait. We don't have to worry that the money will come too late." She choked on the final words, and Maria turned away, afraid she, too, would begin to cry if she did not.

"Every day I'm scared, Mama. Every day I wake up worried that Roberto will have another attack, and this time they won't be able to help him. But this . . . this . . ."

"So just talk to Spanish Louie. You don't have to say yes. Just talk. He said he read about Roberto in the newspaper, and he wants to help us get the money."

"But it's against the law, Mama."

Consuelo shook her head in disgust. "What law? It's all over the neighborhood. Even the grocery store is part of it. Even the bodega downstairs does it. We can do it, too. Just like all those others. What are the police going to do, arrest the whole neighborhood?"

"I don't know, Mama. What would happen to Roberto if we got arrested?"

"Just talk to Spanish Louie. He'll explain it to you. He says he's at the barbershop every night until seven-thirty."

Maria shook her head. "Billy is coming at eight. You know he has to talk to us about another story he wants to do."

"So it's only a little after seven now. Go see Spanish Louie, and you can be back before he gets here." She shook her daughter's arm. "Just talk to him for Roberto. Talking can't hurt anything."

Maria put her hands on her cheeks and closed her eyes. "All right, I'll talk to him. But I'm not promising anything."

Maria felt a tug at the hem of her skirt. She looked down and found Roberto staring up at her. His eyes seemed sunken and hollow, and his small, heart-shaped face was very pale. She reached down and scooped him up.

"I'm tired, Mama," he said. "I want to go to bed."

"Do you feel okay?" She watched him nod. His small head seemed heavy, almost too much for his thin neck to hold up. "You sure? You sure you feel okay?"

"I'm just tired."

Maria looked at her mother over the child's shoulder as she gently rubbed his back. Her mother drew a long breath, and her eyes seemed leaden with grief. It's almost as though we've already lost him, Maria thought. She hugged the child to her and started toward the bedroom. "I'll tuck you in and read you a story," she said.

"Read the one about the three billy goats," Roberto said, switching to English. "It's my favorite. I like that one the best."

She had been distant and nervous, and Burke wasn't sure why. Perhaps it was that brief flirtation with intimacy the night before, he thought. But that didn't feel right. It had to be something else. He continued to think about Maria as the taxi headed south from Whitney's apartment. At Whitney's insistence they were headed to the Palace, the latest and "hottest" of the upscale discos that were just beginning to flood the city. Burke regretted the promise he had made weeks ago—a *delightful* evening among self-inflated celebrities and the ever-present gaggle of celebrity wannabes.

His thoughts turned back to Maria. She had asked again about the money the *Globe* had collected, and he had told her that slightly more than two thousand dollars had come in as a result of the stories. She had seemed disappointed, and he had assured her it was a good sign—that the paper hadn't even begun its publicity blitz and that money would begin to come in more quickly once it had.

He drew a deep breath and realized he felt guilty taking a night off for this silly trip to the Palace. He had stopped at the hospital before he had gone to Maria's apartment and picked up the medical-school information from the flirtatious Wendy.

Then he had spent an hour going through more records. He began tapping his hands against his knees. You should still be there, he told himself. You should be getting this damned research finished as quickly as possible.

"God, you are so morose. You act like you're on your way to the guillotine."

Burke turned to Whitney and offered her an outrageously false smile. "I think you've hit on something. That's exactly what they need at this joint. A guillotine. I can see it now. Anyone who gets inside and is later deemed unworthy is led up the platform by two vapid models." He sliced the edge of a hand through the air. "Then *wop*, off with his head. The clientele would love it. It would say it all for them." He raised his hands and made imaginary quotes in the air. "'You are not beautiful. Therefore, you are not worthy of life. Therefore, you die.'"

Whitney batted her eyes innocently. "Be careful what you suggest, sweetie. You keep that face on and you might find yourself at the head of the line."

"Never. I'll be with you. That alone will make me beautiful and worthy."

"Then stop being so morose. You're with me, and you're worthy. Make believe you're enjoying it."

He leaned over and kissed her cheek. "I am. And it's not the Palace. I'll survive a night in celebrity heaven. And I'll enjoy being with you."

"Then what is it?"

"It's this damned story."

Whitney laughed at him. "Billy, only *you* could feel that way. Anyone else would kill for this story. Everyone in the newsroom must be green. With all the publicity it's going to generate, you'll be the best-known reporter in the city. If things work out, you might even get a book out of it."

Burke stared out the window. "That's the whole problem."

"What is?"

"All the ifs." He turned back to her. "*If* things work out. *If* I can pull it off. *If* there's enough time to do it. And most of all: *If* that sweet little kid doesn't die before there's enough money to save him."

Whitney rolled her eyes. "God, you're impossible. All you can

control is the work you do. The rest of it is out of your hands."
She reached out and squeezed his hand. "But even if the worst
happens, I think there'd still be enough for a book. One about
poor kids dying or living incapacitated lives because they can't
get medical care. It's still a great story, for heaven's sake." Whitney saw him wince and quickly added, "I mean, no one wants
that to be the end result. Everyone wants this little boy to have
his surgery and get well. But there's also a bigger issue than just
one child. I'm just saying you have to look at it from that per-
spective, too. The newsworthiness of the bigger story."

She was prattling, trying to move beyond the crassness of her
initial statement. Burke looked out the window again. It hadn't
hit him before. That Roberto could become a commodity in all
of it. But it was inevitable. And he wondered if he had known
that all along but had refused to acknowledge it. He turned
back to Whitney.

"I can't look at it that way right now," he said. "I know you're
right. It's the way these things work. I also know that ap-
proaching it that way may be the smart thing to do—some kind
of necessary evil, at least on a personal level. It may even be the
best way to make sure the kid has a real shot at getting the operation he needs." He shook his head. "But right now, for me, if
the kid dies, the story fails. That's the bottom line, the only way
I can look at it. The only way I can approach it. And I guess I'm
saying that's more pressure than I want or need."

Whitney looked away. "Big stories mean big pressure. You
know that as well as anyone."

"Yeah, I know it. But there's a personal pressure in this one."

She turned back and stared at him. Then it seemed to register. "You mean your daughter," she said.

He nodded, displeased that his own child had never entered
her thoughts.

"I hadn't considered that," she said.

The cab pulled up in front of the Palace, a converted first-run
movie theater that still had its massive marquee hanging out
over the sidewalk. It was nearly midnight, but a line of
wannabes still stretched down Fourteenth Street a full block, a
menagerie of outrageously hip costumes and hairdos. Whitney

and Burke exited the cab and walked to the head of the line, where a velvet rope benignly barred entrance to the interior. Behind the rope were two far-from-benign bouncers, each of whom had the body of a professional wrestler. One of the brutes took a step forward and glared at Burke as they approached. Billy removed his press card from an inside pocket and placed it in the bouncer's oversize hand. He had called earlier that evening and had spoken to one of the owners.

"William Burke and Whitney Morgan," he told the bouncer now. "We should be on your list."

As the list was consulted, Burke glanced back at the line. A young woman stood directly behind him, her blond hair so heavily sprayed it stood out in spikes, making her entire head look like a sunburst. The woman—no more than twenty, he guessed—was wearing a flimsy black micro-minidress that barely covered her crotch, cut so low in front that the areolas of her breasts were visible above the fabric. The young man standing beside her had long sideburns and was dressed in a white dinner jacket over a black T-shirt. He had finished off the ensemble with a pair of reflective aviator sunglasses. Billy heard Whitney giggle and turned back. She was staring at the young woman flaunting her areolas.

Whitney leaned in close. "Love the dress," she whispered. "Perfect for taking your tits out for an evening stroll." She giggled again. "She's got so much tissue stuffed in there, they're almost falling out. But I guess they're still not good enough to get her in the Palace." She dropped her voice to a lower register. "It's not nice to fool Mother Nature," she intoned, imitating a popular television commercial, and laughed again. "But there's hope. Even for her." She was whispering again. "I hear that little poof Steve Rubell is turning an old television studio on West Fifty-fourth Street into the disco to end all discos. Maybe Miss Tits can try her luck there."

Whitney was also dressed in a revealing black sheath, although far more modestly cut. Burke, slave to fashion as always, was wearing his "uniform"—houndstooth sports jacket, jeans, and a blue work shirt. He thought, You even left your sunglasses at home. Yet another failure in being hip.

"Go right in, Mr. Burke," the bouncer announced. "The front office put you both on our permanent list."

Burke heard a murmur from the line. Envy? Resentment? Perhaps he was hipper than he thought. Or at least his press card was. He leaned in to Whitney. "Wow," he whispered, "now I can come here every night."

Whitney let out a harsh laugh. "You can even drag Little Miss Tits out of the line and take her in with you. God knows what she might favor you with if you did."

The words were loud enough to reach the line, and Burke winced at the retort: "Hey, fuck you, too." The young woman with the exposed cleavage had not been amused. She reached out and grabbed Whitney's arm. "What makes *you* a celebrity?"

Whitney pulled her arm free and gave her an icy stare. "We're not celebrities, sweetie. We're the press. We *make* people celebrities. And I'm afraid you're not on our list."

The young woman's jaw dropped as Whitney spun away. Burke gave the woman a pained expression, then followed Whitney into the club.

They made their way through the lobby and into what had once been the theater itself. The music and the lights hit them as they entered, the low, staccato beat of a bass guitar in seeming sync with the strobe lights that cut through the cavernous main room. There was a crowded bar to the right—one of five scattered throughout—and the flashes of light made everyone appear to move in near-spastic, jittery jumps and starts. They reminded Burke of the marching man, who was so glad to be out of the state hospital.

At Burke's insistence they went up to the mezzanine, where another, less crowded bar was located and where they could look down on the dancers on the main floor. Whitney grumbled at first, accusing Burke of getting as far away from the dance floor as possible, then became mollified when she realized that the mezzanine was where most of the celebrities gathered—to look down upon the masses. There was also—to Burke's displeasure—a second, smaller dance floor, which Whitney immediately dragged him onto amid a crush of gyrating, sweating bodies, doing the Hustle to the strains of "That's the Way I Like It." But many of the bodies were quite good ones, Burke soon realized, and if he had to suffer the indignity of disco dancing, at least he was doing it among the well-shaped bodies of some very fine-looking models.

Whitney slid herself between Burke and another woman, whose dress was cut so low in back the crack between her buttocks was clearly visible.

"Stare at her ass again and I will hurt you," she said.

"I'm a professional observer," Burke said. "I can't help myself."

"Help yourself or you'll be sleeping in your own bed tonight."

Burke winced at the threat. "Now, *that* would hurt me." He raised his eyes to the ceiling and continued to dance.

The music ended, and they fought their way to the bar as the next song blared from the speakers—Bruce Springsteen's "Born to Run."

"Did I tell you I'm trying to get an interview with him?" Whitney was almost shouting to be heard over the music.

"Who?" Burke shouted back.

"Bruce Springsteen."

Burke made a face indicating he was impressed. Springsteen had been on the cover of both *Time* and *Newsweek*, in the same week, the first time the two newsmagazines had ever run simultaneous cover stories. He was being hailed as "the new Dylan."

"I'm going to slice him and dice him," Whitney called out.

"Why?"

She began to drag him back to the dance floor. When they reached the center, she leaned up close to his ear. "I don't know. There's just something about him that pisses me off." When she pulled away, Burke saw that she was laughing.

{ 16 }

Lenny Twist entered the executive editor's office at nine the next morning. Jim McGowan was seated behind his oversize desk, sipping coffee from a large mug that bore the logo ALL THE NEWS THAT FITS, WE PRINT. The mockery of the *New York Times* slogan was a personal favorite of McGowan's, one he felt befitted the defining difference between the two newspapers—the stuffiness of "The Old Gray Lady" versus the tabloid roguishness of the *Globe*.

Before his rise to managing and then executive editor, McGowan had headed the *Globe's* Washington bureau, and to Twist's mind he had all the intellectual flabbiness inherent in those who spent too many years sucking the federal tit—living off official press releases and news conferences rather than chasing down stories themselves.

"Grab a seat, Lenny. Grab a seat," McGowan bellowed. He

had a hail-fellow-well-met attitude that Twist despised. He was also a burly six-foot-three, which Twist despised even more, and his office wall was cluttered with photographs of McGowan with various presidents and heads of state. There was even a picture of Richard Nixon and Elvis Presley, taken during a 1970 White House meeting, that both men had signed under personal inscriptions to McGowan. Twist envied the photos, so he always concentrated on the ship's clock that also adorned McGowan's wall. The man fancied himself a sailor, and Twist wished his sloop would sink one day and drown the son of a bitch. But not until Twist himself had risen to managing editor and was in line to replace him.

Mitch Coffee, the metropolitan editor, was already seated on the long leather sofa that filled one side of the office, and Twist took a seat beside him. There was an easel set up behind McGowan's desk that displayed the subway, bus, and billboard advertising the *Globe* would launch in two days.

McGowan ran a hand through his graying hair, then pointed toward the display. "Whaddya think?"

"Looks great," Twist said. "How long will they be running?"

"Two weeks, with an option for another week if we get the results we expect." McGowan picked up a donation can and held it up. It had a picture of Roberto Avalon and the inscription, HELP SAVE LITTLE BOBBY.

"Our advertisers are going crazy for this. We'll have them in stores by next week." McGowan grinned at both men. "Everybody wants them, but we're only offering them to stores and restaurants and whatever that advertise in the *Globe*. We're going to run a house ad listing all the advertisers who have them, and we're working up a logo they can put in their own advertising that says they support little Bobby. It's a great public-relations gimmick for everyone who has the donation cans, and a big incentive to advertise for those who don't."

"I love it," Mitch Coffee said. He was a large, flabby man in his late forties with thinning hair, a triple row of chins, and the nervous habit of fluttering his eyebrows up and down as he spoke. "We've got a million Hispanics in this city, and anybody who supports little Bobby is going to be seen as an instant amigo."

"And don't think our advertising boys haven't pointed that out," McGowan said. He folded his arms across his bulky body, and his ruddy complexion seemed to take on a satisfied glow. "This is going to be big—for everybody. Circulation is up, advertising is up, and the publisher is creaming his pants over this." McGowan hesitated and looked at each man in turn. "And that brings me to my main point—and the publisher's one concern. We *do not* want this to be a flash in the pan. We want to milk it for everything we can." McGowan extended both arms in the air. "We're the saviors of this kid. And so are our advertisers. Hell, the longer we run these stories, the stronger that image becomes in the minds of the reading public."

"And it gives us another plus," Twist added. "When we get ready to slam the medical profession for their indifference and greed, they'll be up shit's creek for any comeback. We'll be like Christ tossing the money changers out of the fucking temple."

"Exactly," Coffee said. "It'll be take-no-prisoners time."

"But . . ." McGowan stopped and stared at each of them again. "Timing is everything. We've got to have it all in our pockets—all the evidence to whack them hard when we're ready—so when we're through playing out our string, the rest of it is ready to go."

"Burke's only a few days away from having it all," Twist said.

"That's good. But I don't want to have it too fast either. I know Burke. He gets something, he wants to run with it. If there's any tip-off to these doctors or the hospital, they're going to cut their losses and agree to do this surgery gratis. Then our whole campaign is out the window. These people may be greedy bastards, but they're not stupid."

"No problem," Twist said. "As soon as I'm sure we've got enough, I'll slow him down. I could probably even slow him down now and not risk too much. Right now I've got him doing a half dozen more 'Little Bobby' stories so we have them in-house as we need them."

Coffee raised a finger, indicating an idea. "Maybe we should get some more people on the story. It might be easier to slow things down if we're dividing it up."

"Won't work," Twist said. "Burke's already running a scam on the hospital that's got him into their records. I can't send somebody in to replace him on that without risking that access. I could replace him on the stories about the kid. But I haven't got anybody as good as he is for that type of thing. Besides, he's already got the kid's confidence and the mother's."

"But can you control him?" McGowan asked. "I don't want him turning into a loose cannon on this thing. We can't afford that."

Twist gave him a reassuring smile. "Don't worry." He held out an upturned fist. "I've got his short hairs right here. Burke needs to work in New York. And as good as he is, he knows I can make this the only game in town. If we want it, he'll do it."

McGowan glanced at Coffee. "You agree, Mitch?"

Coffee nodded. "I think he's controllable. Five years ago I wouldn't have thought so. But today . . . yes."

"Okay, then we're agreed. We orchestrate." McGowan pointed a finger at Twist. "And you're the conductor, Lenny. Play us a tune the publisher can dance to."

Twist grinned at him. "Just watch my baton, Jim."

{ 17 }

Three days later

"Wounded Knee? Again?"

"Actually it's in Oglala, about thirty miles from Wounded Knee. But it's still on the Pine Ridge Reservation, and it's the biggest story in the country. And come hell or high water, I want you on it."

Burke stared across Twist's desk. "Lenny, this is going to take me away from the 'Little Bobby' story for at least a week. Maybe longer. And I'm close to tying it all up. Really close."

"I'm aware of that. I'm also aware that two FBI agents were gunned down by some renegade Indians, and you've got the best contacts on this paper with the Bureau." Twist glared at him. "You also covered the Wounded Knee siege in '73, so you know the area and have contacts with some of the Indians there. So don't argue with me."

Burke shook his head. "Look, Lenny, Pine Ridge is the second-largest Indian reservation in the country. It's fifty miles by a hundred miles, twice the size of goddamn Delaware. The Indians who did this could be anywhere by now. And even if they're not, even if it turns into another siege, you won't need me *there*. When I was at Wounded Knee, they kept us behind barricades for seventy-one days. Nobody got within two miles of the action. Hell, you can send *anybody* to sit behind a barricade and go to the Bureau's daily press conferences, and I can work the phones from here with my sources. You'll still get the same stuff, and I can stay on top of the 'Little Bobby' story at the same time."

Twist jabbed a finger toward Burke's face. "You're gonna sit behind those barricades, if it comes to that. Period. No more arguments. Got it?"

Burke nodded. "Yeah, I've got it."

Twist sat back in his chair. "Good. Now, you know the Indian lawyers who handled the Wounded Knee trial, right?"

"Yeah, I know them. They work out of the American Indian Movement office in Minneapolis."

"Good. Get on the phone with them and update tomorrow's story with whatever they give you." Twist paused to glare at him again. "And don't tell me it's the same kind of phone work you can use to handle the rest of the story. I've already heard that, and I don't give a shit. You got that?"

"I got it."

Twist sat forward and hunched over his desk. "Good. After you get what you can out of Minneapolis, make your Bureau contacts and set yourself up for South Dakota. I want you there tonight in plenty of time to file something before the last deadline."

Burke let out a long breath. "I was supposed to see my daughter today at the hospital in Westchester. Do I have time for that?"

A small smile played across Twist's mouth. "Your plane leaves for Pierre, South Dakota, at four. You get your phone calls made and file your update, I don't care what the hell you do. Just make sure you're on that plane. Tony Rice is going out there with you. He'll do the color on the dead FBI agents. There's also a dead Indian. That'll be part of his piece, too. Your job is whatever action is taking place and whatever you can find that ties this thing directly in to Wounded Knee." Twist began tapping his fingers against the desk, thinking with them. "What were the names of those two Indians—the ones the feds prosecuted after Wounded Knee?"

"Dennis Banks and Russell Means," Burke said. "The charges were dismissed after the judge found out two FBI agents gave false testimony."

Twist nodded. "If they're back on the reservation, find them. Find out if they were involved in this."

"Am I there for the duration?" Burke asked.

Twist sat back in his chair again. "I'll try to get you back here as soon as I can. But not until I'm sure we've gotten everything out of you and your sources." He held up a hand to ward off a complaint that was not forthcoming. "And don't ask me how long that will be. Just plan for at least a week. Two at the outside if it works out that way." He stared Burke down. "You've got—what?—five stories written and ready to run on the 'Little Bobby' thing?"

"That's right."

"And a couple more days on the investigation?"

"Yes."

"Then you've got nothing to worry about. We'll handle anything that breaks from here, and it'll still run under your byline. The story's still yours, but this is breaking news and you're still a fucking newspaperman. So just do your job and trust me."

Burke bit back a reply. "All right, Lenny. I'll see you in a week."

"Or two."

Burke nodded. "Or two."

Mitch Coffee entered Twist's office five minutes after Burke had left. The metropolitan editor dropped his bulk into the chair Burke had vacated and fluttered his eyebrows in anticipation. "So how'd Billy-boy take the news?" he asked.

"He was pissed. Tried to talk me out of it," Twist said. "Fat fucking chance. What an asshole."

"But a talented asshole," Coffee suggested.

"Yeah, well, it's a talent I can do without," Twist snapped.

Coffee raised an eyebrow. "You plan to get rid of him?"

'The thought's crossed my mind."

"He pulls off this 'Little Bobby' story, he could end up with a Pulitzer in his pocket. He won't be easy to dump then."

Twist folded his hands in front of him. "The Pulitzer nominations won't go in until next December. And I don't think Mr. Burke will be around here then. So we won't be nominating a reporter—just the paper. Hell, that's the gold medal, the biggie. That's the one we want anyway. And I'm not interested in advancing Mr. Billy fucking Burke's career. Or whatever's left of it."

Coffee let out a snorting laugh. "Lenny, you are not a nice person."

"Yeah, I know. Ain't it a bitch?"

Julia was walking across the parking lot when Burke arrived at the Westchester hospital, and she stopped and waited for him as he parked his car. A smile formed as he approached her, his very first of what was already a very long day.

"You look battered," she said when he reached her. "Bad day?"

"Insane. I have to be on a plane for South Dakota in three hours."

"The FBI agents? I heard about it on the car radio."

"Yeah. Wounded Knee redux. I should just get an apartment out there and take up residency. I could become chief of the Wounded Knee bureau. Pardon the pun."

"It's a good story." She was trying to be positive, helpful.

"I've already got a good story. Except now I can't finish it for two more weeks."

"Ah. Have you told Roberto's mother that you're going out of town?"

Burke nodded. "I stopped by the place she works and caught her on her lunch break. God, the look on her face. It made me feel like I was abandoning her child. Just leaving him to die."

"Billy, we both know that's not the case. It's just the way the business works."

They started toward the hospital entrance. "She's scared to death, Julia. She tries not to show it, but the woman's scared every day. Her mother told me how she gets up during the night to check on the kid. Just to make sure he's still breathing. God, can you imagine what it must be like? Wondering each day if your child is still going to be alive? Wondering if this is going to be the day his weak little heart gives out?" He shook his head. "Christ, we've been through a lot with Annie. But at least we don't wake up every morning wondering if it's our last day with her or if the telephone is going to ring at work so someone can tell us that she's gone."

Julia took his hand. "You really like her, don't you?"

There was a hint of concern in Julia's voice, but Burke didn't notice it.

"I love her courage," he said. "I've met a lot of courageous people in this job, and a lot of cowards, too. But I haven't met many as brave as she is." He thought about what he had just said, then added, "Almost all the brave ones I've met have been women."

Julia squeezed his hand. "Do you need someone to stay in touch with her while you're gone?" she asked. "Because if you don't have someone else, I could do that for you."

They had just entered the hospital lobby, and Burke stopped and turned to her. He had thought about something similar, had even considered asking Whitney to give Maria an occasional phone call, just so she'd have some contact with the *Globe* while he was away. He had rejected the idea. Watching her act out at the Palace, he had seen something in Whitney he had never recognized before. She was simply aloof to other people's needs, to their hopes, their frailties. Just too self-absorbed to understand what the average person—let alone a Maria Avalon—went through each day.

"Would you do that?" he asked.

"Of course I would. If she wouldn't mind." The hint of concern was back in Julia's voice again, but again Burke missed it.

"I'm sure she wouldn't. Hell, the woman's ready to accept help from wherever she can get it. I just couldn't think of anyone at the paper who I could trust to give her what she needs."

"I don't have to tell her I'm your wife," Julia said. "I can just tell her you asked me to look in on her and help any way I can."

Burke picked up on the underlying concern now. It made him wonder how Maria would react to his wife's showing up.

But she already knew he was married and separated. And he had told her his relationship with his wife was still a good one—just one that didn't allow them to be together. And it also might help. It might enforce the distance he needed to have with her. "I don't think your being my wife will matter," he said. "There's nothing going on between us besides the boy and the story."

Julia nodded, more to herself than Burke. "I have to admit I wondered about that," she said. "I saw the picture that ran with your last story. She's a beautiful woman." She released his hand. "And she's alone. And she has no one to help her."

"Yeah," Burke said. "She's all of that." He took her arm and started toward the bank of elevators that would take them to their daughter. "But now she has you," he added.

﹛ 18 ﹜

South Dakota, two weeks later

The message from Twist was terse with an undercurrent of anger. Get back to New York. We've got trouble. Burke had been in the field and had gotten the message when he returned to his hotel. He called the city desk, but Twist had already left for the day. He tried Frankie Fabio at home, only to be told by his wife that he was out "doing something for the paper."

Finally, fearing something had happened to Roberto, he called Julia.

"Nothing's wrong as far as I know," Julia said. "I had lunch with Maria two days ago, and everything seemed fine. She was really excited about all the advertising on Roberto. God, Billy, it's all over the city. They even started some radio ads this week." She started to laugh. "The little boy is flying high. People have stopped them on the street and asked him to sign their newspapers."

"So nothing's wrong with the boy?"

"As far as I know, nothing," Julia said. "I went out there two weeks ago and met the boy, and last Sunday she brought him into the city and we went to the Central Park Zoo. He got overtired and had a little tantrum when it was time to leave. But that's what five-year-olds do. Billy, I'm sure she would have called me if anything was wrong. I think she really trusted me, was even grateful to have another woman, another mother her own age, to talk to. Do you want me to call her?"

"No. Let's not get her all worried that something's wrong," Burke said. "If it's got anything to do with the story, it's probably on the other end—the doctors or the hospital. I'm heading for the airport now, and I'll be back at the paper in the morning." He hesitated a moment. "Jesus, Julia, you went all out on this. I really appreciate it."

Julia was quiet for several seconds. "She's a lovely woman, Billy. It's easy to see why you're so concerned." She paused another beat. "And the little boy . . . well, he's just wonderful. A little devil at times, but wonderful. Maybe I'll call her, just to say hello. I won't say anything about any problem. If there is anything wrong with the boy, I'll have you paged at the airport. Which airline are you flying?"

Burke told her, said he'd call again when he got back to New York, then telephoned for flight information. There was only one flight available, a hodgepodge of connections with layovers in St. Louis and Chicago, but it would get him into New York early tomorrow morning. He threw his things together and headed for the airport.

Burke got back to his apartment at seven the next morning. He showered and changed, then tried Frankie again a little after eight, only to find he had already left for the paper. Burke headed there himself, arriving just before nine.

Twist and Fabio were huddled in Twist's office when Burke arrived. Spotting him through the glass partition, Twist waved him in.

"Well, your sweet little *mamacita* fucked us four ways from Sunday," Twist snapped as Burke entered.

"What are you talking about?"

"She got busted," Frankie said. "Night before last." He was fighting a smile, trying to keep Twist from seeing it.

"Busted? What the hell for?"

"She was running numbers for some Mameluke in the Colombo family," Frankie said. "I gather her mother was doing the same thing."

"And you didn't know," Twist snapped. He glared at Burke. "Or did you?"

Frankie saw Burke flush with anger and immediately jumped in. "Wait a minute. Wait a minute. She's only been doing it for a little over two weeks. Billy was out in Indian country. She probably started right around the time he left."

Frankie had an uncle who was supposedly a capo in another crime family, and his contacts within the mob were as good as anyone not directly involved could get. Twist stewed for several seconds, then turned his glare on Burke again.

"Did you know, or didn't you?" he snapped.

Burke returned the glare. "Of course I didn't know. I would have stopped it if I had."

"If I find out different . . ." Twist let the sentence, and the threat it implied, die.

Burke ignored him and turned to Fabio. "How bad is it?" he asked.

"We're fixing it," Frankie said. "I spent last night with the Brooklyn DA. He's moaning and groaning. He's up for reelection this fall, and this bust is a big plus for him."

"So we may have to endorse the son of a bitch," Twist snapped.

"We endorsed him last time," Burke snapped back.

"But it was *our* fucking choice!" Twist's voice had elevated to a shout.

"Hold it, guys. Hold it a minute," Frankie said. He held up a hand, then turned his attention back to Burke, effectively cutting Twist out. "The DA hasn't got squat. Just her." He let out a small laugh. "They leaned on her for a couple of hours at Central Booking. Tried to get her to tell them who she was working for. But the broad was smart. She kept her mouth shut. She called her mother, and her mother called the desk. They got me at home, and I went to the precinct, did a little shuffle, and got her released." He shrugged, minimizing his own efforts. "When the assistant DA found out how much we had invested in this woman, he called his boss, and they agreed to cut her loose. I promised I'd try to get her to talk to them." He shrugged again, made a face indicating how much bullshit was involved in the promise. "Then I met with the DA yesterday."

"So he doesn't know about the Colombo family?" Burke asked.

"Oh, he knows," Frankie said. "Nobody does numbers in that neighborhood who isn't working for them. But he doesn't *know* know." Frankie shifted his weight in his chair. "I did a little checking with my own sources, and she was working for this asshole named Spanish Louie Torricelli. Straight out of the Fifth Avenue Social Club."

"Carmine 'The Snake' Persico's place."

"That's right. The Snake still runs the Colombo outfit from prison, and Torricelli is one of his buttons. He handles all the spic numbers action in the neighborhood and all the way out to Bay Ridge. My people tell me that Torricelli's mother was a greaser—Puerto Rican or Dominican or something—and that's his in with the Hispanics and how he got his moniker. I also gather that the grandmother called Spanish Louie after she called us. Because a few minutes after I got to the Seven-eight, one of their lawyers shows up." Frankie lifted his chin, offered up his "you're full of shit" look. "I told him to take his briefcase the fuck out of there, that I was handling it. That's all we needed, some fucking mob mouthpiece showing up to represent our mother of the fucking year.

"Anyway, I take him aside, let him know who I am, and tell him we got a joint interest here. I tell him not to worry, our mutual client is not about to rat anybody out, and I'm already working with the DA to have the charge disappeared." Frankie shrugged. "He doesn't like it, but he sees the sense in letting us do our thing first."

"And the DA doesn't know anything about the grandmother being involved, too?" Burke asked.

"No. Maria told me about that when I drove her home." He leaned forward, his own stare hard now. "And I gotta tell you, Billy, I laid into this woman pretty hard. I let her know, we can't fix this, she can kiss all our help good-bye, that we kiss her off like she never was."

"Which, of course, we can't do," Twist snapped. "Not without looking like the biggest bunch of assholes in the newspaper business."

Frankie raised his hand again. "Anyway, it's not all disaster. When I was driving her home, she told me all about it. Apparently this moron, Spanish Louie, approaches the grandmother a couple of weeks ago." Frankie started to laugh. He shook his head. "He tells her how he read about her kid in the newspapers." Frankie laughed again and pointed a finger at Burke. "Your fucking stories," he said. "Anyway, he tells her he's touched by her problem, wants to help her, and says she and her daughter can make a couple of yards each month working for him. Maria says they knew it was wrong—that she really didn't want to do it—but they figured they could start giving this Dr. Bradford the money on account and get the operation done sooner." He shook his head again. "They gave him the first payment two days ago. A thousand clams. And this Bradford, he scarfs it up, no questions asked, except how often they can make that kind of payment."

Frankie held out his arms. "So if worse comes to worst, at least we have a story we can peddle that doesn't make her look too bad. I mean, every fucking store and barbershop in that neighborhood takes action. It's not like she was moving heroin or something."

"It's goddamn bad enough," Twist snapped.

Burke shook his head. "Yeah, it is," he said. He stared at Twist. "And it also stinks that this woman has to resort to this kind of thing to try to save her kid's life."

Fabio pointed a finger at Burke before Twist could respond. "That's the angle, my troop. If we need it, that's the fucking angle." He turned to Twist and shrugged. "Hey, it's better than a sharp stick in the eye, right?"

Twist glowered at Fabio. "Yeah, it's terrific, Frankie. And what if the *Post* or the *News* start digging? What if some clown at the *Times* finds out the woman's husband was a stone fucking junkie?"

"Hey, when it comes to cops and crooks, those guys at the *Times* couldn't find their dicks with both hands," Fabio said.

Twist ignored him and turned to Burke. "Did you ever check the husband for a record?" he snapped.

"Yes, I did," Burke said. "He was never busted. At least not here in the States."

"Did you check Puerto Rico?"

Burke looked down at his shoes. "No."

"Do it!" Twist ordered. "Get one of your asshole buddies in the FBI to check him out. I don't want any more fucking surprises. Understood?"

"I'll do it this morning," Burke said.

"That's great, Billy." Sarcasm dripped from Twist's words. "And after you do that little thing, then you go see little *mamacita*. You lay it all out for her again. You make *sure* she understands we have one more problem and we kiss her ass good-bye. You tell her she so much as farts in public, she should turn on her goddamn radio and listen to her son's name disappear. You tell her she can watch the goddamn subways and buses and see how fast his picture can vanish." He drew a deep, angry breath. "Then, when you're sure this stupid cunt understands, then you go see this Spanish Louie, and you make sure *he* understands we're taking care of things. You also tell him this woman doesn't work anymore. You tell him she does, and she gets busted again"—he jabbed a finger into his own chest— "that *we* tell the DA everything *we* know. And you do all this today. Understood?"

"Hey, wait a minute," Frankie said. "Billy can't go busting into their clubhouse and start giving orders." He let out a laugh. "I mean, there's a funeral parlor right next door. Billy goes in there and pulls that shit, he's gonna find himself trying on one of their goddamn coffins."

Twist glared at Fabio. "I don't care how he does it. He can take this asshole out for a cup of coffee. He can lick his goddamn ear. He can give him a fucking blow job. But I want him *told*."

"Okay, okay," Fabio said. "I'll go out there with him after we put the first edition to bed. I'll make a phone call and set it up so he knows we're coming. We'll take care of it." He turned to Billy and shook his head. "We'll do it so we know you're gonna come back alive," he said.

When he left Twist's office, Burke called Dezi at the FBI and asked for the record check in Puerto Rico. Then he called Julia. "I know," she said. "Maria told me when I reached her last night. She's just sick about the whole thing. And she's scared to death about what it will mean as far as the paper is concerned. I tried to get you at the airport, so you could call her, but your flight had already left." She paused. "Billy, they're not going to turn their backs on her because of this, are they?"

"They're close," Billy said. "If Twist could find a way to do it without looking like a fool, he'd dump her like last week's laundry. The only thing she's got going for her is that it would be a black eye for him with the publisher and everybody else down the line. That and the fact that nobody else has picked up on it."

"You think he's told them? The higher-ups, I mean."

"I don't know. He could be screwed if he does. This was his baby from the start. And he could be screwed if he doesn't and it all comes out later."

"He can always blame you," she said.

Billy grunted agreement. "Yeah, there's always that. I'm sure he's got that little plan tucked away in his hip pocket. But he also wants this Pulitzer Prize he thinks he can finally win. I think he might be willing to roll the dice. He pulls it off, his future is pure gold."

"God, I hate to say it—or even think it—but I hope the little weasel comes down on that side of it." She paused a moment. "What do you have to do now?"

Burke told her.

"God, he wants you to confront the Mafia?"

"Hey, if everything works out, he gets his story and he gets rid of me, too. What could be better? But don't worry. Frankie is going with me. I'll come back in one piece."

"It still sounds crazy."

"Just par for the course, that's all."

"Billy?"

"Yeah?"

"When you see Maria, don't be too hard on her. She's really scared. And she was only doing what she thought she had to do."

"I know that."

"Try to think of what you or I would do if we thought we could help Annie."

"I will. I promise, I will."

"And, Billy?"

"What?"

"When you're finished, stop by my apartment and let me know what happened."

"It will be late."

"That's all right. I want to make sure you're still alive."

Fabio and Burke entered the Fifth Avenue Social Club a few minutes after seven. Frankie was in full swagger, playing his Don Cheech role to the hilt. Burke followed like a bodyguard, after being told to "keep your mouth shut and don't offend anybody."

The interior of the club was dimly lit. A long bar took up one wall, with a scattering of occupied stools. A half dozen tables sat opposite, only two of which were being used. It was an exclusively male domain, with ages ranging from thirty to well past sixty, and the members were dressed in everything from flamboyant sports shirts to sweat-stained T's to rumpled dress shirts to the occasional badly cut suit. Two wore hats. There were about fourteen in all, and most had espresso cups before them, mixed in with an occasional shot glass or frosted mug of beer. The majority of the men were overweight, a few slightly emaciated, and taken as a whole they seemed indistinguishable from a gathering at the local unemployment office. They were gangsters as the public never envisions them, a collection of down-at-the-heels former street punks who did the bidding of a handful of bosses who kept everything but the loose change for themselves. Collectively a sorry-looking lot. Dangerous? Very. Intelligent? Hardly. They were a sad breed, Burke thought, men who had grown up on street corners telling themselves they were tougher and smarter than everyone else, and who had ended up with little more than this.

A thirtyish hulk with heavy shoulders, thick arms, and a protruding belly approached them as they entered. He had slicked-back dark hair and long sideburns and wore a flowered polyester sports shirt, the top three buttons undone, exposing three chins and a gold crucifix that lay against a hairy chest.

"This is a private club. You got business here?" he asked. His voice was gravelly—practiced to sound that way, Burke thought—like something out of *The Godfather*.

"We got an appointment with Louie Torricelli," Frankie said. "A call was made." He was giving the man his "you're full of shit" stare.

The man swiveled at the waist and turned his head toward the tables behind him. "Hey, Louie, you expectin' somebody?"

"Yeah, it's okay, Rocco."

Burke watched a short, fat man rise from a table. He was wearing a badly wrinkled sharkskin suit, no tie, and a straw fedora. He waddled as he walked toward them, and Burke noticed that the bottom button of his shirt was missing, showing off a slightly soiled undershirt.

"I'm Louie Torricelli. You Frank Fabio?" he asked when he reached them.

"Yeah. Nice to meet you," Frankie said.

Torricelli turned his eyes to Burke. "You must be Burke, huh? Hey, I read your stories. Nice. Very nice."

"Thanks," Burke said. "Can you spare us a few minutes?"

Torricelli spread out his hands in a benevolent gesture, like the pope granting an audience. Burke noticed he hadn't shaved that morning. "Sure. Sure," Torricelli said. "Let's take a walk."

Frankie and Burke followed him outside.

On the sidewalk Torricelli stopped to light a cigarette. "It's better out here," he said. "The boss, he don't like strangers inside, you know. Like it's a private club, *capisce*?"

"It's not a problem," Frankie said. "We appreciate you taking the time."

"Let's get some coffee. There's a nice little place down the street," Torricelli suggested.

The "nice little place" turned out to be a hole-in-the-wall coffee shop with grimy counters and the smell of month-old grease. They took a table in the rear with an incongruous "reserved" card set out on the top. Torricelli swept the card out of the way and ordered three coffees.

"You guys hungry?" he asked. "They got great cannoli here. Make 'em right in the kitchen." He eyed Frankie. "Just like your grandmother's. You can count on it."

"No thanks," Frankie said. "Just coffee is fine."

Torricelli turned to Burke, playing the benevolent host. "You?" he asked.

"No thanks," Burke said.

Torricelli shrugged, resigned to their error. "You should take some home," he added. "You'll thank me." He folded his hands in front of him. "So what can I do for you guys?"

Frankie folded his own hands, matching Torricelli. "We have a problem," he said.

"So I hear." Another shrug.

"But nothing so bad it can't be fixed," Frankie added.

"That's good to hear. Very good."

"But to fix it, and keep it fixed, we need you to do us a favor," Frankie said.

"If I can, of course."

"It's about this Maria Avalon. There are some people at the paper who are very pissed about what happened to her," Frankie began.

"They're pissed at *me?*" Torricelli had unfolded his hands and placed the fingers against his chest to emphasize the injustice of the suggestion.

"Hey, you know and I know you were just trying to do the right thing," Frankie said. "But these people, who are my bosses"— Frankie shrugged in a "What can I do?" gesture—"they have no fucking idea how a neighborhood works. You understand? All they can see is they've got a lotta clams invested in helping this poor little kid, and how everything is gonna go down the toilet if word gets out his mother was doing this thing she was doing."

Torricelli held up both hands, palms out. "Hey, I understand. But *you* gotta understand that I'm not saying this lady was workin' for me or nobody else. You got that? What I'm saying here is I was just doin' the right thing, you know? Just seein' that a few coins found their way to her purse. You got that?" He offered up another pope-like shrug. "Hey, I'm the lady's bene-factor here. That's all. It's the cops are making it something else. They wanna make this some big Cosa Nostra thing. These cops got Cosa Nostra comin' out their asses, you know?"

"Hey, I understand," Frankie said. "I grew up on Mulberry Street. I know how they think."

"I know you do. Hey, I know your uncle—I mean, like, I met him this one time—and I got a lotta respect for him. You tell him I said that."

"I will," Frankie said. "He already told me you were a man I could do business with."

"Hey, that's good to hear. Very good." He shifted his weight—pleased by Frankie's bullshit, Burke thought. "But what about these bosses of yours at the paper?" he asked. "Are they gonna be, uh, reasonable about this thing?"

Frankie inclined his head. "Hey, I gotta be honest with you. Their first reaction was they're gonna throw this woman to the wolves and turn everything over to the DA."

Torricelli shook his head. "Oh, that would be a bad thing. A very bad thing."

"That's what I told them," Frankie said. "Hey, I had to explain the way the neighborhood works, you know? But now they understand. So they had me meet with the DA, and I explained the situation—about our *personal* interest in all this. And he's willing to take a pass this time if the paper does him a little favor."

Torricelli smiled and nodded. It was the way the world worked, the gesture said.

"And this woman," Frankie continued. "She's a stand-up broad. She kept her mouth shut when the cops leaned on her, and she understands from *me*"—Frankie tapped his finger against his chest—"that she's gotta keep her mouth shut from now on. *Capisce?*"

"Hey, that's only the right thing," Torricelli said. He took a sip of his coffee. "But you said you needed something from me. It sounds like everything is all taken care of."

Frankie smiled. "It is. But we gotta make sure it stays that way. You know what the fucking cops are like—a fucking dog with a bone, you understand?"

"Always. They're fucking mongrels."

"So what we need is to be sure this lady doesn't work for anybody anymore." Frankie shrugged again. "I mean, nothing that's gonna give us a repeat of this unfortunate situation." He paused and stared Torricelli. "Hey, there's only so many times we can fix things up with the DA, am I right?"

"Absolutely."

Frankie tapped the side of his nose and winked, indicating a secret kept. "So what we need from you is some assurance this lady isn't going to work for any*body*, any*place*, any*time*, any*more*. Can you do that for me? As a personal favor?"

Torricelli made another benevolent gesture with his hands. "Hey, consider it done. Like I said, I don't know nothin' about her workin' for nobody. But I'll pass the word. Anybody wants to help this lady and her kid, they should take the coins from their own pockets."

"That's beautiful," Frankie said. "I'll give them the word back at the paper. As long as they've got that assurance, I can promise you nobody will do anything foolish."

"Hey, you tell 'em they got my word on it. It's in the bank, *capisce?*"

Outside the coffee shop Torricelli was all bonhomie. He placed an arm on Frankie's shoulder and pointed to a dark-green, one-year-old Cadillac parked across the street. "Just picked up that baby the other day," he said. "Like sittin' in your fuckin' livin' room when you drive it."

"Beautiful," Frankie said. "I always wanted a Caddy."

"Hey, you want one, you let me know. Maybe somethin' can be worked out."

"Hey, I'll let you know," Frankie said.

Torricelli shook hands with Frankie and Burke, then headed back to the social club. Burke and Fabio went around the corner, where Frankie's Cadillac was parked.

"What are you going to do with two Caddies if he finds one for you?" Burke teased.

"Hey, I got a two-car garage. I can always fit in another one," Fabio said.

Burke shook his head and laughed. "Where does a down-and-out stiff like that end up with a Caddy? A shylock?"

"No, no, no, no," Frankie said. "That clown didn't pay more than five hundred clams for that car."

"How's that?" Burke asked.

"It's simple," Frankie said. "They wait for some car to show up at one of the junkyards the mob owns. A Caddy, a Lincoln, whatever. Then, if the engine's in good shape, they yank it, along with the door plates that have the VIN numbers on them. Then

they get a couple of kids to go out and steal an identical car—
same make, model, color, year, the whole thing. Then they
switch the engines and the VIN plates, and shazam, they got
themselves a new car that they bought from a junkyard with a
legal title and everything. It's simple."

"Fucking wiseguys," Burke said. He shook his head again.
"Hey, they still gotta come up with the five hundred clams.
And for most of them that's a fucking stretch." He paused a moment and smiled. "But, you know, there's something you gotta
ask yourself."

"What's that?"

Fabio waved his arm, taking in the neighborhood. "You got
all these young, upwardly mobile assholes living here now,
right?"

"Right."

"How many of them went to this woman with any kind of offer of help?" Frankie gave Burke a small shrug, then climbed
into his car and lowered the window. "Speaking of which, you
going to see the Avalon woman now?" he asked.

"Yeah. She's right up the street. I called earlier and told her
I'd be stopping by to talk."

"You give it to her straight," Frankie said. "One more time
and it's bye-bye. You got it?"

"I'll tell her."

"Make sure she understands." He held his thumb and index
finger an inch apart. "Twist is this close to pulling the plug to
save his own ass." He paused a beat. "On *both* of you, my
troop." He raised his eyebrows and gave Burke a long stare. "He
needs a scapegoat, guess who's it?"

"I never doubted it for a minute," Burke said.

"That's good. Because if this crap happens again, even I won't
be able to save your ass."

Maria opened the door to Burke's knock. She looked at him,
then at the small gift-wrapped parcel in his hand. She drew a
deep breath, then lowered her eyes. "Come in, Billy," she said.

Maria's mother was seated on the sofa with Roberto on her
lap. The child wiggled free at the sight of Burke.

"Billy! Billy!" he shouted. The boy started toward him, slower than Burke had seen him move before, and he stepped quickly toward him and picked him up.

"Hey, it's the Piece of Work. *¿Qué pasa?*"

Roberto hugged him, then pulled back and stared expectantly in his face. "Mama said you were with the Indians. Did you see Indians?"

"I did," Burke said. "A lot of Indians."

"Were they riding horses and have bow and arrows? Did they have feathers and stuff?"

"Most of them ride in pickup trucks now," Billy said. "And they wear the same clothes as everybody else." Roberto gave him a disbelieving look, and Burke decided not to rain on his fantasy. "Sometimes they wear feathers, mostly for special ceremonies and stuff," he said. "And I did see some with horses."

Roberto smiled happily. "Mama said some of them got into trouble."

"Yes, that's true. But it was only a few of them. Most of them are good, just like everybody else."

"Did they shoot some soldiers?"

"Hey," Burke said, "you've been watching too much TV, haven't you? I thought you promised me you weren't going to watch TV all the time."

Roberto buried his face in Burke's shoulder and giggled. Burke put him down and knelt before him. The child noticed the gift-wrapped parcel and grinned. "Is that for me?" he asked.

Burke looked down at the gift. "It says here it's for the Piece of Work, so it must be for you."

Burke handed it over and watched as the boy tore it open. It was a T-shirt bearing the image of an Indian in full headdress, the words INDIAN COUNTRY printed beneath. Roberto held it up for his mother.

"*¡Mira, Mama! Mira!*" he exclaimed.

Maria came and knelt in front of him. She took the shirt and held it up against his chest, then turned to Burke. "It's the right size," she said. "Thank you, Billy." Her eyes held his. They seemed hesitant, almost as though she expected him to start shouting at her.

"Can I put it on? Can I put it on?" Roberto begged.

"You have to go to bed now. You can put it on in the morning."

"Can I wear it to bed? Please, Mama. Can I, please?"
She pulled the child to her and hugged him. "Yes, you can
wear it to bed. But you have to go to bed right now, okay?"
"But I want to see Billy," Roberto protested. His face formed
a pout, testing her.
"You already saw him." She turned to Burke. "He's been waiting up to see you," she explained. Then back to Roberto, "But
now it's bedtime. Billy will come back again." She turned back
to Burke, her eyes imploring him to say he would. "You'll come
back, won't you?"
Burke nodded. "Of course I will." He reached out and ruffled
the boy's hair. "We still have lots of stories to write." He held the
boy at arm's length. "My wife tells me that people have been
asking you for your autograph. Is that true?"
Roberto's face broke into a broad smile, and his eyes filled
with delight. He nodded vigorously. "My picture's even on the
subways and the buses. I'm a big shot," he said. "Just like you."
Burke laughed. "Okay, big shot." He brought his face close to
the boy's. "But now you have to do what Mama says. Okay?"
"When are you coming back?" the boy demanded, still pushing it.
"Probably tomorrow." He pulled Roberto to him and gave
him a hug. "Now, go to bed, before you get me in trouble," he
whispered. "I'm glad you like your T-shirt."
Roberto kissed him on the cheek and whispered "Thank you"
in Burke's ear. The small, innocent gesture sent a chill down
Burke's spine.
Maria gathered up the boy and took him into the adjoining
bedroom. Burke turned to the boy's grandmother.
"He looks weaker to me," he said. "Has he been ill?"
Consuelo gave him the same shame-filled look Maria had
when he arrived, then looked away. "He is jus' getting weaker, I
think."
"Has he been to the doctor?"
Consuelo nodded. "He says there is nothing to do, 'cept give
Roberto his medicine an' keep him quiet." She shrugged. "Is
still hard to keep him quiet," she added. "But not so much as
before." She looked back at him. "You mad at us?" she asked.
Burke shook his head. "But the people I work for are."

Maria had just come out of the bedroom, and she went to the sofa and sat next to her mother. "Have they changed their mind about helping Roberto?" she asked. "The man who drove me home from the police station said they might."

"I think we're still all right, as long as nothing else happens. The district attorney seems willing to let the whole matter drop." He shook his head, gave each of them a weary smile. "But only if nothing else happens—and if no one else finds out about you being arrested—then I think everyone at the paper will just look the other way."

"What do you mean about someone else finding out?" Maria asked.

Burke gave her a steady, no-nonsense stare. "Another newspaper or magazine could find out about it—or some radio or television reporter might get a tip from someone who knows. If that happens, whoever finds out might decide to use it to embarrass my newspaper. That would be bad."

"They would hurt Roberto jus' for that? Jus' to embarrass jouse newspaper?" It was Consuelo, the look on her face incredulous.

"They wouldn't look at it that way," Burke said. "They would think that *you* hurt Roberto by doing it."

"Oh, God," Maria said. She lowered her face to her hands.

"But I was jus' trying to help him." Consuelo's voice was almost a moan. "I jus' wanted to get some money for the doctor, so the operation could come faster."

Billy nodded. "I understand. And I know your reason for doing it was good." He paused for effect. "Your reason would have been good if you had robbed a bank. But you still would have robbed a bank. That's the way they'd look at it." He smiled at the older woman, trying to soften the words. "Another news organization might even report it with some degree of sympathy. But it would embarrass the people who run my newspaper, and I think they might walk away from you if that happened."

Consuelo's chin began to tremble, and Burke realized she was about to burst into tears. "No one knows yet," he said quickly. "And I think if they were going to find out, they would have by now. So try not to worry."

"It was my fault," Consuelo sobbed. She shook her head hard. "Maria didn't want it, an' I made her. I made her."

Maria reached out and hugged her mother to her. "No, Mama. No. It's all right, Mama. Everything will be all right." "No, no." The sobs came even harder now. "Now . . . Roberto . . . won't . . . get . . . his . . . operation. Is . . . my . . . fault . . . my . . . fault."

"He'll get it, Mama. He will. I know he will." Maria was rocking her now, rubbing her back as though comforting a child.

Burke sat across from them, feeling like a first-class heel. What had these women done, except try to help their dying child? Running numbers—such a petty act in a nation that allowed casino gambling, where various states had started running lotteries that were nothing more than legal numbers games. Sure, the independent action helped provide revenue for organized crime, which then used that money to send its tentacles out into more hurtful arenas. It financed it, just as recreational drug use by middle-class adults and college students financed the murderous South American drug cartels. It was all true, but never black and white. It was an issue so complex, so intertwined with personal predicament that it became a moral morass. Except, of course, when judgment was passed by politicians and judges and cops, and certainly you and your peers in the media, each one handing down easy verdicts, all the while steeped in their own petty, self-serving corruptions.

Julia's words came back to him. *"Try to think of what you or I would do if we thought we could help Annie."* Burke thought about his daughter, the sweet, adoring child she had been before her illness had seized her, changed her into someone he could never know. He wondered how far out of bounds he would go if given even the slightest chance to bring that lost little girl back, to make her whole again. He could think of very few limits.

Burke sat in silence as Maria shepherded her mother off to bed. He wanted to say something that would ease the woman's concerns. But what could he say? The reality was there. The judgment had been handed down. And his job was to deliver the message—play patty-cake with a Mafia grunge, then beat these women into submission. Another job well done by Billy Burke. Success on all fronts. And tomorrow he could report back that all was well, and maybe, if he was lucky, even get a curt nod of approval.

Maria returned and sat on the sofa opposite him.

"Billy. I'm sorry."

"I know that." Still the hard man.

"It was so stupid. But I thought . . ." She shook her head. "I don't know what I thought." She drew a breath and looked away from him. "A few weeks ago my boss offered me a job in the office. It would pay more. But . . ." She hesitated, then hurried to get the words out. "But it would mean I had to go out at night with buyers. Some of them, they like to go out with young women when they're in town." Another breath. "I said no. But mostly because it would take me away from Roberto at night." She stared at him. "Do you understand what I'm saying?"

"Don't take that job either," Burke said. "Don't."

Maria momentarily placed a hand over her mouth, as if trying to hold in something vile that might escape. "It's just that I don't do anything except beg. Sometimes I think about getting another job. I could do that. I could work two jobs. I could. But even that wouldn't be enough to get the money. There's not enough time. And it scares me that if I take another job he'll die, and I won't even have been with him in the time that's left. So I don't do it. I can't give up that time, Billy. Not if it's all that I'm ever going to have. So I beg instead. And I hope some miracle will happen."

Burke wanted to tell her there were no miracles. He knew about miracles. He had prayed for one himself.

"We'll get it done, Maria. I promise we'll get it done."

She looked away, then turned back and smiled. "I liked your wife," she said. She was changing the subject, he thought, not wanting to delude herself with his promises.

"She liked you, too," he said.

Maria smiled, a bit wistfully, he thought. "I think she still loves you very much."

He nodded. "But then there's the hard part. Sometimes love isn't enough."

Maria's eyes became momentarily distant. "Yes, sometimes it isn't."

"Do you think everything will be all right now that they've got what they wanted?"

He was standing in Julia's kitchen, his back against the counter, as she poured them each a cup of decaffeinated coffee. It was ten-thirty. Julia was wearing a pair of lounging pajamas that he had given her years ago. They had still been together as a family then, he and Julia and Annie, and they had joked that all she needed was some time to lounge.

"Who the hell knows?" he said. "It's up to Twist and the people above him." He bit his lower lip, then continued, "I promised her I'd get it done for the boy." He stared at the floor. "I remember, when I was a kid, my father had this expression he'd use whenever I told him I wanted something extravagant. He'd say, 'If wishes were horses, then beggars would ride.'" He continued to study the floor. "You know that's what she called herself tonight—a beggar."

"I know," Julia said. "She told me that, too. It's how she feels."

Burke told her about the "job in the office" Maria had been offered, and what it would have entailed.

Julia closed her eyes and let out a long breath, then brought two cups of coffee to the small kitchen table. "I wonder what I'd do if someone came to me and said I could have Annie back the way she was when she was little—the way I want her to be now—and all I had to do was sleep with some unpleasant men . . ." She paused, as if pondering the question. "Every woman sleeps with an unpleasant man or two," she added. "Except she usually doesn't know it until later."

Burke didn't respond. He didn't want an answer to the question she had asked herself. He didn't want it personalized that way.

She looked at him. "What would you do to have Annie back?" she asked, not letting him escape.

"I guess there isn't much I wouldn't agree to." He brought his hands out to his sides, then let them fall back. "Killing some innocent bastard, I guess. I'm sure there might be some other things, but it's hard to think of many."

She came to him and slipped her arms around his waist and pressed her cheek against his chest. "Oh, Billy, it's all so crazy. Helping this child and these two women should be such a simple thing."

He ran a hand along the soft silk of her pajamas. "Maria told me something else tonight," he said. "She told me she thought you were still in love with me."

Julia smiled against his chest. "She's very perceptive." She tightened her arms around his waist. "Will you stay with me tonight?" Her voice was just above a whisper now.

"I'll always stay with you," he said. "Anytime you want me here."

{ 19 }

Burke spent the remainder of the week making nocturnal visits to University Hospital's records room posing as Dr. John Rourke. It began badly. The irrepressibly flirtatious Wendy—medical student–cum–records clerk—latched on to him the first evening and scared the wits out of him.

"Oh, you're back," she had said as he arrived in white lab coat and stethoscope. "I called your office a little over a week ago, and they told me you were on vacation."

Burke had forced a smile, realizing how close he had come to blowing the whole story. How close he still was if he didn't play it right. "Yes," he had said, fumbling for the right reply, uncertain of what she might have been told by his "office." Wendy watched him, all eyes and smile. "Afraid I had to cut the vacation a bit short." He shrugged with regret. "Patients," he added with a shake of his head.

"I suppose I'll learn about that one of these days," Wendy said. "Now I can't get more than ten feet from my books."

"You will," he said. He nodded reassuringly, then pushed through the gate and into the records area, hoping to escape.

"Still working on the same thing?" she asked, following him.

"Yes, a few more days. Don't let me interrupt your work."

"Oh, it's no problem. There's nothing to do, and I'd love to help you." She moved ahead of him, leading the way, her hips swaying under a long patch-patterned skirt.

Oddly, she did help, and Burke discovered that her familiarity with the system allowed her to search the files twice as quickly as he could himself. By the end of the week—with more than a little help from Wendy—he had compiled the necessary information for yet another year.

So close now, he told himself as he finished the last of that week's work. There was still one year of records to check, but already the degree to which supposed work at Bellevue and Harlem hospitals had been faked was nothing less than staggering. One more year to go, he told himself. He knew he was pushing the envelope, getting close to the end of Dr. John Rourke's vacation. It couldn't be helped. He needed two or three more days next week—four at the outside. Then he'd be ready to put it all on paper.

Yet he knew he wouldn't do that. Not that soon. Not until Roberto's surgery had been scheduled. The writing would take a full day, no more—a series of three articles to start, more undoubtedly to follow later, once they had hit the doctors and the hospital with the first damning articles. For now he wanted to keep the material close to his chest. It wasn't a question of trust. He simply understood how the newspaper business worked. The "Little Bobby" story had become a boon to the paper, with advertisers jumping over each other to join the *Globe's* crusade. There was even talk now of a final advertising campaign on one of the local television stations to augment the bus and subway and radio ads—to push contributions over the top. Once he handed everything over, that could change. Then the main objective— Roberto's surgery—could get lost in the euphoria of impending bloodlust. If Twist had everything in hand, Burke knew he'd lack the hammer to keep Roberto in the forefront of everyone's mind.

He had no reason to believe he'd need a hammer, but he wanted one just in case. The *Globe* had not run any stories accounting for the money collected to date. When he had questioned Twist about it—suggested it be done—Twist had brushed it aside. He didn't want to risk it, he said. There was a fear, he argued, that people would pull back on donations once they thought the goal was in sight. "We don't want to end up ten grand short because we told them too much too soon," he said.

"So how much do we have?" Burke had asked.

"Jesus Christ, you're as bad as that fucking grandmother," Twist had snarled. "She calls here asking that every fucking week."

Burke glared at him. "Her fucking grandson is dying," he snapped back.

Twist had waved a hand, shaken his head in apparent regret of his words. "I know. I know," he'd said. "We're close. We're real close. I just don't have exact figures day to day. The business guys are on top of it. Tell her that, for chrissake. Tell her it's only a matter of a week or two now. Get her the fuck off my back."

Burke made his way to Costello's when he left the hospital. The Fourth of July weekend was about to begin, and Wendy had told him that she would be working Monday, but that both she and her male counterpart would be off Saturday and Sunday, the fifth and sixth. The records room would be open those days, but based on what Wendy had said, it would be staffed by people who were unfamiliar with the nocturnal visits of "Dr. John Rourke." It was an added risk that Burke didn't want to take this late in the game, and he decided to wait until Monday to resume his work.

Burke entered the loud, boisterous bar shortly after ten. It was a typical night, a drunken scene. The Brits and the Aussies had been at it since shortly after three, as usual. The time difference between their respective international desks back home made their lives a little bit of heaven. Outside of stories directly assigned by their foreign desks, their tasks boiled down to little more than rewriting those that had already appeared in the major American papers and those reported on radio and television, then handing them off as their own enterprise. A constant check of wire services also kept them abreast of what was in the works, so they could be ready with answers if their editors queried a specific news item. "I'm right on top of it, old chap" was a refrain that had become a running joke among them.

Burke weaved his way through the drunken horde, until he spotted Eddie Hartman and Frank Fabio at the far end of the bar.

"Buy a weary physician a drink?" he said as he came up beside them.

"My troop," Frankie said. He signaled the bartender, who eyed Burke and immediately picked up a bottle of Jack Daniel's.

"My Cheech. Bless you," Burke said.

Fabio inclined his head toward Hartman. He was fighting off an impish grin. "While you've been out chasing nurses, the Chief here has come up with a yarn that's gonna start the Fourth off with a bang."

"A known fucking piece of shit, no doubt," Burke said.

"I'm outraged at your suggestion," Hartman said. He, too, was grinning, his teeth peeking through his bushy mustache. "But piece of shit or not, it knocked the city's financial crisis off the top of page three."

"With a lead-in photo on the front page," Fabio added.

"So tell me," Burke said.

Tony Rice came up and slipped his arm around Burke's shoulder.

"Have you heard about the Chief's piece of shit?" he asked.

"Shh," Burke said. "He's just about to tell all and make my day."

Hartman spun around on his stool and grinned. "How about"—he made quotation marks in the air—"'Hooker's Diary Reveals Celebrity Sex Secrets: Hollywood Father Figure Gets Golden Showers'?" Hartman's grin widened. "We didn't go quite that far in our headline, but it was close." He raised his glass, saluting the cops who made the arrest. "It seems the boys in vice busted one of our more successful call girls and came up with a little book that details the preferences of her celebrity clients. One of them is TV's favorite father figure. In addition to getting pissed on, Daddy also likes the occasional spanking."

Burke groaned.

Tony Rice giggled. "Such intrepid journalism. I simply tingle in anticipation."

"Fuck you," Hartman said. "You're just jealous this hooker didn't take a whip to your ass, you limey faggot."

"Limey faggot, *sir*, to you," Rice said. He tightened his arm around Burke's shoulder. "I think we should begin covering the sex lives of politicians as well," he teased. "Then we can offer our readers the entire gamut of public life—from oratory to oral sex. After all, dear boy, inquiring minds *do* want to know."

"Up yours," Hartman snapped. "These clowns wanna be celebrities, they gotta take the bad ink, too. It's the name of the game."

Burke turned to Fabio with a raised eyebrow. "Page three, with a front-page photo?" he asked.

Frankie shrugged. "It's like Eddie said. It's the name of the game today. Nail everybody's ass to the wall. It was also a slow news day, so what can I say? A couple of years ago we woulda spiked a story like that. We might have stuck it in one of the gossip columns if we really hated the poor slob. Today?" He rolled his eyes. "The game's changing, my troop. The powers that be can't get enough of it."

Burke could almost see the smirk on Twist's face. He wondered when Tony Rice's suggestion would become a journalistic norm—when even the sex lives of politicians would become fair game. There were already rumblings about one potential presidential candidate, an up-and-coming senator from Colorado named Gary Hart. He couldn't quite imagine it happening, but in the post-Watergate era of "catch anybody at anything," he couldn't discount it either.

Fabio slid off his stool and motioned Burke to follow him to the rear of the restaurant. He took a table, away from their everlistening peers, then hunched forward to keep his voice down even more.

"So what's happening at the hospital?" he asked.

"Close," Burke said. "Two or three more working days at the most."

"You gonna get it all?"

Burke nodded. "It's even better than we thought, Cheech. As time went on, these clowns got even more blatant about it. They even had people working at Bellevue and Harlem hospitals when they were on vacation or attending medical conventions." Fabio shook his head. "Fuckers. Unbelievable. Have you told Twist?"

"No. I'm holding back. I could write it now if I had to, then get the stuff for the final year and add it in later. But I'm afraid they'll lose sight of the kid once they get their hands on the juicier stuff."

"Could happen, but from what I hear, the dough is rolling in. They should be ready to hand it over to the doc in a week or so. Then he can do this little operation, and when it's over you can slam him in the teeth with the rest of the story." He raised a cautioning finger. "Just don't go near an emergency room for the next six months. You're liable to wake up and find your dick's been amputated."

Fabio sipped his drink. "Speaking of which, how are things with you and the lovely Whitney? I haven't seen you guys making the scene lately."

Burke realized that he had hardly thought about the woman in weeks. "I haven't seen much of her since I got back," he said. "Just in the office, really. Before I left, she dragged me to the Palace." He shook his head. "Jesus, what a collection of wannabes and future has-beens that was." He sipped his drink, trying to decide if he wanted to say more. "I started seeing Julia again," he added at length.

Fabio raised his eyebrows. "Is it serious—a rapprochement, as the French say?"

"I don't know. I'd like it to be. But I just don't know. We have a lot of old issues to work through." He stared down at his drink. "We're going up to see Annie together on the Fourth. Then we're having dinner afterward." He gave Fabio a wistful smile. "We've run into each other at Annie's hospital before, but we haven't gone there together in a long time. I think we just have to see if we can handle it. Annie. Being together. Dealing with all of it as a couple, not just individually. I think it's going to take some time."

"Hey, good luck. I mean it. Julia's a great lady. And I don't have to point out that your life hasn't exactly been something to write home about since it ended between you two."

"No, it hasn't," Burke said.

Fabio gave Burke a doubtful look. "You sure you're ready to give up the feminine wiles of Lady Whitney? That won't be an easy thing, my lad."

Burke thought about it. "Not as hard as you think." He paused, looking for the right words. "Hey, Whitney's great. She's beautiful, sexy, and she can be a helluva lot of fun." He paused again. "And she can also be an unqualified, self-centered pain in the ass." He shrugged, as if to say, Who can't? "But she's not exactly the kind of person you discuss your problems with." Burke picked up his drink and swirled the amber liquid. "She's an ambitious lady, and her ambitions don't include a long-term relationship with anyone. Not with the personal problems and the baggage that always go with it. Right now a steady boy-toy and dating are what she's about—nothing heavier. And especially nothing that could get in the way of where she wants to be a dozen years from now." He raised his drink in salute. "But she doesn't promise anything more. She's very up-front about what she wants. And that's okay."

"Look, she needs a new boy-toy when you disappear, you tell her the Cheech is available. I promise no long-term relationship, and no personal baggage. A series of one-night stands would be delightful."

Burke laughed at the idea. "Hey, I'm not sure she could handle you, Cheech."

Fabio leaned back and looked down his nose. "Hey, what woman could?"

{ 20 }

It was a scorching Fourth of July in Manhattan, overcast with a dense, polluted haze. The heat and humidity seemed to drop the farther north they drove into Westchester County, the sky changing to a bright electric blue. Even the car radio added to the mood of escaping the city, offering up John Denver's new hit, "Thank God I'm a Country Boy," and Glen Campbell's "Rhinestone Cowboy," and by the time Burke and Julia arrived at the hospital, all the portents of a perfect day were at hand. Except for their nerves.

Burke had awakened with the jitters and felt them intensify as the morning wore on. He read the morning papers. John Mitchell, H. R. Haldeman, and John Ehrlichman—the last of the Watergate biggies—had finally run out of appeals and were headed to prison. Burke felt as though he were headed there as well. He fought it. The prospect of a full day with Julia—all he hoped it could be—had just put his nerves on edge. He knew that Julia was feeling the same pressure, and he told himself they were both just trying too hard. Relaxation was the key, achieving it the impossibility. Neither of them had ever experienced a relaxing day visiting their daughter.

Annie and the other children at the hospital—Burke could not allow himself to use the word "institution"—were outside when they arrived. Julia hurried ahead, searching out their daughter. Burke moved more slowly, taking it all in. There were a large number of uniformed orderlies, nearly one for every three kids, it seemed. At first the presence of so many "keepers" offended him, but he quickly accepted their presence. They were needed. Among the many and varied symptoms of autism was an absolute fearlessness of real danger. Children afflicted with the disorder had been known to climb trees and then blithely jump twenty or more feet to the ground. They were also prone to erratic, sometimes unintentionally violent behavior— jumping on people without warning or throwing objects without concern about where or upon whom they might land.

It was a maddening syndrome, difficult to diagnose and impossible to cure. In its more benign state it was characterized by feigned deafness, loss of communication skills—primarily speech—and repetitive rocking and hand-flapping. In its more extreme form it involved a complete resistance to learning, avoidance of all eye contact, and an apparent insensitivity to pain.

Annie fell somewhere in the middle, which left some small hope that she might one day live as an independent adult. Many of these children, Burke knew, would require twenty-four-hour supervision for the rest of their lives. Still, the realization that personal "independence" was the only aspiration he had for his child tore at him every day.

Burke knelt before his daughter, hugged her, and stroked her hair. He could tell immediately from the far-off look in her eyes that this was one of her "distant days," as Julia called them. Annie refused to look at either her mother or father—or anyone else. She seemed only to occupy some strange world hidden somewhere in her beautiful blue eyes.

Behind her another child let out a terrible screech that made

Burke and Julia jump, but which Annie did not even seem to hear. Burke allowed his eyes to roam the gathering. A boy, no more than eight, was walking around flapping his arms, a woman Burke presumed to be his mother following him anxiously. Another boy was pulling up clumps of grass, then running toward adults and children alike and throwing it in their faces. Burke turned his back on the scene, unable to deal with it. He took Annie's hand and led her to a quiet bench some distance away. Julia followed, eyes downcast, and Burke knew she felt the same unrelievable sense of hopelessness that filled every part of him.

An hour later the mood had changed. Annie was seated in the grass a few feet away, happily playing with a collection of sticks she had gathered. She was smiling intermittently over a song she was singing to herself, looking very much like any other nine-year-old girl enjoying childish fantasies.

"She looks so happy now," Julia said. They were seated next to each other on the bench, and she reached out and took Burke's hand. "It's hard to imagine her happy after everything she's been through."

Burke thought about the "everything" to which Julia alluded. Myriad tests to diagnose the disorder—seemingly endless speech and hearing exams, repeated blood and urine samplings, CT scans, all followed by month after month of psychological examinations. At first neither he nor Julia fully realized what was being done, that the constantly changing retinue of doctors and psychologists was merely eliminating other diseases, disorders, and syndromes until they could finally settle on this one that they understood not at all. He could still vividly recall the final visit with their primary physician and the hopelessly damning prognosis he had given them. They had sat silently in his office, absorbing his words like blows—stunned, not wanting to believe, yet knowing it was true. Then Julia had begun to weep.

Burke squeezed Julia's hand in return. "If she could always be like this—just this—I think I'd be happy," he said. He drew a breath. "Isn't that awful? When she was born, I thought about so many things for her, things I wanted her to have and experience, things I'd get to see her do in her life." He lowered his head, drew another deep breath to fight back tears. God, he

hated this. Hated it. And yet he so much wanted to have another child—despite the commonly held scientific belief that the
disorder was genetic.

He gathered himself, looked up at his daughter again, then
turned to Julia. "Do you ever think about having another child?"
he asked.

"I want a baby brother."

Burke's head snapped around to the sound of his daughter's
voice. His mouth hung open. Annie was back to her collection
of sticks now and humming again.

"Did she . . . ?" Burke found he could not finish the sentence.

"Yes, she did," Julia said.

It had happened before, clear, cognizant expressions that
seemed to come from nowhere, like fleeting little gifts of coher-
ence and understanding. Burke began to laugh.

"I guess Annie votes yes," he said.

Julia was silent, still studying her daughter. Burke wanted to
ask again but resisted the impulse. After several minutes, Julia
turned to him.

"I think about it all the time, Billy. I was reading the paper the
other day, and I saw that Yoko Ono was pregnant, and I thought,
I'm thirty-four. There isn't a great deal of time left for me."

She didn't say any more, and Burke did not pursue it. He
didn't know if that was an answer for them or not.

A white-uniformed orderly searched Burke out a half hour later.

"Are you Mr. Burke?"

"Yes."

"There was a phone call for you. A Mr. Fabio. He said to call
him at the paper."

Burke debated ignoring the call and claiming later that he
had never gotten the message. It was probably more murder or
mayhem. Something close by, with Frankie recalling that he
and Julia were visiting their daughter that day.

Julia thought so, too. There was a look of disappointment in
her eyes.

"I better see what it is," Burke said.

"I know." She forced a smile. "If we have to go, I'll just tell
myself I'm dating a doctor."

"No you won't. Not when you climb back in my beat-up old Jeep."

"I'll tell myself I'm dating an eccentric doctor," she said.

Burke returned ten minutes later, his face drained of color. "It's Roberto," he said. "They rushed him to the hospital. Frankie said it's bad this time. Really bad. I have to go there."

"How is Maria?"

"Frankie talked to her on the phone. He said she was almost hysterical. He said he's trying to get hold of Twist to see if we can release the money and get this goddamn surgeon there."

"I'll go with you," Julia said. "Maybe it will help her if I'm there."

Roberto was in intensive care in the cardiac unit of Bellevue Hospital. The ambulance had rushed him there, even though other hospitals had been closer. Bellevue was known as the finest emergency-treatment facility in the city. It was the place all cops were taken when they were shot or stabbed in the line of duty. If they could get you to Bellevue alive, it was said, your chances of survival increased tenfold. Burke held on to that thought as they rode the elevator to the cardiac unit.

At the nurses' station Burke explained why they were there, then asked for Roberto's physician, Dr. Salazar. They waited anxiously while Salazar was paged, Burke tapping his foot furiously against the tiled floor.

"It will be all right," Julia said. "I know it will." Burke noticed she was twisting the wedding band on her finger. It was a sign of extreme nervousness that she had periodically affected throughout their marriage.

Salazar came down the hall five minutes later. His tall, slender body seemed weary and hunched, and the soft, gentle brown eyes that had so impressed Burke at their first meeting looked slightly hollow.

"Mr. Burke," he said. He forced a weary smile.

Burke quickly introduced Julia, then hurried on.

"How is he? Roberto? They said at the paper it was bad this time."

Salazar nodded. "Very bad, I'm afraid. We're trying to stabilize him. Then we have to get his strength up a bit. Then . . ." He momentarily let the sentence die. "Then we have to get this surgery performed. There's no choice now. His heart just won't survive another episode."

"Have you . . . ?"

Salazar cut him off, anticipating his question. "I've tried to reach Bradford, but he's off somewhere"—he held up a hand—"just for the day, according to his service. But they *claim* they don't have a number for him." He shrugged, his eyes growing even wearier. "Physicians sometimes tell their services to give out that message. The service gave me the name of another surgeon who's taking his calls, but I want Bradford if at all possible. He's the best man for this, and he knows the case, and we have a little time. We can't do anything until Roberto passes this crisis and gets stronger." He hesitated a moment, seeming almost embarrassed by what he was about to ask. "Will the money be available?"

"I'll make sure it is," Burke said.

Salazar nodded. "I'll tell him that."

"Can we see the child?" Julia asked. "And Mrs. Avalon?"

"Yes, I'll arrange it." He paused again. "Can you stay with her?" he asked. "I think having another young woman here would help her get through this. Especially . . ." Again he let the sentence die.

"Yes, I can stay as long as she needs me," Julia said.

Burke reached out and squeezed Julia's arm. "You go ahead. I'm going to find a phone and call Frankie. I'll find you."

Burke entered Roberto's room twenty minutes later. Maria and Consuelo were seated on either side of the bed. Julia stood behind Maria. She was bending down, whispering something in her ear.

Roberto lay in the bed, awake but unmoving. He seemed smaller and thinner, a bag of sticks covered with flesh. Burke studied his face. It looked beaten, weary of all the pain. He pushed the thought away. No, not that, he told himself. Just battered and weak, something that could be cared for and fixed.

Consuelo was the first to see Billy, and she jumped from her seat. Her face was anxious and pleading, and Burke assumed that Julia had told them he was onto the paper about releasing the money. He gave her a comforting smile, then went to the bed.

"Hey, Piece of Work, what are you doing back here?"

Roberto tried to smile, but it was little more than a slight stretching of his lips. "Sick," he said.

"Well, that's not allowed," Burke said. "You've gotta get better and get out of here. We've got things to do, my man. Places to go, parks to play in, a baseball game up at the stadium to watch. You hear me?"

Roberto's lips stretched a little farther, and his eyes seemed to brighten a bit. But all the spark is gone, Burke thought, all the animation has just slipped away.

He reached out and took the boy's hand. The hand was so small in his, so flaccid, almost as if the bones themselves were losing their consistency. He turned to Maria.

"I called the paper," he said. "All the bosses are off today, but they're reaching out for them." Maria started to say something, her lips trembling. Burke held up his hand, stopping her. "Dr. Salazar also has a call in to Bradford. He'll be coming, too, but probably not until tomorrow." He raised his hand again. "Salazar says they need time to get Roberto's strength up. So he'll be ready when Bradford gets here. It's all going to work out. I promise."

"But what about the money?" Maria asked, the fear audible in her voice. "Is there enough? God, please let there be enough."

"It's close. But don't worry. The paper can tell Bradford it will guarantee the rest. He's not going to say no to a newspaper."

Burke glanced at Julia. Her eyes, too, seemed filled with doubt. And why hadn't the paper guaranteed the money weeks ago? Burke knew that was the question she was silently asking. But he also knew she wouldn't like the answers. They were too stark, too real. Why hadn't they? Because they hadn't, lady, that's all. Because they were a newspaper, not some goddamn philanthropic organization. Because it's not the way the game is played. Because Roberto is just some little spic kid who just happens to be a damned good story right now. Oh, sure, everybody would like to see him live, because then he's an even better story. And after all, we're not monsters. But live or die, he'll still be a story, and let's face it, five years from now no one will even remember his name. Hey, I'm sorry, lady, but that's reality. That's life in the Apple. And like it or not, there's not a damned thing anybody can do about it.

Burke looked at Julia and Maria in turn, then glanced back at Roberto. He had fallen asleep. Burke turned back to the two women. "Let's step out in the hall. I have to leave soon, and I want to talk to you both before I do."

The women followed him out.

"Look, I have to get back to the paper. They want another story about Roberto." He waved his hand in a circle. "About this, about him being sick again." He could see the pained look in Julia's eyes. Maria just seemed bewildered. "It'll help. It will put some more pressure on Bradford and the hospital." He was making up excuses as he went, and he could tell Julia knew it.

"But I thought you said . . ." It was Maria, even more bewildered now.

"I did. I did," Burke assured her. "But I don't want to take any chances on this."

Maria shook her head. She wasn't looking at anyone or anything. She just seemed to be trying to understand everything that was going on around her.

"Let me walk you to the elevator," Julia said. She patted Maria's shoulder. "I'll be right back," she added.

When they were far enough away, Julia took his arm. "What is going *on*, Billy?" She saw his jaw tighten, the muscles begin to dance along his cheek.

"I haven't the slightest idea." They stopped in front of the elevator. Burke drew a deep breath. "I'll be back in about two hours, and I'll drive you home."

"I can take a cab. It won't be a problem." She stared at him, waiting for some further response. "Please tell me what's going on."

Burke studied his shoes. "When I called Frankie and told him what Salazar had said, he reached out for Twist again and finally ran him down. I have no idea what was said, but I was on hold a good ten minutes, and when Frankie got back to me, he didn't sound happy."

"What did Frankie say?"

"Just that Twist wanted me to come in and to do a story about Roberto being rushed to the hospital."

"What about getting the money to Bradford? You told Maria—"

"I know what I told her!" Burke's voice was sharp and angry. He reached out and stroked her arm. "I'm sorry, I don't mean to take it out on you." He shook his head. "I asked Frankie, and all he'd tell me was that Twist would deal with it tomorrow morning. He's busy. He's at some goddamn barbecue or something."

"The insufferable little shit."

"It'll be all right."

Julia stared at him but said nothing. She decided he was trying to convince himself.

"Look," he said as though she had objected. "They need time to stabilize the boy, and they haven't even gotten hold of Bradford yet. When Salazar talks to him, he's going to pass on what I said: that the money's there. I'll force this thing through no matter what, and in the end the paper will back me up."

"You're sure?"

Burke wasn't sure at all. "Yes, I'm sure," he said.

Fabio was in sole command of the city desk. It was the one disadvantage of being the first assistant city editor. You got to run the cityside show on major holidays, when most of the other editors were off enjoying them with their families. It went down the line that way. An assistant managing editor assumed overall responsibility for the paper, the assistant news editor ran the national and international desks, and the assistant chief photographer operated a small group of disgruntled camera jockeys, who would rather be barbecuing hot dogs in their backyards.

It was all done with a skeleton crew—no more than three dozen reporters—and if a major story broke, insanity reigned very quickly.

Fabio eyed Burke as he approached the rim. "Give me two and a half takes," he said. "No more. We got a nasty little murder on the West Side and enough Fourth of July bullshit to fill two papers." He paused a beat. "How's the kid?"

"Still touch and go. No change from what I told you before," Burke said.

Fabio lowered his eyes and shook his head. "We'll get it squared away in the morning."

"What did Twist say about it?"

Fabio gave him a hard stare. "I'm not gonna tell you," he said.

"Then I'll call him and hear it myself."

"No you won't, my troop. He's not home, and I'm not giving you the number where he is. I already told him what *I* thought, and I don't need any company on the shit list." Fabio looked up at the ceiling and shook his head. He knew that Burke would get the number eventually. In the end, all it would take was a sizable enough bribe to the copyboy running the internal switchboard. "All right. Look, I know you'll go ferreting around until you get the number. He said we've been through this before, and the kid's always pulled out of it fine. He wants to wait and see how the kid is tomorrow. He said the mother's probably hysterical and blowing it out of proportion."

Burke stared at him. "You told him what the kid's doctor told *me?*"

"I told him."

"And?"

"And nothing. He'll deal with it tomorrow."

"I already told the kid's doctor we'd make the money available. If he ever locates this fucking surgeon, he's going to tell him that. And if that little shit Twist—"

Fabio listened to the snarl in Burke's voice and held up a hand, cutting him off. "That's exactly why I don't want you to talk to him. You turn this into a pissing contest, you'll cause more harm than good. Now, you wanna find somebody, you find this fucking surgeon. Then tell the kid's doctor where he is." He pointed a finger at Burke. "But do *not* talk to him yourself. Twist was specific about that. Nobody is to talk to this guy until we get a clear picture of what's going on in the morning. You do it and we'll both be out looking for work." Fabio raised his chin, indicating the rows of desks behind him. "Now, go write your story. And when you're finished, find this Bradford guy."

{ 21 }

When Twist arrived at eight-thirty the next morning, he found Burke waiting in his glass-enclosed office.

"Jesus Christ, let me get my goddamn coat off before you start on me," he snarled. He was carrying a container of coffee, and Burke could see his hand shaking. There were heavy pouches under his bloodshot eyes.

Twist slumped into his chair and stared up at Burke. His lips were pressed together in a mean line. "Before you start blowing smoke about the kid, tell me how close you are to wrapping up the hospital side of this story," he snapped.

"We're talking hours," Burke said. "I need less than one final year of surgical records to finish it. If push came to shove, we could start writing—"

"Are you talking about last year or three years ago?" Twist asked.

"Three years ago. I already have all we need on the past two years and the first six months of this year. I still need most of 1972. That'll give us three and a half years that this scam has been going on. With that there's no conceivable way they can write it off as some bookkeeping error." He drew a long breath. "As I was trying to say, we could start writing now and have it in-house, ready to run, whenever we choose. What we have is that solid. Then I could spend one, maybe two evenings at the hospital and I'd have the rest."

"There won't be any problem getting in and getting the rest of it?"

Burke shook his head. "Not until we run that part of the story. Once we do, I doubt anybody will get within ten feet of those records."

"But what we already have is enough, right? Even if they shut us down tomorrow."

"Right. What we're still looking for is just gravy. We've got them cold. We can prove they clipped the city out of several million bucks. Period."

Twist nodded to himself. "And we already have enough on Bradford personally. His income, personal lifestyle, everything." He looked up at Burke for unneeded confirmation, then added an unnecessary "Right?"

"Right," Burke said. "We have all of it. Even photos of the good doctor and his wife arriving at a members-only opening at the Metropolitan Museum. We've got the whole thing wrapped up."

Twist stared through the window surrounding his office. He began stroking his chin with his thumb and index finger. "Okay," he said at length. "Start writing it." His eyes returned to Burke. "And I want you at the hospital the next two nights. I want the gravy, too, and I want it in hand within the next forty-eight hours."

"You'll have it," Burke said.

Twist reached for some papers on his desk, then looked back at Burke as though surprised he was still there. "So get started," he said.

Burke stared back at him. "What about the kid, Lenny?"

Twist's face turned into a snarl. "Oh, for chrissake, that's all I hear from you. The kid, the kid. You're losing track of this story, Billy. The goddamn story. Remember?"

"The kid is dying, Lenny. He gets this operation now or he's dead. Period."

"Bullshit."

"What?"

"You heard me. *Bullshit*. Every time this kid gets a case of the sniffles, he's on his way to the goddamn morgue. You know what I think? I think this cute little *mamacita* of his has you wrapped so tight around her finger that you're starting to get as hysterical as she is."

"*That's* bullshit," Burke snapped back.

Twist's eyes narrowed. "*What?*"

"You heard me, Lenny." Burke put both fists on Twist's desk and leaned toward him. "This doesn't come from the boy's mother. She's so scared right now, she couldn't find her own ass in the dark, let alone offer up a diagnosis about her son's life expectancy." He leaned in even closer. "*I* was at the hospital, and I saw the kid. *I* talked to his doctor. He's not even sure they can get the boy strong enough to *survive* this fucking operation. But he knows one goddamn thing for certain. If the boy *doesn't* get the surgery, he's dead. He doubts he'll even survive the next attack. And you can put a period on that, Lenny. It's a thirty—end of fucking story. And when that happens, *we* end up sitting here with our dicks hanging out, trying to explain how the all-fucking-powerful *Globe* couldn't pressure one doctor into a fucking operating room when people all over this city were sending in their nickels and dimes to save one little kid's life."

Twist looked away, grinding his teeth. He began drumming his fingers on the desk. "We'd still have a story," he said at length. "Maybe even a better story."

"*What?*"

"Don't get bent all out of shape, for chrissake." He held up his hands. "I'm not saying that's what we want. You think I want something to happen to this kid? What am I, some kind of monster? All I'm saying is that if the worst happens, we still have a story." Burke started to object, but Twist waved it away. "Nothing changes the facts, that's all I'm saying." He grabbed his index finger. "Fact one: Doctor Big Bucks and his goddamn hospital turned this kid away weeks ago because his family didn't have the dough to pay the freight, and they did it when a little human decency—that wouldn't put a dent in either of their fucking bank accounts—could have saved his life." Another finger joined the first. "Fact two: Doctor Big Bucks and his goddamn hospital are not only greedy sons of bitches, they are fucking thieves as well. For the past three years they've been ripping off the city with their hospital scam and lining their pockets with John Q. Public's tax dollars." A look of satisfaction came into his eyes. "Now, you tell *me* we don't still have a story."

Burke glared down at him, then raised three fingers and grabbed them with his other hand. "Fact three, Lenny: The *New York Globe*, the biggest daily newspaper in this country, collected thousands of dollars from its readers, but when push came to shove, it didn't have the swat—or the *balls*—to save the life of one little boy." He released his fingers, then pointed one at Twist. "And that's the final story, Lenny. That's the one we'll have to live with."

Twist snorted. "And who's gonna write it?"

Burke continued to stare at him.

Twist flushed as he realized what Burke was telling him. His face contorted into a snarl. "You threatening me, Billy? Are you threatening this goddamn newspaper? Because if you are, you better say it right now."

Burke remained silent, absorbing Twist's stare. "I'm telling you I want the kid to live," he said at length. "That's the bottom line for me. The only bottom line."

"That's wonderful. Egalitarian as all hell." Twist's eyes bored into Burke. "You know what *my* bottom line is? Loyalty to this fucking newspaper. It's my *only* bottom line. And I'm not going to have *anybody* working at this paper who isn't going to give me that to the max. And you can put a thirty on that, mister. So that's the question we have right now: Do you want to work for this newspaper, Billy, or do you want to play fucking Santa Claus?"

Burke felt his stomach knot. Fear? Anger? A combination of both? He drew a long breath, fighting for control. "I want to work here, Lenny. But the bottom line is still the kid. If I have to, I can get a job somewhere else."

Twist nodded, then leaned back in his chair. There was a confident look in his eyes. "I'm sure you can, Billy. No doubt about it." He picked up a pencil and began tapping it against his desk. "I'm sure there are papers in Chicago that would love to have you. Or Philly or Boston. Hell, you might even catch on in D.C." He gave Burke a shrug. "And if that didn't work out, there's no question somebody in Buffalo or Cleveland or St. Louis would snatch you right up." He leaned forward and gave Burke a hard-eyed glare. "But I promise you one thing, Billy: Your next job won't be in New York. And if you want to get here for any *personal* reasons, I promise you, you're going to have one helluva commute."

Burke felt his stomach tighten again. The not-too-subtle threat couldn't be clearer. The man knew just how desperately Burke needed to be close to his own child. He felt his anger rise and fought it down again. "You have that much power, Lenny?"

"Oh, I think my counterparts at the other papers might listen to me. But you know what? I don't think I'd even have to pick up a phone." He began drumming the fingers of both hands on his desk. "I think our publisher would pick up his. Especially after he found out that one of his own reporters fucked him out of a story that he's poured all that money into. I think the man just might get that annoyed when he realized that one of his own people made him look like a goddamn fool."

Burke stared him down. "He'll look like an even bigger fool if Roberto dies." Burke saw a hint of concern cross Twist's face. It was gone almost as soon as he noticed it. But it had been there. He placed his hands on the desk and leaned forward again, deciding to push it. "And he won't have me to blame if that happens, will he, Lenny?"

Twist's momentary concern turned to anger. "Goddamnit, the kid's not going to die."

"You bet your ass he's not," Burke snapped. "He's going to have that surgery, and he's going to have it as soon as they can get him into an operating room. I already told the kid's doctor that we'd guarantee the surgical fees, and that's just what he's going to tell Bradford."

"You *what*? You had no authority to guarantee anything, and you damn well know it. You better get on the phone right now—"

Burke cut him off. "I'm not getting on any goddamn phone. You have the authority to guarantee his fee, and that's just what you're going to do if you want me to write the rest of this damn story."

Twist snorted. "You goddamn arrogant son of a bitch. You think you're the only person who can write this thing?"

"Not at all, Lenny. But I am the only person who's got all the documentation to back it up."

Twist pushed himself forward in his chair until they were almost nose to nose. "You better take a look out in that newsroom, mister. Some of the best goddamn newspaper reporters in this country are sitting out there. And any one of them can document this story if you walk away from it."

Burke nodded slowly. "That's right, they could." His eyes hardened on Twist. "You know, Lenny, when you first told me about this story—when you told me it had the best Pulitzer potential you'd ever seen—I thought you were full of shit." Burke raised his eyes to the empty spot on Twist's wall, the space left for his missing Pulitzer Prize. He let his own smile form. "But you were right, Lenny. This is a surefire contender, the best shot this paper's had in years. And unless something extraordinary comes along, I think you'll win." His eyes hardened. "If it all gets written. And right now I'm the only person who can make that happen."

Twist snorted at the claim. Burke's smile widened. He inclined his head toward the newsroom. "It's like you said, Lenny. You've got a shitload of talented people out there. But not one of them can give you the rest of this story."

"*Really.*"

"Yeah, really. Because I can pick up a telephone, too, Lenny. And once I drop a dime on this story—once the hospital knows what we're really looking to prove—I doubt that anybody out in that newsroom—no matter how good he or she is—will be able to get within a hundred feet of that records room."

Twist sat in stony silence. A twitch began in the corner of one eye. "You bastard," he said. "If you did that, you'd never work *anywhere* again."

Burke stared at him, then shook his head. "That's what you don't understand, Lenny. If that kid dies, I couldn't stomach walking into this newspaper again. I couldn't stomach walking into *any* newspaper again." Twist started to object, but Burke raised a hand, cutting him off. "I'll write your story, Lenny. I'll write the best damned story that's ever crossed your desk. And I'll document the rest of it today, even if I have to stay at that hospital all night." He paused to let the words sink in, then continued, "I'll put that Pulitzer Prize right there on your wall. But the price tag is going to be that operation. That's it, Lenny. No more threats, no further negotiations. Roberto Avalon goes into that operating room as soon as he's strong enough."

"We don't have all the goddamn money yet," Twist snapped. "What am I supposed to do, write a personal check for the balance?"

"You get to Bradford today, and you tell him that the *New York Globe* will guarantee his fee. What the hell is he going to do? Refuse a guarantee from the biggest newspaper in the country? Sue us for nonpayment if we're a month late—after we've hammered his ass into the ground with the rest of the story? And you'll have the story, Lenny. You'll have it in your hands before you even talk to him. And as soon as that boy goes through those operating-room doors, every bit of the documentation will be sitting on your desk."

Twist's face darkened. Burke could see him fighting to calm himself. Slowly he seemed to attain it. "Look, nobody wants anything bad for this kid. You're right. That has to be the bottom line." He ran a hand over his face, then slowly shook his head before looking at Burke again. "I just don't like to be pushed. And I don't like to feel I'm being blackmailed into a decision."

"That was never my intention." Burke was surprised at how easily the lie came. They were both lying now—saving face.

Twist raised his hands, palms out, as if calling a halt to the animosity. "All right. Let's put all the harsh words behind us. You get out there and write the story, and I'll get on the phone and I'll get Bradford in here and I'll promise him the moon and sixpence. Then we'll bury his ass, and everybody else who was part of this thing. But I want the first piece on my desk before I talk to him. Agreed?"

"You got it," Burke said. "You'll have the first piece within the hour."

* * *

Burke slipped into his chair in the newsroom and began assembling his notes. Within minutes Frankie Fabio was standing beside him.

"Well, I don't see you cleaning out your desk, so I take it you survived your little encounter."

Burke let out a small snort. "Barely," he said.

Fabio stared at him, waiting for more. "I could hear the snarling. It didn't sound like you made the man happy. So tell me."

"Let's just say my survival is definitely a temporary condition."

"How so?"

Burke filled him in on the meeting with Twist, ending it with his own prediction that he'd be out the door as soon as the last story hit the street.

"Maybe not," Fabio said. "If the story's as good as we all think it is, getting rid of you won't be that easy. Firing you, then putting the work you did up for a Pulitzer, could be a little risky. It just might put any chance of winning right in the toilet. And I don't think Lenny will want to roll those dice."

Burke inclined his head. "That's only if my name goes on the rest of the stories. Don't be surprised if my byline suddenly gets dropped."

Fabio stared down at him. "I'll make sure your byline is on those stories. Even if I have to go down to the composing room and put it on myself."

Burke nodded. He knew Frankie would do just that. "We could end up on the unemployment line together, my Cheech."

"Hey, my troop. At least we won't be lonely."

{ 22 }

"This is extremely disappointing."

The words sent a chill through Leonard Twist.

Disappointing the publisher of the *Globe* was something Twist had carefully avoided throughout his tenure as city editor. Harold Wainwright was a small, meticulously groomed man in his late fifties, a man who wore a vest and crisply starched white shirt even in the depths of summer, and his attitudes about business—and life in general—corresponded with that austere demeanor. Unfulfilled expectations translated into dis-illusionment, and Wainwright's disenchantment, Twist knew, could bring an abrupt halt to a promising career.

Twist made a regretful gesture with his hands, then let them fall back to the arms of his chair. He was seated in Wainwright's ninth-floor corner office, and the windows behind the publish-er's oversize desk offered an unobstructed view of the Chrysler

Building's phallic spire. Mitch Coffee, the paper's metropolitan editor, was seated beside Twist in a matching leather wing chair. Normally the executive editor also would have been present, but he was currently conducting his annual tour of the paper's various U.S. bureaus, and Coffee had decided they could not afford to await his return.

"The situation is regrettable," Coffee said. "We would have liked to play the story out for a few more weeks at the minimum, but the child's health seems to have deteriorated to the point where that can't be done." Coffee had agreed to take the lead in the conversation. He was free of blame, and Twist had hoped that his lack of direct involvement would deflect Wainwright's anticipated ire.

Wainwright raised a hand and waved off Coffee's words, then used both hands to smooth down the sides of his longish, unnaturally black hair. "I recognize that part of the situation," he said. "Those are simply the vicissitudes of fate." He raised his eyebrows, using them to dismiss the inevitable. "As you know, I, too, would have liked to continue the campaign a bit longer. It's been a boon to both circulation and advertising. But hopefully we'll be able to do some follow-ups about the boy after the surgery." He waved his hand again, this time in a circular motion. "Along with our exposé, of course."

Twist began to assure him that they could, but Wainwright cut him off in midsentence.

"What disappoints me is the fact that this reporter seems to be dictating terms to my newsroom executives." Wainwright had spoken the words to Coffee, but now his cool gray eyes fell on Twist, letting him know exactly where he felt the blame lay.

Twist shifted in his chair. He had urged Coffee not to reveal that part of the story, but the metropolitan editor had insisted it was the only way to deflect blame. Now Twist leaned forward and spoke with all the sincerity he could muster.

"I agree completely. Unfortunately, there was no way to anticipate this outlandish reaction. But I assure you, it is not something we are going to ignore."

Wainwright leaned back in his chair and tapped his lips with one finger. "I seem to recall something about Mr. Burke's background," he said. "I believe when we were considering him for the job of city editor, some personal problems involving the health of his own child became a factor."

Twist let out a breath. "That's true. He has a child who's autistic."

Wainwright nodded. "Yes, that was it. I recall it now." He sat forward and leveled Twist with a steady, unblinking gaze. "Perhaps we should have anticipated this kind of emotional reaction to another sick child."

Twist fought off a shudder. "Perhaps we should have. But at the time it seemed like a plus. We thought he'd bring exactly the kind of passion to the story that was needed."

Wainwright nodded again. "Yes, I see that. It was a judgment call." He fell silent, allowing the words to speak for themselves.

"I assure you we are not going to let this matter pass," Twist quickly added.

Wainwright raised his eyebrows. "What do you have in mind?"

Twist warmed to the topic. He leaned forward again, trying to bring the proper severity to his expression. "First, I intend to remove him from the story as soon as it's practical—"

"Meaning as soon as he completes the stories he is presently holding for ransom?"

"Uhh . . . uh, yes. Once the stories dealing with the exposé are in hand, all follow-up pieces will be assigned to someone else. And then—"

"I wonder if that's wise." Wainwright leaned back in his chair again and pursed his lips.

"I don't understand," Twist said. "We can't just ignore what he's done."

"Oh, no. Of course not." A small smile formed on Wainwright's lips. "But you were right, Leonard. Mr. Burke did bring enormous passion to the story. And it worked very well for us. His stories about the boy are among the best I've ever read. In this paper or any other. His subsequent actions, well . . ." Again he let the sentence die.

Twist saw an opening to curry favor and instinctively grabbed it. "I don't mean to diminish Burke's talent—it's one of the reasons he was assigned to the story. But I think we have to keep in mind that this has been an extremely well-orchestrated endeavor. The promotion, the advertising—these were the things that brought people to the story." Twist waved a hand in imitation of Wainwright's earlier gesture. "Please don't misunderstand. It *is* a great story—well executed and potentially a big prizewinner—but it easily could have passed most of our readers by had it not been for the effort *the paper* put forth. And these were very calculated and creative business decisions. So if prizes come our way, it won't just be Burke's talent that gets us there. To a very large extent it will be due to these decisions."

Wainwright's eyes pinned Twist to his chair. The decisions Twist had praised had been Wainwright's, and Twist now wondered if Wainwright was pleased or if he had gone too far, if his blatant ass-kissing had been a bit too obvious.

"I agree completely," Wainwright said.

"As do I," Mitch Coffee quickly added.

Twist glanced at him. He thought, The fat prick waited to see how the wind would blow before he opened his mouth on that one. He warned himself that Coffee would sell him out in a New York minute. Before Twist could privately acknowledge that he would do the same if the situation were reversed, Wainwright's words snapped him back.

"But that is not my concern," Wainwright said.

Twist and Coffee remained silent, waiting for the other shoe.

Wainwright leaned forward and folded his hands prayerlike on his desk. "Whether Mr. Burke's talents are recognized or not is of little importance to me. His work to date has reflected well on this newspaper, and that in itself has value. What concerns me now is his insubordination, which in this instance is extreme." He took a moment to look at each of his editors. "Insubordination, gentlemen, is something that has a tendency to grow and spread. It is something an organization like ours—any organization, really—tolerates at its peril." He shook his head in an imitation of regret. "I am afraid Mr. Burke has put a very promising career in jeopardy. But that was his choice." He looked at Coffee and Twist in turn. "Now, how you deal with this problem is entirely your decision. If you feel that Mr. Burke can be suitably punished and rehabilitated, I will have no objection. If you decide—*at the appropriate time*—that he should be invited to leave this newspaper, I will support that decision."

Wainwright allowed his eyes to harden on each man. "But whichever solution you choose, I want it done meticulously. I do not want our story placed in jeopardy, and more important, I do not want to be faced with a grievance from the Newspaper Guild. In short, I do *not* want our handling of this"—Wainwright unfolded his hands and made quotation marks in the air—"'Little Bobby' story to be brought into question. We are the champions of the underdog. And very soon we will be St. George slaying the greedy medical dragon. That is the way I want us to be perceived by the great unwashed who buy our newspapers. It is exactly the perception we *need*. It is good for circulation and even better for advertising. What we do *not* want is to have that perception come back and bite us on the ass."

Twist and Coffee left Wainwright's office and headed for the elevator in silence. When the elevator doors closed behind them, both men stared straight ahead.

"What was your take on our meeting?" Coffee finally asked.

"That we better not drop the ball," Twist said.

"What about Burke specifically?" Coffee asked.

Twist let out a loud snort. "I think he told us what he wanted without actually saying it."

"Meaning it's on our heads alone if it goes wrong."

"Exactly."

"What do you think he *wants*?"

Twist looked at Coffee and gave him a small, satisfied nod. "We let Burke finish the stories. Get everything we can out of him." He paused for effect. "Then the man is history."

{ 23 }

Shortly after two, Burke watched Dr. James Bradford enter Leonard Twist's office. He had never met Bradford, but he easily recognized the surgeon from the numerous photographs that had crossed his desk. The man was everything Burke had expected. There was a slight hint of arrogance in his walk and an elevation to his chin that spoke of someone who held himself above the rabble that surrounded him. Dr. James Bradford was someone who took himself seriously, Burke decided, someone who clearly expected all about him to honor that opinion.

As he closed his office door, Twist glanced across the newsroom and offered Burke a confident wink. Burke watched as he then drew the venetian blinds, sealing off the large glass partition. It was part of Twist's technique when hardball was about to be played—a form of intentional isolation, something Burke recognized from personal experience. It made a visitor to Twist's office feel trapped.

Earlier Twist had explained his plan for Bradford. He would tell him that the *Globe's* fundraising effort had not yet reached its goal, but that the drive would continue and the funds be passed on as soon as they were received. He would also tell him that the *Globe* expected him to accept that substantial payment and move ahead with the surgery. Should he decline, there was a second choice. "He can sit back and watch the largest newspaper in the country paint him as five kinds of asshole—a rich doctor who was willing to let a child die because his entire fee wasn't in the bank." A hard edge came to Twist's voice as he touted the anticipated result. "I expect him to fold like a cheap suit—game, set, and match to the *Globe*. Then, of course—after he finishes the surgery—we'll fuck him in the ass anyway."

Burke visualized the confrontation taking place in Twist's office. When it came to intimidation, few newspapermen were better than Lenny Twist, so there was no question in Burke's mind which option Bradford would choose. He only wished he could be there and watch Bradford's self-inflated balloon blow up in his face. Or better still, be there the days following the surgery and watch the good doctor pick up his newspaper each morning and see exactly how his "generosity" had been rewarded.

Burke forced those pleasant thoughts away and turned back to his typewriter. He was almost finished with the second piece of a three-part series detailing the fiscal abuses perpetrated on the city by University Hospital and its well-heeled physicians. The first piece had been finished and handed in to Twist three hours ago. It gave an overall view of the scam that had been operating for the past three and a half years, and it had received Twist's unqualified praise. The second story would detail those abuses and give specific examples of how the hospital and its doctors had been paid for work never performed, and the medical treatments and services they were actually engaged in at those times. The final piece would detail the lifestyles and successful medical practices of the physicians, concentrating in greatest detail on Bradford and his decision to deny care to Roberto Avalon until the *Globe* paid his fee in advance. All three pieces would also include any comments from those involved, from city officials, and from the American Medical Association, if they chose to give them—comments that would not even be sought until hours before each article hit the street, thereby avoiding any premature leaks.

Before the start of the exposé there would be a final story about Roberto and the results of his surgery. That piece would include broad hints of improper medical conduct and would run with a promotional sidebar alerting *Globe* readers that a related series about long-standing medical chicanery would begin the following day. It would orchestrate the series to perfection and guarantee a poor night's sleep for those involved.

Burke drew a deep breath. His adrenaline was pumping, as it always did when a big story was about to break. He had never hunted, but he imagined that this was what a hunter felt when an animal he had stalked for days finally came into view. There was a tinge of fear as well. It centered on Roberto Avalon. The story about the financial shenanigans was there, and it would run no matter the outcome of the boy's surgery. There would be praise and pats on the back and self-congratulations by everyone involved. He only hoped those gestures would not be accompanied by sadly shaking heads and expressions of regret that the story had worked for everyone—except the boy.

He had telephoned Bellevue two hours ago and been assured that Roberto's condition had steadily improved, that plans had already been made to transfer him to the surgical unit at University Hospital when his strength was sufficiently elevated. The news had left him feeling helpless. All he could do now was finish the series and wait. He still had to return to University Hospital that evening and gather the final documentation Twist had demanded. Then he intended to grab a few hours' sleep and go directly to Roberto's bedside. Twist had said he wanted a "personal, gut-wrenching account" of the entire process, "right down to the tears in his mother's eyes as they wheel the little guy toward the knife." Burke had almost gagged on the line, but he knew exactly what Twist meant. It was a story he could write from home—ninety-nine percent fluff and bullshit, tearjerker par excellence. All it needed was an outcome, and that was the one part that scared the hell out of him.

The door to Twist's office opened at three o'clock. They had been closeted inside for nearly an hour, and when Bradford emerged, Burke noticed that a great deal of his earlier arrogance appeared to have melted away. There was a slight bend to his shoulders, and his chin was almost touching his chest. His earlier measured gait had now quickened, as though he wanted nothing more than to get out of the building as fast as possible. Twist stood outside his office, also watching Bradford leave. Then he turned his gaze on Burke, and a smug look spread across his face. Burke raised his eyebrows, questioning the result of the meeting, and Twist responded with a thumbs-up gesture. It was game, set, and match to the *Globe*, just as Twist had predicted. Burke let out a deep breath and turned back to his typewriter.

The third part of the series was passed to the city desk shortly after six o'clock, with instructions that inserts would follow over the next two days. The documentation for the series had been packed in a borrowed briefcase earlier in the day and quietly locked away in the trunk of Frankie Fabio's car. Burke had promised to turn the documentation over after the surgery had been performed, and he had no intention of changing that agreement, even though Twist had apparently fulfilled his end of the deal.

Burke picked up his phone, telephoned Bellevue, and asked to speak to Dr. Wilfredo Salazar. When Roberto's doctor finally came on the line, he explained that the boy was already en route to University Hospital.

"The surgery is scheduled for five A.M.," he said.

Burke's mind filled with the vision of Roberto's small chest laid open by a surgeon's scalpel. "Will you be there?" he asked Salazar.

"Yes. I've asked to be present in the operating room," Salazar said. "Dr. Bradford has graciously agreed." There was a touch of sarcasm in his words. "I'll come out and find the boy's mother when we're finished, so if you're there, I can fill you in on how it all went." He hesitated a moment, then continued. "But there's no point in you being there at five. This procedure will take at least four to five hours. If you're there before ten o'clock, you'll just be cooling your heels."

"I'll be there at five," Burke said.

A soft chuckle came across the line. "I thought you would be," Salazar said. "I'll look for you before we start. I'll be seeing Mrs. Avalon then as well."

Burke entered University Hospital at eight o'clock and headed directly to the records room. He was decked out in his phony medical attire and decided he would miss the impersonation. He was beginning to understand the smugness that permeated the calling. There was a certain public awe that surrounded the title "doctor," and it could be seen in the eyes of those who furtively glanced at his white lab coat and the stethoscope that hung from his neck. His impersonation had made him part of a mysterious cult, the men and women who knew the great secrets of life and death, whose knowledge was shrouded in terminology that few outside the profession could pronounce, let alone understand. Burke smiled at the thought. What the public failed to recognize was that half the men and women bearing that lofty title had graduated at the bottom half of their medical-school class and that their ranks—like those of lawyers or architects or accountants—held just as many dolts as did any other occupation.

Burke recalled a recent conversation with a British correspondent. The Brit had marveled at the high esteem in which Americans held the medical profession, and Burke had asked if that wasn't also true in Britain. "Heavens no," the Brit had replied. "A proper English family would never even consider inviting their family physician to dinner. After all, my dear chap," he had concluded, "why would one wish to dine with someone who spent a portion of each day with his finger up someone else's arse?"

The smile the recollection had provoked disappeared as Burke entered the records room and found two uniformed security guards standing behind the counter. He steeled himself, nodded brusquely, and headed straight for the gate that led into the room's interior. His demeanor, he hoped, held all the self-assured arrogance he had witnessed in Dr. James Bradford that afternoon.

One of the guards seemed to hesitate as he pushed through

the gate, but the other—the younger and seemingly more dull-witted of the pair—immediately stepped forward.

"I have to check your ID," he mumbled, his eyes moving from Burke's face to the hospital name tag that identified him as Dr. John Rourke.

"*What* is going on?" Burke glared at the man with as much irritation as he could muster—a look intended to imply that important physicians should not be accosted by mere guards.

The guard seemed to hesitate, then mumbled something about the hospital and new orders. Burke couldn't quite catch the gist of it.

"Oh, hi, Dr. Rourke."

It was the flirtatious Wendy—to the rescue, Burke hoped. She breezed by the momentarily confused guard.

"Hello, Wendy. How are your summer classes going?"

Wendy made a face. "A drag," she said.

Out of the corner of his eye Burke saw the younger guard turn, look at his partner, then shrug. He kept up his prattle with Wendy.

"This research of mine is getting to be a drag, too," he said. "Can you spare me some help tonight?"

"Sure," she said, sounding pleased at the prospect. She threw the guard a look matching Burke's earlier one, then led him through the gate.

As they walked back to the stacks, Burke leaned toward her. "What's with the guards?" he asked.

"Who knows?" she said. "They showed up at four and said there was some new hospital policy—that they had to check everyone's ID before they were given any information." She rolled her eyes. "As if we didn't already do that. You'd think we'd been handing out information to any bozo who came along." She rolled her eyes again, distancing herself from the obvious stupidity of it all. "Sounds like make-work to me. Either that or they've got some new security boss who's trying to impress everybody."

Burke felt a wave of uneasiness. Had word of the story leaked? It was certainly possible. All it would take was one copyboy or reporter overhearing a newsroom conversation, then shooting his mouth off to some nurse he was hustling in a bar. Burke considered the potential dangers if that had happened. The big danger now was not being caught inside the records room. It would be embarrassing, and there might even be some minor charges if the hospital pushed it. But the *Globe* could take care of that. The danger was the story. He already had enough documentation to run it. That wasn't the problem. The real danger was word getting out to another newspaper or television or radio station that might preempt the story with one of their own, no matter how sketchy or feeble. It was a game the New York media loved to play. Jump your competition, then crow about being first. He decided he would have to alert Twist to the possibility.

Twist. Could Twist have inadvertently said something to Bradford? Burke doubted it. The man was far from stupid. Burke considered the possibility. If he had, no one would ever find out. Burke had never known an editor who had admitted compromising a story, although he was sure quite a few stories had been lost through drunken barroom conversations. It was the reporter who took the weight for those mistakes. Editors joined in when it was time to take a bow, but when failure reared its head, the reporter stood alone in the dock.

Burke glanced back at the guards. According to Wendy they had arrived at four that afternoon, which meant they might be replaced by others at midnight—others who might not be quite so easily intimidated or who might have previously met the real Dr. Rourke. He turned to Wendy and offered her his best smile.

"I've got a ton of records to go through, but I could probably get it all done in a couple of hours if you could help with the copying," he suggested.

"No problem," she said. "I'm yours for the night." She giggled at her flirtatious double entendre.

Burke ignored her. "And if there's any way you can manage it, please keep those guards away from me," he added.

She gave him a momentarily curious look, and Burke hurried on to cover any doubts he had put in her mind. He leaned in close and whispered in his most unctuous doctor's voice.

"I know it's not very egalitarian. But I just cannot *stand* macho minimum-wage men who use their square badges to lord it over everyone else."

Wendy rolled her eyes again. "Tell me about it. You think

they're bad with doctors, imagine how they treat medical students working as file clerks."

He winked at her. "It's us against them," he said.

The idea pleased Wendy. Her entire face brightened.

The work took longer than Burke expected, but with Wendy's help he was able to gather the final documentation and get out the door by eleven-thirty, a half hour before the anticipated changing of the hospital guard. The sudden appearance of the guards still puzzled him, but it was now a moot concern. He glanced at his watch. The first story, the one that would immediately follow Roberto's surgery, would hit the street in twenty-four hours, and the series itself would be in the hands of *Globe* readers the following day. Both those events would have occurred even if the guards had stopped him at the records-room door. This final bit of documentation had been corroborative and noncritical, so-called icing on the cake that just made the story stronger. Still, the question dogged him. He put his concern aside and fought off the temptation to look in on Roberto, who was now somewhere on the surgical floor. He was sure Maria would be there with him, perhaps together with the boy's grandmother, both dozing in chairs if they could manage any sleep at all. He rejected the idea, telling himself the visit would be pointless and would do nothing but interrupt what little rest the two woman would get. It also would require him to stash his phony medical attire and risk reentering the hospital as a civilian at a time when the records-room guards were just going off duty.

The arguments against won out. Instead he would head home and grab a few hours' sleep. Tomorrow would be a long day, and there would be a story to write, and he wanted to have all his wits about him. That story would have to be a killer, a meticulous account of little Bobby's struggle to survive and the close brush with death that had been imposed by the combined greed of doctor and hospital. Done the way Burke intended, it would ignite the natural cynicism of the *Globe's* readers and set the stage for everything that would follow.

When he reached his apartment, Burke checked his service and found he had a message to call Julia "no matter how late." She answered on the third ring, drowsy with sleep.

"The surgery's supposedly set for five A.M.," he said. "Dr. Salazar says Roberto is the first surgical patient on the schedule and that University Hospital runs a pretty tight ship. They don't like to waste any downtime in their high-income operating rooms. So if Bradford is there on time . . ."

"Will you be there?" she asked.

"Yeah, I'd like to see the kid before they take him in."

"Do you want me to come? Do you think it would make it easier on Maria if I'm there?"

"I don't think anything will make it easier," he said. "Salazar said the operation will take at least five hours, so we'll all just be sitting there waiting to hear."

"I'll stop by around nine, on my way in to the magazine," Julia said. "I have a story meeting scheduled for eleven, but if I can get it postponed to the afternoon, I will."

Burke glanced up at his bookcase, at the photo of Julia and Annie. "You're quite a woman, lady."

"Thanks." She paused a moment. "I think you're pretty special, too. If it had been left up to the *Globe* and those medical midgets, that little boy wouldn't be within miles of that operating room. I still can't believe you pulled it off."

Julia was quiet again. She understood newspapers and how they operated. She had lived with him through too many years of it. Burke knew that she also understood the repercussions that were sure to follow. He pushed his thoughts about that away. "Now it just has to work," he said.

"It will. Have faith."

Burke smiled at the sentiment. "Is that like keeping your fingers crossed?"

"It's a little stronger than that," Julia said. Burke thought she wanted to say more, but the words didn't come. "Good night, Billy," she said. "I'll see you in the morning."

Burke said good night and hung up the phone. Have faith, he thought. He glanced again at the photo of his wife and daughter. There had been faith, even prayer, in abundance all those years ago. Julia had clung to those slender threads repeatedly, as had he, each of them desperate to believe in miracles.

Burke closed his eyes in a silent prayer to any listening deity. This time. Please. Just this one time.

⟨ 24 ⟩

Burke walked down the hospital corridor. The walls and floors shimmered under harsh lighting, reflecting his image as though fashioned out of stainless steel. The hallway stretched ahead like a long tunnel, its end seeming to grow smaller and more distant with each step. Nurses and doctors scurried about him, each rushing back and forth from room to room. Several carried large buckets, the contents of which were covered with white towels. Burke tried to stop one, then another and another, each time asking for directions to Roberto Avalon's room. His queries were met with looks of disbelief or disinterest or hostility. Finally, frustrated, he grabbed the sleeve of a passing physician and demanded to know where the boy was. The doctor stared at him, blinked several times, then broke into a wide, maniacal grin.

"He's on the next floor, but you have to hurry," he said. He tried to pull away, but Burke held him fast.

"Why?" he demanded. "Why do I have to hurry?"

"Just hurry," the doctor said. "The next floor. Hurry to the next floor. Room Seventeen-seventeen."

He pointed toward a staircase, and Burke released him and rushed through the door. The interior stairwell was bright, gleaming, the light so harsh Burke could barely see the stairs that rose before him. He hurried forward and began to climb, taking the stairs two, three at a time. He moved up to another landing, then another, then three, then four before a door finally appeared. He pushed through it and found himself in another long hallway. Here the light was dimmer, the walls badly in need of paint, the surfaces smudged with dirt and grime. Burke hurried along the hall, searching out the number the doctor had given him. Seventeen-seventeen. He searched each door as he passed, but none held any number at all. A door opened, and a nurse appeared. She smiled at him.

"Can I help?" she asked.

"I'm looking for a room. Seventeen-seventeen," Burke said. "It's Roberto Avalon's room."

"Oh, yes. That is little Roberto's room. But Seventeen-seventeen's not here. It's in the basement."

Burke began to argue. "But the doctor downstairs said it was—"

The nurse laughed. "Doctors don't know where the rooms are. Trust me. It's in the basement." She pointed down the hall. "Take the elevator," she said. "Turn right when you reach the basement."

Burke entered the elevator and found it was nothing more than a flat platform. He pressed the button marked "B" and watched the platform descend, the sides scraping against the bare concrete walls of the shaft.

The doors slid open, and Burke found himself in a dark concrete corridor, the stark gray walls broken by glass-fronted doors spaced eight feet apart. Finally he reached a door marked 1717. There was no doorknob or handle, so he pushed against the glass and watched as the door swung back with a rush of pressurized air.

Before him was a vast, shimmering room. Here the walls were like those of the first corridor he had entered, seemingly made of glistening stainless steel, each reflecting the light so intensely he could barely make out the far corners.

The room was empty except for a single chair set before an inexplicable window. There was a young girl seated in the chair. She was staring out the basement window, and a long, wide, flowing lawn that Burke could not explain stretched out before her. The child seemed transfixed by the implausible view. Her body remained motionless, and she seemed unaware of his presence. All Burke could see was her outline against the window, and the long, silky brown hair that cascaded along her back until it almost touched the floor.

"Is this Roberto Avalon's room?" Burke asked.

Slowly the child turned, and Annie's blank eyes stared back at him. A small incongruous smile formed on her lips as she raised one hand and pointed toward a distant wall.

"What are you trying to tell me, Annie?" Burke asked.

Annie's smile widened. "Roberto's in there," she said. "But you can't talk to him now. Nobody can talk to him now."

"Why not, Annie?" Burke asked. "Why can't I talk to him?"

Annie looked at him as though he were teasing her with foolish questions. "You can't talk to him because he's dead, Daddy." She gave out a small laugh. "You can't talk to dead people, Daddy. You know that. It's why you can't talk to me. Even though you always try and try. Don't you understand anything, Daddy? Don't you? Don't you? Don't you?"

Burke stared in horror at his daughter, then followed her still-pointing finger to the shimmering wall. He stared, disbelieving, as the wall began to open, revealing a long, narrow room unlike the one in which he now stood. There the walls were stark concrete like those of the corridor he had followed from the elevator, and he suddenly realized that it *was* the corridor. Except now it was different. There, before him, Roberto Avalon lay on a long concrete table, his body naked, his chest cavity opened and spread like an autopsied cadaver's. Roberto looked up at him, then his eyes moved down the length of the table. There, at his feet, a lone nurse sat in a chair with a towel-draped bucket in her lap. The nurse reached into the bucket—once, twice, three times—each dip producing a banded stack of money that she carefully placed on the table.

The nurse turned and smiled at Burke. "Did you bring the rest of the money?" she asked. "You must give it to us now, you know. It's hospital policy. We can't issue the death certificate until we have the rest of the money." She smiled again. It was an encouraging smile, accompanied by repeated nods of her head, urging Burke to comply.

Burke looked back at Roberto. The boy was staring at him, waiting to see what he would do. A voice came from behind, the small, high-pitched voice of a young girl. Burke knew it was his daughter, and he turned to look back, but the light surrounding Annie was too bright, too harsh. He turned back to Roberto's pleading eyes, and the voice behind him came again.

"Give the nurse the money, Daddy. Then Roberto can be really dead. Give her the money for me, too, Daddy. For me, too. For me, too."

Burke squeezed his eyes shut and leaned back against the wall of the elevator, forcing away all memory of the dream that had awakened him at a quarter to four that morning. When the elevator doors slid back, he opened his eyes and stepped out into the hospital corridor. It was now four-forty-five, the dead of night to the still-sleeping city, and the degree of activity along the corridor startled him. Nurses, some in crisp white uniforms, others in green surgical scrubs, darted around lab-coated technicians, who pushed medication carts from room to room. A group of doctors, also dressed in surgical green, stood beside the nursing station, discussing a chart. As Burke approached, he caught a snippet of their conversation.

"We'll take her in, crack her open, and see what we have. Then, if we need Jamison, we can pack her off and call him in. He's on standby, just in case."

Burke stood behind the doctors until he caught the attention of a nurse.

"Roberto Avalon?" he asked.

"Are you family?" the nurse asked.

"Yes," Burke lied, not wanting to waste time with pointless explanations. "His mother is expecting me," he added.

"Four-oh-seven," the nurse said. "He's being prepped for surgery now."

Burke hurried down the corridor and found the room. The door was closed, and he paused, drawing a deep breath. The remnants of the dream still gnawed at him like some deeply rooted superstition he had never before acknowledged, some harbinger of disaster he could not alter.

Burke pushed the door open, almost expecting the pressurized whoosh of air that had been part of his dream. There were two beds in the room, one holding an elderly man who looked at him with open curiosity, the second with a curtain drawn around it. The curtain was pulled back as Burke entered, revealing Dr. Salazar and a nurse, both dressed in green surgical scrubs.

Salazar turned to Burke. "Mrs. Avalon and her mother are in the waiting room down the hall," he said. "They were a little . . ." He shrugged and looked back at Roberto. "We wanted Roberto as calm as possible before we took him in. We'll be giving him his pre-op medication in just a minute."

"How's he doing?" Burke glanced past Salazar. Roberto was in the bed, and he gave Burke a faint, nervous smile.

Salazar glanced at the boy again, then turned his attention back to Burke. "He's doing great. He's just been telling me everything he's going to do after the operation. I'm glad I won't have to try and keep up with him."

"Can I . . . ?" Burke raised his eyes toward the bed.

"Sure. But not too long. The medication cart will be here any minute, then the nurse will have to ask you to leave."

"I'd like to talk with you before the surgery if I can," Burke added.

"I'll wait for you by the nursing station," Salazar said.

Burke walked to the edge of the bed, reached out, and took Roberto's small hand. "Hey, Piece of Work. How ya doin'?"

Roberto gave him another weak smile. "I'm a little scared," the boy said.

The words hit like a hammer. He squeezed the boy's hand, then reached up and stroked his cheek. "It's okay to be a *little* scared. Just try to think about how good it's going to be later." He forced a smile, then raised his eyebrows in expectant wonder. "Nothing's gonna stop you from playing for the Yankees now. And the playground? Wow. You'll just be tearing up the playground."

"Mama said I won't get tired anymore," Roberto said.

Burke perched on the edge of the bed. He held his smile. "She's right. In a couple of weeks you'll be making everybody else tired, just trying to keep up with you."

The boy giggled. "Even you?"

"Especially me. You make me tired now. I don't know what I'm gonna do when *you* don't get tired anymore."

"You can take a nap," Roberto said. He giggled again.

"Hey, I'm too old for naps," Burke said. "I haven't had a nap since I was ten. What are you trying to do to me?"

Burke heard a rumbling noise behind him and realized the medication cart had arrived. The nurse placed a hand on his shoulder, and he nodded without looking at her.

"Look, I have to go in a minute, because the nurse has some stuff she has to do for you. But before I go, tell me one thing: What's the *first* thing you want to do when you leave the hospital?"

"I wanna play baseball. A whole game." Roberto's face brightened.

"Well, you think you might need a new baseball glove?"

"Could I have one? Really?"

"You just tell me what kind you want."

Roberto twisted with excitement. "Can I have a Roberto Clemente model?"

The boy's request for a glove named after a dead baseball player momentarily stunned Burke, given the surgery Roberto faced. He pushed his uneasiness aside. "Hey, wait a minute. He didn't play for the Yankees. He played for the Pirates."

"Yeah, but he was really cool."

"Cooler than Roberto Ramirez? He came to visit you."

"He's cool, too. But Roberto Clemente was cooler. He hit more home runs than anybody. My granma told me all about him."

Burke laughed. He wished the pompous Ramirez were there to hear the sacrilege. "I think so, too," he said. "A Roberto Clemente model it is. I'll bring it to you tomorrow."

"Really?"

"Really."

The nurse placed her hand on his shoulder again, more insistently this time.

Burke stood, then instinctively bent down and kissed the boy's forehead. "You be cool," he whispered. "The doctors are gonna do their thing now, and they need you to be brave so you can help them. You just remember how strong we want you to be, and that a lot of people love you."

"You too?" Roberto's eyes were filled with expectation.

"Yes, me too, Piece of Work," Burke said. He bent down and kissed the boy's forehead again. "I'll see you in a couple of hours."

The boy said nothing. He just smiled. It tore at Burke. He reached down and ran his hand along Roberto's cheek, realizing how much he wanted to see that smile again. Then he turned and left the room.

Dr. Salazar stood behind the nurses' station reviewing a medical chart. When he saw Burke approach, he came out of the station.

"What are his chances?" Burke asked.

Salazar allowed a grimace to express his concern. "We won't really know until we're in there and see what damage was done by these last few episodes. He's strong enough for the surgery, but beyond that it's hard to make a prognosis." He shook his head. "If we had been able to go in there two, three weeks ago, or at least before this last episode occurred, I'd be a lot more optimistic."

"But he'll survive, right?"

Salazar took Burke by the arm. His face was weary, his soft, gentle brown eyes sad. "Mr. Burke, there are no guarantees with any kind of surgery—especially open-heart surgery. Surgery is a highly intrusive procedure for which the body is never really prepared. Unfortunately, one of the best predictors of surgical success is a strong heart, which in this case . . ." He let the sentence die with a shrug.

"So you're telling me his chances would have been better two weeks ago, a month ago."

"Unquestionably. And even better still six months or a year ago, if his condition had been diagnosed that early."

"Son of a bitch."

"If you're talking about a particular son of a bitch, I can't comment," Salazar said. "The medical profession does not take kindly to trash talk about its own, by its own. Even when it's richly deserved."

"Can I quote you about his chances being better if the surgery had been done earlier?"

"Certainly. Just please don't quote me regarding anyone else's decision to delay that surgery. And please be specific that it is my *personal* professional opinion." He drew a deep breath. "That alone will get me in enough trouble. But I have to live with myself, too." He drew another long breath. "Now I have to see Mrs. Avalon. You're welcome to come with me and then wait with her. I'll be coming out to see her as soon as the surgery is completed. Hopefully that won't be for five hours."

Burke accompanied Salazar to the surgical waiting room. Maria sat forward in her chair as though prepared to leap from it at any moment. Her hands twisted together in her lap, further mangling a piece of tissue. Burke noticed that her eyes were red-rimmed, her face drawn and haggard. He doubted she had slept at all.

Maria's mother, Consuelo, sat beside her, and Burke thought the woman's face was as stricken with fear as any he had ever seen. He smiled at the older woman, hoping to comfort her, but was certain the attempt only conveyed his own private fears for her grandson.

Salazar took a chair next to Maria and began to explain carefully what would be done to Roberto over the next several hours. He avoided any technical jargon, keeping his explanation simple and direct. Burke noticed that the doctor's expression remained expectant and hopeful, the doubt that had filled his eyes when they had spoken in the hall now hidden away.

When he finished his explanation, Maria reached out and grabbed his hand. "He will be all right, Doctor? You believe he will be all right?" Every muscle in her body seemed to strain for the right answer.

Salazar reached out with his other hand, covering hers now with both of his. Burke silently hoped he would lie, even if it would do nothing more than ease her anxiety for the hours that lay ahead.

Salazar smiled at her, his brown eyes conveying all the gentleness that seemed so integral to the man. "His chances after this surgery will be better than they have been," he said. "If we did not do this, there would be no chance for him at all."

Maria's jaw tightened, then began to quiver as she fought back tears. "He's so very small," she said, her words so faint Burke was certain he would not have heard them had he not been watching her lips.

"We will do everything we can for him." Salazar glanced at Burke, his eyes seeming to beg for support. Keep up the charade, they seemed to say. It's what she needs right now.

When Salazar left, Maria stood and walked into Burke's arms. She held on tightly, as if his greater size would somehow help her endure what was happening to her son. "Thank you for coming, Billy," she whispered. "Thank you for everything."

"It's going to be fine," Burke said, the banality of his words sounding as hollow as they were. "I spoke to Roberto a few minutes ago, and he's already talking about what he wants to do when he gets out of the hospital."

He felt her breath catch as she fought off a sob. "What did he say?" she asked with difficulty.

"He wants to play baseball. We talked about getting him a new glove." Burke let out a short laugh, still delighted by his conversation with the boy. "He wants a Roberto Clemente model. Not a Roberto Ramirez."

Maria let out something that was half laugh, half sob. "Good," she said, sniffling back waiting tears. "Roberto Ramirez has too much machismo. I don't want my Roberto growing up thinking it's the way a man has to be."

Maria took a step back, and Burke could see her lips trembling. Just talking about her son's future had cracked through the fragile veneer of strength she was struggling to maintain. Burke glanced down at Consuelo. The older woman was rigid in her chair, her hands fisted into tight balls in her lap.

Maria reached out for his hand. "Is Julia coming?" Her voice sounded as though she very much wanted the answer to be yes.

"She'll be here about nine," he said. "She plans to stay with you as long as she can."

"She's been wonderful," Maria said. She hesitated, uncertain if she should continue. "I think you should live with her again,

Billy," she finally added. "Whenever you're together, I can see how much you mean to each other."

They stared at each other. It was as though some silent message—something each had come to realize—had passed between them.

"Let's all go down to the cafeteria and get some breakfast," Burke said, breaking the mood.

Maria shook her head. Her mother began repeating the word no, over and over.

"I'm afraid to leave," Maria said. "What if they come looking for me? What if there's something they have to tell me?"

Burke looked at both women in turn. "It will be hours before there's any news. Believe me." He waited for some response but got nothing. "It'll be better all around if you eat something and try to relax," he added. He smiled at Maria and gave her his best boyish shrug in a blatant attempt to cajole her. "It's going to be a long morning, and I need some coffee. Please come with me."

Julia arrived shortly after nine, and the three women fell into long embraces. Maria and Consuelo seemed to take immediate comfort from her, whereas the four hours they had spent with Burke had only increased their anxiety. Breakfast had been a disaster. Consuelo had steadfastly refused to go, and Maria had spent every minute repeatedly checking the clock and growing increasingly frantic about her absence from the surgical floor. For Burke the four hours that followed had seemed interminable.

Julia broke away from the women and came to Burke. She reached up and stroked his cheek. "You look beat," she said.

"I finished up in the records room last night. Just dotting the final I's on the rest of the story. It took longer than I thought."

"Did you get any sleep?"

"Enough." Julia was dressed in slacks and a ribbed scoop-neck jersey under a tan blazer. The sunglasses she had worn on the street were pushed up on top of her hair, an affectation recently made popular by Jackie Onassis. He thought she looked very stylish, and fetching as hell. "When do you have to go into the office?" he asked.

She gave him a slightly self-satisfied look. "I put the story meeting off until midafternoon. There was some grumbling—

but there's always grumbling. We have as many prima donnas at my shop as you have at yours." A small smile formed at the corners of her mouth. "I think I actually enjoy saying no to them when they start to bitch and moan about something." Burke shook his head. "It's hard for me to envision you as the tough magazine editor," he said. "I don't know why it should be. It just is."

"You've seen too much of the vulnerable side over too many years," she said. She offered him a teasing grin. "If you worked for me, you'd probably be one of the chief grumblers."

Burke narrowed his eyes. "If you're trying to say I'd fit in with all the other prima donnas, I'm offended." He raised a hand. "No, don't say anything. My fragile ego couldn't handle it. Let me get you some coffee instead." He paused a moment. "But come with me, okay?" His look told her there were things he wanted to say away from Maria and her mother.

By the time they reached the elevator, Burke had filled Julia in on what Salazar had told him.

"I can't believe the prognosis is so grim," she said.

"I guess his last attack was even worse than we realized. The kid is just so small and so frail."

They entered the elevator, and Julia wrapped her arms tightly around herself. She shook her head. "I keep thinking about Twist. How he questioned the need to do it now. I mean, I know it's his job to question these things, but the way he wanted to wait until all the money was in." She shook her head again. "The man is such a shit."

Burke took her arm as the elevator doors opened onto the lobby. The entrance to the cafeteria was straight ahead. To its right was a set of double doors bearing the sign PHYSICIANS' CAFETERIA. PHYSICIANS ONLY.

"This thing has a long line of shits, and Twist is at the back of that line," Burke said. "Bradford and this hospital are way up at the front, but they also have a lot of company—including all the doctors over all those years who never took the time to give the kid a proper diagnosis." He guided Julia into the cafeteria. "You know, I think Salazar has been trying to get that message across to me each time we've talked. But he tries to say it without really saying anything flat out."

"What is it that you think he's saying?"

"Just what everyone knows but never says out loud. That when you're poor, the whole health-care system is stacked against you. No matter what you need, you always end up with second best."

They returned to the waiting room with their coffee. At ten o'clock five hours had passed with no word about Roberto. At eleven Burke left to phone the paper and keep the city desk updated.

"The bottom of page three has been left open for you," Fabio told him. "It's enough space for at least three takes, with a jump to the back of the book so you can write another take if you need it." Burke thought about what he was saying. In journalese that meant three double-spaced typewritten pages for page three—the primary news page for a tabloid—with room for another typewritten page in the back of the paper. All together it totaled about a thousand words, a major commitment of space, the kind reserved for stories the editors considered the most newsworthy.

"Let's just hope it's an upbeat piece," Burke said.

Fabio was momentarily silent. "I know it's not what you want to hear, but they plan on the same play whether the kid lives or dies. They consider the story big either way."

Burke ground his teeth, then let it pass. It was the reality of newspapers in its harshest form. "I'll come in and start writing as soon as the kid is out of surgery and I have a chance to talk to his doctor."

"That's fine, but keep me posted," Fabio said. "Twist is pacing around like a caged cat. He also wants to know if you got the rest of the documentation you were after, *and* he wanted me to remind you that you were supposed to turn in *all* the documentation as soon as the kid went under the knife."

Burke let out a snort. "Tell him I decided to see about the kid first. I know he'll think I'm screwing up my priorities again, but he'll just have to live with it. Unless you want to get the stuff out of your car and give it to him."

Fabio let out his own snort. "Fuck him. Let him wait. Just call me when you know what's going on."

Burke was on his way back to the waiting room when he

spotted Salazar at the nurses' station. He hurried toward him. When Salazar saw him, he motioned him into a small room behind the station.

Burke could feel his heart beating in his chest. "How is he?" he demanded even before Salazar could get the door closed.

Salazar let out a breath. "He survived. But it was close. His heart stopped twice during the surgery. If he makes it through the next forty-eight hours, I think he has a good chance. But . . ." He stopped speaking and stared at the floor, almost as though the next words were too painful to speak.

"But what?" Burke demanded. The angry tone of his voice brought Salazar's eyes back to his.

"The damage we found going in was even worse than I expected. That last episode had the effect of a major coronary. I'm afraid that means that if Roberto lives, he's going to have a serious heart problem for the rest of his life."

Burke stared at him. "So we didn't accomplish a fucking thing."

"No, no, no," Salazar insisted. "We accomplished a great deal." He reached out and took Burke by the arm. "There was no chance at all without this hole in his heart being closed. Now at least he has the chance of living into adulthood. And with the medications currently being tested, maybe well into that adulthood. It just may not be as full a life as I had hoped." He shook his head. "Look, the boy won't be an athlete, but if he survives the next forty-eight hours, he can still have a reasonably full life."

It was Burke's turn to stare at his shoes. "Have you told his mother and grandmother?"

Salazar shook his head. "I was waiting for Bradford. But it appears he's not coming out."

Burke's head snapped up. "What do you mean he's not coming out? Where the hell is he?"

"My guess would be that he's in the surgeons' locker room. Changing so he can visit some of his other patients." Salazar held up a hand. "It's not uncommon. There are some surgeons who prefer leaving anything but perfect news to others. They only come out when adulation is expected." Salazar gave him a wry look. "It's a matter of style. It also avoids confrontations and possible accusations by giving family members time to accept results that might have been less than expected. I once attended a conference where an attorney for an insurance company recommended the tactic."

"That's delightful, but I intend to speak with him," Burke said.

Salazar nodded, his eyes suddenly revealing his own anger. "I can't promise you he'll respond, and the area he's in is off-limits to the public. But if someone went through the doors that lead to the operating wing, then turned right at the end of the corridor, he'd find the door clearly marked."

James Bradford was standing before a mirror brushing the sides of his salt-and-pepper hair when Burke entered the surgeons' locker room. Bradford was already dressed in his white lab coat, his stethoscope cavalierly draped about his neck.

"Dr. Bradford. My name is William Burke. I need a few minutes of your time."

Bradford spun around as if fearing an attack. "How did you get in here?" he demanded. His voice was filled with such outrage, it almost made Burke smile.

Burke turned around and stared at the door he had entered. "I came in that way," he said. He watched Bradford try to comprehend the remark. It was so blatantly ridiculous that it seemed to confuse him.

Regaining his composure, Bradford became snappish again. "This area is not open to the public. You'll have to leave at once."

Burke took a step forward and watched Bradford retreat a step. "I'm a reporter for the *Globe*, and I need a comment from you about the surgery you just performed."

Bradford glared at him. "I have nothing to say to you. I said everything I have to say to your city editor."

Burke took another step, and again Bradford retreated. "It's just one question, Doctor. Do you think the outcome of Roberto Avalon's surgery would have been better if you had operated a month ago instead of waiting for your fee to be guaranteed?"

Bradford's face turned scarlet, and he began to huff visibly as he tried to get his words out. "Oh, so that's it, is it? It's not enough that you're going to slander me for the work this hospital has done for the city. Now you're going to castigate me because I didn't operate fast enough on the *Globe's* goddamn poster boy." He began jabbing a finger toward Burke. "Well, let me tell you something. That child got the best surgical care anybody could get *anywhere* in this country. But you people seem to think that surgeons are supposed to be charitable institutions, that it's some kind of goddamn crime when we expect to be paid for our services."

Bradford's tirade flew by Burke in a blur. His comment about the scam he and the hospital had run on the city had momentarily obscured everything else. It had come out of the blue, and Burke immediately realized who its source had been. Twist had sandbagged him. He had used his meeting with Bradford to elicit comments about the hospital scam, not just to push him into the operation for Roberto. He had covered his ass, just in case Burke made good on his threat to hold back the documentation.

Burke struggled to keep his composure and pinned Bradford with his own glare. "Is that your comment, Doctor? That you had a right to be paid? That it was okay for that little boy to wait until you were? Wait so long that his heart sustained enough damage that no amount of surgery could completely fix it?" Burke watched Bradford's color deepen. He softened his voice. "And if he doesn't survive the next forty-eight hours, Doctor, is it still okay?"

"You . . . you . . ."

"What's the matter, Doctor? Is the reality of it just a bit too ugly for you?"

Bradford's face was beet red now, and he took an aggressive step forward. Burke set his feet, hoping that the man would come all the way.

Bradford saw the change in body language and stopped. "It's just like this business with the city," he snapped. "You're out to paint me as some kind of thief—just another greedy physician who's lining his pockets and the hell with his patients. Well, there was nothing I did with that little boy that was in any way wrong. I saved his goddamn life. Me." He held up his hands. "That little boy died on the table twice. *Twice.* And with these two hands I brought him back and gave him a shot at years he never would have had." He started to step forward again, but again he stopped himself. He seemed flustered and began babbling. "It's the same thing with the work I did for the city. Everything you think you found can be explained. It's nothing more than some stupid clerk putting the wrong date on a report. I did every bit of work I was paid for, and so did every other physician and intern and medical student in this hospital."

Bradford was giving him more than he had ever hoped to get, and Burke decided to goad him into even more. "Clerical error. Well, that's something quite different from what I thought I found in the hospital records," he said. He tried to look contrite as he pushed his memory for names he could shove down Bradford's throat.

"Let me see. There was a Winifred Fitzgerald. I seem to recall that you performed a rather lengthy procedure on her when you were actually consulting at City Hospital on another case."

"That's a goddamn clerical mistake. That's all it is." Bradford was raging now, his composure long gone.

"I'm sure you're right, Doctor," Burke said. "And I guess a surgical patient named Walter Marlow was another clerical error. Because you were actually at Harlem Hospital for the entire day when his surgery was performed." Bradford started to speak again, but Burke cut him off. "Then there was—let's see, it's hard doing this without all my notes. Oh, yeah, Rebecca Goldstein and—was it William Monroe? Yeah, that's it, William Monroe. And then there was—"

"Get the fuck out of here, goddamn it. Get out of here right now, or I'll call security and have you arrested."

Burke nodded, as if considering the idea. "Arrest. Yeah, I think that's a distinct possibility, Doctor." He turned toward the door, then glanced back over his shoulder. "But I'll leave now, Doctor. You've given me everything I need. And you? You enjoy the next couple of days, Doc. You're about to get your fifteen minutes of fame."

"You'll hear from my goddamn lawyer," Bradford shouted.

Burke grinned at him. "No I won't, Doc. He'll be talking to one of the twenty-two lawyers who work on the eighth floor of the *Globe*. They're already quite familiar with the stories you'll be reading."

Bradford was still sputtering unintelligible threats as Burke walked out of the room. Fuck you, he thought. And fuck your lawyer and your accountant and anyone else who thinks your medical degree and your goddamn money should keep you from getting slammed.

Dr. Salazar was holding both of Maria's hands when Burke returned to the waiting room. The woman's face was ashen, her eyes hollow and blank, almost as though every other word that Salazar spoke sailed past her without registering.

She looked up as Burke entered. "Billy, is he going to be all right, Billy?" Her eyes were pleading, begging Burke for some words that would counter what Salazar had already told her.

Julia was seated next to her, and she slipped her arm around Maria's shoulder and held her tightly. Maria's eyes continued to stare at Burke. Off in a corner Roberto's grandmother wept silently.

Burke knelt down in front of Maria. He wanted to reassure her, tell her what she needed to hear. He also knew they were past the point of comforting lies. "I don't know if he's going to be all right," he said. "I know Dr. Salazar believes he has a very good chance, and I want very much to believe that. I also know he's a strong little boy . . ."

Maria began shaking her head violently. "He's not strong. He's never been strong. He's small, so very small, and he's—" She began to sob.

Salazar tightened his grip on her hands and began to speak to her in Spanish. Burke thought Salazar was telling her *she* had to be strong, that her son would take strength from the strength of those around him.

Maria drew herself up and stared back at the doctor, but the sobs were still there, along with the fear. "I will be strong," she said.

Burke could see tears forming in Julia's eyes. She tightened her grip on Maria's shoulders, then leaned in and whispered something in her ear. Maria turned and nodded. Her eyes had become harder, stronger.

Maria turned back to Salazar. "When can I see Roberto?" she asked.

"He's in the recovery room now," Salazar said. "He's still

asleep from the anesthesia and will be for at least another hour. But you and your mother can be with him." He gave her one of his gentle smiles. "You can talk to him and hold his hand. There is no medical proof that this helps, but I have always believed that a patient knows when the people who love him are there, and that those small comforts help him to recover."

The words seemed to swell Maria's resolve. "I want to go to him now," she said.

Salazar nodded. "I'll go with you." He turned to Burke, then Julia. "I think for now it would be best to limit the visitors to Maria and her mother. Later, when Roberto awakens and we have a chance to evaluate him, it might be possible for each of you to see him. But that will be several hours at least. So if you have work to do . . ."

Burke nodded. "I'll wait here, at least for a while. At some point I have to go back to the paper. If I have to leave before I can see him, I'll come back later."

"I'll leave word at the nursing station that you're authorized to go in," Salazar said. He reached out and touched Burke's arm. "Thank you for what you did." A small, hard glint came to his eyes. Burke thought it was a hint of the anger he had seen earlier. "And for what you're going to do," he added.

When Maria and her mother followed Salazar out of the waiting room, Julia slid her arms around Burke and laid her head on his chest. "Why don't you go back to the paper now?" she said. "You can get your story written, then you'll be free to spend more time with Roberto later. I'll call you as soon as we can see him."

"I thought you had to get back to the magazine," Burke said.

He felt Julia shake her head. "I'm not going. I'll call the office and reschedule the meeting for tomorrow. And I'll call you as soon as I hear anything."

Burke stroked the back of her head, enjoying the softness of her hair. "Tell me something. Before Maria left, you whispered something to her. What did you say?"

Julia hesitated a moment. "I told her a mother's strength could keep a child safe."

He stroked her hair again. "Do you believe that?"

"Yes, I do," she said. "I've always believed it."

(25)

Burke telephoned Fabio before he left the hospital, and a copy-boy was waiting for him in the *Globe* lobby with the keys to Frankie's car. When he entered Twist's office a few minutes later, Burke laid all the documentation on his desk.

Twist stared at it and nodded. "That everything?" he asked.

"You've got the whole package. Plus you have whatever Bradford gave you during your meeting the other day." He held Twist's eyes. "If there's anything I can use in the story, I'd appreciate having it."

Twist began drumming his fingers on the desk. "I might have a quote or two for you," he said. He glanced at the documentation. "You didn't expect me to let you hold the story for ransom, did you?"

Burke kept all emotion off his face. "Lenny, I'm beyond expecting or not expecting anything."

"That's good to hear, Billy. It's about time you found out how the game is played. By the way, how's the kid?"

Burke pushed down his anger. "It's a coin toss," he said. "The next forty-eight hours will tell the story. He died on the table twice, but they were able to revive him. The worst news is, if he makes it, he'll have serious heart problems for the rest of his life. That last attack did more damage than they thought."

Burke watched Twist's eyes for any sign of anything that approached regret. His words seemed to have gone right past the man. All he saw was a glimmer of excitement over the story Burke would now write.

"Jesus. I want that stuff about the kid dying on the table right up front. All the stuff about the damage to his heart, too. Play it up big. We'll crucify Bradford with it. *And* the hospital. They won't have a chance in hell of talking their way out of it." Burke thought the glint in Twist's eyes approached madness. It was the look of a starving man unexpectedly handed a plate of food. "Speaking of the hospital," Twist continued, "they're sending over a couple of their flunkies to try to convince us that everything they did on the city contract was on the up-and-up." He let out a derisive snort. "Like we give a shit what they say." He tapped his ear. "We'll listen, of course. They just might dig the hole a little deeper. And I've also got a little surprise for them that may make a sidebar to the main story."

"You better be ready for a dance lesson," Burke said. "When I talked to Bradford, he ranted and raved—claimed the hospital scam was nothing but a giant clerical error. And when I went to the hospital last night, there were two security guards standing watch over the records room."

"There were never guards there before?"

"Never. My guess is that Bradford went running to the administration right after he talked to you, and they decided to make sure nothing else got out."

Twist ignored the implied criticism. "What about the additional stuff you were after?" His eyes had hardened, and Burke could tell he was preparing to affix blame elsewhere if the additional documentation had been lost.

"I got it," Burke said. "You have the pertinent surgical records for the past three and half years on your desk."

Twist rubbed his hands together. "Excellent. Excellent." He cocked his head to one side. "You never told me how you were getting the stuff. I always assumed you had somebody inside slipping it out to you. How'd they get it by the guards?"

"They didn't. I got it myself."

"How?"

"I've been going in posing as one of Bradford's partners. Dr. John Rourke. He's been away in Europe. The nurse who gave us the original tip gave me his lab coat, his hospital name tag, even his stethoscope."

"And nobody recognized you weren't him?"

"It was just like she said: Surgeons don't run errands to the records room. They have people who do that for them."

"That is fucking beautiful. God, I wish we could use it. But we'd probably end up in court." Twist held up a warning finger. "Anybody asks, all the documentation was delivered in a plain brown package. We never knew who our benefactor was; we just confirmed its accuracy. They want to know how we confirmed it, we just sit back and smile."

Burke nodded. "I know the drill."

"Good. Then get your tail out to that typewriter and drill a few holes in Bradford and that hospital. And keep checking on the kid's condition. I want a second lead that says the kid died— a couple of paragraphs just in case. I want to have it set and ready to drop in right up to press time. Now, get to it. I'll come and get you when those clowns get here from the hospital. You've earned the right to watch them bleed." There was a glitter in Twist's eyes. "And to see the little surprise I have for them," he added.

Twist came for Burke at three o'clock. Burke handed him the finished copy, along with the second lead that would cover the possibility of Roberto's death. Writing those few short paragraphs had been an emotional nightmare, the most difficult words he had ever pushed through a typewriter.

Twist stood over him, reading the copy. "This is great. Perfect." He read on, then slapped Burke on the back. "Jesus, this Bradford doesn't know when to keep his mouth shut, does he?"

"The man believes what he's saying. He believes what he did

was all right, that it's the way these things are done." Burke stared up at Twist, wondering if he'd ever make the connection, if he'd ever understand that the same attitude prevailed in newsrooms every day.

Twist grinned at him. "You're right. It's the mind-set. Reminds you of Richard Nixon, doesn't it?"

No, Burke thought, the man will never understand it. But that's only part of the point. You understand it, and you still choose to play the game. "It's called spiritual corruption," Burke said.

"Yeah, well, a few days from now he'll be on his knees, praying that the villagers don't show up at his door carrying torches." Twist finished reading the story, held the pages above his head, and shouted, "Copy!"

When a copyboy raced over, Twist handed him the pages and issued a series of commands. "Tell Frankie we may have some inserts coming after our meeting. Tell him the second lead is a 'just in case' job that I want set and held. And tell him I'll write the headline for both stories myself. Tell him I want this off the city desk and at the copy desk as fast as possible, and that I'll go over the copyediting myself before we send it down to the composing room." He turned back to Burke. "Now let's go have some fun," he said.

The attorney for the hospital was a short, balding, grim-looking man who introduced himself as Malcolm MacDonald. His business card indicated he was a senior partner in the firm of Winston, Brancroft and MacDonald, with pricey offices on Wall Street.

MacDonald was shepherding Thomas Prichard, the hospital administrator, and Peter Carangelo, the public-relations officer, and together they occupied one side of a long conference table that completely filled a room off the newsroom reception area. Burke had never met Prichard, who was in his fifties, with a pinched face and permanently pursed lips that went well with his shapeless Brooks Brothers suit. Carangelo was a different story. Burke had dealt with him many times, and Carangelo had always been accommodating. He was the nephew of a Brooklyn congressman who sat on the hospital's board, but he had always proved surprisingly competent for someone who'd gotten his job through political clout.

"Lenny. Billy. It's good to see you guys," Carangelo said. "I wish the circumstances were different, but I'm sure we can clear this up."

Twist stared at Carangelo, letting him know what he thought of his hail-fellow approach. The PR man seemed undaunted. He was dressed in a pale-gray suit with piping along the lapels, a crisp blue shirt with a large butterfly collar, and a striped tie the size of a small flag. He was short and stocky, somewhere in his early thirties, with long sideburns and dark hair that fell across his forehead. He also had the slightly puffy look of someone who enjoyed his lunch-hour martinis. He fixed everyone with a confident smile. "Look, we've helped each other many times over the years," he began. "And I'm certain we can satisfy all the concerns you have."

The lawyer leaned forward, obviously having had enough of Carangelo's glad-handing approach. "Why don't you just ask your questions, and let us provide the answers?" MacDonald's eyes were hard on Twist, and Burke looked down at the reporter's notebook that lay in front of him as he struggled to suppress a smile. There was nothing Twist liked more than dealing with an opponent who considered himself intimidating.

Twist leveled his own stare at the lawyer. "That's a great idea. Let's start with Bobby Avalon and the hospital's decision to withhold services until payment was received."

MacDonald raised his eyebrows to indicate surprise. "Is there something improper about that? University Hospital, as I'm sure you know, is a private teaching institution, not a public facility. When insurance is not available, we always ask for some guarantee of payment. There are, as you also know, public hospitals that regularly care for uninsured or indigent patients."

Twist leaned forward, eyes gleaming. "In this case the care the boy needed wasn't available at a public hospital. It required the kind of specialized surgical facilities that *you* have. It also required the services of a surgeon who specializes in this delicate type of open-heart surgery. If I'm not mistaken, almost all of those surgeons also work for you. It's a little niche University Hospital has carved out for itself."

MacDonald started to speak, but Twist raised a hand, shutting him down. "So what we have is a little boy who is not going to live without a certain type of specialized surgery, and then we have a hospital who says he can't have it until he pays them up front. In effect, we have that hospital passing a death sentence on a child, simply because he has the misfortune of being poor."

MacDonald sat upright, bristling with all the umbrage he could muster. "That's outrageous."

"Yes, it is," Twist snapped back. "That little boy finally got the surgery he needed because the *Globe*, through the generosity of its readers, came up with the cash that your hospital insisted on having before you opened your doors to him." He lowered his voice to emphasize the gravity of his words. "But we were a little late. It took a little too much time to raise your money. Because that little boy died on the operating table *twice* before his belated surgery was completed, and now—*if* he survives the next forty-eight hours—he'll live with serious heart problems for the rest of his life. So, Mr. MacDonald, we have to wonder what this child's condition would be had the hospital taken a more humane stance a month ago."

MacDonald puffed himself up. "You're suggesting the administration of the hospital made a conscious decision to harm this child, when in fact it had no way of knowing this situation even existed. I warn you, such allegations will not be ignored."

Twist sat back and smiled at the man. He lowered his voice even further. "No, I don't think they'll be ignored either, Mr. MacDonald."

Burke leaned forward. "I'm confused," he began. "You say the hospital had no way of knowing about the boy's surgical needs. But it's my understanding that he spent three days in your hospital while that very diagnosis was being arrived at by members of your staff."

"And we never charged him for those three days," MacDonald snapped.

"Take off three days in hell for everyone," Twist sniped. He leaned forward again. "So what is it? Did you know, or didn't you? You sure as hell seem to remember that you provided those three days on the arm."

MacDonald glanced down the table at the hospital administrator, cuing him that it was his turn to enter the fray. Burke decided that their response had been well orchestrated before they arrived.

Thomas Prichard folded his hands in front of him and spoke without moving his upper lip. "That's precisely the point," he began. "We were aware that the child was in the hospital and that the hospital provided certain services on a charity basis— or on the arm, as you say. Which, I may add, we were happy to do. We were not, however, aware of any diagnosis that was arrived at. That remained in the purview of our surgical staff."

"Dr. Bradford," Burke interjected.

"Exactly." Prichard gave a regretful shrug. "It was Dr. Bradford's decision not to go forward at that time. And I'm sure he had sound medical reasons for that decision. However, I also must point out that at no time was the hospital administration advised that this child's surgical needs were in any way critical. Nor do we have any information even now that they were."

"So it was strictly Bradford's decision," Burke said.

"Entirely."

"And had the hospital known, it would have provided the necessary care?" Burke watched Prichard twist in his chair.

"All I can say is that we certainly would have evaluated any request by a member of our staff. And frankly, I can't imagine anyone at our hospital turning their back on a needy child." He raised a cautioning hand. "But I must add: A request would have to have been made by a surgeon affiliated with our hospital. Otherwise . . ." Prichard raised both hands now, then allowed them to fall in a gesture of helplessness.

"So it was Bradford's call not to ask for the hospital's help," Twist said.

"Ultimately, yes," Prichard said. "But I have to say that I have always found Dr. Bradford to be a very competent and extremely caring physician. If you quote anything I have said, I insist you include that as well."

Burke looked down at his notebook again. And, he thought, with that rousing vote of confidence, Thomas Prichard, hospital administrator extraordinaire, and his entire compassionate staff have just sent Dr. James Bradford off to the gallows all by himself.

"All right. That pretty much answers our questions on that point." Twist held Prichard's gaze, taking control again. "And I can assure you that the hospital's position on this will be clearly detailed in our story." He brought his hands together and turned back to MacDonald. "Now let's turn to the service contract University Hospital and its medical school had with the city."

Quickly Twist explained what the *Globe* had found, and its belief that the hospital had collected almost three million dollars for services never performed.

When Twist finished, MacDonald favored him with a look he might give to an errant child. "We've been aware of your concerns for the past two days," he said. "Dr. Bradford explained it to Mr. Prichard after a meeting I believe he had with you."

"Go on," Twist said.

"As I said, we have had the opportunity to look into it just a bit. And it appears—superficially, at least—that there was some apparent basis for your concern. But we have also concluded, after looking at our records, that the few instances you mentioned were the result of nothing more than a series of unfortunate clerical errors."

"Really?" Twist said. He raised a hand. "Just excuse me for a minute. I'll be right back."

While Twist was gone, Peter Carangelo tried his PR best. He told Burke that the hospital would hold daily press briefings about Roberto's condition. Burke felt sorry for the man. He had obviously been brought along for his supposed rapport with the editors and reporters of the *Globe*, and he was working hard—offering up his best tap dance to impress his bosses. But nothing would help him today. When the dust settled, his client would still be fresh meat, and Carangelo's star at University Hospital would undoubtedly suffer a dramatic fall. It was the life of a flack, Burke mused—someone brought in to clean up messes made by others, then held responsible when those efforts failed. He wondered why anyone ever took the job.

Twist returned loaded down with all the documentation Burke had given him earlier that day. He laid the stack on the conference table. It stood more than six inches high.

"So let me get this straight," Twist began again. "Every instance when one of your physicians, residents, interns, or medical students was supposed to be working at a city hospital but was actually elsewhere working for you is nothing more than a few clerical errors? Is that what you're telling us?"

Twist had consciously ignored the stack of papers he had laid on the conference table. MacDonald's eyes, however, had never left them.

"What is that?" he now asked.

Twist glanced at the stack of papers, as if surprised to see them there. "They're your records—or copies, rather. Surgical records, listing when and where your surgeons performed various procedures. Medical-school teaching schedules. Staff schedules. Vacation schedules. The whole ball of wax."

"Where did you get those records?" MacDonald demanded.

"That's not important," Twist said.

"It is vitally important," MacDonald snapped. His umbrage had returned full force. "These are private, in some cases medically privileged records, which you have no right to possess."

"But we do have them. So let's move on."

"No, let's not," MacDonald snapped again. "This is hospital property that has obviously been stolen."

Twist shook his head. "I don't think so. They're all photocopies. So I'm reasonably certain you'll find the originals still in your possession." He turned to Burke, all innocence. "Is that your understanding?"

"I'm reasonably sure that's true," Burke said. He was struggling to keep a straight face. "The photocopies arrived anonymously, but when we asked to have their authenticity confirmed, the people who did that for us had no trouble finding the originals."

"And who authenticated this—this . . . ?" MacDonald kept staring at the stack of papers.

"I'm afraid I can't tell you that," Burke said. "The parties involved asked for anonymity—at least for now."

"So let's get this straight," Twist said, seizing control again. "We have God-knows-how-many hospital documents here, and we've compared them to city records that detail payments made to University Hospital for services allegedly rendered at Bellevue Hospital and Harlem Hospital. Now, it's your contention that any discrepancies showing that members of your staff were elsewhere when these alleged services were being performed are the result of clerical errors." He looked up at MacDonald. "Am I right?"

MacDonald remained silent.

Twist shook his head. "If that's true, you've got one helluva clerical problem." He paused to look at all three men. "You see, when Mr. Burke checked the city's records against your records, he came up with something that astounded us. During those times when your doctors were supposed to be at one of the city hospitals, they were actually at your hospital *seventy-two* percent of the time. In fact, some of your specialists never so much as set foot in one of those city hospitals, even though the City of New York paid them for being there. Now tell me, in all honesty, do you think it's possible that your clerical people make erroneous staffing and surgical entries seventy-two percent of the time?" Twist let out a low chuckle. "Because if that's true, I sure as hell want our readers to know it, so they can stay the hell away from your hospital."

MacDonald sat with his jaw clenched. "I think it is quite possible that our surgical records are correct and that the time sheets submitted to the city erroneously listed the time and dates that our staff was working at the city's hospitals."

"Would you like to show us the correct records?" Burke asked. "I'll be happy to go with you right now."

"Those are private, confidential records   "

"I'll only need the records pertaining to the time spent at city hospitals. We already have the hospital records we can compare them to. Will you show us the correct records?"

"I would have to advise my client not to do so unless served with a subpoena."

The words brought Twist to his feet. "That's a good answer," he said. "Please excuse me again."

Twist returned in less than two minutes in the company of Nicholas Sorrentino. Burke sat openmouthed, stunned by Twist's audacity.

Twist extended his hand toward Sorrentino. "I think you gentlemen know Mr. Sorrentino, the city's commissioner of investigation." He waited while Sorrentino offered each man a curt nod, then continued. "As I'm sure you know, Mr. Sorrentino is in effect the city's prosecutor in all matters involving suspected crimes committed by the city's employees or its contractors. We took the liberty of telling him what we think we've found, and he asked if he could be here."

MacDonald raised both hands in the air. "All right. Let's stop right there. From this point on I am advising my clients to have no further comment on this matter."

Sorrentino smiled down at him. He was tall, slender, and unusually erudite for a career politician, but one hundred percent politician all the same. When Twist had beckoned, he obviously had arrived on the run.

"That's excellent advice, Counselor," Sorrentino began. "I'd like very much to hear the hospital's explanation, but I fully understand that you may need time to consult with your clients." He took a step forward, reached into his suit coat pocket, and withdrew a folded document. "In the meantime, this is a subpoena for all hospital records pertaining to the time your physicians, residents, interns, and medical students worked at the city's hospitals, along with all hospital records that pertain to work done by those individuals at University Hospital and its medical school. That will also include vacation schedules, teaching schedules—everything, in fact, that may prove pertinent. I'd also like to advise you that all of the doctors in question are currently being served subpoenas for their personal records. And further, that uniformed police officers are currently en route to your hospital with orders to safeguard the records in question until the hospital has turned over all of those documents."

MacDonald reached out and took the subpoena, then looked down the table. "Not a word at his time," he warned. He turned back to Sorrentino. "I imagine we are free to go?"

"Certainly," Sorrentino said.

"*I* might have a few more questions," Twist said. He was fighting down a smile.

MacDonald gave him a cold look. "Good day, Mr. Twist. It's been interesting." He turned to Burke. "With you as well, Mr. Burke."

When the hospital trio had left, Twist fell back in his chair and slapped both hands on the table. "I love it. I just fucking love it." He looked up at Sorrentino and extended his hand. "Nick, you were beautiful. When your investigation gets rolling I'm going to have you all over the front page every day. You'll be the biggest thing in this city since Fiorello La Guardia." Sorrentino winced. "He was a Republican, but I guess I can live with it. As long as I don't have to read the Sunday comics on the radio." Twist gave him a broad wink. "You won't have to. We'll get a judge to sentence Bradford to read them."

On the way back to the newsroom Twist slung his arm around Burke's shoulders. "How'd you like my little surprise?"

"It surprised the hell out of me." He reminded himself that he had to alert Gerard LaFrancois that the stories were about to run, so his boss, the city comptroller, could get in on the act.

Twist's self-congratulation continued. "Just wait till we get this thing rolling. We're gonna stand this city on its ear." He gave Burke's shoulder a squeeze. Now, get back to your desk and start churning out the inserts. And give me a sidebar on Sorrentino's subpoena. We're gonna tear this town up tomorrow. Then we're gonna win this newspaper a goddamn Pulitzer Prize."

{ 26 }

Twist took one of the wing chairs that faced Harold Wainwright's desk. He was alone this time. The executive editor was still touring the paper's farflung bureaus, and Twist had decided to bypass Mitch Coffee and see the publisher alone. The good news he had to deliver did not, in Twist's view, require the company of the metropolitan editor.

Wainwright, as always, sat rigidly behind his desk, a clothing-store mannequin dressed in starched white shirt and vested suit, despite the July heat. But what did it matter, Twist thought, since the man went from air-conditioned office to air-conditioned limo to air-conditioned restaurant to air-conditioned home? He doubted Wainwright had broken a sweat in the past ten years.

The publisher smiled across his desk, his unnaturally dark, plastered-down hair sitting like a helmet over unfriendly eyes. "My secretary tells me you have some favorable news," he began.

"Very favorable, I think." Twist ran through the events of the day, then laid a proof of the first story on Wainwright's desk. The publisher glanced at the headline, which read:

LITTLE BOBBY CLINGS TO LIFE
Delayed Surgery Leaves Child Critical

A thin smile formed on Wainwright's lips as he read the first few paragraphs of the story. "What is the prognosis?" he asked at length.

"It was fifty-fifty immediately after the surgery. It's about sixty-forty in the kid's favor as of an hour ago. His chances get better each hour he survives, but the hospital tells me it's still a crap-shoot." Twist raised a cautionary hand. "I've had a thought about that," he began again. He wanted to choose his words carefully. "If the worst happens, and the kid doesn't make it, I think we should consider starting a fund in his name."

"To help other children in similar circumstances," Wainwright interjected.

"Exactly. It's not the ideal solution, but it would allow us to keep the ball rolling with our advertisers."

The publisher nodded. "Yes, that could work. But it is definitely a less attractive alternative." Wainwright tapped his chin with one finger. "After all, Leonard, we created this campaign for the lad, and I think everyone concerned—our readers, our advertisers, certainly everyone here at the paper—would like to see it fulfilled." He paused, thinking again. "So let's keep that in the forefront of everything we do—for now." He raised an instructive finger. "No expense is to be spared. Make that very clear to the hospital." He tapped the proof sheet with one finger. "It sounds as though a great deal of aftercare will be needed, and that the child may require medication for the rest of his life if all goes well."

Twist nodded agreement. "We'll have a sidebar about that with our second-day story. It should allow us to prolong our fundraising campaign for several weeks."

Wainwright steepled his fingers in front of his face. "Even longer, perhaps. I'll advise our advertising and promotion departments to renew their efforts." He dropped his hands beneath his chin as he appraised Twist. "You seem to have pulled this together nicely, Leonard. I take it from what you told me that Mr. Burke is now under control."

"Completely."

"And your plans for him?"

"I think there's plenty of time for the other shoe to drop," Twist said.

"Yes. He's doing some exceptional work. We wouldn't want to discourage that. Tell me about your plans for the doctors and the hospital and the tawdry little scheme they were running on our city."

Twist handed over another set of proofs, including the sidebar on Sorrentino's investigation. Wainwright read each piece through, finishing with the sidebar. That final piece produced a restrained chuckle.

"This Sorrentino business was a stroke of genius. Your doing?"

"Yes, it was."

Wainwright tapped his chin again. "It could garner us some criticism for involving the city in our investigation, but it will certainly stop the competition from trying to knock down our story."

"It sure as hell will. It validates our story from day one," Twist said. "And it will force the competition to follow our lead on the stories *they* run."

"They could ignore our story, of course."

"They wouldn't dare. Not with Sorrentino involved. Plus, the hospital has assured us they'll hold press briefings each day on the boy's condition."

Wainwright chuckled again. "How did you . . . cajole them into that?"

"They're hoping we'll use a velvet glove with them and let Bradford take the fall all by himself."

Wainwright laughed openly now. He tapped the series about the hospital scam. "When they read this, they may decide they've been hoodwinked and call an end to their press briefings."

"By that time they'll already have held one, and every newspaper and television station will be demanding more. Besides, they'll want to do everything they can to make the public think they give a damn."

Wainwright leaned back in his chair, mulling that premise. "Yes," he said. "Of course they will." He leaned forward and leveled Twist with his stare. "But the only one who truly cares is the *Globe*. Let's make that clear every single day. We are the newspaper of the people. Our advertising department has been coining money with that phrase. And I see no reason for that to stop."

"I see no reason either," Twist said.

Roberto's small five-year-old body seemed almost lost in the sheets that enfolded him. A tube carrying oxygen ran to his nose; another ran to a bag hung from the bed to capture his waste. There was an intravenous tube in one arm, steadily dripping a saline solution into his veins, and wires ran from his chest to the monitor that hung above the bed, sending out a regular beep with each beat of his heart.

Burke looked from the child to the monitor, both captivated and unnerved by the repetitious arcs of light that moved across its screen. The boy's heart had stopped twice before, and the knowledge that it could happen again raced through his mind.

When he looked back at the bed, Roberto's eyes were open. The boy kept drifting in and out of sleep under the lingering affects of the anesthesia. Burke stroked his forehead, then gave him a thumbs-up gesture. Maria had taken his hand, and Consuelo was cooing soft, encouraging words in Spanish.

Julia stood beside Burke, and she slipped her arm around his waist and leaned her head against his shoulder. Burke reached into the bag he had brought with him and withdrew the Roberto Clemente baseball glove he had bought on the way to the hospital. He held it up for the boy to see.

A small glint came to Roberto's eyes, but his face remained slack, too weak to form any expression of pleasure. Burke pointed to the signature on the glove, mouthed the words "Roberto Clemente," and watched a slight curve come to the corners of the boy's mouth.

A nurse moved swiftly into the room and inserted herself between Roberto and his grandmother. She quickly checked his vital signs, then began adjusting the flow on the intravenous solution. Glancing back over her shoulder, she eyed Burke and Julia.

"Only a few more minutes," she said. "I need to limit the number of visitors to two. Roberto needs his rest."

Turning back, the nurse began to check the bandage that held the intravenous needle in the boy's wrist. Suddenly Roberto's body arched, and his arms and legs began to thrash violently. The nurse pressed his shoulders down, pinning him to the bed, but the child's arm flailed, striking her face, and she reeled back into the rack holding the IV bottle and sent it crashing to the floor. She rushed forward and again tried to hold him to the bed, but the child's small body continued to buck.

Burke stepped forward and placed his forearms against the boy, one across his shoulders, the other across his legs. The nurse activated an intercom beside the bed, her voice suddenly shrill. "Code blue. Stat. Code blue. Stat."

Squeezing in between Burke and the child, she pressed her fingers against Roberto's carotid artery. A crash cart slammed through the door, followed by two nurses and two doctors. One of the doctors brushed Burke roughly aside, snapping the word "Out!" as he did.

Burke staggered back, and a nurse drew the curtain around the bed. Behind him Maria and Consuelo were sobbing hysterically. Burke turned and found Julia holding both women tightly, her eyes wide, her face rigid with fear.

"Oh, God, no. My baby, my baby. No, no, no, no." Maria's wail filled the room, and Julia gently pulled the woman's face to her shoulder, muffling the sound. Consuelo had dropped to her knees in prayer.

Burke stood there, helpless, impotent. Every organ in his body seemed constricted, and he suddenly felt his arms and legs trembling.

Dr. Salazar rushed into the room and hurried behind the curtain. Medical orders were barked out, each one blurring in Burke's mind. He looked back at the curtain but could see only a flurry of legs moving about the bed. Then one of the legs kicked out, and the Roberto Clemente baseball glove he had dropped came skidding under the curtain. He reached down and picked it up. His large hands squeezed the leather as though it were a lifeline he did not dare release.

Five minutes passed, then ten, before Salazar stepped through the curtains. He held up his hands and spoke soothingly in Spanish. Maria rushed to him, and the doctor engulfed her in his arms. Salazar looked at Burke and Julia, both frozen in place.

"He's all right. He's stable again," Salazar said. Burke dropped the baseball glove, and both hands went to his face as he exhaled a long, frightened breath. Next to him he heard Julia fighting back sobs.

As Burke removed his hands from his face, the curtain was drawn back from the bed as the nurses and residents prepared to remove the crash cart. Burke stared at the small, sleeping figure, eyes riveted on Roberto's chest until he saw it rise and fall. He raised his eyes to the boy's face. It was drained of all color, a ghostly white, and it forced Burke's eyes back to the boy's chest to be certain the life he had seen was indeed there.

Salazar took Burke's arm, then Julia's. "I have to ask you to leave now," he said. "Only his mother and grandmother can stay. I'm going to have a nurse stay here with him."

Burke stared at the doctor, his eyes demanding more. Salazar shook his head.

"It's not because I expect anything more to happen," he said softly. "I just want the room as quiet as possible so he can rest." He raised his chin, indicating the hall. "Come out with me, please."

Burke and Julia followed Salazar into the hall. After the chaos they had just witnessed, the intensive-care floor seemed unnaturally hushed. The doctor put both hands to his face and rubbed softly. When he lowered his hands, his face seemed suddenly drawn and haggard.

"It was close," he said. "If the nurse hadn't been there, I don't know if we would have gotten to him in time."

Burke had to fight his next words out. They seemed to catch in his throat, and his voice sounded strange in his ears.

"How bad is it now?" He drew a breath. "Is he worse?"

Salazar shook his head, but the gesture seemed filled with uncertainty. "It was a setback, but he seems to be rallying. We've increased his medication, and that should help." His eyes suddenly hardened, and Burke could see the simmering anger he seemed to hide so well.

"If we had operated a month ago, even two weeks ago—anytime before that last episode . . ." He stopped himself and stared at the baseball glove that Burke had retrieved from the floor and now held tightly again in both hands. Salazar let out a long breath and seemed to have his anger under control again.

"If we had had that time, Roberto would be playing with that glove now." He reached out and took the glove from Burke, fitted it onto his hand, and punched a fist into the pocket. "It's a good glove," he said. "I intend to see that he gets to play with it."

Julia reached out and placed a hand on Salazar's arm. "Will we be able to see him again today?" Her voice, too, sounded choked, strange and unfamiliar to Burke's ear.

Salazar shook his head. "Not today. Maybe tomorrow. We're going to monitor him very closely now." The doctor's eyes shifted back to Burke, anger filling them again. "You know, a few days ago I was very worried about what you would write, what you would say about my profession, and how it would be perceived by the people who read it." His jaw tightened momentarily, then he continued. "You go write your story, Mr. Burke. You let them know that there are some in my profession who think hospitals and medical degrees are nothing more than licenses to make money."

Burke returned to the newsroom at eleven the next morning. He had remained in the hospital waiting room until midnight, when a nurse had come and told him that Roberto was "resting comfortably" and that Maria and Consuelo were asleep in the child's room. He and Julia had spoken with Maria earlier, after he had brought them all dinner from the hospital cafeteria. Maria and Consuelo had barely touched their meals. Both women were exhausted—physically, mentally, emotionally—their faces lined with all the fear that was now part of every waking minute.

Maria had taken Burke's hand, thanking him again for everything he had done, everything he was still doing, and he could feel her hand tremble as he held it. Helplessness, he had thought then, the same helplessness he had known years ago when Annie was being diagnosed by an ever-increasing number of doctors. But worse for this woman. Annie's prognosis had never included the possibility of death, never the frightening realization that in an instant she could disappear from his life and never return. He sat at his desk, feeling just as drained as he had when he and Julia had left the hospital eleven hours ago. He had called that morning and received the usual medical babble. Roberto was stable. Translated, it meant nothing more than that he was still alive, and Burke had told himself that was all that could be expected. A full recovery was no longer possible. Hope that the frail little boy would one day have a normal life was now out of the question. Salazar still held out limited possibilities— medications that were being developed that might improve the quality of that life. Other words came back. A month earlier, two weeks earlier—anytime before the child's last crushing episode—and so much might have been different. That last episode had been only five days ago.

Burke thought about Bradford, his daily existence in a comfortable Westchester home, the affluence that surrounded every hour of his life. "*A god*," his nurse Jennifer Wells had said, one whose judgments and decisions were never to be questioned. "*A license to make money*," the words Salazar had used, the anger he hid so well finally coming off him like cold sweat.

Burke glanced at his story in that day's edition of the *Globe*. He had pilloried Bradford, but they were only words. Pompous words that served the *Globe* and meant nothing, changed nothing. A year from now hundreds, perhaps thousands, of "Little Bobbys" would have passed by unnoticed, only a very few helped by men like Salazar who struggled against the greed that permeated not only medicine but every profession, every life.

Tony Rice came up behind Burke and laid a hand on his shoulder, evaporating his thoughts. "You look depressed, dear boy. Is it bad news about the lad?"

Burke shook his head. "No, he's still the same." He glanced up into Rice's sympathetic eyes. "I was contemplating the concept of futility." He added a self-deprecating smile to his words.

"Ah, futility," Rice said. "I know that lady well. Translated, you know, it means feeling sorry for oneself."

"I suspect there's more than a little of that, too." Burke shook

his head again. "I thought I could pull it off, Tony. Actually started
to believe it somewhere along the line. Then the vagaries of fate
arrived."

"They always do, my dear chap. The philosophers tell us it's
what makes life interesting. But philosophers are always full of
shit, aren't they?"

A burst of invective drew their attention. Pete Stavos's chair
had turned up missing again, and he was ranting at the top of
his lungs.

"There, my dear chap, is reality. Children lie close to death,
people rummage through trash cans for food, our subways are
covered with mindless graffiti and cleaned each day with urine-
scented disinfectant, crime rules our streets, and the city is in financial ruin. And here, in the midst of it all, our beloved Greek
fruitcake still fumes over a missing chair. The world is mad,
dear boy, and our comrade Stavos is the harbinger of insanity
yet to come."

Burke began to laugh. "God, Tony, you are truly an uplifting
voice with which to begin the day."

"I do try, dear boy." He slid into his chair and spun back to face
Burke. His eyes were coldly serious. "Just remember, you did
everything you could for the lad. And I for one am proud of you."

Burke was about to thank him, when Twist's voice bellowed
across the newsroom. When Burke looked up, he saw he was
being beckoned to Twist's office.

"Thy master's voice," Rice snapped. "Run along now, there is
bidding to be done."

Twist was pacing behind his desk when Burke entered. "I expected you in here at ten," he began.

"I was at the hospital until midnight," Burke said. "I needed
eight hours."

Twist held up the copy Burke had filed from the hospital after
Roberto's seizure. "I had them hold this," he said. "I want to run
it as a box with tomorrow's story. It'll have more impact that way.
And I want you to keep it updated, right up to the six-o'clock
deadline for the bulldog. I'll have the night and lobster shifts
check on the kid every hour after that so we can keep current for
the city edition and the final." Twist stopped pacing and jabbed a
finger in Burke's direction. "The hospital is holding a press brief-

ing at three. I want you to cover it. See if you can't encourage some questions from the TV clowns." He waved a hand in the air. "About Bradford and the hospital delaying the surgery until they received their thirty pieces of silver. Something along those lines." Burke nodded but said nothing about Twist's suggestion. "I'll be there. I'll also be at the hospital tonight. So I can keep nightside up to speed."

"Let's not go crazy on overtime here. Once the glow wears off, everybody'll be chewing my ass, claiming that I spent too much money."

"I'll take it as comp time," Burke said.

"Good." Twist added a nod of approval. "Oh, and what's the latest on the kid?"

"Still the same. I was with him when he had the seizure last night. I thought it was all over."

Twist grunted, stared at his shoes, then back at Burke. "The publisher has put in some calls to people he knows on the hospital board. He's made it clear that University Hospital has one chance to save a small part of its ass, and that's by keeping this kid alive."

Burke stared at his own shoes now. He wanted to ask if Wainwright had placed a call to God as well—just to let Him know how the *Globe* wanted everything to turn out.

"I'm sure that will keep everyone on their toes," he said instead.

Twist eyed him, searching for any hidden sarcasm. "You're off everything else until further notice," he finally said. "I want you to stay on top of the kid's condition and keep checking for any new developments on the series." He let out a low cackle. "Like, maybe Bradford will hang himself in a broom closet."

Twist gave up on that bit of merriment and continued, "Also, you should keep checking with Sorrentino's office to see if anything new develops in his investigation. It's probably too early, but we may be able to get a photo of somebody carrying boxes of records out of the hospital."

"You got it," Burke said.

Twist stared at him as though surprised he was still there. "Okay, that's it," he said. "Get cracking."

At one o'clock all was quiet on every front, and Tony Rice and

Eddie Hartman cajoled Burke into joining them for lunch at Costello's. "I only eat with journalistic stars," Hartman said. "And with today's story, yours is definitely in the ascension." Burke received other congratulations as they entered Costello's. The place was its usual lunch-hour mob scene. The Brit and Aussie correspondents at the bar were regaling each other with stories they had told each other the night before but had been too drunk to remember. Burke, Rice, and Hartman took a booth near the bar and watched as Costello's infamous waiter, Herbie, served an adjacent table with his thumb firmly submerged in one customer's bowl of soup.

"God, why do I continue to come here?" Rice muttered as he watched Herbie wipe his dripping thumb on his trousers.

Hartman eyed Herbie, who was short and fat and sixty and vaguely resembled the actor Charles Laughton. He wore a battered tuxedo almost as old as he was. "It's the ambience," Hartman said. "You'd never find a Herbie at La Côte Basque."

Herbie spun away from the table he had just served and turned to them. "Herbie's here, Herbie's here," he intoned. "What can I get you?"

Rice glared up at the aging waiter. "Anything but the soup," he snapped.

"The soup's good today," Herbie said, his face all innocence and confusion.

"How would you know?" Rice demanded. "Have you been sucking your infernal thumb again?"

Herbie blinked several times, then wiggled his pad at Rice. "It's busy, busy," he warned. "If you don't order, I have to go to other people's tables."

Rice growled out an order for "a hamburger untouched by subhuman hands," and Hartman and Burke said they'd have the same. Each also ordered a bottle of St. Pauli Girl beer.

"I am never eating here again," Rice snapped as he watched Herbie retreat toward the kitchen. "And I swear, if there is a thumbprint on my hamburger bun, I will slay that little gnome right here in front of everyone."

"I hear Herbie licks the pickles before he puts them on the plates," Hartman said. He watched Rice shake his shoulders and shudder. He grinned at Burke. "Lord Haw Haw will be eating here again before the week is out." He inclined his head toward the bar, where the Brits and Aussies were still babbling to each other. "It's the only place he can get the latest news about the queen," Hartman added.

Burke laughed, suddenly glad he had agreed to come to lunch. Rice and Hartman were just what he needed, a break in the tension that had been building for days. He looked toward the bar, at the gaggle of newshounds, each one impressed with what he did for a living, each doing all he could to convince his peers that he was well suited to membership in that elite group. Burke's eyes roamed the bar, taking in the flamboyance of the collective egos, and he silently admitted that none was any larger than his own.

His eyes stopped when he spotted Frankie Fabio at the middle of the bar. Fabio was seated next to Ben Rostantino, the comptroller for the news department, and he decided to walk over and find out what intelligence Fabio had on Twist's plans to follow up the hospital series.

As he approached the pair, Burke noticed that Rostantino seemed unusually downcast. He had rarely seen Ben without a smile on his face. Despite his impossible job of managing the news-department budget, he was one of the most likable and even-tempered men Burke had ever known. Today Rostantino seemed deeply depressed as he stared into his drink. Fabio looked nothing short of livid.

Burke slipped his arm around Rostantino's shoulder. "What's the matter, Ben, you saw my expense account for last week?" he began. He glanced at Fabio. "You don't look exactly overjoyed either, my Cheech," he added.

Rostantino looked up at Burke, his eyes surprisingly fearful. "How's that little boy?" he asked. The words seemed choked.

"He's still fighting his way back," Burke said. "The doctors think he'll live, but it won't be the life everybody was hoping for. They got him to the table a few weeks too late."

Ben turned away and shook his head. Burke glanced back at Fabio. The man's face was red with anger.

"You better listen to what Ben has to say," Fabio said.

Rostantino's face was still turned away, and Burke pressed in closer to the bar to get a clearer view of him. Ben looked up at him, making it easier. His face seemed ashen to Burke.

"I have a grandson the same age as that little boy," he said. Anger suddenly infused his face. "It wasn't just the doctors who screwed Roberto over, Billy. And it wasn't just the hospital."

Burke felt a sudden chill. "What are you talking about?" he asked. He could feel a knot forming in his gut.

"It was the *Globe*, too."

For a moment Burke couldn't speak. "What, Ben? Tell me," he finally managed.

"The fund they started for the kid," Ben said. "I was in charge of it. It was put under the news department for tax purposes." He paused as though the next words were too much for him. "They've had the money for three weeks. All of it. Everything they needed for the doctors and the hospital." He shook his head. "It just poured in after your first stories. We couldn't count it fast enough." Rostantino's mouth twisted in anger. "Ninety thousand bucks. It was nothing. Christ, we have almost twice that now."

Burke felt rage building. Sweat broke out on his forehead. "Then why the stall? Why all the claims that they needed more time? Why the lies that another department was handling it, and nobody knew what the total was?"

"Because advertising and circulation were going through the roof," Ben snapped. "When I told Twist we had the money we needed, he just stared at me and told me, 'No we don't.' He said circulation was sky-high, and advertisers we hadn't had for years were coming back into the fold, and that he had no intention of pulling the plug any sooner than necessary. He said the publisher would tell us when we had enough."

"It has to be why he sent you out to Wounded Knee," Fabio snapped. "You were getting too close to wrapping everything up on the hospital scam, and he wanted to get rid of you for a couple of weeks and slow everything down. If I had known. If I had fucking known . . ." Fabio let the words die.

"Those cocksuckers." Burke could feel his body trembling. He could see Roberto thrashing in his bed. He could hear Salazar's words: *"If we had gotten him to the table before the last episode . . ."* Only five days ago. It had been only five days ago. And even then Twist had tried to stall for more time.

He felt Rostantino grip his arm, and he looked down into the man's guilt-ridden eyes. "I tried, Billy. I really did. I even went to Mitch Coffee, and he told me the same thing Twist did. He told me to run my department and let the city desk handle it. So I did what I was told, goddamn it. And now . . ." He shook his head again and turned away.

"I'll break that rotten little bastard in half," Burke growled. He made a move toward the door, but Fabio's hand hit his chest, stopping him. "No. Don't be stupid. Get the fucking evidence and make those bastards pay for it," he snapped.

The words stopped Burke. Rostantino spun around on his stool and grabbed his arm again. "The fund was in a special account," he said. "The monthly statements are sitting on my desk. They show the daily deposits, right down to the last nickel."

Burke stared at him as the words sank in. Then he spun away and raced for the door.

Burke ran the three blocks to the *Globe*. He ran across the lobby and into a waiting elevator. When the doors opened on the seventh floor, he raced through the reception area and down the hall that led to the newsroom. Thelma, the receptionist, sat with a stunned look on her face, then shrugged, deciding that Billy Burke had joined the ranks of lunatics she dealt with every day.

Rostantino's office was at the end of the hall, and Burke went straight through the door to his desk. The bank statements were sitting on top, and he picked them up and began mentally calculating the figures. It was exactly as Ben had said. The money had been sitting in the account for weeks.

Burke folded the statements and placed them in his jacket pocket, then turned and walked slowly across the newsroom, his eyes fixed on Twist's glass-enclosed office.

Twist was seated at his desk when Burke entered. He was reading copy spread out on his desk, and Burke was beside him before he looked up. There was a sneer on Twist's face, but it instantly disappeared when he saw the glare in Burke's eyes.

Before Twist could speak, Burke had him by the throat. He jerked Twist up, sending his chair crashing to the floor, then slammed him back into the wall. Several of Twist's awards tumbled to the floor.

"You miserable little cocksucker." Burke's voice was ragged, barely more than a hoarse whisper. Twist stared at him in shocked disbelief. His eyes bulged in his head, and he struggled to gag out what words he could.

"What . . . ? What . . . ? God . . . you're choking . . . me."

Burke reached into his jacket pocket and withdrew the bank statements. He shook them open with one hand and held them in front of Twist's face. "You had it all," he hissed. "You had every fucking penny weeks ago. You played craps with that kid's life, and you lost, you son of a bitch. Not Bradford. Not that fucking hospital. *You*. You and this goddamn newspaper. You pissed that kid's life away. You took the one miserably desperate chance he had, and you said, 'Fuck you. Not today, kid. Not until we suck every dime we can out of your story.'"

Burke pulled Twist toward him, then slammed him back against the wall. He did it again and again, emphasizing his words with each thump of his body. "You used *me*. You made *me* your fucking *shill*. Every *pain* that kid felt *you* caused. Every *tear* that came out of his mother's *eyes* came from *you*."

Twist's hands flailed at his own throat, trying to break Burke's grip. Then his eyes began to roll back in his head. Burke released him and watched him slump to the floor. He leaned down, forced Twist's chin up, and stared into his eyes.

"Mrs. Avalon is going to get these bank statements, Lenny. She's also going to get the name of the best fucking lawyer in this town. And when it's all over, if I ever see you on the street, you better start running as fast as your skinny little legs can take you. And you better pray to God it's fast enough."

Burke turned and started for the door.

"You can't have those . . . statements," Twist gagged. "That's . . . *Globe* property. You can't take them . . . out of this . . . building."

Burke turned. Twist was on his hands and knees, crawling toward him. He stared down at him and laughed at the sight. "Fuck you, Lenny. They came in a brown paper wrapper. I'm just gonna help the lady find out if they're real or not. If they're legitimate, I'm sure her lawyer will send them back to their rightful owner."

Twist began to pull himself up, then fell back on the seat of his pants, still gasping for breath. "You'll never work . . . in another newspaper . . . *anywhere*," he gasped. "I'll make sure nobody . . . hires you. *Nobody*."

Burke shook his head. "Lenny, you are a pathetic little shit. But if you never do anything else in your miserable fucking life, just be sure to make good on that promise." He gave him a broad wink. "See you on the unemployment line."

Burke left Twist's office and walked across the newsroom. Frankie Fabio stood at the city desk. He was slightly out of breath, and Burke realized he had rushed back to witness Burke's confrontation with Twist. There was a broad grin spread across his face. As Burke passed, Fabio gave him a thumbs-up gesture.

"Good luck, my troop," Fabio said.

"Thank you, my Cheech. Have to run. There's a lady I know who needs to find a lawyer."

"Sounds like a plan to me," Fabio said.

EPILOGUE

The *New York Globe* did not win the Pulitzer Prize in 1976. When the awards were announced that year, the champagne was ready in the newsroom but remained unopened. The Pulitzer committee, in its wisdom, awarded that year's Meritorious Public Service Medal to the *Anchorage* (Alaska) *Daily News*.

Leonard Twist was not one of the disappointed editors who filled the newsroom that day. He was not even invited to the hoped-for party, although Frank Fabio made a point of telephoning him at home to deliver the news. Two months after Billy Burke walked out of his office, Twist resigned as city editor of the *Globe*. The resignation came one day after the *Globe* quietly settled a threatened lawsuit on behalf of Roberto Avalon. Today Twist runs a small weekly newspaper in upstate New York. The space on his wall remains empty.

The amount of Roberto Avalon's settlement, though never disclosed, was said to be five million dollars, payable with interest over a ten-year period. A short time after the settlement was reached, Roberto was released from University Hospital. He remained under the care of Dr. Wilfredo Salazar and with the help of medication was soon able to play a subdued game of baseball with Billy Burke. He told Burke that his Roberto Clemente baseball glove was "the coolest glove anybody ever had."

Roberto subsequently moved back to Puerto Rico with his mother and grandmother. Years later he returned to New York, where he graduated from Columbia University and New York University Medical School. Today he is a physician working with the poor of San Juan. Roberto Avalon, M.D., still corresponds with Billy Burke several times each year. He signs each of his letters "Piece of Work."

Billy Burke and his wife, Julia, again took up their life together.

It was difficult at first, but time and patience and the memory of a little boy who had almost died kept them at it. Without fail they spend each weekend with their daughter, Annie.

In 1978 Julia gave birth to a son. Together they agreed to name him Bobby. Today Bobby Burke works for a small newspaper in Vermont and dreams of making his way to the "big time" in New York. The genes, according to Billy, are just too strong to fight.

Billy Burke never again worked for a newspaper, but his freelance articles still appear regularly in various national magazines. In 1979, with Maria Avalon's permission, he published his first book. It told the story of Roberto Avalon, and it was not well received by newspaper reviewers. Even so, the book spent a few weeks on the *New York Times* bestseller list and led to three subsequent books that did nearly as well. But, like everything else Burke had written in his career, the Roberto Avalon story never accomplished all that he had hoped. Specifically, it did nothing to change the profession he had loved and had left.

BEULAH HILL by William Heffernan

281 pages, trade paperback; $13.95, ISBN: 1-888451-40-8

A novel of rare literary distinction—an erotic thriller combined with a true mystery, and a look back at a little-known part of the American societal patchwork.

"The whispered revelations that come spilling out of *Beulah Hill* are like ghostly voices you sometimes hear in the attic—soft, sad and disturbingly urgent." —*New York Times Book Review*

ADIOS MUCHACHOS by Daniel Chavarría

Winner of a 2001 Edgar Award

245 pages, a trade paperback original, $13.95, ISBN: 1-888451-16-5

"Daniel Chavarría has long been recognized as one of Latin America's finest writers. Now he again proves why with *Adios Muchachos*, a comic mystery peopled by a delightfully mad band of miscreants, all of them led by a woman you will not soon forget—Alicia, the loveliest bicycle whore in all Havana." —Edgar Award-winning author William Heffernan

THE EYE OF CYBELE by Daniel Chavarría

413 pages, hardcover, $27.00, ISBN: 1-888451-25-4

Equal parts historical epic, whodunnit-style thriller, highbrow erotica and philosophical discourse. Set in fifth-century B.C.— during the reign of Pericles—the novel fictionally recreates the behind-the-scenes scandals and political intrigues that occupied the Athenian home front at the height of the Peloponessian War.

SPY'S FATE by Arnaldo Correa

More Cuban Noir from Akashic.

302 pages, hardcover, $24.95, ISBN: 1-888451-28-9

"A captivating thriller based on the murky U.S.-Cuban spy wars. Correa deftly paints the history of Castro's Cuban intelligence service and the changing face of the Miami exile community . . . The insightful sociopolitical picture, the nasty maneuverings of both services, and the credible spy plot make this a fascinating read." —*Publishers Weekly*